ON
THE
BEACH

The pretender to the Emperor's throne was a fat thirty-seven-year-old Chinaman called Artie Wu who always jogged along Malibu Beach right after dawn even in summer, when dawn came round as early as 4:42. It was while jogging along the beach just east of the Paradise Cove pier that he tripped over a dead pelican, fell, and met the man with six greyhounds. It was the sixteenth of June, a Thursday.

CHINAMAN'S CHANCE

ALSO BY ROSS THOMAS

Cast a Yellow Shadow
The Singapore Wink
The Fools in Town Are on Our Side
The Eighth Dwarf
Out on the Rim

Published by
THE MYSTERIOUS PRESS

CHINAMAN'S CHANCE

a novel by

ROSS THOMAS

MYSTERIOUS PRESS

THE MYSTERIOUS PRESS

New York • London • Tokyo

For Rosalie

PART
I

Chapter One

The pretender to the Emperor's throne was a fat thirty-seven-year-old Chinaman called Artie Wu who always jogged along Malibu Beach right after dawn even in summer, when dawn came round as early as 4:42. It was while jogging along the beach just east of the Paradise Cove pier that he tripped over a dead pelican, fell, and met the man with six greyhounds. It was the sixteenth of June, a Thursday.

Artie Wu and the man had often seen each other before. In fact, nearly every morning for the past two months, except on weekends, they had passed each other, Artie Wu in his blue sweat suit, the man in shirt and slacks, both of them barefoot. At first they had merely nodded, but later they spoke, although it never went much further than "Morning" or "Nice day."

The greyhounds, all brindle colored, traveled in a tight, disciplined pack at the man's heels. But sometimes, at the man's silent hand signal, a kind of choppy, almost brutal gesture, they would leap forward and race one another to the pier, streaking along at sixty miles per hour, or however fast greyhounds run. After they reached the pier they would stop, turn, and trot back to the man, their mouths open, their long pink tongues licking their muzzles, as they seemed to laugh and josh each other about what fun the race had been.

After Artie Wu tripped over the dead pelican, he felt himself falling and said, "Shit" just before he hit the sand. The man with the six greyhounds wasn't far off, not more than forty feet away, and when he saw Artie Wu fall he thought, There goes the fat Chinaman.

The man had always assumed that Artie Wu was a neighbor, or at least lived somewhere nearby, perhaps in one of the trailers in Paradise Cove. For a while he had tried thinking of Artie Wu as the fat Chinese, but for some reason that hadn't rung true, so after about a month the man had gone back to "fat Chinaman," although the description still made him just a bit uncomfortable.

When Artie Wu bothered to think about who he was, which was seldom, he usually thought of himself as a fat Chinaman. He had thought of himself as such ever since he was six years old and they had dumped him into that San Francisco orphanage where he had stayed until he ran away at fourteen. Sometimes, of course, when it suited his purpose, he also thought of himself as the pretender to the throne of the Emperor of China.

The man with six greyhounds hurried over to where Artie Wu lay half sprawled on the sand and asked, "Hurt yourself?" One of the dogs, as though to express his own concern, gave Wu's face a wet lick.

"I don't know yet," Wu said as he sat up, bent forward, grasped his bare left ankle with both hands, and squeezed hard. The pain was there, all right, not blinding, but sharp, almost searing, and Artie Wu said, "Shit" again—but in a rather noncommittal way, so that the only other evidence of pain that he offered was the film of sweat that popped out on his forehead. One of the greyhounds gave the sweat a quick lick and then smacked his lips as though he liked the taste.

"Get away, Franchot," the man said, and the greyhound promptly moved back, sat down on his haunches, and gazed out at the ocean as though he had discovered something wonderful and strange out there.

"Franchot?" Wu said.

"After Franchot Tone."

"Cute," Wu said, and then got into a kneeling position to find out whether he could rise using only his right leg. He was two and three-quarters inches over six feet tall and weighed 248 pounds, but only twenty of that was really lard, most of which had settled in around his gut, although enough had spread to his face to make him look fat and jolly and almost benevolent. Laughing Buddha was what a number of persons, mostly women, had told him that he looked like, and he had long ago grown sick of hearing it.

That which wasn't fat was mostly big bone and hard muscle, and on any normal day Artie Wu could easily have raised himself to a standing position using only one leg. The pain, however, had done something to his balance, and he found that he had to put his left foot down for support. When he did, the pain shot through his lower left leg and ankle, even worse than before. So he said, "Shit" for the third time that morning and sank back down into a sitting position on the sand.

"Let me give you a hand," the man said.

Artie Wu nodded and said, "Okay. Thanks." The man helped him up and in doing so learned from Wu's grip that there was far less flab to the fat Chinaman than he had thought.

"You live around here?" the man said.

"My partner does," Artie Wu said. "The yellow house there."

The sand that they were standing on was at the edge of the water and had been packed down hard by the surf. A few yards beyond this the beach rose sharply, not quite straight up, for three or four feet and then leveled off for sixty or seventy feet until it ran into a high bluff of tan earth that was partly covered with green succulents and gray weeds. The yellow house had been built at the base of the bluff and rested on creosoted piling that raised it about a dozen feet above the sand, which was probably high enough to keep it dry from anything except a tidal wave.

A flight of wooden steps ran up from the sand to the broad redwood deck that edged out from the house on three sides. Most of the front of the house was glass. The trim was a very pale yellow, and the roof was of dark green composition shingles. The house didn't look very large to the man with six greyhounds. Two bedrooms, one bath, he thought. No more.

"Ever any good at hopscotch?" he asked Artie Wu.

"Not bad."

"Ready?"

Artie Wu nodded. He had his right arm around the man's neck and shoulders now, and with the man's support he started hopping on his right foot toward the house. Going up the steep three-or-four-foot sand incline was hard, but they managed it, and then when the beach leveled off it got easier until they reached the stairs. The greyhounds had followed along in their tight cluster, alert and interested and looking quite ready to offer advice if but asked.

The two men eyed the stairs for a moment and then, without speaking, shifted positions so that Artie Wu's left arm, rather than his right, went around the man's neck and shoulders. They started up the stairs then, Wu using his right hand on the banister to give a lift to his hops.

Once up on the deck they moved past the round redwood table with the Cinzano umbrella sticking up out of its center and over to a half-glass door that led into the kitchen—dining area.

"It's not locked," Artie Wu said. The man nodded, opened the door, and helped Wu hop inside.

The dining area blended into a living room whose far wall was covered, floor to ceiling, with books. Next to the wall of books was the wall of glass that looked out toward the sea. A man who wore nothing but a pair of faded blue jeans, their legs apparently sawed off at the thighs, stood in the corner that was formed by the walls of books and glass. He stood next to a newsprinter that was clacking away with the sharp, gossipy sound that all newsprinters have. The man was tall, taller even than Artie Wu, but lean—almost, indeed, skinny.

The man turned quickly from the newsprinter to stare at Artie Wu. He wore the deep tan of an old lifeguard, which made his white grin seem whiter than it was. "What the hell happened to you?" he said.

"I tripped over a dead pelican," Artie Wu said.

"Let's get him over here," the man with the deep tan said, and moved quickly away from the newsprinter to help the other man ease Artie Wu down into a black leather Eames chair that was so worn and used that it almost looked old fashioned.

The tall, lean man then knelt down before Artie Wu and gently felt and probed the injured ankle. Artie Wu said, "Shit."

"Hurts, huh?" the man said.

"You damn right."

"I don't think it's sprained."

"It feels sprained," Artie Wu said.

The lean man sat back on his heels and studied the ankle for a moment. His name was Quincy Durant, and he was fairly sure that he was thirty-seven years old, give or take a year. He and Artie Wu had been partners ever since they had run away from the John Wesley Memorial Methodist Orphanage in the Mission District of San Francisco when they were both fourteen years old—although in Durant's case you had to give or take a year.

Durant rose and frowned down at the ankle. "I'll go get something to put on it," he said. "Maybe some Oriental impassivity." He turned to the man with six greyhounds. "You like some coffee?"

"Sure," the man said. "Thanks."

"It's on the stove," Durant said, turned, and left through a door that led down a short hall. When he turned, the man with six greyhounds saw for the first time the network of long, crisscrossed white scars that spread over most of Durant's back. They were ridged scars, frog-belly white against Durant's tan, and had he had time to count them the man would have learned that there were an even three dozen.

"You want some coffee?" the man said to Artie Wu.

"Yeah, I would, thanks."

The man moved into the small kitchen. On the gas stove was a large, old-fashioned coffeepot made out of blue-and-white-speckled enamel. It looked as if it would hold a gallon of coffee. At least a gallon, the man thought. He felt the pot and almost burned his hand. He found a pot holder and used it to lift up the lid and peer inside. The pot was almost full, and a small piece of eggshell floated on top.

The man opened a cabinet, found two cheerful yellow mugs, and filled them with coffee. It smelled just the way he liked it, strong and rich.

"How do you take yours?" he called to Artie Wu.

"With a shot of brandy this morning," Wu said. "He keeps his booze in the cabinet above the refrigerator."

The man reached up, opened the cabinet, and examined the bottles. The tall guy with the scars isn't exactly a boozer, he decided. There were a bottle of fairly good bourbon, some halfway expensive Scotch, some so-so vodka, a bottle of Tanqueray gin that looked unopened (nobody drinks gin anymore, the man thought), and a fifth of Courvoisier.

The man took down the Courvoisier, poured a shot by guess into one of the cups, hesitated for a moment, shrugged slightly, and then poured another, smaller measure into the cup that he had chosen as his own.

He put the brandy back, thinking that the man with the scars must have been fairly well off at one time and perhaps not too long ago. The furniture in the living room indicated that. There was the Eames chair, for example, which was the genuine article, not just some Naugahyde imitation, and Eames chairs didn't come cheap. Then there was the couch, upholstered in what seemed to be a rich, patterned velvet. Fifteen hundred bucks for the couch at least, the man thought, although he had noticed that it too looked a bit worn and beat up, as though it might have been stored often, moved frequently, and even slept on for many a night. And also there was that other chair, the man remembered, the one that looked as if it might be covered with pale suede. That hadn't been bought at Levitz either.

The rug was the real clue, of course. The man thought of himself as something of a minor authority on fine Oriental rugs. He felt that the one in the living room should be displayed on a wall someplace instead of being spread out on the floor of a beach house, for God's sake, where everybody would track sand into it. Well, if the guy with the scars ever goes broke he can always sell the rug. The man estimated that it would bring fifteen thousand easily. Maybe even twenty.

Carrying the two mugs of coffee the man moved back into the living room and handed one of the mugs to Artie Wu, who thanked him. The man nodded; took a sip of his coffee, which tasted even better than it smelled; and sent his gaze traveling around the room again. He gave his head a nod toward the newsprinter that was still clacking away in the corner.

"Reuters?" he said.

Artie Wu twisted around in the chair to look at the newsprinter. When he turned back he said, "Yeah, Reuters."

"The commodity wire?"

Artie Wu shook his head. "The financial wire."

The man nodded thoughtfully, took another sip of his coffee, and was trying to decide how to phrase his next question when Durant came back into the room carrying a shoe box with no top. The box contained a roll of gauze, some surgical cotton, adhesive tape, scissors, and a big, dark brown bottle with no label.

Durant knelt before Artie Wu again, uncapped the brown bottle, and started sloshing a dark purplish liquid on to the injured ankle. The liquid had a bitter, pungent odor that made Artie Wu wrinkle his nose.

"Jesus," he said, "what's that?"

"Horse liniment," Durant said. "Best thing in the world for a twisted ankle."

"Mine's sprained."

"No, it's not. It's just a mild twist, but when I get done you won't even have that."

He sloshed more of the dark liquid on to the ankle, rubbing it in carefully with his long, lean fingers. Then he made a neat pad of some of the gauze, soaked it with the liquid, and wound the pad around Artie Wu's ankle, fastening it in place with two small strips of adhesive tape. After that he cut two long, wide strips of adhesive tape and wound them tightly around the ankle over the gauze, working carefully but with quick, seemingly practiced movements.

When done, Durant sat back on his heels. "Okay," he said. "Put some weight on it."

Artie Wu rose and gingerly put some weight on his left

foot. He smiled broadly, and it was the first time that the
man with six greyhounds had seen him smile. He noticed
that Artie Wu had very large, extremely white teeth and automatically assumed that they were capped, although they
weren't.

"Jesus," Artie Wu said, still grinning, "that's not bad. Is
that stuff really horse liniment?"

"Sure," Durant said with a small, careful smile that made
it hard to tell whether he was lying.

"You've done that before, haven't you?" the man with six
greyhounds said to Durant. The man was still standing in the
middle of the room with his mug of coffee.

"You mean tape up a bum ankle?" Durant said, and then
answered his own question. "Once or twice. Maybe more.
Why don't you sit down and finish your coffee?"

"Thanks," the man said, and headed for the couch, but
stopped. "By the way," he said, "my name's Randall Piers."
He watched carefully to see whether the name meant anything. It was a name that got into the papers often enough,
and he was used to having people recognize it and even
prided himself on the fact that he could usually tell when
they did. But there was nothing in either Durant's or Wu's
face. Not a glimmer or a glint.

Instead, Durant said, "I'm Quincy Durant, and this is my
faithful Chinese houseboy, Artie Wu."

Randall Piers grinned, but didn't offer to shake hands because he somehow felt that they already knew each other too
well for that. Instead he said, "You guys are partners, huh?"
and then sat down on the couch.

"That's right," Durant said. "Partners."

Durant was putting the scissors, tape, and gauze back into
the shoe box. Wu was still on his feet, testing his taped
ankle. He placed all of his weight on it; smiled again as if
satisfied, or even delighted; and then sat back down in the
Eames chair. Randall Piers nodded toward the newsprinter.

"You in the market?"

"In a small way," Durant said.

"It can't be too small with Reuters in your living room."

"We're keeping our eye on one particular little item."

"Oh?" Piers said, refusing to push for the name, but curious.

"Something called Midwest Minerals," Durant said.

Piers's mouth went down sharply at the corners—a petulant expression that somehow made his fifty-year-old face look younger. Or perhaps just childish. "Christ," he said, "that's dropped thirty-two in the last five weeks."

Artie Wu got up again and moved over to the newsprinter, hardly even limping. He grinned happily and said, "Should be down thirty-three when it opens this morning."

"You guys went short," Piers said, making it an accusation, but an admiring one.

"Yeah," Durant said, "we did."

"Where's bottom?"

"We think around twenty-seven, maybe twenty-eight," Artie Wu said as he moved back to his chair.

Piers nodded thoughtfully. "Way too late for me, even with an uptick."

"Probably," Durant said.

"Is this all you do?" Piers said. "Sell short?"

Durant shrugged. "We sort of fiddle around with this and that now and again."

"That's not overly explicit."

"No," Durant said, "it's not."

Piers nodded as if he found that perfectly understandable. He shifted his gaze from Wu and Durant to the ocean and, still staring out at it, said, "Once in a while—not every day, of course, or even every month, but once in a while—just for kicks or maybe even a little excitement—I'll go in on something that's just a bit—" He stopped to choose his next word carefully, finally settling on "dicey." He switched his gaze back to Wu and Durant. They returned it with no more expression than could be found in a saucer of milk.

Piers didn't mind. "I'm a curious sort of guy," he went on. "I mean I have a lot of curiosity, so I ask questions. Sometimes it pays off."

After a long moment Artie Wu said, "Dicey, I think you said."

Piers smiled. "Dicey."

Keeping his face perfectly grave, Artie Wu leaned forward, tapped Piers on the knee, and in a low, confidential tone said, "Like to buy a map to the Lost Dutchman gold mine, mister—or is that too dicey for you?"

"Jesus," Piers said, and smiled again.

"A bit rich, huh?" Durant said.

"A bit. Have you really got one?"

"We've got two," Wu said. "Both very old, very worn, and nicely stained and tattered."

"What else?" Piers said.

"You sound serious," Durant said.

Piers shrugged. "Try me."

Durant looked at Wu, who made his big shoulders go up and down in a small, indifferent shrug. Durant nodded and looked at Piers.

"How about buried treasure?" he said.

"Pieces of eight?" Piers said, and smiled, but not so that the smile would cancel out anything.

"Hundred-dollar bills," Durant said. "Some fifties. A lot of them."

"Whose?"

"Nobody's now," Durant said.

"How much?"

"A couple of million," Artie Wu said.

"Where?"

"Saigon," Durant said. "Or Ho Chi Minh City, if you prefer."

"I don't," Piers said. "Where in Saigon?"

Artie Wu looked up at the ceiling and in an almost dreamy voice said, "When things got tight at the embassy toward the end, they found themselves with six million dollars in cash. They decided to burn it. Well, four million got burned and two million got buried, and for five thousand bucks we can buy a map of the embassy grounds with an X on it."

"Well, now," Piers said. "Who buried it?"

"The guy who wants to sell us the map," Durant said.

"You check him out?"

Durant nodded. "We spent fifteen hundred bucks checking him out. There are, of course, a few obvious problems.

That's why we've decided that perhaps keener minds than ours should take over. We'll sell you our contact for—say, two-fifty."

"We might even part with him for two hundred," Artie Wu said.

Piers rose, a grin on his face. He was a medium-tall man with a wedge-shaped head and gray, smooth, thick hair that lay flat on his head. He had some interesting lines in his face—perhaps too many lines for fifty, but he had both worried and laughed more than most people and perhaps the lines could be blamed on that. His eyes were gray and smart, his nose slightly hooked, his mouth wide and thin, and his chin firm without too much sag. All his life he had just escaped being handsome, for which he was mildly grateful, and now almost everyone thought of Randall Piers as being distinguished looking, which he was just vain enough not to mind.

Still grinning, Piers said, "I think you've got yourselves one hell of a deal."

Durant looked at Wu and said, "I think he just said no."

Wu shook his head sadly. "The chance of a lifetime."

"If it works out for you," Piers said, "I'd like to know. But then, if it works out for you, you won't be letting anybody know, will you?"

"Not right away," Durant said.

Piers grinned again. "Thanks for the coffee—and the offer," he said. Piers started for the door, and then almost on impulse, but not quite, because he never did anything entirely on impulse, he stopped and said, "My wife's having some people over for drinks this evening. Maybe you guys would like to come."

"What time?" Artie Wu said.

"Around six."

Wu looked at Durant, who after not quite a second of hesitation said, "Sure, I think we can make it. You live down the beach?"

Piers gave Durant a quick, careful look, but there was nothing in the lean man's face other than the desire for an address.

"My house is the one where the white steps lead down to the beach from the top of the bluff," he said. "You know it?"

Durant nodded. "Those steps. They're real marble, aren't they?"

"That's right," Piers said. "Real marble."

Durant watched from the deck as the man with the six greyhounds made his way down the beach toward the glistening white steps. When Piers started up the steps, Durant turned and went back into the living room.

"Well?" Artie Wu said.

"I think," Durant said, "that we just got our nibble."

Wu nodded slowly. "Yeah," he said after a moment. "That's what I think too."

Chapter Two

The 182 steps that led to the top of the seventy-foot-high bluff where Randall Piers had built his house three years before were fashioned out of an Italian marble that came from a quarry in Carrara—the same quarry, Piers sometimes told people, that Michelangelo had liked to do business with. Piers wasn't at all sure that this was true, but it made a good story.

The steps were eighteen inches deep and six feet wide, with gentle six-inch risers that made for easy ascent because of the way they zigzagged back and forth across the face of the bluff. The marble was a lustrous white with a faint pinkish tinge to it that sometimes, when the sunset was just right, made the steps look like a jagged, blood red scar running down the pale gold of the sandy bluff.

Piers usually made the journey up and down the steps with the six greyhounds twice each day, just after dawn and just before dusk. He walked and ran the dogs along the beach for almost three-quarters of a mile in the direction of Point Dume and back. That was three miles a day, and he counted going up and down the steps as another two miles in effort, if not in distance, and that was all the exercise he got except for an occasional set of tennis on one of his two courts. For those who didn't like to walk up and down the steps there was an electric boxlike affair, something like a ski lift, which had seats in it for those who were too weary to stand. Piers had ridden in it only once, just to make sure that it worked.

The land on which his house stood ran from the sea to the Pacific Coast Highway. It was approximately two acres wide and six acres deep, and when he had paid not quite a million dollars for it five years before, it was generally agreed that he was crazy. There had been a house on the land when Piers bought it, a sprawling fourteen-room California Mission–style affair that had been well built at low cost back in 1932. The house had been considered a showplace, if not quite a historic-cultural monument worthy of preservation, and almost everyone was properly horrified when Piers brought in the bulldozers, leveled it, and had the rubble carted off to a dump.

In its place Piers had built a thirty-two-room house that was usually referred to as a mansion for lack of a better description. It had been designed by a young Japanese architect in Tokyo who had worked on its plans full time for almost two years. The problem had been to comply with Piers's insistence that every room must have a view of the sea. The architect had cleverly managed this by designing the house around a series of three staggered, open-ended, U-shaped courtyards. The architect had done his job so well that he had been written up in the *Los Angeles Times* as a genius, which made him happy because he was now getting a lot of work from the Arabs.

The house was built of Burmese teak and Pittsburgh glass and Italian marble and Mexican tile and Philippine mahogany, and exquisite was the word most often used to describe it. It had two swimming pools, one indoor and one outdoor; three Jacuzzis; two saunas; fifteen fireplaces; two kitchens; a six-car garage; nineteen bathrooms; and a dozen living suites, not counting rooms for the servants and kennels for the greyhounds.

The original estimated cost of the house had been $2.6 million, but because of inflation and what the architect and the contractor had come to call Piers's "mizewells," its final cost had topped out at $4.9 million. The mizewells were Piers's unchecked proclivity to suggest, in the form of an order, that "we mizewell use marble here instead of tile, and while we're at it, we mizewell put in another bathroom over there."

When word got out about how much the house was costing, most Piers watchers were publicly shocked but secretly delighted. For a time, a lot of people went around calling the place "The Six-Million-Dollar Goof." That lasted until late 1975, when a Beverly Hills real estate agent, representing what she chose to call "certain interested parties in Kuwait," offered Piers a firm $10.6 million cash money for the place, which was almost exactly twice what it had cost.

It was a quarter till seven by the time Piers reached the top of the marble steps. He turned the greyhounds over to Fausto Garfías, the bowlegged thirty-nine-year-old Mexican gardener who was also the dogs' schoolmaster. It was Garfías who had taught them the silent hand signals, which he later had taught Piers to use. Although the dogs pretty much had the run of Piers's twelve acres, they usually roamed around all bunched up in their tight, disciplined pack. Piers had hired another Mexican, Angel Torres, nineteen, not only to help Garfías out with the gardening but also to pick up the dog shit.

The rest of Piers's household staff consisted of a butler; a Korean who served as a combination chauffeur-bodyguard; an Austrian housekeeper from Vienna; two young Mexican maids who were in the country illegally; and a cook who claimed to be French, but was actually Swiss. The staff, with the exception of the butler and Fausto Garfías, kept hours that were scheduled around Piers's wife, Lace Armitage, who seldom got up before eleven unless she was working in a picture, which she hadn't done in seven months.

The butler, who liked getting up early because he was still enthralled by California sunrises and suffered from insomnia anyhow, was Styles Whitlock, a forty-four-year-old English-man who had been born in Islington and, on a scholarship, had taken a degree in engineering from the University of Warwick. In 1960 he had emigrated to the States as part of what he still liked to think of as the brain drain. Whitlock had worked in the space program in Los Angeles until the cutbacks began in the early '70s, when he had been one of the first to be fired because he was, at best, only a mediocre engineer.

After six months, Whitlock's American wife had got sick of his hanging around the house all day staring at television. So she had hired herself an acerbic lawyer with an intimidating snarl, filed for divorce, and taken Whitlock for his last dime. After that he drove a Yellow Cab for a while and then in desperation placed an ad in the *Hollywood Reporter* that read: "Experienced English butler available for catered parties." Because he was tall and dour and spoke with what most Americans thought of as a properly received accent, he soon had more work than he could handle.

When Randall Piers married Lace Armitage in 1973 they had moved into the new house in Malibu, and Styles Whitlock had been one of the bride's wedding presents. Piers paid Whitlock almost as much as he would pay a halfway brilliant engineer, but after getting into several technical discussions with the Englishman, Piers was always relieved that he had hired him only as a butler.

Whitlock was waiting for Piers just outside the huge room which the architect had designed as a library, but which Piers used as an office, although the butler insisted on calling it "the master's study."

"Coffee is on your desk, sir."

"Thanks," Piers said. "Mr. Ebsworth here yet?"

"Just arrived, sir."

Piers nodded, started into the room, but paused. "Get

somebody to pick up a coffeepot," he said. "I want the big old-fashioned kind that'll hold a gallon and is made out of speckled enamel. Blue and white. They can probably find one at Sears."

Whitlock gave Piers a grave nod of assent, which he had practiced for hours in front of a mirror after studying the nods of English butlers in old movies. The Public Television series *Upstairs, Downstairs* had proved to be a treasure trove of information on buttling, and Whitlock had watched each program at least three times and often took notes.

When Piers entered the library-office, he didn't bother to say good morning to the twenty-nine-year-old lawyer with the streaked blond hair, cautious blue eyes, and thin, skeptical mouth that always looked to Piers as if it were about to issue a dire warning. The lawyer's name was Hart Ebsworth, and he had been graduated second in his class at the University of Chicago. He had been Randall Piers's executive assistant for nearly five years now and didn't at all mind coming to work at seven in the morning because Piers paid him almost $76,000 a year.

Ebsworth had gone to work for Piers instead of joining his uncle's Chicago law firm, which was the kind usually referred to as stuffy but prestigious, because when Piers offered him the job he had said, "If you come to work for me, you won't starve, but you won't make any money, not for the first three years. After that, if you work out, I'll pay you exactly what the Chief Justice of the U.S. Supreme Court gets. If he gets a raise, so will you, because by then you'll be worth it."

Piers settled himself behind his carved oak desk, picked up his cup, and took a sip of the coffee. Ebsworth watched him, waiting, not saying anything. Piers decided that the coffee wasn't nearly as good as that which he and the fat Chinaman had had that morning. He put the cup back down, looked at Ebsworth, and instead of saying good morning, said, "Midwest Minerals."

"A dog," Ebsworth said.

"We could have gone short."

"We could have bought Avon at nineteen."

"Two guys up the beach in that little yellow house. You know it?"

Ebsworth nodded.

"They've got Reuters, the commercial wire, in their fucking living room. How much does that cost?"

"About two hundred a month; maybe a little more with line charges."

"They're going to ride MidMin down to twenty-seven, which they claim is bottom."

Ebsworth nodded again, thoughtfully this time. "Good luck," he said.

"You don't like it?"

Ebsworth shrugged. "They got inside somehow."

Piers thought about it. "Probably."

"You want me to find out how?" Ebsworth said.

Piers thought again for a few moments and then shook his head and said, "Don't bother. Let me tell you how I met them instead."

"Maybe you should," Ebsworth said, and took a sip of his own coffee. Piers leaned back in his chair and stared out through the floor-to-ceiling glass wall that offered a view of the curving shoreline and, in the far distance, Santa Monica, which seemed to be trying to grow a fresh batch of morning smog.

"I'm going along the beach with the dogs like I do every morning," Piers said, "and I see this guy who's a jogger. He's a fat Chinaman, a big guy, and I see him every day and sometimes we say hello or how are ya or some shit like that. Well, this morning he trips over a dead pelican and either twists or sprains his ankle. He didn't ask me to, but I give him a hand up and it turns out that he's not as fat as I thought. I mean there's a lot of muscle there, too. So I help him up and into this little yellow house that turns out to be his partner's. How much would a house like that go for?"

Ebsworth looked up at the ceiling. "If it's the one I'm thinking of—"

"Yellow with a green roof."

"About a hundred and fifty thousand."

"Jesus, for two bedrooms and one bath?"

"It's on the beach. In East L.A. it would bring thirty, maybe. When they built it twenty years ago it probably cost twelve, if that."

"What would it rent for?" Piers said.

"Six, seven, maybe even eight hundred."

Piers nodded his receipt of the information and went on with his tale, still staring through the window across nineteen miles of ocean to Santa Monica.

"Well, anyway, I get the fat Chinaman into the house and there's his partner standing by the newsprinter, which is the first thing I notice. The partner's a real tall guy too, sort of skinny with a hell of a tan and somewhere around thirty-six or thirty-seven. I think maybe they're both around thirty-seven or so, although with the Chinaman you can't be sure —and if I keep on calling him the Chinaman, I hope you and the ACLU will pardon me all to hell."

"I'll try to think of him as the Chinese gentleman," Ebsworth said.

"Wonderful. Well, they offer me the best cup of coffee I've had in twenty years, and the tall, skinny guy bandages up the Chinaman's ankle like he knows what he's doing—I mean like maybe he's had medical training somewhere. It was as good as any doctor could've done. Anyway, we get to talking and they tell me they're going short on MidMin and that they sometimes fiddle around with this and that. We're kind of kidding back and forth, but I'm pressing just a little because, hell, I'm curious, and so they come up with this real pisser."

"What?"

"A couple of million that was supposed to be burned but got buried instead somewhere on the embassy grounds in Saigon."

"And they have a map?" said Ebsworth.

"They know where to buy one—for five thousand."

"And sell it to you for how much?"

"They didn't try to sell it to me. That's when I got interested. In fact, I got so interested that I invited them over for drinks this evening."

Piers shifted his gaze from Santa Monica to Ebsworth,

who stared back at him for a moment and then worked his face up into an expression that was even more dubious than usual. "The Chinese gentleman," he said slowly. "Do you think he was really hurt?"

Piers gave it some thought. "He was hurt," he said finally. "Either he was hurt or he's the best goddamned actor in the world. Nobody could underplay it just like that and make the sweat pop out on his forehead and everything."

"Did you get their names?"

"Artie Wu and Something Durant. Quincy Durant. Wu's either W-u or W-o-o. He's the Chinaman."

"Really," Ebsworth said, making a note on his pad and not bothering to keep the edge out of his tone. About the only thing Ebsworth could fault his employer on was Piers's penchant for going into excruciating detail. Piers would sometimes justify it by explaining that experience had taught him that most people, present company excluded, of course, couldn't pound sand down a rathole without printed instructions. Ebsworth had often wondered whether or not he agreed with this assessment and finally had decided that he did.

"So," Ebsworth said, "did you pick up anything else I could use?"

"Scars," Piers said. "The tall, skinny guy, Durant. He's got scars on his back."

"What kind of scars?"

Piers reached into a drawer, took out a sheet of thick, creamy paper, and using a ball-point pen, quickly drew the outline of a man's nude back. The drawing was remarkable for its anatomical accuracy as well as for its economy of line. Piers thought a moment and then sketched in the scars as he remembered them. The only mistake he made was that he drew only thirty-two scars instead of three dozen. Finished, he handed the drawing to Ebsworth.

The lawyer looked at it and said, "Interesting." Then he said, "I'll try to find out how he got them. You want it all?"

"Everything you can get."

"Five-thirty be okay?"

"Yeah," Piers said. "Fine."

Ebsworth rose. He looked at the drawing again and then at Piers. "Why these two?"

Piers locked his hands behind his head, leaned back in his chair, and resumed his thoughtful inspection of Santa Monica.

"Hunch, mostly," he said. "Sometimes you can just tell about a guy—just like you can sometimes tell whether he's ever had the clap or been in jail. You just know. These two —well, these two just might do."

"And if you're wrong?"

Piers shrugged. "If I'm wrong, we'll keep on looking."

Chapter Three

They broke McBride's left thumb that morning at a quarter to eleven in the back booth of Sneaky Pete's Bar & Grill, a place as shoddy as its name that was located three blocks from the beach in Venice, a failed paradise in Southern California.

They broke it casually, almost as an afterthought, the way a reasonably conscientious camper might break a match. McBride neither yelped nor yowled when they broke it, nor did he implore any particular deity's intercession. All he said, very quietly, was "Motherfuckers." If he felt any pain, which of course he did, he offered no evidence other than the single tear that formed in the inside corner of each eye and then trickled slowly down his cheek until he licked them away with a coated tongue.

The black man who sat next to McBride in the booth was the one who had pinned his wrist and arm to the table while the white man, sitting across from them, had reached over with only one hand, his right one; grasped McBride's thumb; and bent it back quickly until the second joint went with a faint, moist popping sound. The black man was called Icky Norris, although his parents had named him Harold Ickes Norris when he had been born thirty-six years before on a farm near Muscle Shoals, Alabama.

Icky Norris smiled faintly without showing any teeth as he watched McBride lick away the two tears. "Go ahead and cry, man," he said. "Shit, we doan blame you."

McBride looked at him. In a soft voice that just escaped being gentle he said, "Get stuffed, Icky." The black man smiled again, just as faintly as before, and then gave his head a couple of sorrowful shakes as though to demonstrate that he bore McBride neither grudge nor malice.

"Saturday," Icky Norris said, although the way he said it made it sound something like "Saa'dy," but not quite. "Saturday," he said again, "noon."

"Yeah," McBride said, "noon."

"You get behind like you got behind, Eddie," the man across the table said, "and it gets hard to catch up. When you borrowed that five thou from Solly you said right up front that you maybe couldn't pay it back for a couple of months on account of things being a little tight for you just then. Well, hell, Solly appreciated that. He really did. Some of these jerk-offs will come in and say, 'Hey, Solly, lemme have five thou for a week, I got a real sweet deal goin'.' Well, shit, they ain't got no deal goin' and they can't pay no five thou back in no week, but Solly, because he's a sweetheart, he really is, will say, 'Okay, here's five thou, but I gotta have it back in a week.' Well, you know what happens."

The man shook his head glumly, as though suddenly struck by the realization that all was perfidy. "What happens is that the jerk-off starts playing hide-and-seek and me and Icky here have to drop what we're doing and go find him and try and convince him that if he can't pay the nut, then he's gotta pay the vigorish. And lemme tell you that some of these jerk-offs are so dumb that it takes just one hell of a lot of convincing."

The man delivering the cautionary monologue was Antonio Egidio, sometimes called Tony Egg because of both his name and his shaved skull, which, along with his muscles, made him look very much like Mr. Clean. He often complained that if he hadn't lost his hair ten years ago when he was twenty-three, he would have had a clear shot at the Mr. America title. Icky Norris, who wasn't quite as tall as Tony Egg's six-two, but whose bulging muscles were just as overly developed, claimed that the only reason he had never got to be Mr. America was because of what he darkly described as "politics."

Both men spent most of their days working out at a gymnasium called Mr. Wonderful on Lincoln Boulevard not too far from Muscle Beach. The gymnasium was owned by Salvatore Gesini, an occasional lender of modest sums—never more than $5,000—for which he charged 10 percent a week, or 520 percent in simple annual interest. Eddie McBride, into Gesini for the maximum $5,000, had fallen behind in his payments. The broken thumb was a Please Remit notice.

McBride now had the thumb down underneath the table pressed lightly between his thighs. It seemed to help the pain a little, but not much.

"I've gotta go find a doctor," McBride said.

Icky Norris made no move to let him out of the booth. "Finish your drink, man. Hell, that's good Scotch."

McBride picked up the shot glass and drained the whiskey. They're not through yet, he told himself. They haven't got to the real horror stuff yet. That's what they always leave you with, the horror stuff.

"Now, Eddie, we know you're gonna be here Saturday noon just like you said," Tony Egg said. "Hell, me and Icky here trust you, don't we, Icky?"

"Sure, man."

"But Saturday's only a couple of days away and you gotta come up with at least a thousand bucks by then and we're just sort of curious about how you're gonna do it. I mean, we don't want all the details or anything like that. We just want something that we can tell Solly, on account of you know how he worries."

McBride started to speak, but stopped because he felt that if he spoke the words would come out high and scratchy. He cleared his throat. "A couple of guys out in Malibu," he said. "We've got a deal going. I'm gonna go see 'em at two o'clock this afternoon."

"Out in Malibu, huh?" Icky Norris said. "Well, that's nice out there. Real nice."

"Lot of money in Malibu," Tony Egg said. "Lot of money." He shifted in his seat, leaned forward across the table, and dropped his deep voice down into an even deeper tone, which gave his confidential whisper a rumbling sound something like distant artillery. Enemy artillery.

"Are these two guys you're gonna go see thinking of buying something off of you maybe?"

"Maybe."

"Maybe like a map?"

"Maybe."

"Maybe like a map of where all you've gotta do is take a shovel and dig up maybe two million bucks?"

"It's there," McBride said.

Tony Egg leaned back in his booth, picked up his glass of Tab, and took a swallow. "Oh, hell, I don't doubt it's there, not for a minute. I mean, when you told me and Icky and then Solly about it, well, shit, you know, you convinced everybody, didn't he, Icky?"

"Convinced me," the black man said.

"There was only this one thing, and that was the thing Solly raised, which was really sort of a minor point, like they say, but hell, there it was, and what bothered Solly sort of was that he never could figure out how you'd get into Nam and then out now that the fucking Commies and all have kind of taken over. I mean, it's just a minor point, but there it is."

"One of these guys is Chinese," McBride said.

Icky Norris turned his mouth down at the corners, stuck out his lower lip, and nodded comfortably as though to testify that that made sense. "Lot of Chinese folks in Nam," he said. "Was when I was there, anyhow."

"Well, hell, that's different, then," Tony Egg said. "All the Chinaman's gotta do is get into Saigon somehow. Just how he's gonna do that I haven't got figured out yet, although maybe it'll come to me in a minute. But anyway, once he's in nobody's gonna notice him, because all those slopes look alike, right? So all he's gotta do then is buy himself a shovel and maybe a flashlight somewhere, wait till it gets dark, then sneak into the embassy grounds and dig it up. Two million bucks. Just like that. Right, McBride?"

"It could be done," McBride said in a soft, stubborn voice.

Egidio stared at McBride for a moment, sighed heavily, and slumped back in the booth. He played with his glass of Tab, moving it around on the table. Still playing with it, he said, "You know what I hope, McBride?"

"What?"

"I hope for your sake that these two guys you're gonna go see this afternoon are just half as dumb as you are. Because if they are, maybe you got a half-ass chance of coming up with Solly's thousand by Saturday."

"Noon," Icky Norris said. "Saturday noon."

"We knew a guy one time who had a little trouble coming up with his money," Egidio said, looking at Norris. "Remember old Toss Spiliotopoulos?"

"Shit, man, he was something else, wasn't he?"

"He was a Greek," Tony Egg said to McBride. "Toss Spiliotopoulos. Took me about a month to learn how to pronounce his name. Well, all Greeks have got what's called an Achilles' heel. They like to gamble. You know what an Achilles' heel is, don't you, McBride?"

"Yeah, I know," McBride said, and knew it was coming now. The horror stuff.

"Well, there's also something called an Achilles tendon. But anyway, to get back to old Toss, he got behind in his payments and took off for Vegas to try to double up and catch up, but that didn't work out because it never does, and so he just got more and more behind. Well, the first thing you know old Toss the Greek has got himself a severed Achilles tendon. Now, if you ain't ever seen a guy trying to walk around with a severed Achilles tendon, then you've missed one of the funniest fucking sights in the world."

Icky Norris chuckled. "Old foot's flippety-floppin' back and forth and up and down and ever which way." Norris flopped his hand around to demonstrate. "He sure was some sight."

"And the thing about it is that sometimes they can't fix it, can they, Icky?"

"Couldn't fix old Toss," Norris said. "Last time I seen him he was scootin' along the street on crutches, over on Wilshire in Santa Monica, his left foot just a wiggly-wagglin', flippety-floppin' up and down and back and forth and ever which way. He sure was some sight."

Tony Egg yawned and stretched. "Well, hell, McBride, we don't wanta make you late for your appointment. How's your thumb feelin'?"

"It hurts like hell," McBride said. "I've gotta go find a doctor."

"Yeah, he can fix it up and maybe give you a pill or something." Tony Egg slid out of the booth and stood up. As he moved, his huge muscles bunched and rolled and threatened to burst through his tight white T-shirt. McBride looked up at him and thought, He's got a pea head. He grew all those muscles and they make his head look like a pea. He looks like a fucking freak, he decided, finding comfort in the thought.

Icky Norris was now up and standing beside Egidio. Norris also wore a T-shirt. He stretched and yawned, making his muscles ripple and roll. McBride watched as Norris sneaked a glance toward the bar to see whether any admirers were watching. None was, and McBride caught Norris' flicker of disappointment. Another fucking freak, McBride decided.

Icky Norris turned and leaned down and across the table, supporting himself on his two huge, thick forearms. He leaned forward until his face was only a few inches from McBride's. There was something on Norris's breath, and

McBride decided that it was cinammon. The black man
made the muscles of his forearms jump and roll a couple of
times for McBride's benefit.

"Saturday, man," Icky Norris said. "Saturday noon—unless you wanta try walkin' wiggledy-waggledy."

"Yeah, sure," McBride said. "Saturday, noon."

Chapter Four

Because she loved the touch and feel of fine things, but
knew she would always be too poor to possess any, Ophelia
Armitage had rather wistfully given her three daughters the
names of some things that she admired most.

By early 1963 the Armitage sisters, Ivory, Lace, and Silk,
were the hottest folk group in both the United States and
England. But on Christmas Eve of that same year, Ophelia
Armitage was found dead of a stroke, alone in her tiny house
near the Black Mountain Folk School in the Arkansas
Ozarks. Those who came looking for her discovered that one
room of the house contained almost nothing but fine silk,
costly lace, and rare ivory.

Also found tucked away out of sight underneath her bed in
a slop jar was a Hills Brothers coffee can stuffed with
$19,439 in cash. Thus, when she died Ophelia Armitage had
been poor no longer, and nearly everyone agreed that the
girls had been awfully good to their mama.

Ivory, the oldest sister, was dead now too, having died in
1970, alone like her mother, and again like her mother,
dying on Christmas Eve, but in a Miami Beach hotel room
—dead from an overdose of heroin that she had bought from
a grinning Cuban bellhop.

By mid-1970 the group had already disbanded—nearly, but not quite, at the height of its popularity. A little less than six months later, Ivory was dead and Lace had just finished her first picture. It had been a small, nothing-much role, but there had been one particularly meaty scene that Lace had handled so superbly that she had been nominated for the Academy Award for best supporting actress.

She didn't win the award, but her roles grew steadily larger and her popularity soared. By 1973, when she married Randall Piers, Lace Armitage was one of the two bankable actresses in the world. The other was an eleven-year-old girl with a foul mouth who could also wiggle her nose like a rabbit.

Lace, the second oldest, was usually considered to be the most beautiful of the three sisters, although it was hard to decide, really, because all three were stunning—even Silk, the youngest, who had been only sixteen when she had made her first million dollars in 1963.

But even at sixteen Silk had been the one best able to cope with all of that sudden fame and big money. That's probably because she was the one most like Papa, Lace Armitage sometimes thought. Papa never gave a damn about money either. The only thing the self-ordained Reverend Jupiter Armitage had ever really given a damn about was the coming of the peaceful socialist revolution, which, he sometimes swore, was due next year or, at the latest, the year after that. The Reverend Mr. Armitage had gone to his grave in late November of 1960, poor as Job's turkey, but convinced that Jack Kennedy would be sworn into office with a socialist blueprint in his hip pocket.

"When we were growing up," Lace had once told her husband, "I sometimes think politics was half of our diet along with cole slaw and black-eyed peas. And corn bread. We ate a lot of corn bread, too. But Ivory never did care about politics or about what she ate either, or even if she ate at all. Poor Ivory. Sometimes I think she must have lived where all the sad poets live, in that secret place where everything hurts all the time. Then she finally discovered dope, which must have been what she'd always been looking for, and she had enough money to buy as much as she wanted, so that's what she did. I never tried to stop her. I don't know, maybe I should've, but I didn't."

"But Silk," Randall Piers had said. "Silk's different, right?"

God, yes, Silk's different, Lace Armitage had told him. "Silk was always just like Papa, all mouth and brains and both of them going wide open and full out from get up till go to bed. She was his favorite, and she was always with him from the time she was four going on five. You know what she did? She listened. You never saw a child listen so hard. And then, somewhere around 1958, when Silk was about— oh, hell—eleven, I reckon—she started talking; I mean talking just like a grown-up. And by golly, you know they all listened to her. They had to, because she was so smart and made such damn good sense."

Piers had nodded understandingly. "Life at the bomb-throwing school," he had said.

When Lace Armitage awoke that morning at eleven she awoke as she always did, quickly, almost abruptly, and Randall Piers was where he usually was, in the cream-colored chair near the window that looked south and west toward Little Point Dume. She smiled at him.

"Have you been there long?"

"Not long." He rose, picked up a freshly poured cup of coffee from a table, and carried it over to her. She propped herself up in the bed against the pillows and accepted the cup gratefully.

"You shouldn't bother," she said, "but I'm glad you do."

"I like to do it," he said. "What time was it this morning?"

"When I got to sleep?"

Piers nodded.

"About five, I think. Maybe a bit later. It was just beginning to get light."

"You should try those new ones he gave you."

"No pills," she said.

"He swears they're not addictive."

"No pills," she said again. "When we get this thing with

Silk straightened out I'll start sleeping fine again." She took a sip of her coffee and then looked at her husband again. "Today's Thursday?"

Piers nodded. "The call came about nine. A man."

"How much?"

"The same as always, a thousand."

"What'd he use this time?"

"Calliope the calico. Was that okay?"

Lace smiled. "That was a kitten Silk once had. A calico kitten that became a cat. She called it Calliope because it sounded like one. Did Kun drop it off?" Kun was Kun Oh Lim, the Korean bodyguard-chauffeur.

Piers nodded.

"Where?"

"Somewhere over in Gardena."

"She's moving around."

"Maybe not," Piers said. "Maybe she's just moving the drop around."

Lace frowned and chewed on her lower lip. "What's it been now, two months?"

"About."

"God damn it, I want to do something."

"Silk made the rules."

"If I could just talk to her."

"She doesn't want you involved."

"I'm already involved. I'm her sister, damn it."

"I had those private detectives, remember? They thought they were getting close and then she found out and made me call them off."

"Those ass-holes. I don't blame her. Look, I just want to see her and talk to her. Maybe we should go at it from a different angle, another approach."

Piers sighed. "Two guys I've just met. They might do. As you said, a new approach."

"Where'd you meet them?"

"On the beach."

"Just like that?"

Piers sighed again and nodded. "Ebsworth's checking

them out. You can meet them this evening. They're coming over for drinks."

"What're they like?"

"Well, one's sort of tall and fat and Chinese, and the other one's sort of tall and skinny with scars on his back."

"Where'd he get the scars?"

"I don't know."

"What do they do?"

"Well, they play the market a little."

"Oh, swell, marvelous. What else?"

"I don't know, but somehow I've got the feeling that they go in for chancey stuff."

"How chancey?"

"I'm not sure."

"You didn't say anything about Silk to them."

"No."

Lace frowned, took another swallow of her coffee, and then placed the cup and saucer on the bedside table. "Well, we've got to do something."

"I know," Piers said. "It's interfering with my sex life."

She grinned at him. It was the crooked, charming grin that was almost her trademark. "Nothing wrong with your sex life last night, old man."

"There's nothing wrong with the fucking," he said. "Hell, I'm fucking Lace Armitage. That's what fifty million guys out there dream about—as they damn well should. But afterwards I like a warm ass for my cold feet."

"What do you want me to do, lie there wide awake and stiff as a board all night so you can warm your feet?"

"You could take a pill."

"A pill's not going to cure what's wrong with me," Lace said, staring at Piers.

He shook his head. "I wasn't talking about that."

"You want to talk about it? If you want to talk about it some more, I will."

Piers shook his head again, a small, pained expression on his face. "Talking about it never does much good, does it?"

She shrugged. "Not much. I just keep on making the same mistake over and over."

For a while they were silent, both thinking about some of those past mistakes and the men they involved—men whose names filed through Piers's mind in perfect chronological order.

Lace knew how to break the somberness of his mood. She threw back the covers and swung her feet to the floor. She was naked, and Piers experienced the same pleasant shock with which the sight of her still affected him, even three years after he had first seen her, as she liked to describe it, bare assed and buck naked.

At thirty-two, Lace Armitage's body was still almost perfect, at least in her husband's opinion, although there were some who carped about the high breasts' being a bit large and even argued that the long legs were a touch thin. But no one had ever faulted the smooth, perfect shoulders or the narrow waist that rounded out into the melonlike hips that she could make roll, when she was fooling around and talking Arkansas, "like two bull pups under a blanket."

But if her body was nearly perfect, there was enough wrong with her face to make it haunting if not beautiful. People remembered that face. To begin with, there was all that thick auburn hair, which grew so that it was nearly always flopping down into those green eyes. The eyes were probably too green and too large and set too far apart, although they had to be that far apart to rest properly on those high cheekbones, which were so pronounced that they would have made her face seem hollow had it not been for her wide mouth with its sensual, almost too thick lips that seemed to promise all sorts of interesting oral sex. Except when she smiled. Randall Piers called it her "fuck tomorrow" smile, and it was what people remembered about her most and made them wish that they knew somebody who could smile like that.

She moved over to her husband, tousled his gray hair, leaned down, and kissed him on the crown. He put his arm around her, squeezed one of the cheeks of her buttocks, and kissed her on the stomach.

"I've got to go pee," she said.

"You always make it sound like a news flash," he said.

She started across the room toward the bath.

"Papa always told us that the body had certain natural functions that—" The closing of the bathroom door cut off the rest of her sentence.

Piers waited, knowing that when his wife came out she would finish the sentence as if there had been no interruption. It was the way her mind worked. Sometimes she would start a thought one week and finish it the next. If you didn't pick up on it, she would look at you as though you were a fool. She had never once looked at Piers that way, because he was certainly no fool and had the kind of mind and memory that could connect up his wife's thoughts even if their beginnings and ends were separated by as much as a month, which occasionally they were.

When Lace came out of the bathroom, she was wearing a white cotton voile robe with small buttercups woven into it. "—they shouldn't be any more embarrassed about than a car's backfire," she continued. "People have to cough, hiccup, fart, sweat, cry, pee, and move their bowels, Papa always said, and if England hadn't tried to pretend that none of these things existed, it would probably still be the greatest country in the world."

"I don't quite follow his last thought there," Piers said.

"Well, I didn't either, but Silk said she did. If they find her, they'll kill her, won't they?"

Piers's mind worked quickly, the way it always did. "Her" was Silk, of course. "They"—well, he wasn't absolutely sure who "they" were, although he had a fairly good idea.

"Your sister's a very smart, competent woman," he said. "She laid down the rules and we agreed to play by them."

"That was two months ago."

"They're Silk's rules and it's her life."

"I want to talk to her. I've just got to talk to her. You understand?"

"I understand."

"These two guys, what makes you think they might be able to find her?"

Piers shrugged. "Mostly hunch, I guess."

Lace stared at him and then smiled. "Is it one of those real gut ones that you get sometimes?"

He nodded.

"Down in here?" She bent over and poked him in the stomach.

"It's not located any one place, dummy."

"You know what I mean."

"It's a real strong feeling, but I could be wrong."

"What's it like?" she said. "I mean, why do you think they might be able to find her?"

"Well, it's simply this feeling I have," he said slowly, "that these two guys are the kind who just might know where to look."

Chapter Five

It was three minutes until two when McBride turned his yellow 1965 Mustang convertible left off the Pacific Coast Highway and started down the narrow, winding asphalt lane that led to the Paradise Cove pier.

The top was down on the convertible, and if his thumb hadn't throbbed so much, and if he hadn't been brooding about the fact that he wasn't still in the Corps and stationed at the embassy in either Paris or London or Bonn, which was where he could have been if only he'd kept his nose clean, McBride might have been able to admire or at least notice the tall green pines and the handsome eucalyptus trees that lined either side of the lane.

But preoccupied as he was with both fate and pain, McBride noticed nothing, not even the pothole. He hit it at twenty miles per hour. The resulting jolt made the front wheels start to shimmy. Without thinking, McBride grasped the steering wheel with both hands. When he did, the pain from his bandaged left thumb flared up, and the hot tears that filled his eyes almost blinded him.

"Assholes!" McBride screamed. It was a broadside indictment, aimed at the world in general, but in particular at the U.S. Marine Corps; Tony Egg and Icky Norris; McBride's landlord, who wanted to evict him; the young doctor at the free dope fiends' clinic in Venice who had reset and taped up his thumb, but who had refused to give him anything for the pain, implying that McBride had probably broken the thumb just to get himself some free dope; and finally, the last asshole on the list, the management of Paradise Cove, whose clearly culpable negligence had created the pothole.

At one time, back in the '20s, Paradise Cove had been a rumrunners' haven. But now it was a trailer park that boasted a seafood restaurant, a pier where you could either launch your boat or rent one, and three-quarters of a mile of private beach that you could spend the day on if you could afford the price, which that year was $3 a car. McBride's immediate objective was to talk his way past the guard at the gate without paying the $3.

At the end of the lane McBride braked his car and waited for the guard to come out of the small office.

"I'm going to see Mr. Durant," McBride said.

The guard, a tall, skinny man with disappointed eyes, swallowed something, and McBride got to watch his Adam's apple bob up and down. The guard shook his head. "Durant, huh?" He shook his head again. "Durant." The name meant nothing to him.

"He lives in that small yellow house at the end of the parking lot," McBride said.

"Oh, yeah, he's the guy that the Chinaman comes to see all the time."

McBride nodded. "That's him."

"Du-rant," the guard said slowly, stretching the syllables out. "Durant. I guess I better try to remember that."

"Work on it," McBride said. He let in his clutch and pulled away, heading toward the beach. Directly in front of him, about a hundred yards away, was the pier. To his right was the parking lot that served the restaurant, which was a white, one-story structure built for some reason along faintly colonial lines, perhaps because it sold a lot of what its menu described as New England clam chowder. To the left of the pier was another large parking lot, about the size of a narrow city block, and at the end of that was the yellow house with the green roof.

McBride drove to the end of the parking lot, pulled into a space, switched off his engine, and listened to it as it kept on running for a few moments. The engine hadn't done that before, and McBride automatically took it as a portent of awful things to come.

He got out of the car, remembering not to open the door with his damaged left hand, and walked up the driveway that led from the parking lot to a small garage that was attached to the yellow house. Guarding the driveway were some signs that read, KEEP OUT, PRIVATE PROPERTY and NO PARKING, VIOLATORS WILL BE TOWED AWAY. Ignoring the signs was a large green Chrysler station wagon that McBride recognized as belonging to Artie Wu. He needs it for all those kids of his, McBride thought, and tried to remember whether the Wu clan numbered four or five.

When he reached the half-glass door, McBride knocked and waited until Artie Wu opened it. Wu nodded, and McBride went in. He followed the slightly limping Wu into the living room, where they turned and inspected each other's damage.

"I tripped over a dead pelican," Wu said. "What happened to you?"

McBride looked down at his taped-up thumb. "I owe a couple of guys a little money. This here's the past-due notice."

"They break it?"

"They broke it."

"The bastards," Wu said, and McBride was a little surprised at how much compassion went into the comment.

"Sit down some place while I go get Durant." Wu turned to leave, but stopped. "You want a drink?"

"Got any beer?"

"In the fridge. Help yourself."

Wu left, and McBride went over to the refrigerator, opened it, and took out a can of Schlitz. He popped it open, took a swallow, and then moved over to the newsprinter which was still clacking away in the corner. He glanced at what was coming off the printer, found it dull, drank some more beer, and inspected the titles of several of the books that lined the wall. They looked dull too. There were *The Emperor Charles V* by Brandi, George Antonius' *The Arab Awakening, The Age of the Reformation* by Preserved Smith, and the U.S. Government Printing Office's *Investigation of Senator Thomas J. Dodd—Part I.*

McBride decided that the books were there for decorative purposes. He was almost sure that nobody would ever read them, not unless they were forced to. On the other hand, Durant might have read every one of them. McBride found Durant hard to figure and had to remind himself constantly not to "sir" him when they spoke. That's what eight years in the Corps'll do to you, he told himself. Make you wanta say "sir" to any ass-hole who's ever cracked a book.

He turned when Wu and Durant came into the living room. Durant was still barefoot and wearing his sawed-off jeans, but he had a shirt on now, a frayed blue oxford-cloth one with a button-down collar, although the buttons were long missing. He wore it with the tails out and the sleeves rolled halfway up to his elbows. Artie Wu, also barefoot, wore white duck shorts and a gaudy green-and-gold shirt that was big as a tent, but still not big enough to conceal his gut.

"Artie told me about your thumb," Durant said. "Does it still hurt?"

"Some," McBride said.

"Want some pain-killer?"

"You got any?"

Durant nodded. "I'll give you a couple when you go. Just don't take them before you drive and don't mix with booze."

"I'll take 'em tonight," McBride said. "Things always hurt worse at night."

"Sit down," Durant said.

McBride sat down on the Eames chair, but didn't lean back. He sat hunched forward, his arms resting on his knees, the can of beer in his right hand. He watched closely, trying to read something into the way Durant chose the couch and Wu the suede chair. Nothing to read, he decided. Just two guys sitting down, one of them fat and the other one skinny.

Artie Wu produced a long, slim cigar from a shirt pocket, cut off its end with a tiny knife, stuck it into the left side of his mouth, and lit it with a kitchen match that he struck with his right thumbnail. He looked at McBride as he blew some smoke out, and McBride noticed that he inhaled.

"No deal, Eddie," Artie Wu said. "Sorry."

"Shit," McBride said.

Wu and Durant watched as McBride took a long draught of his beer. "Well, shit," he said again.

"You were counting on it, I suppose," Durant said.

"Yeah, I was counting on it."

"We checked it out," Durant said.

"If you checked it out, then you know it's there."

"That's not the problem," Wu said.

"You guys could do it," McBride said.

"I'm thirty-seven," Wu said. "That makes me too old to try because I'm too young to die."

"You guys could do it," McBride said stubbornly.

"We called somebody we know in Zurich," Durant said. "He goes in and out of Saigon."

"Jesus, you didn't tell him about the whole thing, did you?"

"We told him just enough," Wu said. "No more."

Durant stared at McBride. "He wouldn't touch it, not even for half."

"You tell him how much half was?"

"We told him."

McBride gave his lower lip a couple of bites. "Well, shit," he said again. He looked at Durant and then at Wu. "Why don't you look at it like this. Maybe you can't get in this year—or maybe even next. But at the end of a couple of years they're gonna have diplomatic relations with Nam again. Hell, you know it and I know it. They're already talking about it. So why don't you look at it as a long-term investment? For five thousand bucks you can have every-thing—my ten percent, the map, everything. Then when things calm down, hell, maybe even three years from now, you can find some ass-hole on the embassy staff and cut a deal with him. Even if you cut it fifty-fifty, you'd still be a million bucks ahead."

Eddie McBride had been selling, something that he didn't do very well and, worse, knew that he didn't. The effort had made his armpits sweat, and they felt cold and damp and nasty. They can probably smell it, he thought. Even from where I'm sitting they can probably smell it.

Durant fished an unfiltered Pall Mall cigarette out of his shirt pocket. He looked at it for a moment with something like revulsion, then sighed, put it into his mouth, and lit it with a disposable lighter.

"You're forgetting something, Eddie," Durant said.

"What?"

"There were two of you, right?"

"Yeah, two of us."

"Who was he?"

"Some spook. He'd been out in the boonies and he came in at the last moment and they assigned him the money."

"And you were shotgun?" Wu said.

"That's right."

"Was it his idea?" Durant said.

McBride stared at them for a moment. "I was a Marine sergeant. He was a CIA heavy. Who the fuck's idea do you think it was?"

Wu blew a smoke ring. "And you were to split it how—fifty-fifty?"

"Yeah."

"When?" Durant said.

"He said we'd work it out."

"How?" Wu said, and blew another smoke ring and stuck his right forefinger through it.

"He said he had some connections that he was leaving behind."

"Did you believe him?" Durant said.

McBride took another swallow of beer. "No."

"So how much did you take out with you?" Wu said.

"We both grabbed about twenty thousand."

Durant nodded as if that were sensible. "Then what?"

"It was fucking panic after that. The slopes were coming over the goddamned walls. I was on the last chopper out."

"And the spook?" Wu said.

McBride shook his head. "We were supposed to let everything simmer down and then meet here in L.A. six months ago—January fifteenth. We were going to meet in the lobby of the Beverly Hills Hotel. He didn't show on the fifteenth —or the sixteenth, or the seventeenth. He just didn't show. I spent a month in that lobby."

"Did you try to find him?" Durant said.

It was a pained look that McBride gave Durant, who shrugged and said, "Maybe more to the point, did he ever try to find you?"

"I just told you that. No."

Durant put his cigarette out. He did it carefully, and while he was doing it and without looking up he said, "What was his name?"

"Who?"

"The spook."

"Why?"

Durant shrugged. "Maybe it might be worth something."

"Who to?"

"To you," Wu said, and blew another smoke ring, a fat one. It was time to be smart, McBride told himself. The trouble is that you're just smart enough to know that, but not smart enough to do anything about it.

"How much?" he said.

"This jam you're in," Durant said. "How bad is it?"

"Bad."

"You're in how deep?"

"Five thousand."

"And you're what, a week behind?"

"Almost two. Two, Saturday. Noon."

"Who's the shylock?"

"Solly Gesini."

"Jesus," Wu said.

Durant looked at him. "You know him?"

"I've heard of him," Wu said. "He's the worst, the real basement."

"Is he lined up with anybody?" Durant said.

McBride shrugged. "Solly drops a lot of names. He's always talking about all the Wop gongos he knows in Chicago or Miami or Vegas or someplace."

Durant studied McBride for several moments. He looks exactly like what the taxpayers pray that the Marine Corps looks like, he thought. Not too tall, not too heavy, and tough without being mean. Fairly competent, maybe even half clever, but certainly not brilliant. Presentable, almost handsome, but far from pretty. It's Eddie McBride, the can-do kid, the perfect embodiment of the American ideal that lies somewhere between a shorter Gary Cooper and a taller Steve McQueen.

"You weren't too smart, Eddie," Durant said finally.

"Smart?" McBride said. "Smart's got nothing to do with it. Nobody goes to a loan shark because it's the smart thing to do. They go because they're desperate. They go because they got no place else to go."

He jerked his head at the newsprinter. "You guys," he said. "You guys take a chance every now and then, don't you?"

Durant nodded.

"Okay, and the bigger the risk the bigger the payoff, right? Sure. You can look it up. Well, you take a risk when you go to a loan shark, too. You know that something awful's gonna happen to you if you don't pay 'em back, but it's not as awful as what's gonna happen if you don't get the money. You follow me?"

"So what's going to happen to you, Eddie?" Wu said.

McBride bent over and pulled up his pants leg, peeled down his sock, and pointed to his Achilles tendon. "They're going to cut it," he said, "right about there."

Durant sighed. "How much would it cost to keep you from getting cut?"

"A thousand."

"That would keep you out of trouble for how long?"

"A week, maybe two."

"That's not long."

McBride snorted. "If you've been living the way I've been living, a week's forever."

He watched as some silent message passed between Wu and Durant. Wu shrugged slightly, reached into his pocket, and brought out a flat, thick, folded sheaf of bills that were pressed together by an oversized solid-silver paper clip. Wu counted out five one-hundred-dollar bills and then ten fifties, folded them lengthwise, and almost, but not quite, offered them to McBride.

"Who was the spook, Eddie?" Wu said.

McBride swallowed. Then he cleared his throat before speaking, because he was again afraid that what he was going to say would come out high or maybe even squeaky.

"He had a funny name."

Wu waved the sheaf of bills, not much, just a little. "So."

"Childester," McBride said. "Luke Childester."

Wu handed him the money without comment. Durant leaned back on the couch, clasped his hands behind his head, and stared up at the ceiling. He seemed thoughtful.

"I—I don't know when I can pay you guys back," McBride said.

"That's for services rendered," Durant said, still staring up at the ceiling. "We took up your time and time's worth something, so we pay for it."

McBride automatically tried to figure their angle. He knew that there had to be one, and he put all of his cunning to work in an attempt to determine what it was. And then it occurred to him that there just possibly might not be an angle. That made him experience the almost totally foreign emotion of gratitude, which he wasn't at all sure that he liked because it made him swallow a lot.

"Look," he said, and this time his voice did squeak a

little. He forced it down into its normal register. "Look, if you guys ever need anything—I mean anything—well, shit, you know where to find me."

"That's right, Eddie," Artie Wu said. "We know."

Chapter Six

It was exactly 5:32 that evening when Hart Ebsworth, carrying a small stack of three-by-five cards, entered Randall Piers's study and took his usual seat in one of the brown leather chairs that faced the carved oak desk. Piers watched as Ebsworth carefully rearranged the cards, getting them into the exact order that he wanted.

For a few moments Ebsworth said nothing as he concentrated on the cards, shuffling and rearranging them, frowning a bit as he worked. The cards were filled with the lawyer's cramped scribblings that were virtually indecipherable to anyone but him. Ebsworth liked to work from cards because he found them neat, concise, and logical.

Finally, Piers grew tired of waiting and said, "Well?"

Ebsworth looked up. "A couple of real hot-doggers," he said. "Hardball players. They've done it all. Or almost all."

"Oh?" Piers sounded pleased. "What haven't they done?"

"Well, they've apparently never killed anybody and they've never been caught stealing and they've only been in jail twice, once in Mexico and once in Djakarta. And the Chinese gentleman, if you're still with me, is the pretender to the throne of China. The last of the Manchus. Or so he says."

Piers nodded and grinned. He looked pleased. "Tell me," he said.

"About Artie Wu?"

"Yeah. Pretender to the throne of China. Damn, I like that. By God, I do."

"Well, according to Wu—and he has some pretty fancy documentation to back him up, although I guess it could be faked—he's the illegitimate son of the illegitimate daughter of the Boy Emperor who was called P'u Yi by most Westerners. You want more?"

"Absolutely."

"The Boy Emperor—and he was the last one they ever had—ascended to the throne in 1908 when he was not quite three, I think. In 1912 he was forced to abdicate by Sun Yat-sen, but they let him hang around the palace in Peking until about 1924. Well, in 1922, just before he got married, there was this fourteen-year-old girl in the palace who had an illegitimate daughter. P'u Yi, it seems, had knocked her up. The fourteen-year-old, I mean, not the one he married. So all the high pooh-bahs in the court wanted to get rid of the baby—strangle her or throw her out with the garbage or whatever. But P'u Yi—you'll like this next part—got one of his faithful eunuchs—"

"You're making it up," Piers said happily.

"I'm not."

"A faithful eunuch, by God!"

"Well, the faithful eunuch smuggled the kid out of the palace and turned her over to Mr. and Mrs. C. Howard Hempstead, a couple of Methodist missionaries who were both about forty and childless."

"And they took the kid in."

"Right. They adopted her and took her to San Francisco with them when they went back in 1926."

"Whatever happened to the Boy Emperor?"

"He got married and finally they chased him out of Peking and he wound up in Tientsin and then, about 1931, after the Japanese took over Manchuria, they made him emperor of that, which really wasn't much of a job, but he stayed with it until the Russians dragged him off the throne in 1945. Then when Mao came along in 1949 or '50, P'u Yi got thrown into jail—actually, it was a labor reform camp—but finally they let him out and he wound up as a tourist guide in Peking—at the Heavenly Palace, in fact. He died in '66."

"And the girl?"

"She grew up in San Francisco with the Hempsteads. Then in early 1939 this old friend from China visited them on some kind of a fund-raising trip. He was a Chinese Methodist bishop, and if I've got it right, his name was Bertrand Sooming Liu. It seems that the bishop had an eye for the ladies."

"The girl was how old by then?"

"In '39? Seventeen, I guess. Sixteen, maybe."

"And the bishop snuck into her bedroom, huh?"

"Somebody did. Anyway, she got pregnant and died giving birth to Artie Wu. By then the Hempsteads were in their late fifties, but being good Christians they adopted the new baby and gave him the name Arthur Case Wu—which was his mother's surname. I don't know where they got the Arthur Case."

"Then what?"

"Well, on August 9, 1945, the Hempsteads got killed in a car wreck in Oakland. They had no relatives, close or otherwise, so Artie Wu was dumped into the John Wesley Memorial Methodist Orphanage in San Francisco. Guess what six-year-old was there to show him the ropes?"

"Durant," Piers said.

"Right. Quincy Durant—and that's all anybody knows about him. He got left on the orphanage steps in the usual bassinet or basket when he was about six weeks old. He had a tag around his neck that read Quincy. Nobody knew whether Quincy was his first name or his last, but the guy who ran the orphanage had once had a Durant car—was there a Durant car?"

"Yeah, I think so," Piers said.

"So he named him after this car that he'd once had."

"Jesus," Piers said. "Then what?"

"Well, they stuck it out at the orphanage until they were

both fourteen, which would be around 1953. August of '53, in fact. And then they simply took off and never went back. They've been partners ever since."

"And afterwards?" Piers said. "I mean after the orphanage."

"There's a blank between 1953 and 1956, but by late '56 they're down in New Orleans shucking oysters in some place just off Canal Street. So one night they're going home. It's late, maybe two in the morning. They're going up Chartres, and they decide to cross Jackson Square because they live in a flophouse on Decatur—1021 Decatur."

Ebsworth looked down at his notes to make sure of the address. Piers tried to remember whether Ebsworth had looked at them before and decided that he had, but only once.

Ebsworth glanced up from his notes and frowned—a small, disapproving frown. "Now it gets a bit like Dickens or maybe Horatio Alger." From his tone it was apparent that he didn't think much of either one.

"More," Piers said.

"Comes now Henderson Hodd Belyeu, doctor of philosophy—Princeton '16, it seems—Southern scion, minor poet, one-time associate professor of Greek at the University of Mississippi, and elderly fag. He was sixty-five then, and the first time Durant and Wu saw him he was getting himself beaten up by a couple of deepwater sailors that he'd tried to cruise."

Piers grinned, clasped his hands behind his head, and leaned back in his chair. "Well, now."

"So Durant and Wu waded in and took out the two sailors. They got Dr. Belyeu back up on his feet and brushed him off, and he was so grateful that he invited them up to his apartment. He lives in one of those big old red brick buildings that are on either side of Jackson Square."

"Lives?"

"Lives. I talked to him this afternoon. He's eighty-four and a militant activist in the Vieux Carré chapter of the New Orleans Gay Liberation movement. But it apparently wasn't like that between him and our two heroes, although I sup-

pose he tried. He didn't say. What he did say was that the
first thing he noticed about both Wu and Durant was that
they were bright—very, very bright. Well, they talked almost the entire night—the old man's fascinating, by the
way, he really is—and finally he asked them if they wanted
to be oyster shuckers for the rest of their lives. They said no,
and he offered to tutor them. Which he did."

"Tutored them for what?"

"For college. For Princeton, in fact."

"They're Ivy Leaguers?"

"Well, Wu is, sort of, although he didn't graduate. Durant
was the real scholar, except that he didn't go—not offi-
cially, anyhow, although he went."

"It gets better and better."

"The old man used his influence and that of some of his
friends to get Wu in. One of the letters of recommendation
came from Edmund Wilson, who was an old classmate of
Dr. Belyeu's."

"Jesus."

"The stipulation was that since Wu was the last of the
Manchus, he had to be accompanied everywhere, even to
class, by his faithful bodyguard-companion. Durant."

"The Manchu thing," Piers said. "Who thought that
up—Dr. Belyeu?"

"Right. He started digging into Wu's background and
somehow came up with what I told you." Ebsworth made his
voice go slightly prissy and somewhat Southern. "'There are
a couple of leaps of faith that one has to take, my dear Mr.
Ebsworth, but although it all started out as a rather elaborate
hoax, I now feel that Arthur might very well be the last of
the Manchus. And it is such a delicious story.' He talks like
that. Fascinating old guy."

"So what happened?"

"Well, Dr. Belyeu paid their expenses for the first year."

"And after that?"

"Poker."

"Are they good?"

Ebsworth riffled through his cards. "In 1969 in a table-stakes game at the Leamington Hotel in Minneapolis they walked out with eighty-three thousand dollars."

"But that was later," Piers said. "What happened in between?"

"They dropped out of Princeton in 1960 and went to Mexico. They were messing around with pre-Columbian art, but somehow got into trouble and wound up in jail. The charges were dropped and the next thing you know they're in the Peace Corps."

"The *Peace Corps?*"

"Yeah, they got sent to Indonesia in late '61 and about a year later they're back in jail again. In Djakarta. For smuggling. But again the charges were dropped, although they did a couple of months. Well, after that they wandered around the Pacific for a while, doing God knows what, until they finally wound up in Papeete, population then about nineteen thousand."

"This was when?"

"Early 1963."

"Oh Tahiti, huh?"

"Yeah."

"So what did they do in Papeete?"

"Well, they had a little money and they talked Air France into putting up a little more and they leased this old waterfront bar. Guess what they called it?"

"What?"

"Heyst's."

Piers chuckled. "My God, Conrad's Axel Heyst. I haven't thought of that name in years."

"So let's say you're an ordinary tourist and you wind up in Papeete with nothing much to do and you're looking for a little action. Well, some guy at that Air France outfit, UTA, tips you off to this place called Heyst's down on the waterfront. You know the kind of place. No tourists—just beachcombers, remittance men, and stranded chorus girls."

"I like it."

"So you wander down to Heyst's, and sure enough, there's this fat Chinaman sitting at a table in his white linen suit and Panama hat, looking like a young Sidney Greenstreet, brushing the flies away with his ivory-handled fly whisk, and right away you know that he's up to no good. And the other guy, the thin one, his partner, looks like a failed poet with an impossibly desperate past. And even better are all the good-looking broads who're sitting around the place."

"How'd it go over?" Piers said.

"Big. They ran the place for a little more than a year and then sold out to a syndicate from Sydney."

"That brings them up to when?"

Ebsworth looked at his notes. "The middle of 1964. After that they moved around the Pacific a lot for a couple of years—all over—and then in 1967 they showed up in Bangkok and went into the import-export business. That lasted a couple of years."

"And then?"

"In 1969 they were in Minneapolis for a while and then they turned up in Key West. They went in with a syndicate that was looking for sunken Spanish treasure. They found some—maybe even a lot—but there was a problem with the state, and so by 1970 they were back in Bangkok in the trucking business."

"Trucking?"

Ebsworth looked at his notes. "That's what I got. Well, they used to go in and out of Bangkok a lot. And one time Durant went out and he didn't come back and then Wu went out and when they both came back, Durant went into the hospital."

"For what?"

"Exhaustion is what I got. But actually it was that time that he got the scars."

"You find out how?"

Ebsworth shook his head. "No."

"That was when, now?"

"The spring of '72. When Durant got out of the hospital, they unloaded the trucking business and a month later turned up in Scotland."

"Why Scotland?"

"Maybe because it was a long way from Thailand. They wound up in Aberdeen."

"And what was in Aberdeen?"

"A lot of Texans and Oklahomans."

"For the North Sea drilling?"

"Right. Well, the next thing you know Wu and Durant have opened up something called the Nacogdoches Chili Parlor featuring Texas Jailhouse Chili, the recipe—according to the menu—courtesy of Mrs. Lyndon B. Johnson. Well, it was a smash, even with the Scots. I suppose if you can eat haggis, you can eat anything. Well, a month after they opened the place Wu got married."

"This was, now?"

"The middle of '72."

"Who'd he marry?"

"An impoverished Scottish lass with a trace of royal blood who can trace her family back to before 1297. Agnes Garioch was her maiden name. Now she's Aggie Wu. They had twin sons in '74 and twin daughters in '75. Artie Wu spent a little money with a genealogist in London, and they've figured out that with maybe three revolutions and about ten thousand or so providential deaths, the older of his twin sons, Angus, could be both Emperor of China and King of Scotland."

Piers grinned. "That it?"

"Just about. They sold the chili parlor earlier this year at a big profit and then they all came back to the States. They were in San Francisco for a while and then came down here. Wu rented a house in Santa Monica. Durant has the one on the beach. He pays six hundred and fifty a month for it."

Piers was silent for a moment, thinking, and then he said, "Good job. It must have taken a lot of digging."

"I hired some help," Ebsworth said. "I also used up a couple of big favors in Washington."

"I don't think I'll ask what favors."

"No," Ebsworth said. "Don't."

There was another silence until Piers said, "Well?"

"I think they just might do," Ebsworth said slowly. "But they'll cost."

Piers nodded.

"And," Ebsworth said after a moment, "they're probably going to take just one hell of a lot of convincing."

Piers nodded again. "Well," he said, "that's what I do best."

Chapter Seven

It was the usual mixed bag that had been invited to Randall Pier's for drinks that evening. In addition to a Nobel Laureate, who supposedly was the third-smartest man in the United States, there were a prominent criminal lawyer; a Democratic National Committeewoman; a former child actor turned union business agent; an ex-Governor; a producer who couldn't quite stop reminding people that he had been to Yale; a one-time Rose Bowl queen; and a tall, pleasant man of about thirty-five, a TV producer, who told Artie Wu that he was Boris Karloff's godson and wondered whether Wu would like to join him and his handsome wife in a run up to Oxnard for the world's best burritos in a Mexican joint that they knew. Artie Wu declined with regret, but got the name of the restaurant because he was very fond of Mexican food.

As the party wound down and the guests began to leave, Lace Armitage came up to Durant, put a tentative hand on his arm, and said, "You'll stay for a while longer, won't you, Mr. Durant—you and Mr. Wu? My husband and I really haven't had a chance to talk with you."

Durant looked at her and she gave him her best smile, one that contained an amazing amount of what seemed to be genuine warmth. Durant said, "All right, I'll go talk to Artie."

She smiled at him again, touched his arm gratefully, and moved off to say goodbye to the rest of her guests. Durant went over to Artie Wu, who stood by the pool, drink in hand, staring at the house.

"How do you like the way the rich folks live?" Durant said.

"I like it. Damned if I don't."

"They want us to stay."

Wu nodded. "Piers mentioned it to me."

"Maybe they're just being neighborly."

Wu shook his head. "If you had a hundred and sixty million, would you invite us over?"

"No," Durant said, "now that you mention it, I wouldn't."

Randall Piers took a sip of his drink, looked at Wu and then at Durant, and said, "How much do you know about me?"

They were in Piers's office-study. Lace Armitage was behind her husband's big desk, playing with a silver letter opener. Piers was on a couch, and Wu and Durant were in two of the brown leather chairs. Hart Ebsworth, the lawyer, was in another chair beneath a very good oil portrait of Lace Armitage.

Durant answered Piers's question. "Not much," he said.

"How much?"

"You went through MIT on the GI bill, got your doctorate in '51, started teaching at Cal Tech, got fascinated by electronics and symbolic logic, eventually set up a company called International Data Systems, and nine years later sold out to IBM for roughly one billion dollars. You had almost fifteen percent of the stock, so your cut was about a hundred and fifty million. After that you sort of dabbled in things— politics, a couple of films, a record company, and that magazine you founded, *The Pacific,* which always looks to me like an uneasy cross between the *National Enquirer* and *Arizona Highways*."

"You've been busy," Piers said.

Durant shook his head. "Not really. Artie took a run over to the Malibu library this afternoon."

"We ran a check on you two," Piers said.

Artie Wu frowned. "What does that mean?"

"You've been around."

"That doesn't answer my question," Wu said.

"It means I was interested in your bona fides because I'm going to make you a proposition."

"What my husband is saying is that we'd like you to help us," Lace Armitage said.

"To do what?" Durant said.

Piers looked out through the huge window at Santa Monica, whose lights were just beginning to come on. "I have a sister-in-law whom you've probably heard of, Silk Armitage."

Wu looked at Lace Armitage. "She was the Silk in Ivory, Lace, and Silk, right?"

Lace nodded.

"And she's in trouble," Piers said.

"I'm sorry to hear that," Durant said, "but I can't see what it has to do with us. We're not exactly in the trouble business. In fact, we try to avoid it."

"Not always," Ebsworth said.

Durant looked at Ebsworth and then at Piers. "What does he do?"

"As I said, he's my lawyer."

"You need a lawyer for this?"

"Maybe."

Durant shook his head. "Then I don't think I'm going to like it."

Lace Armitage tossed the silver letter opener on to the desk with a clatter. "This is becoming a waste of time."

"Probably," Artie Wu said.

"Maybe we're going a little fast for you," Piers said to Durant.

"Maybe. We meet a guy in the morning. We have a cup of coffee together and a few laughs, and being neighborly, he invites us over for drinks that evening. By the time we get here he's run a check on us. Whatever it is he finds out about our pasts—something unsavory, probably—convinces him that we're the kind who can get his sister-in-law out of some jam she's in. As you say, it's a little swift for me, a little sudden."

"Mention money," Ebsworth said to Piers.

Piers shook his head. "Not yet. We'll get to that later."

"How much money are we going to get to later?" Artie Wu said.

Piers looked at him. "Enough."

Wu shrugged and grinned. "I'll listen."

"What about you?" Piers said to Durant.

Durant sighed and rattled the ice in his glass. "I think I could use another drink first."

Ebsworth rose and took Durant's glass. "Scotch?"

"Anything."

"You care for one?" Ebsworth said to Artie Wu.

Wu shook his head. He produced one of his long cigars. "I'll just smoke this if nobody minds."

Nobody did, and Wu used his tiny knife to slice off the end, stuck the cigar into his mouth, and lit it with a kitchen match.

Piers waited until Durant had his drink. Then he said, "What do you know about Pelican Bay?"

"Not much. It's a city down the coast on the other side of Venice. About a hundred and fifty thousand in population. Sort of ugly. And I hear it's a little like Philadelphia used to be, corrupt and contented."

"Pelican Bay," Piers said, "was part of the district of a Congressman who died a couple of months ago. Congressman Floyd Ranshaw. Know anything about him?"

"I know how he died," Wu said. "He died messy. His wife shot him and then shot herself."

"So they say."

"Who's they?" Durant said.

"The Pelican Bay cops. The Ranshaws had been separated for a year. His wife checked into a motel room with a bottle. She'd been having trouble with the booze. The Congressman was back in town from Washington. She called him. He went over, probably to see if he could get her into a drying-out place. She pulled a gun and shot him and then shot herself. Suicide-murder. Case closed."

Piers waited for the question he knew would come.

"What's this got to do with your sister-in-law?" Durant said.

"Silk was living with Ranshaw," Lace Armitage said. "She had been for not quite a year."

"In fact, she was waiting outside the motel in her car when he was killed," Piers said. "And that's the last time anyone's seen her."

"But you've heard from her?" Durant said.

"Just once."

"What'd she say?"

"She talked to me," Lace Armitage said. "It was two days after it happened. My sister is usually a very relaxed person, calm as clams. But this time she was nervous, all tensed up, and very, very scared. I could tell. She said it didn't happen the way the cops said it did. She wouldn't say how she knew that, but she did say she was in just one hell of a lot of danger, so much so that she was going to have to disappear.

"She said she knew some people who would help her and that she would need money, but not too much because too much might draw attention to her. She said she would have somebody call us every week. It would be in a kind of code. Whoever called would mention something that only she and I would know about, something from when we were kids. Then whoever called would tell us where to drop the money off. The same amount every week, one thousand dollars. And that's the last time I ever talked to her."

Wu nodded and inhaled some of his cigar. "And this was when, two months ago?"

"Just about," Piers said.

"You'd better tell them about the other thing she told you," Ebsworth said to Lace.

She nodded. "Silk said that we should look into how the Congressman's wife felt about guns."

"Did you?" Durant said.

"I hired some private detectives," Piers said. "They learned that back in 1947 when the Congressman's wife had been six years old, she found her father's service pistol. A forty-five automatic. He tried to take it away from her. It went off and blew his brains all over the bedroom wall. Ever since then she was frightened of guns. She was more than frightened. They terrified her."

"You told the Pelican Bay cops about this?" Wu said.

"Ebsworth did," Piers said.

"I took a copy of the report," Ebsworth said, "and drove down to Pelican Bay and personally handed it over to the chief of police, a guy called Oscar Ploughman. I sat there and watched him read it. When he was through he made me a nice little speech about how much he always liked to meet a public-spirited citizen. Then he very politely told me that he would take the report under advisement and that perhaps it might be better if I went back to L.A. and waited until I heard from him. I'm still waiting."

Durant took a Pall Mall out of his shirt pocket, looked at it regretfully, and lit it.

"You trying to quit?" Piers said.

"Not really," Durant said. "I just go through a bit of self-loathing every time I light one." He pulled some more smoke down into his lungs, blew it out, and said: "So what you're saying is that both the Congressman and his wife were probably murdered; your sister-in-law may or may not know who did it, but thinks she's in trouble; and the Pelican Bay cops may or may not be sitting on their hands. Is that it?"

"Roughly," Piers said.

"What do you want us to do about it?"

"Find her."

"Why don't you use private detectives? We're not in the people-finding business."

"I know. That's why I want you to do it. I tried private detectives. They got close, she found out, and she made me call them off."

Artie Wu blew a smoke ring. "If we find her, what then?"

"You'd ask her to set up a meeting between her and Lace. Anyplace Silk says, anytime."

"And if she won't?" Wu said, and blew another ring.

Piers looked at his wife. Lace Armitage sighed and picked
up the letter opener again. "If she won't, she won't. But I'll
give you a letter—which will be part begging, part personal
entreaty from one sister to another. Family stuff. I think I
can make it strong enough so that she'll agree to see me."
Lace paused. "I hope I can, anyway."

Piers looked at Wu and then at Durant. "Now I'll mention
money, all right?"

"All right," Durant said.

"One month of your time, twenty-five thousand dollars. If
you find her, another twenty-five. If she agrees to the meeting a total of seventy-five thousand."

Durant stared at him and then smiled slightly. "You can
afford it, can't you?"

"That's right," Piers said. "I can afford it. But I don't
throw money away. Finding Silk is awfully important to
both me and my wife."

Durant looked at Wu. "Well?"

Wu grinned. "I'm a miner, I'll go down."

"What does that mean?" Piers said.

"Probably yes," Durant said.

"You don't want to talk it over?"

Durant shook his head, another slight smile on his face.
"We have a rule never to talk it over when somebody offers
us twenty-five thousand dollars for a month of our time."

"By the way," Wu said, "will it be cash or check?"

Piers nodded at Ebsworth, who rose, moved over to Durant, and took a check from the breast pocket of his jacket.
He looked at the check as though to make sure that the
amount was correct and handed it to Durant, who glanced at
it, nodded appreciatively, and then looked at Piers.

"You're taking just one hell of a chance," he said.

Piers nodded. "As I told you this morning, I sometimes go
into things that are just a bit dicey."

Durant shook his head, not bothering to hide his disbelief.
He shifted his gaze to Wu. "Have you got any ideas about
how to find a strayed sister-in-law?"

Wu thought about it for a moment. "Maybe we'd better start in Pelican Bay."

"We know anybody useful there?"

Wu thought some more, reached into his hip pocket, and brought out a small black address book. He leafed through it for a moment, then stopped, smiled happily, and looked up at Durant. "Otherguy Overby."

"Well, now," Durant said.

"Is that someone we should know about?" Piers said.

"I'm not sure," Durant said. "We first met Otherguy where—in Manila?"

"Yeah, Manila," Wu said.

"He was always just a couple of jumps ahead of the law, but when the cops sometimes caught up with him, he always managed to blame it on some other guy. The San Francisco cops hung the name on him, and now he hardly answers to anything else." Durant looked at Wu. "What's his real name —Maurice?"

"Uh-huh," Wu said. "Maurice."

"Is he a thief or what?" Ebsworth said.

"I suppose he's stolen a few things in his life," Wu said. "But mostly he's a hustler who tries to work a medium-size con. He's also a dedicated gossip. That's what we've sometimes used him for. Information."

"Do you think he might know where Silk is?" Lace Armitage said.

Durant put his drink down and rose. "No, but he might head us in the right direction. You said something about a letter."

Lace nodded. "I'm going to write it tonight. I'll get it to you tomorrow. Will ten be all right?"

"Ten's fine," Durant said.

Wu rose, went to the huge window, and stared out at the distant glitter of Santa Monica. He turned to look at Piers, who was also up now. "We're a long shot, you know."

Piers thought about it. "Ten to one, at least."

"Probably more."

"Probably."

"When the banks open tomorrow, I'll be there with your check."

Piers studied Wu for a moment. Then he smiled. "If you weren't," he said, "I'd start worrying about my judgment."

Chapter Eight

Salvatore Gesini, the moneylender, didn't like to drive. Despite having lived for the past thirty years in California, where driving is a minor dogma laid down in the public schools, Gesini drove the way that they still drive in his native Manhattan—nervously, irascibly, grimly.

Usually, Gesini had one of his older catamites chauffeur him around, but none was in attendance at Mr. Wonderful's when the call came that Friday morning, so Gesini had climbed into his Oldsmoble 98 and driven off, grumbling to himself about how the fuckers were never around when you needed them.

A short, squatty man of fifty-five, Gesini was almost remarkably ugly, with a bald head and a squeezed-together face in which nothing seemed to fit. The bulging brown eyes were too near the huge, waxy triangle of a nose that hovered over the sweet little rosebud mouth. And the mouth was so round that it always seemed in danger of rolling off the ledgelike chin which, even freshly shaved, was invariably blue with beard.

Although he was the sole owner of Mr. Wonderful's, the Venice gymnasium whose motto was We Build the World's Best Bodies, Gesini had let his own body go to hell. He was fat, grossly so, with gray skin almost the color and nearly the texture of wet plaster. And although he didn't smoke, he sometimes wheezed and gasped and fought for breath, especially when servicing one of his string of muscular young men—a sexual inclination he had picked up in San Quentin, where, fifteen years before, he had served sixteen months for second-degree manslaughter. The father of four, Solly Gesini no longer bothered much with women, particularly his wife, because he didn't like the way women looked at him when he took off his clothes.

Gesini was thinking about the call that had come that morning. He thought about it as he drove south on the San Diego Freeway, keeping stubbornly in the fast lane at a dogged forty-five, oblivious to all traffic except the car directly ahead of him.

The call had come at 8:30 from Mr. Simms—or rather, from someone who had said that he was Mr. Simms' executive assistant. Gesini had been slightly irritated by the voice and its tone, because it had been one of those snotty Hollywood voices, all la-di-da, the kind that says "terrific" a lot and calls you by your first fucking name even if they're thirty years younger than you. Solly liked to be called Mr. Gesini, by God, at least for the first two minutes.

Nobody that Gesini knew ever called Mr. Simms anything but just that—Mr. Simms—although his first name was Reginald. Gesini wondered what kind of name Reginald Simms was and decided, after some thought, that it was a lucky name because it obviously was neither Jewish nor Italian. Gesini had little ethnic identity and often wished that his own name were something different. Years ago he had settled on Lawrence Parnell because he thought it sounded kind of classy, and sometimes he even covered sheets of paper with it just to see how it looked as a signature.

Gesini knew very little about Reginald Simms other than his name. He knew that Simms had been brought in from back East a little more than a year ago to smooth things over in Pelican Bay. Gesini wasn't quite sure what smoothing things over actually entailed, but he had a fairly good idea, although he hadn't pursued it because what went on in Pelican Bay was really none of his business.

Gesini was curious, however, about why Mr. Simms would want to see him. Gesini had no illusions about his own ranking in the scheme of things. On a scale of one to a hundred, Gesini felt that he himself was very small change —four bits probably, sixty cents at best. Gesini always ranked everyone like that. A real success was, to him, a ninety-nine-center. A failure was a nickel-dime guy.

At the sign that read PELICAN BAY—NEXT 3 EXITS Gesini decided to switch lanes. He did it without either signaling or looking into his rearview mirror, and as usual, he was a little surprised by all the frantic horn blowing. The fuckers oughta look where they're going, Gesini told himself as he swung down the curving ramp that led to Park Avenue.

When it had been founded a little more than ninety years ago, Pelican Bay had been laid out on a stern grid. It was a narrow, oblong coastal city, almost totally surrounded on three sides by Los Angeles, which it poked up into like a long, exploring finger. More of its streets ran north and south than east and west, and the city's founding fathers, not noted for imagination, had numbered all the east-west streets.

The north-south streets, however, had presented something of a problem because they had to be given names. The founders had solved the problem by giving them the names of states. As the town grew it eventually ran out of states and started borrowing the names of other famous thoroughfares. Now there were a Park Avenue; a Peachtree Street; a Downing Street; a Bourbon Street; a Broadway, of course; and for a time even a Kurfürstendam, although in 1917 that name had been changed to Champs-Élysées, which nobody could ever pronounce, and the street was now called Champ Street.

There was no park adorning Park Avenue, which could boast nothing more than a long line of dusty-looking bungalows. Most of the bungalows seemed to have campers parked in their driveways, as though to advertise that their owners liked to get out of Pelican Bay and go somewhere else as often as possible.

Gesini drove along Park Avenue until he came to Fifth Street, which was one of the city's main thoroughfares. He turned right on Fifth Street and headed toward the ocean. Gesini prided himself on his ability to read a street and determine its level of prosperity. Fifth Street, he decided, was on an economic bummer.

The street was lined largely with small stores which occasionally were interrupted by five- and six-story office buildings all wearing SPACE AVAILABLE signs. Here and there a brassy fast-food chain had set up shop. But mostly the small stores seemed to be marginal businesses: tired junk shops with cute names; a couple of used-paperback bookstores with no customers; four palm readers in one block, which to Gesini meant Gypsies; a hopeless-looking VD clinic flanked by two massage parlors; and bars. Far too many bars.

They oughta at least wash their fucking windows, Gesini thought. Mr. Wonderful's was located on Lincoln Boulevard in Venice, an unlovely street in an unlovely town. But Gesini kept his place spruced up and freshly painted—not out of civic pride, but because it was good for business. When it came to Venice, Gesini had no civic pride. Besides, he lived in Brentwood.

Pelican Bay seemed to grow a little more prosperous as Gesini neared the ocean. But he still didn't like the looks of the pedestrians. Too many spics and too many spades, he thought as he pulled into a parking lot and snapped at the black attendant to "Watch the fucking fenders." He waited until the car was safely parked. Sometimes, when he suspected that an attendant was drunk or doped, or possibly both, Gesini would rent two spaces, park the Oldsmobile himself in the center of them, and take the keys. Gesini trusted few people. Perhaps none.

The building where he was to meet Mr. Simms was called the Ransom Tower, and Gesini remembered that it had been named after one of Pelican Bay's dead city councilmen. He also remembered that there had been some scandal attached to the construction of the building, but other than a vague impression of civic graft, he could recall no details.

The Ransom Tower was a little more than two years old and exactly fifteen stories high. Built out of steel beams and tinted glass, it suggested, in design, a box of cereal. It was located two blocks from the ocean, and the occupants of its west side could look at that if they wished. Those on the east side had nothing much to look at but the streets of Pelican Bay or, if that palled, Los Angeles.

Gesini found the number of Reginald Simms, Inc., Consultants, on the building directory and took the elevator up to the fifteenth floor, which was actually the fourteenth floor. There was no thirteenth floor. And the top floor, the sixteenth, which was really the fifteenth, was occupied by what Gesini had heard was an exclusive private club, which in Pelican Bay, he decided, meant that they didn't let any Jews in. Or Italians either, probably. Gesini could understand that.

The first thing Gesini saw when he got off the elevator was a redheaded receptionist, who smiled at him and asked whom it was that he would like to see. When he told her who that was and who he was, she smiled again, picked up her phone, and said, "Mr. Gesini is here."

A few moments later, to Gesini's right, a voice said, "Hel-lo, Solly."

Gesini turned. He saw a tallish man of about thirty-two with the sleek looks of a male model. The man had a fat mass of carefully styled brown hair, and he wore a three-piece grayish-blue suit with a cream-colored shirt. The shirt was open and tieless, and the man had spread its collar out over the lapels of his jacket. Gesini thought it looked silly.

The man bore down on him, his hand outstretched. Gesini gave it a limp shake.

"I'm Chuck West," the man said, and automatically Gesini didn't like him because he didn't like anyone who had a nice name like Charles and then went and fucked it over into something like Chuck. Gesini hated it when people called him Solly, although he never made any fuss about it because he didn't much care for Salvatore either.

Gesini was steered toward the ocean end of the hall by

Chuck West, who chattered smoothly about how busy we know you are and how grateful everybody is that you could make it on such short notice. Gesini grunted "Uh-huh" and "Sure" in reply and kept on wondering what it was all about.

At the end of the hall they reached a doorway. West took out a plastic card, something like a credit card, and inserted it into a slot. The door, which looked like wood, slid open, and Gesini assumed that the door was some kind of metal, probably steel.

Gesini's impression of the room that they entered was one of deep carpet, paneled walls, and a blond secretary at an antique desk who looked up from her typing, smiled slightly, and then went back to her machine. West used the card again to open yet another sliding door. West was talking about the weather now, something to do with rain or the lack of it.

The first thing Gesini noticed when he entered the big room was the gray stone fireplace. On his left were the tinted windows which looked out over the Pacific and on the right was the fireplace with four-foot logs in it that crackled and blazed. Gesini wondered who brought the logs up and how the chimney worked and whether they used a gas jet to light the logs and keep them going.

The second thing Gesini noticed was the man who rose from behind the big spindly-legged desk and advanced to meet them: handsome as an actor, tall, somewhere in his mid or late forties, tanned, and at least in Gesini's estimation, dressed fit to kill.

The man had his head cocked slightly to one side and a warm but strangely shy smile on his face. "Mr. Gesini," he said. "I'm Reginald Simms. How splendid of you to come." They shook hands, and Gesini gave him a little more grasp than he had given Chuck West. Simms seemed to notice West then, nodded at him politely, smiled again, and said, "Thank you, Charles."

"Yes, sir," West said, and left.

Gesini examined Simms carefully and liked everything that he saw. He liked the dark gray, almost black suit with its pearl gray vest. He liked the starched white shirt and the carefully knotted, richly patterned tie and the plain black shoes with their gleaming toes. He liked Simms' face, too, with its heavy dark brows, gray eyes, bold nose, firm mouth and chin, and just enough lines here and there to make it all look thoughtful and intelligent.

"Do you like a fire, Mr. Gesini?" Simms said, gesturing Gesini into one of the big, comfortable-looking leather chairs that were drawn up to the fireplace. "I suppose it's rather ridiculous to have a fire in Southern California in June, but I somehow find one rather comforting, don't you?"

"Fires are okay," Gesini said, settling himself into the chair. They were barely seated when the door opened and a black man in a white jacket entered, carrying a tray that held cups and a silver coffee service. He served the two men silently, Gesini first. Gesini didn't much like coffee. He usually drank Tab for breakfast. But he could stand coffee if he put enough cream and sugar into it. He helped himself liberally to both and then noticed that Simms took his black. He also noticed how Simms dismissed the black servant with a small, but very polite, nod. The fucker's got class, Gesini thought. You gotta admit that.

Simms took a sip of his coffee, gave Gesini another of his warmly shy smiles, and said, "It seems, Mr. Gesini, that we have some mutual friends who speak most highly of you."

"Oh, yeah? Who?"

"Vince Imperlino has some very kind things to say about you."

Gesini nodded carefully. "Yeah, I know him." He had met Imperlino just twice, the second time at a big, fairly secret meeting at La Costa. Gesini had felt both lucky and surprised to have been invited to the meeting, because a lot of the ninety-nine-centers had been there.

"And then Mr. Minuto down in Palm Springs also has some awfully nice things to say about you."

Gesini knew that Simms was lying then, but he didn't care. There are lies and lies. Gesini had shaken hands with Ulderico Minuto just once, and that had been nearly thirty years before, when Gesini had just arrived on the Coast from New York and the newspapers were still calling Minuto Richie Minute. Now Minuto was a retired aging myth that was baking itself to death in the desert sun down in Palm Springs. Shit, Gesini thought, he must be eighty now.

"Well, I met Mr. Minuto a long time ago."

"He still keeps abreast of things," Simms said. "A most amazing old gentleman. He's almost eighty-three now, of course."

"I figured he was up there somewhere like that."

"As you probably know, what we do here in our little shop is try to serve as liaison between certain business groups and the city government. I suppose what we really are is an intelligence-gathering organization. We collect the odd bits and pieces of information, feed them into the computer, and from that we can make our projections."

"Sounds interesting," Gesini said because Simms was looking at him as though he expected some kind of response.

"It is, actually. Sometimes a comment here and a snippet of gossip there will be just what we need to head us in the right direction."

Simms put his coffee cup down on a small, highly waxed table, reached into his pocket, and brought out a silver cigarette case. He opened it and offered it to Gesini.

"I don't smoke."

"Good for you. Do you mind terribly if I do?"

"Go right ahead."

Simms lit his oval cigarette with a lighter that Gesini assumed was real gold. He blew the smoke out, fanned it away with his left hand, and gave Gesini another almost shy smile. "Let's see, where were we? Oh, yes. Snippets of information. Well, yesterday—or was it the day before? No matter. What is important is that from all the bits and pieces that were fed into the computer some names cropped up. Among them were yours; two of your associates, a Mr. Egidio and Mr. Norris, I believe; and a Mr. McBride. Edward McBride, I think. Do you know him?"

"Eddie McBride," Gesini said. "Yeah, I know him."

"You've lent him a small sum to tide him over, I understand."

"Five thousand bucks."

"That much? Is he a suitable risk?"

"He'll pay."

"I'm sure he will. However, what really caught our eye was this marvelous story about a buried two million dollars that Mr. McBride seems to be bruiting about. Are you familiar with it?"

"Yeah, he came to me with it. I thought it was a lot of cock."

"I don't blame you, Mr. Gesini. I don't blame you at all. That was exactly my reaction. Exactly. Still, one must poke about in all the dross. So we did some extremely discreet checking up on your young Mr. McBride, and to our surprise there seems to be a measure of truth in his remarkable tale."

"No shit," Gesini said.

"Again, my reaction exactly."

Suddenly, Gesini smelled money. Not a lot, of course, because if this smooth fucker is in on it, although he seems like just one hell of a nice guy, well, there's not gonna be much left over for yours sincerely. Occasionally, Gesini got his cliches mixed up. But there'd be a payoff of some kind, he knew. A tiny slice; a few crumbs; peanuts, probably—but what the hell, it all added up.

"That's kinda interesting," he said.

"Mmm. Isn't it? Profitable, too, although perhaps not in the immediate future. More of a long-term investment, I should think, wouldn't you?"

"Yeah," Gesini said cautiously, "I guess so."

"However, there does seem to be a tiny problem. Your two associates, Mr. Egidio and Mr. Norris, are such talkative chaps. I'm not sure that you shouldn't caution them. Of course, if they weren't so garrulous, we would never have heard of Mr. McBride, now, would we?"

It was said with a charming smile, but it was still a rebuke, and Gesini immediately went on the defensive. "Well, when you're in the kinda business I'm in, you hear all sorts of crazy stories and all of them are gonna make you a million at least."

"It must be a trial," Simms said. "However, I was wondering if you would be interested in a proposal?"

"I'll listen."

"Good. My proposal is that you get all the information that Mr. McBride has. I must stress *all*. It seems, according to your talkative two colleagues, that Mr. McBride, after you rejected his overtures, decided to take his proposition to two other gentlemen."

"Yeah, I think Icky and Tony told me that."

"And one of these two gentlemen was Chinese, I believe."

"I think I remember that they said one of 'em was a Chinaman. I wasn't listening too close."

"Did they mention where they live?"

Gesini thought about it. "One of 'em lives in Malibu, I think. I don't know which one."

"I would think that the names of these two gentlemen along with their addresses should be included in the information that you get from Mr. McBride. They are a couple of loose ends and I don't like to leave such things dangling. Of course, after Mr. McBride has been debriefed he would become surplus, wouldn't he?"

"What do you mean, surplus?"

"I would think he could be disposed of, don't you? Nowadays, we do live in such a throwaway world. Could you handle all this—with your usual discretion, of course?"

"Yeah," Gesini said, "I can handle it."

"And now to compensation. I do hate to haggle, so I'm going to be what I hope is generous. Say, twenty thousand?"

"Yeah, that's all right. That's fine."

"Good."

"What about the other two guys, the Chinaman and the other one?"

Simms seemed to think about it for a moment and then gave Gesini another of his shy, pleasant smiles. "I do think, Mr. Gesini, that I might have to look after them myself. You do understand, don't you?"

"Sure," Gesini lied, "I understand."

Chapter Nine

Artie Wu was at the Crocker Bank in Santa Monica that Friday morning at two minutes until ten, which was when the bank opened. At five minutes past ten, just after he had cashed Randall Piers's check for $25,000, he used a pay telephone in the bank's lobby to call Durant.

Durant was in the bedroom of the rented beach house making his bed. He picked up the phone on its first ring and said hello. As he did, he heard the knock at the front door.

"It's me," Artie Wu said after Durant said hello.

"Hold on a second. Someone's at the door."

Durant put the phone down and went into the living room. Through the door's glass he could see Lace Armitage—at least, her upper half. She was bearing a white blouse that he couldn't quite see through, with four of its top buttons undone and no brassiere. Durant opened the door to discover that the six greyhounds were with her. They had gathered around her in a tight bunch and seemed to be waiting for an invitation to bound inside.

"Well," Durant said. "Good morning."

"Morning," she said. "Am I early?"

"Not at all. Come in."

"*Siéntense!*" she said to the dogs with a passable Spanish accent, and they promptly lowered their haunches to the deck and prepared to await the morning's next development.

Inside, Durant gestured toward the stove. "Help yourself to some coffee," he said. "I'm on the phone, but I'll be through in a second."

"No hurry," she said.

Durant was wearing only his sawed-off blue jeans. When he turned to go back into the bedroom she saw the thirty-six scars on his back, although she didn't count them. In the bedroom Durant picked up the phone again and said, "Okay."

"Who was it?" Wu said.

"Pier's wife."

"With the letter?"

"Probably."

"I'm at the bank."

"And?"

"We're in business—although I'm not sure what kind."

"Profitable, I'd say. So far."

"What do you want to do next, take a run down to Pelican Bay and look up Otherguy?"

"We might as well."

"Lunch?"

"Who's cooking today?"

"I am."

"Then I'll be there," Durant said, and hung up the phone. When Durant came back into the living room he was wearing an old gray sweat shirt with DENVER ATHLETIC CLUB stenciled across its front in faded letters. Lace Armitage was seated in the suede chair, a yellow mug of coffee in her hands.

"My husband was right," she said. "You do make a damn good cup of coffee."

"Thanks."

She nodded at the burled-walnut coffee table, where another mug of coffee rested on the current issue of *Foreign Affairs*. "I poured you some too."

"Good," Durant said, and sat down on the couch.

"My husband sent someone out yesterday to get a coffeepot like yours, but when they tried it this morning it turned out awful. What's your recipe?"

"Let me think," he said. "I have to think about it because I always make it automatically and half asleep." He thought a moment and then said, "Well, first you fill up the pot and bring it to a boil. Then you throw in a couple of handfuls of coffee, crack an egg, and toss in the shells. Then you boil it till it's done. If you don't know what to do with the egg, you can drink it. I always do."

"Raw?" She made a face.

"It's not bad with a little Worcestershire and a dash of Tabasco. Some salt and pepper."

"How do you know when it's done?"

"The coffee?"

"Yes."

Durant shrugged. "You just know."

Lace shook her head in a kind of mock despair, reached down beside the chair, and picked up her large leather draw-string purse. She opened it and took out a thick buff envelope, which she handed to Durant. He noticed that the envelope was unsealed. On its front was written the one name *Silk* in a firm, rather pretty hand.

"This the letter you mentioned?" he said.

"Yes. You can read it if you like."

Durant thought about it. "Would it help us to find her?"

"No."

"Then I won't read it. If I do find her, she might not like having had the postman read her mail. And that's about really all I am, isn't it—a postman?"

He licked the flap of the envelope, sealed it, and placed it on the coffee table.

Lace looked at him for a moment and then smiled. It was her best smile. "That was a damn decent thing to do."

"What?"

"Not reading it. Most people would've."

"You think so?"

"I know so."

Durant grinned. "Then we share an opinion of most people." He picked up his coffee and sipped it. "Tell me about her," he said as he put the mug down.

"Silk?"

"About her and the Congressman."

"Silk," she said and bent down to fish into her leather bag again. She came up with a red box of Sherman cigarettes, the long brown kind; took one for herself; and then offered the box to Durant. He took one, nodded his thanks, and lit both of them with a disposable lighter. Lace blew some smoke out and said, "Silk" again. "Well, Silk and I have always been very close. That's not to say that she and Ivory weren't close, but both of them felt closer to me than they did to each other. Does that make sense?"

"Sure."

"You have any brothers or sisters?"

"I thought your husband checked me out."

Lace shook her head slightly in a kind of small apology. "I almost forgot. You grew up in an orphanage, didn't you?"

Durant nodded.

"You and Mr. Wu?"

"Yes."

"What's it like, growing up without knowing who your folks are?"

"You usually get used to it."

"And if you don't?"

"Then you invent something."

"Like Mr. Wu?"

"He didn't invent anything."

"You mean he's really the pretender to the Emperor's throne?"

Durant nodded slowly. "When he needs to be, he is."

There was a silence for a moment as Lace examined Durant's answer. "I think I understand what you're saying," she said after a moment.

Durant smiled. "Maybe you do."

"But Silk," she said. "To understand Silk I reckon you'd have to understand how we grew up." She started putting out her barely smoked cigarette in an ashtray. She did it carefully, turning it into a painstaking task as she thought about what she was going to say. "We grew up poor on eighty acres in the Arkansas Ozarks that my papa called the Black Mountain Folk School. My husband always calls it the bomb-throwing school."

"Was it?"

Lace smiled. "No. My papa was a socialist and a preacher, but looking back on it now, I reckon that what he was most of all was a teacher. He thought there had to be some place in the United States that taught all the things that were dying out. You know, folklore and crafts. Things like how to make a chair out of white oak splits. How to cure the itch with just sulfur and lard. How to cure a bee sting with mashed ragweed. How to build a log cabin, even. How to cook possum. You ever eat possum?"

"Never."

"It's good—if you cook it right. The head's the best part. When we were little, Ivory, Silk, and I'd fight over who got the head. You eat everything but the eyes. Well, anyway, during the Depression when Papa was still single he traveled all over the South preaching wherever he could, but mostly back in the mountains, and he learned all this stuff and wrote a lot of it down. And songs, too. He collected songs. He could play almost any instrument there was, and of course, he never had a lesson in his life. And sing! He had one of those big old fine country church baritones that you could hear damn near over in Joplin. 'Loud, girls,' is what he used to tell us. 'Folks don't care much what you sing as long as you sing it good and loud.'" She stopped and smiled at Durant. "Maybe you remember how we used to sing."

Durant smiled back. "Good," he said, "and loud."

"Well, anyway, Papa wound up in Arkansas in 1940 when he was about thirty-two or -three, I reckon. He had this idea for a folk school even then, so when he met Mama he set to courting her, not just because she was the prettiest girl in three counties, but also because she just happened to own an eighty-acre farm that her folks had died and left her. Well, they got married and Papa founded the school."

"Who came to it?" Durant said.

"That's the funny part. Mostly city people came. Papa had the idea that it'd be mostly country folks, but not many of them seemed too interested. Then word sort of got around and people started coming from the cities—New York especially, Chicago, Boston, Saint Louis, all over. After a while, even some college professors. Of course, almost nobody ever had enough money to pay the whole tuition, although, God knows, it wasn't much. But that didn't bother Papa as long as they could pay just some, or if they couldn't even do that, well, he'd let them help out around the school. Those who did come then were talkers, and sometimes I think Silk must have listened to every word."

"Even as a child?" Durant said.

"Even then. She drank it in. And then in early 1960, well, she and Ivory and I sang at that fair in Fort Smith and Don Pennington heard us and signed us up with Papa's blessing and we became Ivory, Lace, and Silk and that fall, just before Papa died, we went on the Sullivan show and after that you know what happened. We got rich and famous."

"You were very good," Durant said. "Some of those songs were tremendous."

"That was Ivory. She wrote all of our really good ones. She was actually a poet, I suppose, and terribly shy. Silk had the brains and the voice, and I—well, I always sang loud and wanted to be someone else, which is how I wound up in films, I reckon. I don't know, but sometimes I think that if it hadn't been for Vietnam, we'd all still be back in Arkansas."

"But you were doing well in the early '60s, before anyone really gave a damn about Vietnam."

"We were singing pure folk then. All those old songs that Papa had collected over the years. Then in '63 Ivory wrote that song about Kennedy after he got killed, and after that we really took off. Funny when you think about it—how we made all that money off of assassination and war. I think that's what really got to Ivory finally. She just couldn't do it anymore. So we broke it up, and Silk went on as a single and really got into the antiwar movement, and Ivory—well, you know what happened to Ivory."

"Yes," Durant said. "I'm sorry. Would you like some more coffee?"

"I sure would," she said.

Durant rose, picked up the cups, and started for the kitchen, but paused. "How'd your sister meet the Congressman?" he said, and went on into the kitchen.

Lace Armitage raised her voice a little. "He used to be a cop, you know."

"So I recall," Durant said, pouring two more cups of coffee. He came back into the living room and handed her one of the mugs. "I don't think I got them mixed up." He sat back down on the couch. "Floyd Ranshaw, the singing cop —wasn't that what they called him?"

"He wasn't bad, either," she said. "Not good, but not bad. He sang his way through college, club dates, weddings, what have you, and then joined the cops in Pelican Bay and became the youngest lieutenant in its history—the *padrón* of the East Side. It's almost pure ghetto over there, you know. Part black, part Chicano, part poor white. And he knew them all. Or a lot of them, anyhow, and they liked him because he was honest and fair, and on Saturday night he had this radio program where he'd sing, play the music they liked, and take calls from anybody who wanted to bitch about something. City Hall didn't bother him because he didn't interfere with their graft, and besides, he was helping keep the East Side quiet. Well, in 1968 the Congressman from that district up and died, and Ranshaw decided to run. He didn't have any money, and there were fifteen in the race. But he came in second, and so they had to have a runoff. The man who came in first was the pet of City Hall. Well, just ten days before the runoff election Ranshaw came up with a briefcase full of solid evidence that could've put his opponent away for twenty years. Or so they say. Well, there was a quiet meeting and the opponent withdrew four days before the election for reasons of ill health and Ranshaw found himself elected."

"Where'd your sister meet him?"

"At an antiwar rally in Washington in '72. Somebody came up with the cute idea of having Silk and the Congressman sing a protest song together. Well, you know how those things go. They started seeing each other, and then the Congressman left his wife, and he and Silk set up light housekeeping about a year ago, sometimes in Washington, sometimes out here. She was mostly working Vegas and New York at the time. Then something happened in Pelican Bay and the Congressman started spending more and more time out here."

"What happened?"

"I don't know. Something to do with politics. All Silk ever said was that he was in trouble."

"She didn't say what kind?"

"No."

"Then he died."

"Two months ago."

"How active was your sister in the antiwar movement?"

"She worked at it. She really did."

"She didn't have anything to do with the really far-left nuts, did she?"

"Like the Weather Underground?"

Durant nodded.

"You mean you think that some of them might be helping her to keep out of sight."

"They know a lot about it."

She shook her head. "Silk is a pretty devout anti-Communist. Most old-line socialists are. Papa was."

"They have reason to be."

"You a socialist?"

Durant smiled. "No, I'm a registered skeptic."

"But you keep up, don't you?" She nodded toward the wall of books. "All those books and *Foreign Affairs* on the coffee table. Or is that just for show?"

"I'm just curious about what they did then and what they'll do next. Politicians, I mean."

Lace dug the box of Shermans out of her purse again and lit one, after first offering the box to Durant, who shook his head no. "You're not married, are you?"

"No."

"You like women?"

"Why?"

"Well, I've been sitting here for half an hour and nothing's happened—not a look, not a leer. So I just got curious."

Durant stared at her a moment, then smiled slightly and said, "There're clean sheets in the bedroom, Mrs. Piers, if you'd like to fuck."

The pink flush started in her smooth neck and rose rapidly to her face. Some kind of reply sprang to her lips—something bitter, Durant decided—but she bit it back, actually clamping down on her lower lip. "None of that was necessary," she said.

Durant shrugged. "It cleared the air."

"Your private life is none of my damn business."

"That's right," he said. "It isn't. All I am is a hired hand who might or might not find your sister."

"Do you think you can?"

"I have no idea."

"When will you start?"

Durant let his eyes roam up and down her body. His gaze unbuttoned her blouse and took it off and then removed her pants. She crossed her legs.

"When will you start?" she said again.

He smiled. "To look for your sister?"

"Yes."

He kept the smile on his face. "I've already started."

Chapter Ten

Artie Wu lived in a four-bedroom Spanish Mission—style bungalow on Ninth Street in Santa Monica, a sunbaked, somnolent city so quiet and devoid of commerce that it could offer free indoor parking to the occasional shopper who happened to stray within its limits.

The house on Ninth Street had a red-tiled roof, white stucco walls, arched windows, and a neat green lawn that was kept in shape by the heavy tribute Wu paid to the twelve-year-old buccaneer who lived next door. The backyard, which was the real reason Wu had rented the house, had a high fence, a sandbox, a nice grove of six tall eucalyptus trees, and some bare patches in the lawn that, after a rain, were useful for making mud pies. It was in the back-yard that the two sets of Wu twins spent a lot of their time, watched over by nineteen-year-old Lucia Reyes, an illegal emigrée from down Sonora way who was teaching them Spanish, which the older twins had already begun to speak with a slight Scottish accent.

Durant parked his car in the driveway behind Wu's Chrysler station wagon. The car was a five-year-old 280 SL Mercedes two-seater that was beginning to show its age. Durant had paid too much for it secondhand because he had liked its lines, and since then it had given him nothing but trouble. When he got out he slammed the door hard, hoping it would fall off so that he would have an excuse for trading it in on something sensible like a Volvo. Durant had never owned an American car. He wasn't quite sure why.

The front door to the Wu house wasn't locked, so Durant went in and called out, "Hi, honey. I'm home."

"In here," a female voice said from the living room.

Durant moved from the short reception hall into the living room, where he found Agnes Wu seated in a chair, an open book in her lap. She was a tall woman in her late twenties, nearly five-ten, with a cap of short, curling blond hair that framed a strong, handsome, full-lipped face softened by large gray eyes that looked innocent, but weren't. She wore jeans and a yellow T-shirt. When Durant came in she closed her book, using her thumb to mark her place.

She looked up at Durant and smiled. "Ah, the misanthrope of Malibu."

"Aggie," Durant said, and twisted his head around, trying to read the title of her book.

She held it up for him. "Trollope's *Barchester Towers*." There was a soft burr to her r's, but so slight that unless it was listened for it might be missed.

"That's pretty racy stuff."

"That's all I'm reading—the dirty parts. We're having a drink, aren't we?"

"Sure. Where's Artie?"

"Back in the kitchen preparing something Oriental and exotic called Reuben sandwiches, I believe."

"Artie," Durant called.

"Yeah," came the answering call from the kitchen.

"You want a drink?"

"Sure."

Durant moved over to a table that held a tray of bottles, an ice bucket, and some glasses. He put ice cubes into a glass pitcher, poured in some gin, added a dollop of vermouth, thought about it, added a drop or two more, and started stirring the mixture with a glass rod.

"How're the bairns?" he said.

"Growing up straight and tall in true California style." Agnes Wu loathed California. "They'll all probably reach seven feet. Did I ever tell you I had an uncle who was seven feet tall? My uncle Jacob."

"Old Jake Garioch," Durant said. "Used to play for the Lakers, didn't he?"

"The only thing Uncle Jacob ever played was cards, which he did incessantly and very badly and died broke, like all Gariochs."

Durant poured the martinis into three glasses. "Have you got any olives?"

"No olives."

Durant shrugged, picked up two of the drinks, moved over to Agnes, handed her one, and then sat down on the red-and-white-striped couch. Artie Wu had rented the house furnished just after its owners, in a seizure of patriotism, had redecorated it in red, white, and blue. The couch was red and white, the rug was blue, a couple of easy chairs wore slipcovers of red-and-white and blue-and-white stripes, and the draperies, until Agnes had rebelled, had been red, white, and blue. Now they were a soft off-white.

Agnes Wu held up her glass and said, "To the California life-style."

Durant grinned. "The next wet, cold, rainy day we have you ought to bring the kids out to the beach."

"There's never going to be another wet, cold, rainy day," she said. "Forever and ever it's going to be nothing but sunshine with tanned, smiling faces all insisting that I have a nice day whether I want one or not."

"You didn't like San Francisco either."

She took a sip of her drink. "San Francisco. You know what San Francisco is?"

"What?"

"It's Glasgow with hills." She took a cigarette from a box of Parliaments, lit it, and looked at Durant. "What was she like, Quincy?"

"Who?"

"You know who. Lace Armitage."

"Didn't Artie tell you?"

"Artie didn't have her over for coffee this morning. What was she wearing?"

"How'd you like a gift subscription to *Modern Screen Romances?*"

"I've got one. What was she wearing?"

"Well, she was wearing blue-and-white-checked pants and a white shirt that was unbuttoned down to here and no brassiere, and she seemed to think that since I wasn't married or anything I might be a little gay."

"You went into your macho act then, I bet."

"Yeah, I did a little, I'm afraid."

"Get anywhere?"

"You mean into her panties?"

"Now, this is my kind of conversation," Artie Wu said as he came in from the dining room carrying a tray of sandwiches. He put the tray down on a glass-and-chrome coffee table. "Whose panties are we getting into?"

"Lace Armitage's," his wife said.

"Remember what they used to say at Princeton back in the '50s when we'd come in from a date?" Wu said.

Durant nodded. " 'Get any tit?' "

"I don't believe that," Agnes said.

"Quincy and I never said it, of course, but the cruder types did." Wu looked around. "Where's my drink?"

"Over there," Durant said.

Wu picked up a plate that held one of the sandwiches, handed it to his wife, and moved over to the drinks tray. He took a sip of his martini and looked at Durant, who was just biting into his sandwich. "I got a call," Wu said.

Durant chewed and then swallowed. "Who from?"

"McBride."

"And?"

"He's had an offer for his map."

"How much?"

"Five thousand."

"Well, now," Durant said. "Who's buying?"

"The moneylender."

"Solly Gesini?"

Wu nodded and took another sip of his drink. "There's just one stipulation to the offer."

"What?"

"Gesini wants our names."

Durant smiled without either showing his teeth or putting any humor into it. "Things seem to be moving right along, don't they?"

"They do indeed," Artie Wu said.

It was two o'clock by the time Durant and Wu arrived at the address on Alabama Avenue in Pelican Bay. Located three blocks from the beach, Alabama Avenue was lined with blighted palms and aging apartment buildings. Number 256 was a seven-story, thirty-nine-year-old, weary-looking structure that called itself the Catalina Towers.

They drove by in Durant's Mercedes, turned right at the end of the block, and found a place to park on Fifth Street. They got out of the car, locked it, and started walking back toward the Catalina Towers.

Wu examined the apartment buildings, most of which seemed to be losing their battle to hang on to a few shreds of respectability, although several of them had tried to camouflage their decline with coats of pastel paint and cheaply remodeled entrances. But nothing could be done to disguise the tenants. A lot of them were oldsters in their sixties and seventies who, primly dressed, sat outside in the sun and watched with reproving eyes and pursed lips as their neighbors hurried into and out of large, shiny cars. The hurrying neighbors seemed mostly to be young, pretty women who wore too much eye shadow.

Wu looked around again as they approached the Catalina Towers. "Faded splendor," he said. "Otherguy's kind of neighborhood."

"He never was much for high overhead."

"Who shall we be?" Wu said as they turned into the walk that led to the apartment's entrance.

"I think we're probably from the finance company," Durant said.

"Here for the car?"

"Why not?"

Inside the small lobby, Durant and Wu approached the counter that enclosed the switchboard. Behind the counter sat a canny-looking old gentleman with glittery blue eyes and pure white hair so long that he wore it in a ponytail bound by a red rubber band.

Wu and Durant leaned on the counter for a moment, looking around the lobby. It was empty.

The old man cleared his throat. "Help you gents?"

Artie Wu turned and smiled. "Like to make an easy twenty bucks?"

The old man thought about it. "Who do I have to mug?"

"We're from the HFC," Wu said.

The old man turned his mouth down at the corners and nodded knowingly. "Repo, huh?"

"That's right," Durant said.

The old man examined them with the shrewd eyes that seemed never to have needed glasses. "Well, you guys are big enough," he said. "Who's the victim?"

Artie Wu took a folded letter-size sheet of paper from his pocket, unfolded it, glanced at it quickly, and then looked at the old man. "Maurice Overby."

The old man snorted. "Him."

"He giving you any trouble?" Durant said.

"Nah, he's just an all-around prick. Car?"

"Car," Wu said. "How'd you know?"

"Well, it's always either the car or the TV. Although sometimes you guys come for the stereo, too. You start fucking around with that stereo stuff, adding all those woofers and tweeters and what have you, and before you know it you're in over your head. Speaking of which, you said something about twenty bucks."

Wu slid a twenty-dollar bill across the counter to him. The old man picked it up, folded it lengthwise, folded it again and yet again, and then tucked it into his watch pocket. "Maybe the old lady won't find it there before I get it spent on something nice. Maybe a blow job. Got a twenty-year-old hooker living here who's sorta sweet on me. Gives me cut rates when she's feeling good."

"Sounds cozy," Durant said.

"Yeah," he said dreamily. "Twenty years old. Well, hell, I guess you guys wanta go on up. Apartment 522. Try not to start a ruckus, but if you have to bust him a couple, I sure as shit ain't gonna say nothing."

"Thanks for your help," Artie Wu said, giving the counter a farewell slap.

He snorted again. "For twenty bucks I'll do almost anything. Make it fifty and I'll do even that."

Durant gave the old man a small salute and a goodbye grin, and the two men moved down the hall, got into the waiting elevator, and rode it up to the fifth floor. When they reached Apartment 522, Wu knocked on the door.

"Who is it?" a man's voice called.

Wu made his voice go down an octave. "It's the FBI, Mr. Overby. Open up."

There was a silence followed by some scurrying noises and then the faint sounds of a woman's voice that seemed to be protesting something. After that the door opened slowly until it was stopped by its security chain. A man peered out cautiously. Artie Wu jammed his foot in the space.

"Ah, shit," said the man who had opened the door.

"Hello, Otherguy," Wu said cheerfully.

"I'm busy," Overby said. "Come back tomorrow. Maybe next week."

"You don't want to lose the chain, do you?" Durant said. "Artie's picked up a few pounds since you last saw him. All he has to do is lean on it and, bang, you're out a new chain."

"Well, shit," Overby said. "Get your goddamned foot out of the door, Artie, so I can close it and get the chain off."

Wu withdrew his foot. The door closed and then reopened. Wu and Durant went in. Overby, a medium-tall man of about forty with a sour look on his hard, seamed face, stood barefoot in the middle of the apartment's living room dressed in what obviously was a hastily donned white shirt and a pair of expensive fawn slacks. The shirt was unbuttoned, and its tails hung down over the slacks, whose fly was unzipped.

"We didn't interrupt anything, did we, Otherguy?" Durant said, looking around the room, which had an indisputably furnished look to it. There were a couch covered with some kind of green, shiny fabric; a couple of overstuffed chairs that failed to match either the couch or each other; some scarred occasional tables; another table in the dining area with four chairs around it, only three of which matched; a few ugly lamps; and on the white walls a couple of prints, one of a China Clipper under full sail and the other of some snowcovered mountain peaks that looked, to Durant, like Colorado. On the floor was a brownish wall-to-wall carpet that bore the scars of spilled drinks and careless cigarettes.

"I like your place," Wu said.

"This going to take a while?" Overby said.

"It could," Durant said. "You might as well zip up your pants and get rid of her."

Overby looked down to see whether his fly was really open, zipped it up, turned toward a closed door, and not quite yelled for Brenda to come out.

The door opened and a young woman of about twenty-three or -four came out of the bedroom. She wore only a wispy pair of bikini panties. Pale green. She had a face that would have been almost pretty except for its wised-up expression. Her hair was long and black, her breasts were nice, and her feet were dirty, especially around the ankles.

She examined Wu and Durant carefully and then turned to Overby. "Well?"

"Come back later," he said.

She again looked Wu and Durant over with her antique eyes. "I'll fuck all three of you for fifty bucks."

"Later, Brenda," Overby said.

She shrugged, turned, went into the bedroom, and came out carrying a pair of sandals, a blouse, and a pair of shorts. Wordlessly, she went to the hall door, opened it, and left.

"That was Brenda, huh?" Wu said.

"Yeah."

"She always walk around like that?"

Overby sighed. "She lives across the hall."

"Well," Durant said, "it's been a while."

"Not long enough," Overby said. "How'd you know I was in town? My phone's not listed."

"We were up in San Francisco—when was it, Quincy, a couple of months ago?"

"About that," Durant said.

"Well, we were sitting in the Fairmont lobby waiting for my wife—you didn't know I was married, did you?"

"I heard."

"Well, we were sitting there and who should walk in but Run Run Keng. You remember Run Run?"

"Yeah," Overby said, "I remember."

"I thought you would," Wu said. "Well, Run Run's just in from Singapore and we started talking about mutual acquaintances and what they were up to and Run Run mentioned you and how if he had time, which he didn't, he'd like to look you up for both auld lang syne and that five thousand bucks you owe him."

"Four thousand," Overby said.

"Whatever. So we told him we had a somewhat similar interest in paying you a call and he was good enough to give us your address."

"How much did you finally get for the pearls, Otherguy?" Durant said.

"Let me explain about that. You guys want a beer?"

"Sure," Durant said. "You can tell us about the pearls over a beer."

Overby walked into the small alcove that held the kitchen, opened the refrigerator, and took out three cans of Pabst. "I was supposed to fly down from Manila and meet you guys in Cebu, right?" he said, closing the refrigerator door with his knee.

"Right," Wu said.

Overby came back into the living room and handed Wu and Durant each an unopened can of beer. He popped open his own can and tossed the top at an ashtray on the coffee table. He missed.

"Well, everything was all set. I was at the airport. I had my ticket, the money, and everything. And then I came down with this attack of malaria."

"Jesus, Otherguy, we're sorry to hear that," Durant said, opening his beer. He walked over to the coffee table, put his top in the ashtray, and picked up Overby's and dropped it in.

"Still the fusspot, isn't he?" Overby said to Wu.

"Neat as a pin."

"So what happened after you came down with the malaria attack?" Durant said.

"Well, hell, they threw me in the hospital, what do you think? Ten fucking days. Then when I got out I tried to find you guys, I really did, but you'd disappeared. I looked everywhere."

"Of course you did," Wu said. "So how much did you get for our pearls?"

"Ten thousand," Overby said promptly.

Wu sighed. "Otherguy."

"What?"

"After you had your—uh—'malaria attack,' we flew up to Manila looking for you."

"I was probably in Hong Kong by then, looking for you. We probably just missed each other."

"Uh-huh. And when we got to Hong Kong you were in Singapore, and when we got to Singapore you'd just left for Kobe. But in Manila guess who we talked to?"

"Who?"

"Sonny Lagdameo."

"Oh."

"Yeah, Sonny," Wu said. "Well, Sonny said he paid you twenty thousand for the pearls because you were in a hurry, but if you'd dickered with him, he'd've gone twenty-three, maybe even twenty-five."

"Which means," Durant said, "that deducting your commission, an overly generous fifteen percent, as I recall, you owe us exactly seventeen thousand dollars."

Overby took a swallow of beer. A defiant, stubborn expression spread over his face. "I ain't got it."

Durant sighed. "Then we're going to have to work something out, aren't we?"

"What?"

"Not what, but how," Wu said.

The defiant expression slid off Overby's face. In its stead came the hungry look of the born gossipmonger, the quidnunc who would almost rather die than be the last to know.

"You guys," he said, "you've got one going, haven't you?"

"Maybe," Durant said.

"And you're gonna cut me in."

Wu swallowed some beer. "We're thinking about it."

"For how much?"

"For just what you owe us, Otherguy," Durant said. "Seventeen thousand."

Overby's face fell, but then it brightened as he glimpsed the angle. "Plus expenses," he said.

Durant sighed again. "Okay, plus expenses."

Chapter Eleven

Durant, beer in hand, stood by one of the windows in Overby's apartment, staring out at the view, which consisted largely of the rooftops of some grimy two- and three-story buildings. The stripped frame of a bicycle, probably stolen, had been abandoned on one of them. Two blocks beyond the buildings a pair of coupled, nearly empty gondolas inched their way up toward the summit of the highest hump in the old roller coaster at the Bayside Amusement Park. The gondolas reached the top of the hump, paused to catch their breath, then plunged down out of sight. Beyond the amusement park, glittering in the afternoon sun, more gray than blue, was the Pacific.

Durant turned. "You never stray too far from the ocean, do you, Otherguy?"

Overby sniffed. "It's good for my sinuses. Keeps 'em open."

Overby was seated on the couch and Wu in one of the chairs. Wu took out one of his long cigars and, after snipping off an end, lit it with his usual kitchen match. When he had it going he critically examined its burning end and said, "Tell us about it, Otherguy."

"About what?"

"Pelican Bay and how you happened to light here."

Overby finished his beer. "It's ripe."

"Oh?" Durant said.

"Yeah. Very ripe."

"Tell us," Durant said.

Overby rose and started for the kitchen before he stopped, remembering his manners. "You guys want another beer?"

Both Wu and Durant shook their heads no.

"Well, when the war ended in Nam things went dead as a doornail out there," he said, opening the refrigerator and taking out another beer. "Out there" to Overby was the Far East—everywhere from Seoul to Sydney. He popped open his beer and tossed the top at the sink. Again, he missed.

"Where were you when it ended?" Wu asked as Overby came back into the living room and sat down on the couch again.

"Me? I was in Saigon. I mean, I wasn't there when it ended, not when they were knocking the slopes off the planes and all, but I was there two or three weeks just before the end. Hell, you could smell it ending, and in a situation like that you never know what might turn up."

"You did all right, huh?" Durant said.

Overby shook his head. "I did a little business. Some diamonds, some gold, but shit, the competition was something awful. You know who was in town then?"

"Who?"

"Well, Pancho Clarke was there; and Jane Arden, she came in all the way from Seoul, fat as ever; and old Tiger Madrid was there from Cebu—"

"I thought the Tiger was dead," Wu said.

"Nah, he ain't dead. Well, he was there, and Run Run was there—that's how come I happened to owe him that four thousand bucks that he went and lied to you and said was five thousand—and the Pommie Bastard was there. Old as he is, he flew in all the way from Adelaide, and everybody said he cleaned up. Well, he was there, and lemme think who else; oh, yeah, the Niggerlick Kid was there— you knew him in Papeete; and Gyp Lucas, he was there too; and a whole bunch of others that I can't remember right off."

"And everybody got rich, huh?" Wu said.

"Well, they say that some of 'em did, and I know for a fact that Gyp Lucas got out of there with at least two hundred grand in emeralds that he traded fifteen first-class seats to Paris for. But all I managed to score was a little walking-around money. Well, after all that I went to Singapore for a while, but that's been turned into a fucking YMCA, so I left there and tried Hong Kong, but you gotta be a goddamn millionaire to live there now, so I went back to Manila, which ain't much better, but at least it's where I belong, and that's where I heard about Pelican Bay."

"Who'd you hear it from?" Wu said.

"Billy Prospect."

Durant grinned. "What's Billy got going, his pirate-picture scam?"

"Yeah. I figured it's the same fucking deal he pulled off in Ceylon two years ago, although this time he was trying to get Manila to put up the development money. Anyway, Billy showed up carrying this script around, and it looked to me like it had the same old coffee rings on it. Of course, Ceylon's still looking for Billy and that two hundred and fifty thousand they advanced him, but he figures that maybe

Manila hasn't heard about that. So anyway, we were sitting in Boy Howdy's place out on Mapa Boulevard, and Billy, who's just in from L.A., starts telling me about Pelican Bay. He tells me money's lying around in the streets."

"What kind of money?" Durant said.

"Billy's kind."

Wu examined his cigar again. "What do you have to do to get it?"

"You have to do what you always have to do," Overby said. "You have to see the man."

"Did Billy say who the man was?"

Overby nodded. "Reginald Simms, and nobody ever calls him Reggie. Not even Billy. Well, Billy paints me this picture and it sounds so good that I flew in here a couple of months ago."

Durant looked around the shabby apartment. Overby caught the look. "That's right," he said. "I ain't quite got rich."

"What happened?"

Overby thought about it for a moment. "Well, you know how I am. I'm not bragging, but usually I can fly into a town at nine in the morning and by noon I can tell you what the Mayor's taking for his piles. You guys know that."

Wu knocked half an inch of ash from his cigar. "We know how wonderful you are, Otherguy. Just tell us what happened."

"Well, I got here and I nosed around a little, but I didn't turn up anything interesting, so I decided to go see this guy Simms and tell him that I'm ready to help him pick up some of the loose change that's supposed to be lying around in the streets. Well, Simms has got the whole fifteenth floor of the Ransom Tower here. But I don't get in to see him. All I get to see is Simms' assistant, a real smooth number called Chuck West. So this guy West goes through a whole riga-marole which is sort of the fine print, if you know what I mean. Then we get to the bottom line, which is if I wanta talk to Simms about doing a little business it's gonna cost me ten thousand bucks. Just to talk. Well, I tell Chuck baby that although I'm sure it's just one hell of a fine offer, I'd like to think it over. And that's what I've been doing ever since—thinking it over."

"That's all?" Durant said.

"Well, I've been nosing around here and there."

"And you've turned up what?"

"That they had an election here last November."

"They had one all over the country."

"Not like they had here. They dumped a majority of the old city council here, and the first thing the new one did was fire the city manager and the police chief and bring in Simms as sort of an industrial-civic consultant. At least, that's what the newspaper here calls him when it mentions him at all, which it don't hardly ever do."

"Where's Simms from?" Durant said.

"Back East, although nobody seems to know for sure. At least, he's supposed to have a lot of connections back there."

Wu blew a smoke ring. "After Simms got here—what happened?"

"Well, the first thing he did was find 'em a new city manager. He found 'em this guy who'd been fired off his last job, some place in Idaho—Boise, I think—for being a lush. And he ain't no reformed lush, either. Then Simms brought in the new police chief, a guy named Ploughman who's from Jersey. Well, I don't have anything better going so I do a little checking on Ploughman, and it turns out he's had a touch of trouble with a grand jury back in Jersey, if you know what I mean."

"Well," Durant said.

"You getting the picture?"

Wu smiled. "As you said, Otherguy, it sounds ripe."

"It gets better."

"How?"

"Well, the first thing I always do when I hit a cold town is try to get in tight with a reporter. I try to find the kind who covers either the police or politics. I especially try to find one who's maybe fifty years old and making two-fifty, three hundred a week and who's just woke up to the fact that he ain't never gonna win any Pulitzer Prize like everybody said he was when he was editing the college paper back in '49.

Well, you find a guy like that and buy him a good steak and all he can drink and you can learn a lot. So I found one. A guy called Herb Conroy. And one night he's had his thirteen-dollar steak and his twenty-two-dollar bottle of wine and is working on his fifth or sixth drink and I bring up Simms and the police chief and the city manager and ask him how come I haven't read anything nasty about 'em in the *Times-Bulletin,* which is the rag he works for. Then I go on to tell him that if he doesn't know anything real juicy about 'em I'd be glad to drop a couple of hints in his lap, at least about the police chief and the city manager, which I dug up all by myself with just two or three long-distance calls."

"So what did he say?" Durant asked.

Overby shook his head in a kind of wonder. "Well, he started crying. So, shit, you know how you feel when you have to sit there and watch a fifty-year-old man start bawling in public. You sorta squirm around and see if anybody's noticing, and of course, everybody is, and, Christ, well, it makes you embarrassed."

"Why was he crying?" Durant said.

"That's what I asked him. I sorta patted him on the arm and gave him my handkerchief, and he went and blew his nose in it and then started apologizing all over the place. And then, in between sniffs, he tells me how he's been a reporter on the *Times-Bulletin* for twenty-five years; in fact, it's the only job he's ever had, although if it hadn't been for his mother-in-law, who lives with him and his wife and who won't leave California, he could've been working for *The New York Times* or *The Washington Post,* or UPI anyway. Well, I don't know how many times I've heard that story. All these fucking reporters claim that the only reason they're not all dressed up in trench coats and reporting from Paris or some place on the six-thirty news is because they've always refused to kiss ass. Anyway, I buy him another drink, which he sure as shit don't need, and he starts telling me that he don't need me to tell him about what's going on in his town." Overby thought about what he had just said. "You follow me?"

"Sure," Wu said.

"So I say what do you mean, and he says he knows all I've told him about the police chief and the city manager and more besides. And that if I don't understand why I'm not reading it in the paper, then maybe I'd better do a little more checking and see who really owns the fucking paper. Well, by now he's mad. You know how drunks get. He's mad at me, and he's mad at himself for not living in Georgetown and having Kissinger over for dinner every week, and he's mad at his mother-in-law and his wife and God knows who-all. Himself mostly, I guess. Well, I figure if I get another drink or two in him he'll really turn confidential, you understand what I mean?"

Overby seemed to be expecting some sort of comment, so Durant nodded and said, "Perfectly."

"So I order us both a couple of double shots of the best fucking cognac they've got, which set me back twelve bucks, and he tosses his down like it's Diet Cola or something. Well, the cognac hits him pretty good and in a few minutes he leans forward and asks me if I know when Reginald Simms really showed up in Pelican Bay. So, I tell him sure, it was right after the election, when they brought him in as a consultant. He shakes his head and goes on shaking it, and I'm starting to worry that maybe it'll fall off when he says, no, it was before that. Then he tells me that Simms was the guy who brokered the sale of the *Times-Bulletin* four months before the election that they had last November. The paper'd been in the same family for years and a lot of chains had tried to buy it, but the family always said no. But Simms arrives in town, makes 'em an offer, and a week later it's sold. And no sooner's it sold than it starts coming out against the city council and the Congressman and everybody else who's in office. Well, like I already told you, the city council got rolled. But the Congressman got back in because Pelican Bay is only about half of his district. But he didn't last long—the Congressman, I mean—because his wife shot him a couple of months ago, but you probably heard about that."

Wu nodded. "We heard. So who bought the paper, Other-guy?"

"That's what I asked him. But by now he's drunk himself about half sober and he's mad again, so he shakes his finger under my nose and tells me that since I'm so fucking smart I can find out for myself. Then he gets up, stumbles, grabs to keep from falling, gets hold of the tablecloth, and goes down flat on his ass—drinks, dishes, glasses and everything all over the floor." Overby shook his head. "It was a mess. The goddamn bill for the two of us—guess how much?"

Durant sighed. "How much?"

"Eighty-three fucking dollars plus a twenty-five percent tip, which I had to give 'em on account of the mess he made. Can you imagine, eighty-three dollars for two people —for *dinner?*"

"Who owns it, Otherguy?" Wu said.

"What?"

This time Wu sighed. "*The Times-Bulletin?*"

"Oh, yeah, that. You know, sometimes I think if I'd gone to college, I'd've made just one hell of a good librarian. They got men librarians, don't they?"

"Lots of them," Wu said.

"Well, there's nothing I like better than to get back some place where they keep old records. You get back there with maybe just one fact to go on and that leads you to another one, and before you know it it's turned into kind of a chase and you really get all excited, you know what I mean?"

"Sure," Wu said.

"Anyway, I started checking out this outfit called Oceanic Publishing, Inc., which bought the *Times-Bulletin*. Well, it seems Oceanic Publishing is owned by something called the Glassman Products Company, which is a do-nothing corporation that's owned by the Golden Bear Manufacturing Company, which is owned by Nightshade Records. Well, hell, everybody's heard of Nightshade Records on account of all that publicity it got when it was set up back in the late '60s by that scientist guy who made a billion dollars or whatever it was out of that electronic doodad he invented. You remember him; he even married what's-her-name, the one who used to be a singer, Lace Armitage. His name starts with a P. Uh—"

"Piers," Durant said.

"Yeah, Randall Piers. Well, he sold Nightshade Records about five years ago for a ton of money. And everybody knows who put up the cash for that deal, although his name sure don't show up on the records anywhere."

"Otherguy," Wu said.

"What?"

"Durant and I, we don't know his name."

"Yeah, that's right. You guys've been out of the country."

"So have you," Wu said.

"But I keep in touch." Overby managed to make it a mild accusation.

"Well, we all have our failings," Wu said, "but even so, maybe you'll tell us the name."

The cunning expression that appeared on Overby's face was that of a man who knew he was about to serve up his choicest morsel. He savored the moment and then said, "Vince Imperlino."

If Overby expected his announcement to produce a reaction, he was disappointed. Wu and Durant stared at him impassively, their expressions polite and interested as if they were quite willing, but not terribly anxious, for him to go on with his story.

Overby's expression became one of exasperation. "Christ, you guys at least know who Vince Imperlino is, don't you?"

Durant nodded. "Something to do with organized crime, I think."

"Or perhaps better yet, 'prominent mob figure,'" Wu said, giving his voice a quoting tone.

Overby started nodding his head up and down quickly, as a man might when he suspects that he may be the butt of a joke. "Okay, you guys, go ahead. Have fun. You know all about Vince Imperlino. For all I know, you're ass-hole buddies."

Durant rose and moved over to Overby and looked down at him. He stared at the seated man for several moments and then said softly. "What's he going to do with it, Otherguy?"

"What?"

"He bought himself a newspaper and now he almost owns himself a town. So what's he going to do with it?"

Overby stared up at Durant. "What the fuck you think he's going to do with it? He's going to make himself some money."

"How?"

Overby shrugged. "I could think of a million ways."

"And not one of them legitimate," Wu said.

Overby smiled—a wise, tight, cruel smile. "Funny thing about Vince—and I'm gonna call him Vince, although if I ever met him, I'd sure as shit call him Mr. Imperlino. But like I was saying, it's a funny thing about him. He runs things west of Denver, except for Vegas. I mean, none of 'em makes a move unless they check with Vince first. But Vince don't get his name in the paper hardly at all. And the L.A. cops, they don't even seem to know he's alive. Even the Feds leave him alone. You'd almost think old Vince had the fix in all the way to Washington."

"One might think that," Durant said, "but it still doesn't tell us what plans Imperlino has for our fair city."

Overby looked at both men suspiciously. "What do you guys really care?"

Wu smiled, showing most of his big, broad white teeth. "We might want in. Quietly, of course."

"Then again, we might not," Durant said. "So why don't you front for us, Otherguy. Why don't you see the man?"

Overby looked at them again, his gaze more suspicious than before. "It'll cost."

"We know," Durant said. "Ten thousand, wasn't it?"

"That's just to talk."

Durant nodded. "We know. Pay him, Artie."

Wu took a thick manila envelope out of his breast pocket and counted a stack of one-hundred-dollar bills onto a table. "Ten thousand."

Overby rose, moved over to the table, counted the bills, then looked at Durant. "Expenses," he said. "You guys mentioned something a while back about expenses."

Wu counted some more bills onto the table. "Two thousand. Expenses."

Overby looked around the room and frowned. "Maybe I oughta move into a better place. Maybe like all of a sudden I came into some big money. It'd look good."

Wu glanced at Durant. Durant's expression didn't change, but Wu started counting out some more bills. "That makes four thousand in expenses."

"You want a receipt?"

"Well, no, I don't think so, Otherguy." Durant smiled. "But we'd certainly like you to stay in touch."

Wu took a notebook from his pocket and wrote two phone numbers on it. "You can usually reach us at one of these."

Overby nodded and pocketed the numbers. He took the sheaf of bills, shaped them into a roll, found a rubber band in an empty ashtray, and snapped it into place. He tossed the roll up into the air a couple of times, but not far, and then tucked it away in his pants pocket. "Okay, I see Simms, keep you out of it, find out what I can, and then get back to you, right?"

"Right," Wu said. "But there's one more thing you can do for us."

"What?"

"This Congressman who got killed."

"What about him?"

"Find out about it."

"His wife shot him. Everybody knows that."

Wu shook his head patiently. "Find out about it."

Overby stared at him and then licked his lips. "Why?"

Wu smiled, but not very pleasantly. "Because we told you to."

PART
II

Chapter Twelve

It was nearly seven o'clock that Friday evening when Icky Norris cautiously swung the big twenty-nine-foot Winnebago Custom into Sea Breeze Lane—a narrow, one-way alley in Venice that separated some rambling, patched-up beach cottages from a row of two- and three-story houses, all of which needed paint and nearly all of which wore faded ROOM FOR RENT signs.

Norris stopped the motor home and looked down the alley, which was choked with cars. Most of the driveways and garages that faced the alley bore stern signs warning, NO PARKING—VIOLATORS WILL BE TOWED AWAY AT OWN EXPENSE.

"Where we gonna park this mother?" Norris said.

Tony Egidio, who was seated in the swivel seat next to him, searched the alley until he found what he wanted, a small, crudely hand-lettered sign that said PARKING 50¢.

Egidio pointed. "There."

Norris eyed the narrow alley, made even narrower by the parked cars. "Shit, man, I don't know if we can make it."

Egidio stuck his head out the side window to look and judge. "You got plenty of room."

Icky Norris made his own assessment. "Maybe we got plenty of room on your side, but we damn near scrapin' on mine."

"You want me to drive?"

"Shit, man, I don't want you to drive. I can drive this

101

mother all right. Just askin' how much room we got, that's all."

Norris slowly drove the big vehicle down the alley and carefully turned it into the unpaved parking lot that seemed to be empty except for two derelict Ford sedans, both of them products of the early 1960s. Using his rearview mirror, Norris backed the Winnebago into place. Then he switched off the engine and sighed his relief.

"You had plenty of room," Egidio said.

"Yeah, well, maybe you wanta explain to Solly how you went and got his brother-in-law's new Winnebago all scratched up, but I sure as shit don't."

They climbed out of the motor home and locked it. As they started to move away, the door of one of the derelict Fords opened and a slight, starved-looking man of no more than twenty-two got out. He had a long, matted beard that clean might have been ash blond in color. Now it was a gritty gray, as was his equally long hair. The hair stuck up from his head in a crown of carefully twisted spikes. He was twisting a new spike into shape, apparently not conscious of what he was doing, as he shuffled slowly toward Egidio and Norris. He wore a filthy green tank top and old, patched jeans. He could have used a bath.

"That'll be a dollar," he said.

Egidio looked at him and then at the sign. "Sign says fifty cents."

The man with the spiky hair turned to look at the sign. His eyes were a wet, glittery gray and probably a bit mad. They examined the sign—or perhaps something a thousand yards on the other side of it. Then he turned back to Egidio and Norris.

"The printed word," he said bitterly, and then shook his head to express his contempt. The spikes writhed—a bit like snakes. "That'll be a dollar."

Egidio started to argue, but Norris said, "Pay the fucker."

The man accepted the bill, looked at it curiously, then examined Egidio and Norris. He shook his head again and the hairy spikes danced once more. "You eat meat, don't you?" he said, turned, and shuffled barefoot back to the 1962 Ford that was his home.

Egidio grimaced, spat, and said, "Fucking dope fiends."

When they reached the alley they paused. "Which one?" Norris said.

Egidio nodded. "That one."

The building Egidio had nodded at was a moldering six-story apartment hotel built out of red brick. It was located on the ocean side of the alley, and the black-and-white sign that stretched across one side of it just below the roofline had been painted there in 1928. The sign, almost obliterated by time, read, SEASHORE HOTEL—VENICE'S FINEST—ROOMS $2.50 AND UP.

Egidio and Norris walked along the side of the hotel until they reached its front, which faced a broad cement sidewalk and beyond that the beach. They went through a glass door into a vacant lobby. An elevator with a green door was to the left of the alcove that once had been the hotel reception area. The area held garbage cans now, most of them full.

The elevator's red IN USE sign was on, but Icky Norris punched the Up button anyway. Then he sniffed a couple of times, wrinkled his broad nose, and said, "Dead cat some-wheres."

Egidio sniffed, frowned, and then nodded his agreement.

The elevator hit the first floor with something of a bump, the red IN USE sign went off, and the door clanked open. An almost pretty girl started out of the elevator, but hesitated when she saw Egidio and Norris. She was young, very young, probably still in her teens, with wary brown eyes and a small mouth that was now shaped into a terrified O. She at first shrank back from the two men and then forced herself to sidle around them.

"Boo!" Icky Norris said.

The girl yelped and fled across the lobby and out the door.

"That little mama done been raped once or twice already, I bet," Norris said as they entered the elevator. Egidio punched the 6 button and nodded, not speaking. Many times he didn't bother to reply to Norris, who usually had some

totally unfounded observation to make about almost everything. Sometimes, Egidio thought, the nigger just talks too
much.

On the sixth floor they walked down the uncarpeted hall
until they reached number 611. It was toward the front of the
building, near the beach. Egidio knocked.

A man's voice called, "What?"

"It's us," Egidio said, "me and Icky." He raised his voice
to make it go through the door.

The door opened and Eddie McBride stood there, dressed
only in white boxer shorts. He looked at both men and then
frowned.

"Saturday, you said." McBride frowned some more. "Saturday, noon."

"Saturday, Friday, it don't make no difference now,"
Norris said. "Shit man, you in clover."

"The deal still on?" McBride said.

"Sure it's on," Egidio said. "We just came by because
Solly wants to see you."

McBride stepped back, and Norris and Egidio entered the
room. It was a typical cheap hotel room, but far neater than
most. The bed was almost primly made; the chair in front of
the small, scarred writing desk was exactly in place; a comb
and brush were precisely centered on the dresser. Eddy
McBride felt better when things were neat. The Corps had
taught him that, and he had learned that when the Corps
teaches you something, it dies hard.

"Why's he wanta see me tonight?" McBride said. "Why
not tomorrow?"

"He's going outa town tomorrow," Egidio said. "Up to
Big Bear for the weekend. We got his brother-in-law's
camper outside. We'll run it over to Solly's place, you can
talk to him, and then we'll bring you back in his car."

McBride thought about it. He didn't much like the way
it sounded, but when he thought it over it sort of made
sense, especially if Solly was going out of town. At least
they couldn't stiff him out of any money. Solly's first
offer for the map had been the $5,000 that McBride owed
him. That was already gone, of course—long spent.

McBride had then held out for the interest that he owed, and after some bickering over the phone, with Egidio serving as intermediary, Solly had agreed to cancel that too. That had bothered McBride a little. Solly had given in too easily.

"Well," McBride said, still hesitating, "I guess I better get dressed."

He pulled on a pair of white duck pants and was slipping a dark blue T-shirt over his head when Egidio took a small piece of paper from his pocket and looked at it.

"Those two names you gave me over the phone this afternoon," he said.

"What about 'em?"

"I don't know if I got 'em spelled right."

"Durant," McBride said and then spelled it. "Quincy." He spelled that too.

"And the Chinaman's?"

"W-u."

"Shit, I spelled it W-o-o." Egidio borrowed a ball-point pen from Norris and corrected his spelling. "And you said his first name's Artie?"

"Yeah."

"Real name's Arthur probably, huh?"

"Arthur Case," McBride said as he pulled on a pair of socks and slipped his feet into carefully burnished loafers.

"Funny fuckin' name for a Chinaman," Icky Norris said. "Arthur Case Wu. He half Chinese or what?"

"He's all Chinese, but I don't think he talks any. At least, I never heard him talk any."

"Well, you ready to go?" Egidio said.

McBride patted his pockets to make sure he had everything.

"Yeah, I'm ready."

"Got the map?"

McBride reached behind the mirror on the dresser and withdrew a No. 10 envelope that had been Scotch Taped to the mirror's rear.

"That ain't too slick a hidin' place," Norris said.

"Yeah, well, my wall safe's busted."

Egidio held out his hand for the envelope containing the map that had the X where $2 million had been hidden somewhere in the U.S. Embassy complex in Saigon.

McBride stared at him. "I think I'll give it to Solly," he said. He pulled up his shirt, stuck the envelope halfway down his shorts, and then used the still sticky Scotch Tape to fasten it to his lean, flat stomach. Once the envelope was in place McBride pulled his shirt back down, but not before Egidio noticed that McBride still wore his Marine Corps belt with the big, heavy buckle.

Egidio shrugged. "Okay by me," he said.

McBride led the way out of the room. Icky Norris was the last to leave. He paused and examined the room with his eyes as though to make sure that nothing incriminating had been left behind. Then he closed the self-locking door and grinned at McBride. "You got a real nice little place here."

"It stinks," McBride said.

"Well, least you keep it nice."

They took the elevator down to the empty lobby and then walked along the side of the Seashore Hotel until they reached the parking lot. The camper was still the lot's only customer, although its superintendent was now atop his derelict Ford, seated cross-legged, the spikes of his hairy crown waving gently in the sea breeze as he stared raptly out over the ocean south and west toward Bora Bora.

"Shit, he's out of it, ain't he?" Icky Norris said.

"He always is," McBride said.

Norris unlocked the Winnebago and waited for McBride to climb in first. Then Norris got in and slipped behind the wheel, followed by Egidio. McBride, now halfway to the rear of the camper, stood looking around.

"It's the first time I've ever been in one of these things," he said. "They're sorta neat, aren't they?"

"If I was your age and single, this is sure what I'd have," Icky Norris said as he headed out of the parking lot. "I'd live in it. Got plenty of room for one. Got plenty even for two."

"Mind if I sort of look around?" McBride said.

"Help yourself," Egidio said.

McBride inspected the three-burner stove and opened the small refrigerator, which seemed to be fully stocked. He then opened the cabinet doors and read the labels of some canned goods, took a look at the head, turned the taps in the sink on and off, and even looked underneath it where somebody kept the Spic and Span, the 409, the Clorox, the Windex, the Dove, and a glass bottle of blue ammonia and another one of white gasoline.

"Jesus," he said, his tone full of admiration, "you wouldn't need anything but this. It's kind of like a boat."

"Don't cost as much as a boat, though," Norris said. He had stopped the Winnebago at a red light and was waiting to turn left onto Lincoln Boulevard, which he would stay on until he reached Colorado Avenue in Santa Monica.

"How much they cost?" McBride said.

"You almost bought one, didn't you, Tony?" Norris said.

"Yeah, I was thinking about it," Egidio said. "You can get a new one, maybe not quite as big as this, for fifteen, twenty thousand. Get a used one, though, a lot cheaper'n that."

"What kind of mileage they get?" McBride said.

"Terrible," Norris said. "Four, five, sometimes not even that much."

McBride had sat down on one of the upholstered benches that could be made into a bed. He reached over and turned one of the taps in the sink on and off again as though fascinated by the fact that it worked.

Egidio turned his swivel seat around so that he could face him. "How's your thumb?"

McBride glanced down at his left hand. The bandage was becoming soiled. "It's okay."

"It wasn't nothing personal, you understand?" Egidio said.

"Sure."

"Just business."

"Sure."

"Well, we just didn't wantcha to think it was anything personal."

They didn't find much to talk about after that. Norris turned right off Colorado Avenue in Santa Monica onto Seventh Street. He put the big machine up to thirty-five to make the lights and actually made most of them. They went through a business district that turned into an area of three-and four-story apartment houses, fairly new, with SORRY, NO VACANCY signs out in front of most of them. Seventh also had some very nice eucalyptus trees along that stretch, but they disappeared when the area of one-family houses began.

At San Vicente Boulevard, Norris stopped for the light. But when it turned green, instead of turning right he went straight ahead as Seventh became East Channel Road.

For a few moments McBride didn't say anything. Then he said, "Solly lives in Brentwood."

"That's right," Egidio said. He had turned his swivel chair back around so that he was again facing the front.

"This isn't the way to Brentwood." McBride's voice was flat and even a little sad.

"That's right," Egidio said, and swung around in the swivel chair. He held the automatic in his right hand. With only a glance McBride automatically classified it: a .45 Colt automatic, service issue. A lot of gun.

"Well, shit," McBride said.

Egidio shook his head—a small, commiserative shake. "It's the way things work out sometimes, Eddie."

"Just business, huh?"

"That's right," Egidio said. "Just business."

"You better get him to give you the map now," Icky Norris said as he twisted the Winnebago around the sweeping curves that led down Santa Monica Canyon to the Pacific Coast Highway.

"Yeah, we don't want any holes in the map," Egidio said, and then chuckled at his own little joke.

McBride pulled up his shirt so that he could get to the envelope. But before he could touch it, Egidio said, 'Don't touch your belt buckle, Eddie. Don't try for the knife. In fact, just take it out real nice and easy, like they say in all those dumb cop shows."

"Now?" McBride said.

"Yeah, now. Real slow."

McBride did something to his belt and the buckle came away. It formed the handle for a wicked, 4 1/2-inch stiletto. He handed it carefully, buckle first, to Egidio. Without removing his eyes from McBride, Egidio handed the knife to Icky Norris, who grinned at it and laid it on the shelf in front of the steering wheel.

"I told you he had one of those mothers," Norris said. "Shit, everybody in Nam used to have one, especially those fuckin' jar-heads."

"Now the envelope, Eddie," Egidio said.

McBride peeled the tape away from his skin and handed the envelope over just as carefully as he had handed the knife. Then he pulled his shirt down, slumped back onto the bench, and stared out the window. They were on the Pacific Coast Highway, heading north.

Nobody spoke until they reached the Getty Museum, and then Icky Norris said, "We sure gonna have us one pretty sunset." McBride looked, but Egidio didn't.

Instead, Egidio decided to lecture McBride. "You know what the trouble with guys like you is, Eddie?"

"What?"

"You don't get nothing steady. I mean, guys like you come back from the war and you don't try to get yourself lined up with something steady. You try to make cute deals, and shit, you ain't smart to make a living doing that. Now, Icky here, he was over in Vietnam, weren't you, Icky?"

"Sixty-four to '65," Norris said. "Hell of a time."

"But when he came back, he lined himself up with Solly. He didn't run around trying to pull off any half-ass deals. He got hisself something steady."

"Breaking thumbs," McBride said.

"Ain't no use talkin' to him," Icky Norris said. "Hell, he know it all."

"Yeah," Egidio said. "You're probably right. Try to give somebody a little good advice and what do they hand you back—smart ass, that's what."

Nobody spoke for the next dozen miles, not until they were passing through the heart of Malibu.

"That Durant guy," Egidio said. "He lives out here, don't he?"

"Farther out," McBride said.

There was more silence until they passed Pepperdine University, whose somewhat futuristic campus belied its fundamentalist underpinnings. "You know where you've seen all those buildings before?" Icky Norris said.

"What we're looking at?" Egidio said, not taking his eyes off McBride.

"Pepperdine University."

"I've seen it when I've come by here before."

"Nah, I mean where you seen it on TV."

"Where?"

"*The Six-Million-Dollar Man*. You watch that, don't you?"

"Yeah, I watch that all the time." Egidio thought about it. "By God, you know, you're right, Icky."

"Course I'm right."

A mile or so past Pepperdine University, Norris turned the camper right into Latigo Canyon Road, a narrow strip of blacktop that snaked its way up and back into the mountains. A highway sign with a long, wiggling black line on it read, NEXT 9 MILES.

Most of that nine miles was uphill, one curve after another. After three or four miles the houses ran out and there was nothing but the blacktop road and the sheer drop-off into the canyon below. The sun had gone down behind the mountains, but it was not quite dark. McBride picked his time carefully.

It was on a particularly treacherous curve, a blind one. He took a deep breath and yelled it: "Look out for that fuckin' car!"

Icky Norris hit the brakes. Despite himself, Egidio turned away from McBride, then caught himself and started turning back. But McBride was already squatting beneath the sink. He had the door to the cabinet open, and the bottle of gasoline was in his left hand. His right hand was digging into his pants pocket.

He came up fast in one smooth motion, cracking the top off the bottle of gasoline with a sharp, rising blow on the sink. He yelled, because it made his thumb hurt. But he kept his movement going, even as Egidio brought up the automatic. The gasoline, nearly a pint of it, sloshed over Egidio's face and head and into his eyes. He yelled.

McBride's right hand came up out of his pants pocket. It held a Zippo lighter, the one with the Marine Corps emblem on it. Its top was already open. McBride was thumbing its wheel as it came out of his pants pocket. The lighter caught, and he tossed it against Egidio's gasoline-drenched shirt.

The flames shot up, igniting the film of gasoline that still covered his face and bald head. Tony Egg screamed, dropped the automatic, clawed at his eyes, and slapped at the flames.

Icky Norris finally stopped the camper, slamming on its brakes. The camper skidded dangerously close to the sheer drop-off at the left edge of the road. Norris glanced back, swiveling his head quickly, trying to see what needed his attention more, Egidio or the camper. He decided on the camper. It was a mistake.

McBride snatched up the .45, thumbed off the safety, and shot Icky Norris in the back of the head. Most of the left side of Norris' head smeared itself over the windshield, already cobwebbed by the .45 round. Norris slumped down over the wheel, and his foot slipped off the brake. The camper started creeping toward the long drop down.

McBride moved quickly. He scrambled over the still smoking Egidio, who, with the flames finally out, had drawn himself up into a tight, quivering, screaming ball on the floor. As he stepped on Egidio's head, McBride thought it all looked strangely familiar, and then he remembered some burn victims he had seen in Vietnam. They had all scrunched themselves into tight little balls like that.

McBride fought with the door latch and hurt his broken

thumb again. The motor home was still moving, five, perhaps ten, miles per hour, a dead man's foot on its accelerator. The door finally came open. McBride jumped.

He picked himself up just in time to see the Winnebago go over the edge of the canyon. It kept to its wheels for almost ten seconds and then started rolling, sideways at first, then end over end. It came to rest in the bottom of the canyon, almost a thousand feet down. It rested there for a moment and then burst into flames.

McBride looked at it. Then he looked at the .45 he still held in his right hand. He wiped it off with his shirt and then threw it by the trigger guard as far as he could. McBride watched the gun fall, and for a moment longer he stared down at the burning motor home.

"Burn, you fuckers," Eddie McBride said.

Chapter Thirteen

The coyotes followed McBride for nearly an hour. There were five of them, and they never came closer than twenty yards, although the biggest one sometimes loped in just a little closer than that—showing off, McBride thought.

The coyotes had picked McBride up fifteen minutes after he left Latigo Canyon Road. He was now trying to work his way along the bottom of the canyon back to the ocean. It was hard going, and McBride had stumbled and fallen several times, and once he had fallen so hard on his left hand that he thought he had broken his thumb again. When he fell that time, he got mad and yelled and picked up a rock and threw it at the coyotes. He missed, and they had laughed at him. Or at least it looked as though they were laughing at him.

After that it got dark and McBride could no longer see the coyotes, but he knew they were there. It was just like in one of those crummy Westerns that he sometimes read, McBride thought. The cowboy's stumbling around in the desert or somewhere after dark, and although he can't see it, he knows that the mountain lion's out there. Or the Indians or whatever. McBride had a sudden, new respect for Westerns.

The coyotes escorting McBride were just five of the hundreds who ranged over the Santa Monica mountains living mostly off snakes, rodents, and rabbits and whatever else they could catch. But sometimes they would raid a sparsely settled residential section and dine on fat tabby and pampered poodle. There was many a three-legged dog and tail-less cat in Malibu who had been patched up by the local veterinarians after a brief and painful encounter with a couple of coyotes.

The five that had picked up McBride followed him until he could see the lights of some houses high up. After that, the coyotes turned and trotted off back into the hills. Again, McBride could only sense that they were gone.

The going got easier after that, and McBride didn't stumble nearly so often and fell only once more. An hour later he was standing on a bluff overlooking the Pacific Coast Highway about a mile north of where Icky Norris had turned into Latigo Canyon Road.

McBride found a defile and followed it down until he reached the highway. He waited until he could see no cars in either direction and then raced across. On the other side of the highway was a high chain fence. He moved along it until he found a place that had been pried open. He slipped through and carefully felt his way down to the beach. Then he stopped and rested, sprawled on the sand. He estimated that he had walked for a little more than two hours and that he had covered at least six miles. Maybe seven.

Feeling the need for a cigarette, McBride fished a box of

Marlboros out of his left pants pocket, wincing at the pain
that it caused his thumb. He put the cigarette in his mouth
and then swore softly, remembering what he had done with
his lighter. Shit, he thought, they'll find it, and with that
emblem on it they'll figure out that it belonged to some
Marine or ex-Marine, and it won't take Solly long to tell 'em
which one, either. He wondered if the burned Winnebago
had been discovered yet. If it had, he speculated about how
long it would take the police to trace the license and get to
Solly's brother-in-law and then to Solly. An hour, probably.
Maybe two.

McBride tried to think what he should do. There was no
sense in going back to his room in Venice. By the time he
got there they would probably be waiting for him—either
the cops or some of Solly's boys, some he hadn't even
met yet. He tried to look down at his clothes to see how
presentable he was, but it was far too dark. He knew,
however, that the white duck pants were soiled and stained
and that the blue T-shirt wasn't in much better shape.
Then too, he was probably scratched and bruised all over
from where he had fallen. If he walked into a motel with
no car, they would take just one look and call the cops.

McBride tried to think his way out of his predicament—
logically at first, but he was really no problem solver, and
dimly he realized this. So he rose and dusted the sand off the
seat of his pants and headed north almost intuitively toward
someone another mile or so up the beach who was smarter
than he was and who might have some ideas. He headed
toward Quincy Durant.

Durant was seated on the couch in the living room, a
secretary's spiral notebook in his lap, and on the record
player the Cleveland Quartet was doing extremely well with
Mozart's *Adagio and Fugue in C Minor* (K. 546). Durant
started when over the Mozart he heard the clump of
McBride's leather-heeled loafers on the flight of wooden
steps that led up from the beach. But because there was so
much noise Durant relaxed as he realized that someone was
trying to announce himself.

He glanced at what he had written in the notebook. There was a heading in printed, almost architectural lettering that read, SILK ARMITAGE. After that there were four paragraphs of no more than three lines each, all of them numbered. When he heard the steps on the stairs, Durant had just written number five. He closed the notebook, tucked it away out of sight under the cushion on the couch, rose, and went over to the sliding glass door. He switched on the outdoor light and slid the door open just as McBride reached the top of the stairs.

McBride stopped and grinned weakly. "How're ya?" he said.

Durant examined him. "Well, I'd say I'm just one hell of a lot better off than you are."

McBride nodded wearily, suddenly realizing how tired he was. "Yeah," he said. "Can I come in?"

"Sure."

Durant stepped back to let McBride in. Once inside the living room McBride stood for a moment, quite still. He closed his eyes, swayed a little, and then opened them. "That music," he said. "That's nice. Classical, isn't it?"

"Uh-huh," Durant said. "Classical. Try that one over there," he said, indicating the Eames chair. "If you bleed on it, the blood'll come off the leather."

"Am I bleeding?"

"Not much."

"I didn't know I was bleeding."

"You've got a couple of deep scratches up here," Durant said, touching his own left temple.

McBride, accustomed, as is everyone, to a mirror image, touched his own temple, but the right one. Then he remembered and touched the blood that was trickling down from the two inch-long scratches that were almost gashes along the side of his left temple. He looked at the blood on his fingertips and said, "Huh." Then he sat down on the chair.

"What do you want," Durant said, "Scotch or bourbon?"

"Gin," McBride said. "You got gin?"

"I've got gin," Durant said. He turned and went into the

kitchen, reached up and opened the cabinet above the refrigerator, and took down the still unopened bottle of Tanqueray gin. He also took down the bottle of Scotch.

"Straight?" he called to McBride.

"Yeah. Straight."

Durant found a couple of tumblers, put some ice into one of them, and poured a measure of Scotch into it, adding some water from the tap. Then he opened the bottle of gin and poured almost three ounces by guess into the other tumbler. He put the bottles back, picked up the glasses, and went back into the living room.

"Here you go," he said, "a hooker of gin."

"Thanks," McBride said. He sounded grateful. He swallowed a big gulp of the gin and made a face. "Jesus." He started to fish the pack of Marlboros out of his left pants pocket, but snagged his thumb and said, "Oh goddamn son of a bitch, oh Jesus H. Christ."

Durant picked up his own package of Pall Malls from the coffee table, shook one out, and offered it to McBride. "Here," he said.

McBride took the cigarette and let Durant light it for him. He drew the smoke far down into his lungs, coughed, and said, "These fuckers are strong, aren't they?"

Durant looked at him carefully. "Are you okay now?"

"Yeah, I'm okay."

"You're not going to faint or anything?"

"No, I'm okay."

"I'll be right back."

McBride drank gin until Durant returned with his open shoe box of medical supplies. McBride's scratches weren't as bad as they had first seemed, not even the two gashes on his forehead. Durant cleaned the blood off and dosed the scratches with an antiseptic. Then he sat back on his heels in Oriental fashion and studied McBride for a moment.

"I don't even think you need any Band-Aids."

"Yeah, well, thanks. I appreciate it."

"How about your thumb?"

"It hurts like hell. I think maybe I busted it again."

"I doubt it. You want me to look at it?"

"You know about busted thumbs?"

Durant smiled. "A little. Enough, probably."

McBride frowned as he debated about whether he should trust his thumb to an amateur physician. When he decided finally that he should, he thrust his left hand out at Durant and said, "Here."

Durant smiled again and examined the job that the dope-clinic doctor had done on McBride's thumb. Careless, he thought. Even slapdash. The thumb stuck out from McBride's hand at a thirty-degree angle. Using a pair of surgical scissors, Durant quickly snipped away the old tape and, using the same splint, fashioned a new bandage that pressed the broken thumb against the side of McBride's left forefinger. His movements were quick and deft and curiously gentle. McBride yelped only once. When finished, Durant sat back on his heels again, and McBride examined his freshly bandaged thumb as though it were a new and highly prized toy.

"Jesus, that's neat. That's a hell of a lot better than that dopers' doctor did."

"I brought it in against your hand. Now you won't snag it as much."

"Yeah, that's right, isn't it? I was always catching it on something before. Where'd you learn how to do that?"

Durant shrugged. "You pick it up here and there."

"You never were a doctor, were you?"

Durant smiled and shook his head. "No. Hardly."

"You do it just like a doctor does it. You can tell. What I mean is, you got the same moves."

Durant studied McBride for a moment. Then he said, "How'd it happen, Eddie?"

"You mean tonight."

"That's right. Tonight."

McBride got his cigarettes out of his pants pocket without discomfort and lit one with a table lighter. He also took another swallow of gin. Then he looked away from Durant and said, "I had to kill both of them. I ain't making it up, either. It was either them or me and I couldn't think of any good reason why it should be me."

Durant nodded as though he understood perfectly. "But that was later, wasn't it? That was toward the end."

"Yeah, that was toward the end."

"Go back to the beginning. Take your time."

"You gonna call the cops?"

"I don't know. I won't decide that until after you tell me."

McBride had to think about Durant's reply. He turned it over in his mind, and as he did he saw his alternatives slipping away. I haven't got any choice, he realized. I haven't got any choice at all. After that he sighed and said, "Well, this is exactly what happened."

It took Eddie McBride fifteen minutes to tell his tale. He told it in a low monotone that gave the same emphasis to both the coyotes and Icky Norris' exploding head. He left nothing out, and in leaving nothing out he created no villains and invented no hero. It was a flat although bloody account, curiously lacking in either anger or passion. He's doing what he unconsciously set out to do, Durant decided. He's making it dull.

When done, McBride leaned back in the leather chair, finished his gin, and said, "And that's it. That's what happened."

Durant nodded slowly and said, "You left out one thing."

"What?"

"Why. You left out why they wanted to kill you."

"The map. They wanted the map."

"You were going to give them the map anyway."

"Well, maybe they thought I had a copy of it and I'd try to sell it to somebody else."

"You do, don't you?"

"What?"

"Have a copy."

McBride smiled—a grim, hard, utterly mirthless smile. "I got a dozen copies. Or had. They're all in my room. The cops've probably found 'em by now."

Durant shook his head. "You don't have to worry about the cops."

"You mean you're not going to call 'em."

"I won't and neither will Solly Gesini. He'd have to explain too many things. It wouldn't wash."

"And you're not gonna call 'em either?" McBride had to be sure.

"No."

"Why? I mean, I'm grateful as hell, but we're not exactly buddies."

"No, we're not, are we? But then, I'm not Malibu's most upright citizen, either. It's a failing, probably. One of my many. Anyway, let's say that's reason number one. Reason number two is that I think maybe we can use you."

"To do what?"

Durant stared at him. "Do you care?"

For a long moment, McBride didn't answer. "No," he finally said. "I don't care."

"Three hundred a week, Eddie?"

"Yeah. Okay. Three hundred a week."

Durant rose. "Let me call Artie. We'll find you a place to stay—at least for tonight."

Durant dialed Wu's number. It was answered on the ninth ring by Artie Wu, who said, "What do you want?"

"Did I interrupt something?"

"Not really," Wu said. "Nothing important, anyhow. I was just making love to my wife, but I'm finished, although I'm not sure that she is."

Durant heard Aggie Wu say something that sounded sharp. Then Wu said something that Durant couldn't quite make out, and after that Aggie Wu giggled.

"I could call you back," Durant said.

"No, it's all right. I was going to call you anyway."

"You want to go first?"

"No, go ahead. I can listen to you and tickle Aggie at the same time. It gets her over her postcoital sadness."

Again Aggie Wu said something that sounded sharp, and again Wu made some reply that Durant couldn't hear. But after that he could hear both of them giggle. Durant sighed.

"Okay," Wu said.

"It's Eddie McBride."

"Oh?"

"He's in a jam that I'll tell you about later, but I've put him on the payroll at three hundred a week. I think we can use him."

"Maybe down in Pelican Bay?"

"That was the idea."

"It makes sense," Wu said. "How bad is the jam?"

"Bad enough. We've got to keep him out of sight, though. Tonight, anyhow."

"Let's put him in with Otherguy," Wu said. "They can be roomies."

"I'll let you call Otherguy and tell him."

"I'll like that," Wu said. "Anything else?"

"No, nothing that can't wait."

"Well, I got a call—about an hour ago. He's in town."

Durant didn't have to ask who *he* was. "Where?"

"The Beverly Wilshire."

"Let me guess. He wants a breakfast meeting."

"What else?"

"When?"

"Nine tomorrow. He started by suggesting seven, then eight, but I worked him down to nine."

"He just couldn't let it alone, could he?" Durant said.

"Did you expect him to?"

"No. Not really. Well, I'm going to have to let Eddie have my car, so you'll have to pick me up."

"Ah, shit," Wu said. "I'll have to leave by seven, then."

"What time does Randall Piers usually come by here with those dogs?"

"Between five-thirty and six. Why?"

"I though I'd invite him in for a cup of coffee tomorrow morning and see what he can tell me about the guy that he sold his record company to."

"Vince Imperlino?"

"That's right," Durant said. "Vince Imperlino."

Chapter Fourteen

Eddie McBride's toilet kit, which was now contained in a small plastic bag, consisted of a razor, a hairbrush, a comb, a toothbrush, and a bar of soap. There was no shaving cream, mouthwash, deodorant, after-shave lotion, or toothpaste. Eddie McBride brushed his teeth with salt when he had it; with nothing when he didn't.

He put the toilet articles into the shopping bag that sat in the middle of the floor of Room 611 at the Seashore Hotel in Venice. Almost everything McBride owned in the world was in that shopping bag—except his car. He worried about the car for a moment, the 1965 Mustang convertible, because he was convinced that it would become a classic in just a few more years. But since he wasn't at all sure that he would be around quite that long, McBride said goodbye to the car with a silent Fuck it, picked up the shopping bag, and moved to the door.

He paused to make sure that nothing had been forgotten. He was leaving behind no television set or radio. They had been pawned long ago. He examined the room once more and then went out the door of Room 611 for the last time with everything he had acquired in thirty-one years—the entire McBride estate, contained now in a Safeway shopping bag that held one jacket, three pairs of slacks, five shirts, some underwear, a pair of shoes, some socks, a passport, an honorable discharge from the Marine Corps, and a dozen Xerox copies of a map that purportedly told where a stolen $2 million was hidden. Tucked up his rectum in an aluminum capsule was the rest of the McBridge fortune, the $875 that remained from the thousand that he had been paid for his time by Durant and Wu.

McBride had taken a risk, a quite calculated one, by coming back to his room. But after he had talked it over with Durant they had agreed that the police would almost certainly not be waiting for him. Whether Solly Gesini would have someone waiting was the chance McBride would have to take. It had seemed unlikely. With a mind like Solly Gesini's in charge of the hunt, McBride's room could well be virtually the last place that any trackers would come searching for him. Nobody's gonna think I'm that dumb, McBride had told Durant. Not even Solly.

McBride made it down in the elevator and out the door of the hotel without incident. A block away he climbed into Durant's Mercedes, placed the shopping bag on the seat beside him, and drove off. Forty minutes later he was knocking on the door of Otherguy Overby's apartment.

Overby opened the door and inspected the man who stood there with the shopping bag in his hand. They stared at each other for a moment, searching for common points of reference, and found them in a kind of mutual recognition. McBride would become Overby in another ten years—if he lived that long.

"You're McBride, huh?"

"Check."

"What the hell does that mean—check? You're McBride or you're not, yes or no. I don't need any of that cutesy check-and-double-check shit. I'm too old for that."

"Okay, I'm Eddie McBride, unless it makes your piles hurt."

"Yeah, well, come on in, I guess."

Overby stepped back to let McBride enter. Carrying his Safeway shopping bag, McBride went in, put the bag down, and looked around, allowing his gaze to pause only for a second on the girl who sat in the overstuffed chair wearing nothing but green bikini panties, a can of beer in her hand.

"Jesus," McBride said, "just like the Hilton."

"The Hilton would like that fancy luggage of yours."

McBride looked around some more. "At least it looks right at home here."

"Well," Overby said, "that's Brenda. This here's Eddie McBride, my new assistant."

McBride looked at him. "I am, huh?"

"That's what they tell me."

"What do I do—assist you across the street?"

"That's pretty big-time stuff," Overby said. "We're gonna have to see how you work out first."

McBride nodded agreeably as though to signify that thus far the exchange of diplomatic protocols had been both extremely frank and highly productive. He changed the direction of his nod so that it took in Brenda.

"Who's that?"

"Like I said, that's Brenda."

The girl waved her beer can. "Want some of my beer?"

McBride shook his head, rejecting both the girl and her offer. "Brenda looks like she might have a lot of friends. And friends talk a lot."

Overby frowned. "Yeah, that wouldn't be too good, would it?"

"No."

"I guess maybe I'll have to explain things to her."

"Explain what?" Brenda said.

Overby moved over to Brenda. He looked down at her for several moments. "You never heard of any Eddie McBride, did you, sugar?"

The girl shrugged. "What's an Eddie McBride?"

"Get rid of her," McBride said.

Brenda pouted. "I don't wanta go home. I just got here."

Overby turned to McBride. "You wanta fuck her first?"

McBride shook his head. "I don't take wet ducks," he said. "Get rid of her."

Overby turned back to the girl. "Brenda," he said.

"What?"

"Out."

The girl put her beer down and got up. "You got some real weird friends, Otherguy, that's all I gotta say." She started toward the door, but paused when she reached McBride. She put her hands on her hips, arched her back, and thrust her crotch up against McBride's, rotating it slowly. Her mouth was open, and she let her long pink tongue run slowly around her lips.

"You got any idea what you're missing?" she said.

McBride stared at her coldly for a few seconds, not responding to the bump and grind of her pelvis. After another moment or two he said, "Go wash your feet, Brenda."

The girl stopped her efforts and, pouting again, moved quickly to the door. She opened it, then turned back to look at Overby. "You know what, Otherguy?"

"What?"

"You suck." With that she was gone, carefully slamming the door behind her.

Overby sighed. "She lives across the hall."

"Handy."

"You want a beer or something? I've got bourbon."

"Beer's fine."

Overby moved across the room to the kitchen alcove and opened the refrigerator door. "You known 'em long?" he said as he took out two cans of beer.

"Who?"

"Durant and the Chinaman."

"Not long. Have you?"

Overby didn't answer until he had handed McBride a can of beer. "About nine years. Maybe ten." He popped his beer open and tossed the top at an ashtray. He missed. McBride opened his can and placed its top in the ashtray, then bent down and picked up Overby's top and placed it beside his own.

"What do they do?" McBride said. "I mean, what do they really do?"

"How'd you meet 'em?"

"They came looking for me. I had something to sell and they thought they might buy, but it didn't quite work out."

"What was it, something tricky?"

McBride nodded. "Yeah. A little."

Overby took a swallow of his beer. "Well," he said, "I've

known 'em for damn near ten years and that's what they've always done—something just a little bit tricky."

McBride drank some beer and then sat down on the couch. "But they're smart, aren't they? Both of them. I mean, they're the kind of guys that don't make too many mistakes."

After thinking about the question for a moment, Overby took another swallow of his beer and said, "Well, now, I don't know if they never made any mistakes, but they're smart, all right. Especially the Chinaman."

"I thought Durant sort of had the edge."

"Well, he's no dummy either, but that Artie Wu is one smart Chinaman, and a smart Chinaman is just about twice as smart as anybody else."

"I don't know if you're gonna believe this, but I don't even know what they're up to."

"Well, I don't either exactly, but as long as the money's okay I don't care just one hell of a lot. What about you?"

"No," McBride said after a moment, "I don't guess I really care either."

At 5:30 that morning, the eighteenth of June, a Saturday, Solly Gesini was asleep in his bedroom on the second floor of his house on Medio Drive in Brentwood when the phone began to ring.

Gesini came awake slowly. He didn't snatch up the ringing phone. Instead, he lay there alone in his bed trying to divine what misfortune had struck. He knew with absolute certainty that it wasn't going to be good news—not at 5:30 in the morning.

Finally, on the tenth ring, he picked up the phone and said hello.

The man's voice that replied was both loud and excited. "I'm gonna sue you, you cocksucker!"

Solly Gesini woke up. "Who's-this-who's-this?" he said, running the words together, even stumbling over them a little.

"It's me, you dirty wop son of a bitch, that's who."

"Oh," Gesini said. "You. How're ya, Ferdie?" Ferdie was Ferdinando Fiorio, his brother-in-law.

"I'll tell you how I am. I just called my lawyer. That's how I am. He's gonna sue your ass."

"Sue? What's all this sue shit?"

"They're on the way, Solly. I didn't know nothing about it. I told 'em that. I told them they wanta find out about it, you're the guy. That's what my lawyer says, too. Boy, are we gonna sue your ass."

"You don't make sense, Ferdie. But you don't make sense at noon, so why should you make any at five-thirty in the fuckin' morning? Just calm down and tell me one thing—who's on the way?"

"The sheriff, that's who."

"What sheriff?"

"*What* sheriff? The sheriff who found it, that's who. I don't know if it was the real sheriff. There were two of 'em. Young kids with mustaches. Maybe deputy sheriffs. Anyway, they found it."

"Found what?"

"My thirty-two-thousand-dollar Winnebago, that's what."

"Where'd they find it?"

"Down at the bottom of a canyon all burned up, not a fuckin' thing left, everything ruined, and you said you were gonna borrow it to go up to Big Bear and I oughta know by now never to believe anything you ever tell me, and you just wait, am I gonna sue your ass."

"What canyon?" Gesini said.

"What canyon? I don't know—Latigo Canyon out in Malibu. I think it's Latigo. I think that's what they said. And those two guys you sent over to borrow it, that big nigger and that other one with the bald head, the white guy, Tony what's-his-name. There ain't nothing left of them neither. I shoulda known better. The only reason I did it was because of Anna-Maria, you never take her anywhere, and I thought she'd like to get up to Big Bear and—"

Gesini cut him off. "There were just two guys in it?"

"Yeah, two guys. I told 'em that the nigger and that other one, Tony, had borrowed it for you and they asked me how big they were and when I told 'em they said they think that they probably're the two who got burned up in it. I don't think my insurance is gonna cover this. One of 'em was shot. I don't know which one. I told 'em I didn't know anything. I told 'em to go to talk to you about people getting shot. I told 'em you knew all about that. I told 'em—".

Solly Gesini didn't listen to what else his brother-in-law had told the Los Angeles County deputy sheriffs. Instead, he slowly hung up the phone. They fucked it up, he thought. Tony and Icky. They let the kid take 'em somehow. Jesus, I'm gonna have to tell Mr. Simms something. I'm gonna have to figure that out. But later. Yeah, I'll do that later.

Gesini nestled slowly back in the bed. He drew his knees up as far as he could, pulled the sheet up over his head, and waited for the deputy sheriffs to arrive.

Chapter Fifteen

At a little past six that Saturday morning Quincy Durant was standing out on the redwood deck of his rented yellow house dressed in a pair of light gray slacks and a blue lamb's-wool pullover sweater. He stood with a mug of coffee in one hand, a cigarette in the other, and watched as Randall Piers came down the beach at a brisk walk, the six greyhounds bunched at his heels.

When he was still some distance away, perhaps fifty yards, Piers waved at Durant, who waved back and then held up the coffee mug, pointing at it with the hand that held his cigarette. Durant could see Piers nod his head at the invitation.

Neither man spoke until Piers started up the steps. Then he said, "You know something?"

"What?"

"They miss half of it."

"Who?"

"People who live on the beach. They pay a lot to live here and then they never get up in time to watch the sun rise. What a waste."

"You've got a point," Durant said politely.

Piers shook his head. "Not much of one. Just my thought for the day. You got any of that coffee of yours left?"

"Sure."

Piers made one of his abrupt, nearly brutal hand gestures and the six greyhounds promptly flopped down on the deck. Two of them yawned at each other, one of them gnawed at something that seemed lodged in his paw, and the other three looked around with the interested, curious gaze of the knowledgeable tourist who never gets bored.

Inside the house, Durant poured Piers a cup of coffee and warmed up his own. They moved into the living room, where Piers looked around, a slightly puzzled expression on his face. Then the puzzlement vanished and he turned to Durant. "You had them take it out, didn't you?"

"What?"

"The Reuters ticker."

"Yesterday. We had them take it out late yesterday."

"You covered, huh?"

"Yeah, we did. It seemed about time."

Randall Piers ran yesterday's closing prices through his head. "You made some money."

"A little. Our broker said we should have hung in there awhile longer, but what the hell. We made enough."

"So," Randall Piers said, lowering himself into the leather chair that Eddie McBride had bled on a little the night before. "You said you were going to take a run down to Pelican Bay."

"We did. Yesterday."

"What'd you find out?"

"Something's happening down there."

"What?"

"We're not sure," Durant said, and lowered himself to the couch. "We're trying to put a man inside."

"Inside where?"

"Reginald Simms—consultants. Mean anything to you?"

"No. Should it?"

Durant shrugged. "Let me try another one. Vince Imperlino."

Piers's face grew still. He put his coffee mug down on a small table with a white marble top. He had to turn slightly to do it. When he turned back, his face had become more stiff than still. He stared at Durant for a moment and then said, "What about him?"

"They say you sold your record company to him."

"It was a complicated deal. Very complicated. By the time Imperlino surfaced it was too late to pull back. Too many commitments had already been made. You want the details?"

"No."

"It was a complicated deal."

"You said that."

"There was a lot of pressure on me then."

"Okay. Fine."

"How did Imperlino's name come up?"

"He's bought himself something else. Or so they say."

"What?" Piers said.

"The newspaper at Pelican Bay. The *Times-Bulletin.*"

Piers's face relaxed. "How'd he buy it?"

Durant shrugged. "For cash, I suppose. Probably a lot of it."

"I mean, what device did he use?"

"I think there was a company that owned a company that owned a company and so forth that bought it. Imperlino's name doesn't appear anywhere. Or so we're told."

"That's usually the way they work."

"Who's they?"

"Who do you think?"

Durant smiled. "The ones whose names all end in vowels."

"That's close enough. They're buying a lot of things."

"For instance?"

"I could name you a couple of movie studios that if they don't own yet, they control."

"So I've heard."

"Yeah, I guess that is pretty common knowledge. Maybe I'm just trying to rationalize my letting them grab off Nightshade. There was a certain point after I finally found out about Imperlino that I could have still said no. It would have been difficult, very difficult, but I still could've killed the deal."

"But you didn't?"

"No."

"Did your sister-in-law ever know him?"

"Which one?"

"Silk."

"Yeah, Silk knew him. So did Lace. But Ivory knew him best of all. She was living with him for a while. That's really why they broke up the group. Silk wouldn't put up with it. I mean, she wouldn't record for him. She didn't object to Ivory's being shacked up with him. She didn't like it any more than Lace did, but neither one of them would ever have dreamed of telling their sister who she could sleep with. He kept her in dope, of course. Ivory, I mean—but she finally left him. Went off by herself, just wandering around the country, and then wound up dead of an overdose down in Miami Beach."

"What kind of affair was it?" Durant said.

"What do you mean?"

"Well, was it public or private? Did the press pick up on it? You know, Mob Boss Squires Folk Star—that kind of thing."

"You don't know much about Imperlino, I take it."

Durant shook his head. "Not a hell of a lot."

"He's a hermit. Well, maybe not exactly a hermit. Recluse would be better. And Ivory, except when she was singing, was probably the world's most private person. They got along alone, if you follow me. Imperlino has three guys on his payroll who do nothing but try to keep his name out of the paper. They did a good job then and they do a good job now."

"What's he like?" Durant said.

"I only met him twice."

"What about when the negotiations were going on for the record company?"

Piers shook his head. "He was never a part of those. Even today, I doubt that anyone could actually prove that he controls Nightshade. Everybody knows it, of course, or thinks they do."

"But you met him?"

"Twice, as I said. Once he and Ivory had Lace and me over to dinner at his place in Bel Air. They'd wanted Silk to come too, but she refused. Silk has—well—principles. Lace and I went because Ivory asked us to." Piers smiled —a crooked, rueful smile. "And I suppose our principles are a little more, well, flexible than Silk's. Also, I was just curious as hell. I take a lot of kidding about that place of mine, you know. But it's what I wanted, I paid for it, and I live there, so to hell with them. But this place Imperlino built himself in Bel Air. It's got everything but a moat."

"A castle, huh?"

"Not exactly. He built it in the '60s and it looks as though it's been there since 1647. There're some who claim that he had a guy on Disney's staff design it for him. It's sort of half fairy tale and half English country house. But it works. God knows how much it cost him. So anyway, Lace and I went to dinner there that time."

Piers paused as though remembering, then picked up his coffee and finished it. "Jesus, that's good."

"Like some more?"

"Yeah, I would, thanks."

Durant picked up the two mugs and took them into the kitchen. When he came back, Piers said, "That recipe you gave my wife. It's not bad, but it's not like this."

"I'm not sure I told her to put in a pinch of salt."

"Salt?"

"Just a pinch."

"I'll tell her."

"What was he like?"

"Imperlino?"

Durant nodded.

Piers took a sip of his coffee first. "Smooth," he said. "Not slick smooth, but gracious smooth, if you know what I mean. Somewhere he's acquired a lot of polish—the effortless kind. I mean, he doesn't have to remember his manners, and let me tell you something, they're perfect. And he also must have gone to a voice coach at one time, because he skips his r's a little and the a's are slightly broadened, but not much. Lace claims to know for a fact that he hired George Sanders to give him elocution lessons, but Lace knows more apocryphal tales than anyone I've ever met."

"You didn't talk about the record company, I take it?" Durant said.

Piers shook his head. "It never came up. Well, all four of us were there in what he called the Big Hall with the fireplace blazing in July and the air conditioning keeping the temperature down to sixty-five and Imperlino and I in black tie and the two ladies in party dresses and four servants and six courses, or maybe seven, I don't remember now, and Imperlino orchestrating the conversation."

"What'd he talk about?"

"Eliot."

"T.S.?"

"Right. Imperlino delivered a nice little fifteen-minute lecture on how Ezra Pound's editing saved Eliot's—uh—"

The Waste Land?

"Right. Well, Christ, I hadn't read Eliot since I was in college and I didn't much care for him then. But Imperlino managed to make him and Pound sound fascinating as hell. I don't know. Maybe they are. It seemed so while he was talking, at least. After that he somehow very smoothly, very gently coaxed Ivory into reciting some poetry she'd written. I didn't know she wrote poetry. I knew she wrote lyrics, of course, but the poetry was a surprise.

And it was good. Damned good, although, of course, I'm no critic, but that's not the point. The point is how he got Ivory to recite it. Then he starts drawing Lace out on growing up in Arkansas. Well, that was no big deal. Lace'll go on about that for hours if you'll let her. But she made it funny and amusing, and the next thing I know he's got me going on about how brilliant and clever I am. I must have gone on for ten minutes all about me before I realized what was happening. But even then I didn't mind. Who would?"

"And that was the evening?"

"Yeah, that was it. A good time was had by all and delicious refreshments were served. I came away with the impression that I'd just been had. I think he must have studied charm the way I studied electronics—except that he's better in his field than I am in mine, and I'm not exactly a slouch."

"A charming recluse?"

"It's a paradox, isn't it?"

Durant nodded. "It would seem so. What'd your wife think?"

"Well, we weren't married then. This was back in '70. But she thought that if she ever needed her throat cut, she would go to him because he would not only know how to do it, he would also make her enjoy it."

Durant lit a cigarette, his third for the morning. "You said you saw him once again."

Piers nodded slowly and then drank some more coffee. "The end of 1970. Down in Miami. I went down to claim Ivory's body. Neither Lace nor Silk could face it, so I went. He showed up. He and Ivory'd split by then, but he was there anyway. He wanted to see her. He also wanted me to go with him. Well, what the hell, I did. He went in and looked at her. I waited for him outside. Ivory wasn't very pretty by then. She'd quit eating, and the dope and the horrors had finally got to her.

"Well, when he came out he was crying. He wasn't sobbing or anything, but he was crying in this quiet, dignified manner. I don't know. Maybe he learned how to do it in charm school. But, by God, he did it well. He told me that he wanted Ivory's body. He wanted to take it back and bury it at his place in Bel Air. I told him that that wouldn't be possible because the sisters had already made arrangements to bury her in the family plot in Arkansas next to her mother and father. He nodded as if that were perfectly understandable. He was still crying, but not apologizing for it or anything.

"Then he asked if I knew what the police had found out. Well, I told him that they thought Ivory had bought some bad dope off a Cuban bellhop who worked in the hotel she'd stayed at. But they didn't have any proof. He nodded as if he found that sort of interesting, but not terribly, and then we shook hands, and that's the last time I ever saw him. But there's a postscript."

"Oh?"

"Yeah. Two days later they fished that Cuban bellhop out of the ocean. He'd had his throat cut. Then there's the post-postscript."

"What?"

"Two weeks after they buried Ivory in Arkansas, some-body dug her up and made off with the body. You like it?"

Durant shook his head slowly. "Not much."

"Neither did Silk. She wanted to raise all sorts of hell until Lace and I talked her out of it."

"So he's a sentimentalist."

"Or weird."

"Maybe both," Durant said. "What about his Washington connections?"

The question surprised Piers, and his face showed it. His eyebrows went up and his mouth turned down at the corners. "I hadn't heard," he said. "Are there any?"

"There's a rumor, but it's pretty low-grade stuff."

"Where'd you hear it?"

"The name wouldn't mean anything to you."

A new expression slid across Piers's face, one that was both skeptical and wary. "You spend one day down in Pelican Bay and you come back talking about a mob boss and his Washington connections. Is that really possible?"

"Anything's possible. We're just looking for your sister-in-law, but to do that we have to poke around to find out where to look. Any objections?"

Piers rose. "None. I'm not paying you to be orthodox." He started for the door, but paused. "By the way, when my wife was here the other day, did you make a pass at her?"

Durant examined Piers for several moments before replying. There was something in Piers's eyes, Durant thought. A sadness perhaps. Finally, Durant said, "No."

"I guess that's what she was complaining about." He grinned then, but not very merrily. "She likes to play little games like that," he said. "I wouldn't take her too seriously, if I were you."

Durant kept his expression grave. "I'll try to remember that."

By seven o'clock that morning Randall Piers was seated behind his desk in his combination library-office-study. Before him was a three-page, single-spaced memorandum from his executive assistant, Hart Ebsworth. The memorandum was entitled RUNDOWN—DURANT AND WU. Piers picked up a blue pencil and circled one paragraph consisting of four lines. He then picked up his phone, pressed a button, and said, "Come on in."

Ebsworth came in and took his usual seat. Piers slid the memorandum across to him. Ebsworth glanced through it and said, "The paragraph you circled?"

"Right."

"Early '70 until early '72. When they came back to Bangkok from Florida and Durant got his scars."

"Yeah," Piers said. "It's a little sketchy there."

"You want more."

Piers nodded. "I want it all."

Ebsworth leaned back in his chair and sighed. "It'll cost. And I don't mean money, either."

"Get it," Piers said.

Chapter Sixteen

Because it was Saturday the traffic was light, and they made it from Malibu to the Beverly Wilshire Hotel in a little under thirty minutes, which may have set some kind of record. Artie Wu drove the way he always did—with what Durant usually thought of as wild abandon. When Wu drove, Durant kept his eyes closed much of the way.

He opened them once just in time to see Wu fake out a white Rolls-Royce at the corner of San Vicente and Gretna Green. Durant caught a glimpse of the Rolls's driver, open mouthed and apoplectic, as Wu whipped the big Chrysler past with not much more than a quarter of an inch to spare.

Durant closed his eyes again and said, "I think you hit him."

"I didn't hit him."

"You nicked him."

"Never."

His eyes still closed, Durant said, "Your driving—"

Wu interrupted. "Don't tell me again."

"It's just that I've come up with a theory that might explain it."

"What?"

"Somewhere in your ancestry, and not too far back, there must have been some Chinese bandits."

Artie Wu nodded as though pleased by the suggestion. "Yeah," he said, "I'd like to think so, anyway. You know how you drive?"

"I'm an excellent driver," Durant said. "No, not excellent. Superb."

"Bullshit. You toodle along like it's always Sunday morning and you're early for church."

"But I get there."

"We'll get there. On time, too."

"He does like promptness, doesn't he? Probably a fetish."

"Along with his bow ties."

"At least he ties them himself."

"Yeah," Wu said. "There's that."

Wu covered the next four miles in a little less than seven minutes, and they arrived at the Beverly Wilshire at three minutes until nine. Wu turned into the drive that separated the new section of the hotel from the old and handed the car over to an attendant.

"He's in the old section, I bet," Durant said.

"Where else?"

They got out of the elevator on the sixth floor and turned left, heading down the richly carpeted hall toward the suite numbered 617-19.

"You know, I read somewhere that they've got a rating system in this hotel," Wu said.

"Oh?"

"Yeah. If you're almost somebody, or at least make out like you are, you get fresh flowers in your room. But if you really are somebody, which means that maybe you got your name on Cronkite once, then they send up a bottle of champagne. I don't remember whether it's French or not."

"Probably California," Durant said.

"Probably."

"I wonder whether he got champagne or flowers?"

"Well, he was an assistant secretary of state once."

"And ambassador to Cambodia," Wu said.

"Not to forget Togo."

"Plus a few other things. Five bucks he got champagne."

"No bet," Durant said just as Wu knocked on the door.

The man who opened the door was Whittaker Lowell James, who was sixty-four years old and used all three names whenever the opportunity presented itself. He was white haired and very tall, just a little over six-three. He held himself stiffly erect, almost in a brace, and it gave him a somehow distant, almost forbidding air that his wintry smile, which he had just turned on, did nothing to dispel.

"Gentlemen," James said, and looked quickly at his watch before offering his hand first to Wu and then to Durant.

"Hello, Whittaker," Wu said, because he knew that James hated for anyone to call him Whit.

"Arthur," James said. "You're looking fit. And you, Quincy—you, I think, could use a few pounds."

"How've you been?" Durant said, wondering how long it had been since anyone had called Wu anything but Artie. Not since Mrs. Billington at the orphanage, he decided. She had always called him Arthur.

James told Durant he had been fine—splendid, in fact— and then Artie Wu said, "I like your flowers."

James turned toward a blue, glazed vase that held an artfully arranged assortment of carnations, chrysanthemums, Dutch iris, and delphiniums touched up with some baby's breath.

"The management sent those up," James said. "Along with a quite good bottle of champagne."

Wu and Durant didn't look at each other because they knew that if they did, James would catch it. At sixty-four, Whittaker Lowell James was as alert as he had ever been, which was very alert indeed.

"Why don't we sit over here," he said. "At least, until breakfast arrives, which should be within"—he glanced at his watch again—"the next minute or so. I took the liberty of ordering for all of us." He looked around as though ready to fend off any challenge to his judgment, and when none came, he smiled his December smile again.

James had waved Wu and Durant over to a striped maroon-and-white couch with overly delicate legs. Durant sat down on the couch. Wu chose a boxy easy chair covered in some kind of nubby pale gray fabric. James hesitated and then decided to sit in the chair that matched the couch. He sat as stiffly as he stood.

"Quite a nice hotel, this," he said. "They even have

kippers, which I thought we might have. You like kippers?"

"I do," Wu said, "but Quincy hates them, although you don't have to worry about it. All he ever has for breakfast anyhow is a raw egg."

"You're not as much of a gourmet as is our plump friend here, are you, Quincy?"

"I just don't like to cook."

"You still do quite a bit of fine cooking, Arthur?"

Wu smiled. "Whenever I get hungry."

"I like to cook, you know. But rather simple fare, I'm afraid. A chop now and then, a salad, or perhaps an oyster stew. I do that quite well."

The conversation had begun as it always began whenever Wu and Durant met with Whittaker Lowell James. They invariably talked about nonessentials at first—about nothing, really. And as they talked James inspected them both, measuring their posture and pauses and eye movements for possible signs of disenchantment and sloth and even incipient treachery. James was an extremely suspicious man, and he prided himself on his ability to read the small, telling signs that a body made. His guideposts were a tremor, a tic, a stammer, a gesture, a glance—even a silence.

James searched for them now as he talked about nothing. He had long made it a rule to talk about nothing before he hired anyone. Or fired them.

They were still talking about hardly anything at all when the knock came. James rose and opened the door. The Mexican waiter pushed the wheeled table into the room, smiling as though he enjoyed his job. James fussed for a moment about where the table should be put. When that was settled, the waiter started bringing the dishes up from the hot boxes underneath, and he and James chatted with each other in rapid Spanish.

Durant half-listened to the Spanish and felt grateful that James was talking to the waiter about the warm weather. Perhaps he'll spare us that. Durant noted that James had made a concession to California informality by abandoning his usual dark gray or blue suit for a navy blue blazer and gray slacks. But he had clung to the bow tie—butterfly, of course, blue with white polka dots. And his gleaming black shoes were the kind that needed laces. Durant tried to remember when he himself had last worn shoes that demanded laces. At least ten years, he decided. Probably more.

When the waiter had gone they sat down at the table. Artie Wu took a lot of everything, including the kippers. James had a soft-boiled egg, some bacon, a bit of kipper, and a piece of dry toast. Durant took nothing but a piece of toast, which he buttered carefully.

After he had finished his egg, James patted his lips carefully with a napkin and said, "I must confess, gentlemen, I'm a little disappointed."

"I thought it was good," Wu said, helping himself to another portion of scrambled eggs.

"He's not talking about the food," Durant said, and lit a cigarette.

"No kidding," Wu said. He finished the last of his eggs, used his napkin, leaned back in his chair with a sigh, and produced one of his long, slim cigars, which he held up to James.

"Mind?"

"Not at all."

Wu carefully clipped an end off his cigar, then lit it with his usual kitchen match, and when he was sure that he had it burning nicely, he peered through the smoke at James and said, "Tell us about your disappointment, Whittaker."

"In two months not a single report."

Wu shrugged. "We had nothing to tell you."

"Even that would have been interesting, if not useful."

"Well, we were busy," Durant said.

"How?"

"We had to set it up," Wu said.

"I should have liked to know what steps you were taking."

"What'd you want us to do," Wu said, "call you up and tell you that we were looking for a dead pelican?"

James frowned, and when he did the chill in his pale gray eyes seemed to drop several degrees. "Perhaps we should review," he said. "Would you like to start with the pelican?" He came down hard on "pelican," almost biting the word in two.

Artie Wu smiled. "Let's start before that. Let's start with Aberdeen."

"All right," James said. "Let's. And since I was privy to at least that part of our little venture, perhaps I should take the class." He looked at both men as if again expecting a challenge. What he got from Durant was a slight smile and an even slighter nod. Wu waved his cigar a little.

"In Scotland—in Aberdeen, to be precise—we met and I explained the problem. From a short list of several names my little group had selected yours because we naively had thought that you—especially you, Quincy—might be highly motivated. I think it took only five minutes of conversation with you both before I realized how sadly mistaken we had been."

Durant rubbed his left eye. "Revenge is an awfully old-fashioned motive, Whittaker."

"Apparently."

"But when you mentioned money," Wu said, "I think we perked up considerably."

"Yes, you did, but my little group is not the government and we don't have unlimited funds at our disposal."

"What is it again that you call yourselves?" Wu said. "Something cute, as I remember."

James seemed almost embarrassed, but not quite. "The R Street Fudge and Philosophical Society," he said, and then glared at the two men defiantly.

Artie Wu grinned cheerfully. "Cute, like I said."

"How many are there, a couple of dozen of you?" Durant said.

"Approximately."

Durant started putting out his cigarette. "And how many of you are ex-Cabinet members. A dozen, fifteen?"

"All of us have served in government in one capacity or other."

Durant nodded. "And all of you are millionaires or better. Much better."

"A number of us are comfortably fixed," James said a little stiffly, trying to make it neither a boast nor a confession.

"And used to it," Wu said.

There was no warmth in James's look. "To a comfortable living?"

Wu shook his head. "To running things. Let me put it another way. If a pot starts to boil somewhere, you guys are right there with a lid."

James sighed. "You overestimate both our scope and our influence, Arthur."

Wu smiled. "Do I?"

"I'm afraid so. We have limited resources, far more limited than you think. And for purposes of security we decided that this particular project had to be self-financing. I made that clear in Aberdeen."

"What you made clear in Aberdeen," Wu said, "was that if anything went wrong in Pelican Bay, your R Street bunch would come out with hands so clean that they'd be almost antiseptic."

"You're not complaining about the financial arrangements, are you, Arthur?"

Wu shook his head. "No. You found us a quick buyer for the chili parlor, and then we took what we got and went short on Midwest Minerals, the way you advised, and we made ourselves a bunch of money. I'm not complaining about that. It's just that my teeth hurt whenever you start talking poor-mouth."

James smiled another of his bleak and chilly smiles. "I'll try to be less parsimonious in my future remarks. In any event, after selling your—uh—establishment in Aberdeen—what was it you called it? The Something Chili Parlor."

"The Nacogdoches Chili Parlor," Durant said.

"Yes, to be sure. Interesting name."

"My wife thought it up," Wu said. "She likes American names."

"And how is that splendid woman?"

"Okay, except that she loathes California."

"She rises even higher in my estimation. But to continue. After leaving Aberdeen, you gathered up kith and kin and came to Washington, where we three met several times and devised a general strategy. It was about then, of course, that the Congressman was killed out here, which presented us with an alternative avenue of approach in the form of Randall Piers and through him to his sister-in-law, Silk Armitage. Are we still of the opinion that she could be the key?"

"It depends on what she's got," Durant said.

"Well, we're pretty sure of what the Congressman had," James said. "After all, he had been a policeman and, from what I understand, a very good one. What a pity that his wife killed him."

"Maybe she didn't," Durant said.

A new layer of frost settled over James's face. "Well, now," he said. "That little bit of information might've been included in one of those reports that you didn't send me."

"We only learned about it yesterday," Durant said, and looked at Wu. "Or was it the day before?"

"Yesterday."

"I see," James said. "Perhaps you gentlemen should continue the review—from when you left Washington until now. Provided, of course, that there is something to review other than a general description of life at the beach."

"Okay," Durant said, and lit another cigarette. "We went to San Francisco first. You know that, of course. We went there because we knew some people there who knew who was in L.A. and who wasn't. By that I mean who was down here that we might use. After that I came down to L.A. first. Since Randall Piers and I don't travel in the same circles, the problem was how to make the approach without letting him know that he was being approached. I decided on proximity. Then I had some luck and found the house on the beach."

"You sent me a postcard of that, I believe," James said, "with something like 'Keeping busy, having fun' on it. Oh, yes, and your address and phone number, too."

"See, we did keep in touch," Wu said.

"Okay. After I found the house," Durant went on, "Artie came down and got settled in Santa Monica. Then using the information you gave us we looked up Eddie McBride and opened what he thought were negotiations."

"He thought the money was still there, I take it?" James said.

"Yes."

"And you didn't disabuse him of that notion?"

"No," Durant said, shaking his head. "Well, after we established proximity to Piers, the next thing was to create familiarity. Piers walks his dogs nearly every day along the beach, so Artie started jogging along the beach."

James's silver eyebrows went up. "I thought you hated exercise, Arthur."

"I do. I especially hate it right after dawn, which is when Piers walks his dogs."

"What kind of dogs?"

"Greyhounds," Durant said. "Six of them."

"Six?"

"Six."

"My word. But why did you decide that Arthur should do the jogging? Why not you, Quincy? After all, it was your house."

"I'm more exotic," Wu said.

"Yes. Yes, I see."

"It was part of the whole mystique," Durant said. "The come-on. Finally, when we decided that Piers was ripe, we had to set up the accidental meeting."

"That's when we went looking for a dead pelican," Wu said.

"There really was a dead pelican?"

"Sure," Wu said. "I needed something to trip over."

"To be sure," James said, murmuring the words, not even bothering to hide his disbelief.

"Dead pelicans are hard to find, by the way," Wu said. "But we finally found one down at Zuma beach, and I planted it the next morning. Then when Piers came along I tripped over it and sprained my ankle. I mean, I really sprained it."

"It wasn't a sprain," Durant said. "It was a mild twist."

"It felt like a sprain."

"And Piers came to your rescue?" James said.

Artie Wu nodded. "He helped me into the house. We'd really worked to give it the right atmosphere. The furniture was all very good stuff, but just a little worn. We even rented a twenty-thousand-dollar Oriental rug and put it on the floor. Also, Quincy here kept his shirt off so that Piers could get a good look at his scars. And finally, over in a corner, we had the Reuters financial ticker clacking away."

"A nice touch," James said. "Very nice indeed. And?"

"He nibbled at first, and then he bit," Wu said. "We used MidMin to let him know how smart we were. Then we brought up Eddie McBride and his two million—just mentioning it, of course; a throwaway almost, certainly not a sell. And there you have it—a house on the beach with a twenty-thouand-dollar Oriental rug on the floor, a wall of books, a news ticker in the corner, and a fat Chinaman and his mysterious, scar-backed partner getting rich by riding the wire. Not to mention a map of where a stolen two million bucks might be buried. Now, if you had a missing sister-in-law and needed a couple of hard cases to find her and ran across us at six-thirty in the morning, what would you think?"

"That I'd stumbled across a nest of brigands," James said.

"Exactly," Artie Wu said, and smiled.

Chapter Seventeen

Whittaker Lowell James was an expert listener. As Durant and Wu talked, James sat quietly in his chair, moving almost nothing but his eyes except when he occasionally sipped cold coffee from his cup.

The report was delivered almost in relays, Wu and Durant spelling each other off with some kind of silent system that seemed to James almost prearranged. They skipped nothing and they embellished nothing, and James's only interjections were an occasional "I see" and "Of course" and "Indeed." When Durant came to the deaths of Icky Norris and Tony Egidio a brief frown wrinkled itself across James's forehead, but it lasted only a second. Perhaps less.

After Wu and Durant were done, James looked at his watch and said, "There should be fresh coffee here within the next few minutes."

They waited in silence then. James toyed with a spoon. Durant sat quietly, slumped back in his chair, his lean hands locked behind his head.

Artie Wu's cigar, forgotten while he talked, had died from neglect in an ashtray. Wu picked it up, looked at it fondly, and stuck it into the left side of his mouth. As he chewed on his cold cigar, Wu examined James for evidence of the reaction that would soon be due. A patrician, Wu thought, if there is such a thing. He could be coming to a boil, but you'd never know it.

If there were any clues to James's thinking, Wu felt that they would be found in the eyes and the mouth. But the eyes had all the expression and color of ice cubes forgotten in the refrigerator since last summer. And the mouth, underneath the slightly beakish nose, was stretched into a tight, reproving line that could mean either stifled rage or trouble with the kippers.

Wu was about to break the silence and say, "Well?" when somebody knocked at the door. James rose and admitted the same room waiter as before. The waiter put the fresh pot of coffee down, and James complimented him on his promptness and tipped him a dollar. When the waiter asked if they would like the table removed, James shook his head no.

When the waiter had gone, James served the coffee in fresh cups. He almost made it into a ceremony, and when it was over he leaned back in his chair and looked first at Wu and then Durant.

"Well, it's better than I expected," he said.

"Durant, his hands still locked behind his head, stretched and looked at the ceiling. Wu simply chewed on his cold cigar some more.

"He knows you're here," James said. "That might be good."

"Simms?" Durant said.

"Yes. Reginald Simms." James said the name as though he were biting into it for the first time and were not at all sure that he would like what he found.

"We assume that he knows," Durant said.

"Well, yes, he probably does. I would say that it's a safe assumption. After all, someone wanted your names from McBride, didn't they? We can assume, then, that it was Simms. Or one of his henchmen."

"Henchmen," Wu said. "My God, I don't think I've heard that used in twenty years. Not since Princeton."

"It almost goes back that far, doesn't it? You and Simms, I mean."

"Almost," Durant said.

"It all began in Mexico, didn't it—in '61 or thereabouts."

"In '61," Durant said, still staring at the ceiling.

"And exactly what were you doing in Mexico then?"

"Exactly?" Wu said.

"Yes."

"We were in jail."

"Yes, I remember, but I don't recall the details."

"You mean why?" Wu said.

"Yes. Why."

"We were involved in pre-Columbian art," Durant said, shifting his gaze from the ceiling to James and smiling a little.

"Counterfeiting it, you mean."

Durant shrugged. "Some of the pieces we sold are still in museums. Old Carrasco was a real artist. A genius, probably."

"You were how old then?"

Wu did some mental subtracting. "Twenty-two."

"And Simms showed up," James said. "And he recruited you."

Wu shook his head. "He didn't recruit us. He gave us a choice. We could either stay in a Mexican jail or join the Peace Corps and go to Indonesia for him."

James smiled, and for the first time a small amount of mirth crept into it. "I can think of no two less likely candidates. For the Peace Corps, I mean. What did he see in you—did he say?"

"Our youth," Durant said with a grin.

"Yes, of course. For two so young you hadn't led an exactly sheltered existence."

"Not quite," Wu said.

"And so you went to Indonesia for 'the Peace Corps.'" James carefully put the name in quotes. "Java, wasn't it?"

Wu nodded. "About seventy miles out of Djakarta."

"Who was your contact?"

"A Dutchman called Jonckheer. Simon Jonckheer."

James sipped his coffee. It had grown cold, but he seemed neither to notice nor to care. "Yes, Jonckheer. The Chinese doubled him, didn't they?"

"That wasn't until later," Wu said. "In late '62."

"How long did it take for him to burn you?"

Durant shrugged. "He let us run awhile."

"Why?"

"We were cutting him in."

James nodded. "Cigarette smuggling, wasn't it?"

"Partly," Wu said.

"What else were you feeding him?"

"Jonckheer?"

"Yes."

Durant smiled again. "We made things up. If we caught a rumor, we'd fancy it up and pass it along to him. He liked us."

"And the Peace Corps?"

"They were happy as hell with us," Wu said. "We increased the per capita income of the village we'd been assigned to by five hundred percent in the first six months. Of course, we had almost the entire village on our payroll by then."

"How was the jail?" James said.

"You mean the one in Djakarta?"

James nodded.

Durant shrugged. "It was Dutch built. Solid. Lousy, of course, but we got to meet Sukarno."

"Did he come just to look?" James said.

Artie Wu thought about it for a moment. "He talked to us a little. About Hollywood. He was a film nut."

"But nothing else?" James said.

Wu shook his head. "They had us cold. On the smuggling, anyway. They would have had us on the other except Jonckheer was found dead with a bullet in his back, and after that they couldn't prove anything."

"That was just about the time that our Mr. Simms appeared on the scene again."

"Right," Durant said.

There was another long silence. James's face had acquired a dark, almost brooding look as he stared down at the tablecloth. Finally, he looked up and said, "Simms killed him, of course—Jonckheer, I mean—and then worked a deal with Sukarno to let you go. An expensive deal, I might add."

"Money?" Wu said.

"No, not money."

There was another silence, and then James said, "And

after Indonesia came Tahiti, didn't it, and Simms pulled the strings with the French for your licensing and so forth. That was your payoff, wasn't it?"

"That's right," Durant said.

"Or you would have gone public?"

There was nothing pleasant in the smile that Wu formed around his dead cigar. "We mentioned it to him in passing, I think. Once or twice."

"Would you have?"

Wu shrugged. "Maybe. But probably not."

"But he still had you on his string?"

Durant shifted in his chair. He leaned his elbows on the table and stared at James. "Let's get one thing straight. We were never on anybody's string. We were never anything but pea pickers—casual labor, seasonal help. We got into it because we were blackjacked into it, and afterwards we played along because sometimes it was useful, but not very. And finally, there toward the last, we did what we did for money and for nothing else. But as for being spies, if that's what we ever were, Artie and I were pretty much of a bust."

Wu grinned around his cigar again. "Everybody in Papeete used to tell me I looked like a spy. What the hell, it was good for business."

"After Papeete, then?" James said.

Wu moved his heavy shoulders slightly in a shrug of sorts. "We moved around the Pacific for a while and then to Bangkok.

"He was there, wasn't he? In Bangkok. Simms."

"Yeah, he came through a few times."

James looked as if he wanted to pursue that further, but then abruptly changed his mind. "And from Bangkok you went back to the States and finally down to Key West. This would be '69 by now, right?"

"About then," Durant said.

"Who made the approach?"

"He sent somebody," Wu said.

"Who?"

"One of your old buddies from your OSS days. Simms's gray eminence. The Frenchman."

"Lopinot?" James said.

Wu nodded. "That's right. The sly fox himself. What was he then?" he asked Durant.

"In '69? Fifty-three probably. Maybe fifty-four."

"And Lopinot made you the proposition?"

"Right," Durant said.

"Tell me about it."

Durant leaned back and looked at James curiously. "You know all about it."

"I think we should review."

Durant rubbed his nose and sighed. "All right. He and Lopinot had teamed up, and the Agency had sent them into Cambodia with God knows how much money. They set up their own fiefdom and sent out the word that they were looking for recruits. Well, they all showed up from all over —Germans, South Africans, old Foreign Legion types, a lot of the scum from the Congo, a few Biafra veterans, some English, even some Americans. Their job was to soften things up for the Cambodia—what did they call it—incursion. The problem was supply. Lopinot offered us the contract."

"And you took it," James said, making it almost an accusation rather than a question.

"That's right," Wu said. "We took it."

"For the money, of course."

Wu nodded. "It was a fat contract."

"So you set up shop in Bangkok again."

"We had an office and a warehouse and some trucks in Bangkok and a jumping-off place at the border. We leased two helicopters from one of the CIA fronts, hired some pilots, and flew the stuff in at night. Either Artie or I would go along on every trip."

"How many men did he have?" James said.

"He had about five dozen mercenaries, not counting what he'd had rounded up by press-gangs. It wasn't an unusual situation. The Agency had a number of guys like Simms operating out there then, although most of them were in

Vietnam. And most of them had smaller operations than Simms, but not all. He controlled about a fifty-mile-square area, and they'd started calling him the Dirty Duke." Durant paused. "With good reason."

"And you ran him supplies until when—'72?" James said.

"May fifteenth," Durant said automatically as if the date were as familiar to him as his birthday.

James nodded slowly. "You had known Mlle. Gelinet for quite some time then, hadn't you?"

"About a year," Durant said. "A little more."

"And she was with—"

"*Paris-Match*."

"Yes. She was quite an excellent journalist."

"And photographer," Wu said.

"Yes, of course." James used his right hand to smooth his thick white hair. It was the first even slightly nervous gesture he had made. His second one came when he cleared his throat before saying, "You were quite fond of each other, I understand."

Durant stared at him for a long moment, for nearly five seconds, and then nodded slightly, just once.

Artie Wu took his stub of a cigar out of his mouth, looked at it, and said, "They were sweet on each other. They were going to go back to Paris and get married. Or live together. Whichever."

Durant glanced at Wu. "I'll tell it."

Wu shrugged. "Sure."

"The rumors started filtering in. About Simms, I mean. The Dirty Duke. All sorts of rumors. Christine wanted to do a story on him, an interview. The next time I went in I checked it out with Lopinot. He liked the idea—maybe because she was from *Paris-Match*. Lopinot liked publicity. You remember that book he wrote."

"Yes," James said. "Rather self-serving, I always thought."

"Anyway, Simms wasn't around, but Lopinot gave the okay. We set the drop zone for a week later. Well, when I got back to Bangkok another old friend of ours had shown up. Jack Crespin of CBS. We'd known him in Papeete and then later down in Key West. He'd heard about the Dirty Duke too. I said okay, fine, he could go along when I took Christine in. So we went in and they were waiting for us." Durant paused.

James waited for him to go on. When Durant didn't, James cleared his throat again and said, "They?"

"It was a crack combat team. North Vietnamese. A long-range group led by a Captain Kham. We came in at night, of course, and the signal lights were right. They knew we were coming."

There was another silence. "I got out of the chopper first. Then Christine. They shot her a second later. I don't know why. Kham later said it was a mistake. Jack Crespin, well, he was half out and half in and he was trying to get all the way back in when they shot him too, and he fell back in. The pilot didn't wait around for me."

James shook his head and murmured, "Most unfortunate."

"Wasn't it, though?" Durant said.

"Then came the interrogation?" James said.

"They used a whip," Durant said. "That was later, of course. They wanted to know a lot of things that I didn't know, so I tried lying. Making things up. Well, I wasn't too good at it—not good enough, anyway—so the Little Shit brought out the whip."

"The Little Shit?"

"He was their intelligence officer. Very smart, very mean, very little—about five feet high, maybe less. His name was Lieutenant Nguyen Van Dung. The Little Shit. He had a seven-foot-long whip made out of water buffalo hide. I got three dozen of the best over a period of three days. They got everything out of me that they wanted and after that they left me alone. It was seven feet deep. The hole, I mean. Maybe two feet wide and five feet long. What it really was, I guess, was my grave."

James looked at Wu. "How did you manage it?"

Wu shrugged. "I knew where he was—or where the drop zone was, anyhow—so I hired some help and went in and got him out. It was hit and run just before daylight. Nothing fancy."

"It sounds extraordinary."

Wu clamped down on his cigar as if to cut off any further discussion. "It wasn't."

"And afterwards?" James said.

"Artie cancelled us out of everything after we got back to Bangkok," Durant said. "I was in a hospital for ten days. After that we went to Honolulu. And from there to Aberdeen."

"Why there?"

"It was cold and wet and far away and it seemed like a good idea." Durant passed. "And it was."

"And Simms?"

"What about him?"

"Did you ever figure out why?"

"Sure," Artie Wu said. "Lopinot should've checked first before he agreed to let Quincy bring Christine in. When Simms found out, he cancelled everything and moved—except he didn't bother to tell us."

"Kham caught a straggler," Durant said. "That's why the landing signals were right."

"How did you feel?" James said.

"About what?"

"Simms."

Durant smiled slightly. "I would've killed him. Then."

"And now?"

Durant shook a cigarette out of his pack and lit it. "It all happened a very long time ago, didn't it?"

James brushed a few crumbs off the table. "That was quite a mess you two left behind."

"But you cleaned it up, Whittaker," Wu said. "You sat on it and most of it never got out."

"After Cambodia, Simms kept operating, you know. Right up until the very last. In Vietnam."

"Till '75, you mean?" Durant said.

James nodded. "Lopinot finally got killed in rearguard action during the retreat from Phuoc Long."

"We heard," Durant said.

"He'd become an anachronism by then, almost. Simms, I mean. He showed up at the embassy at almost the last moment. From what I've been able to gather, he was considerably shaken. His world was collapsing around him. He still had a lot of friends, of course, so to keep him busy—almost therapy, I suppose—they let him burn the money."

"Six million dollars," Wu said.

"Yes. They bagged it first, you know."

Wu shook his head. "I didn't."

"They used green plastic garbage bags."

"And he pulled a switch, right?" Durant said.

"He and your young friend. The Marine."

"McBride."

"Yes. McBride. Who still thinks it's there."

"How'd he get out?" Wu said. "Simms, I mean."

James shook his head. "We can only speculate. He waited until the embassy was completely evacuated, of course. But getting out of Saigon would have been no problem. Not for him."

"The name he was using then?" Durant said.

"It was the same one he'd used all through the war," James said. "Childester. Luke Childester." He cleared his throat for the third time and patted his hair again. "Tell me, how did you two feel about it?"

"About what?" Wu said.

"The war."

Wu glanced at Durant, who shook his head and shrugged. "What did we think about it?" Wu said, not caring about the amazement that coated his tone.

"Yes."

"Tell him we were steadfast in our opposition," Durant said. "That's what he wants to hear."

"You would grant that it was an immoral war?"

"Immoral?" Wu said. "What the hell has morality got to do with it? The only moral wars are the ones you win. After that you can have a parade and make speeches about not dying in vain. But if you lose one, you try to forget it like a bad mistake—which, because you lost, it sure as hell was."

"You just made a speech," Durant said. "Although I

thought you might have had a line or two in there about the Yellow Peril."

"You share Arthur's views, I take it?" James said.

"Oh, sure, I'm opposed to war—along with famine, pestilence, flood, earthquakes—the lot."

"Yet you went?"

"To the war?"

"Yes."

The smile that came to and went from Durant's face was so bitter that it almost made James flinch. "I didn't have to go," Durant said. "If they had tried to make me go, I probably would've gone somewhere else. Sweden, most likely, for the girls and the politics, which I find rather sensible. The girls, I mean. But I went to the war to make money, not to get shot at. When I got shot at, I went home."

James shook his head several times in what seemed to be both disbelief and disapproval.

Durant watched him, then smiled again, quite skeptically this time, and said, "What about you, Whittaker? Any regrets?"

"No," James said. "None."

"If you hadn't gone on record against it," Durant said, "at least not quite so vehemently, you probably would've been Director today. You had a clear shot at it. There was no one better qualified—according to all the pundits."

"I'm enjoying my retirement," James said.

"Sure," Wu said. "Lots of time to read, I bet."

"We want Simms stopped," James said, ignoring Wu.

Durant nodded. "We know."

James rose and paced toward the window that looked out over Wilshire Boulevard. He peered out, then turned and paced back to the table. He was on his way back toward the window again when he said, "We had a meeting just before I came out here."

"The Fudge and Philosophical Society?" Durant said.

"Yes. Something bad is about to come out."

"About the Agency?"

"Yes."

"How bad?"

"Lies and more lies." James sighed. "He was such a liar, you know."

"Yes."

"Well, we're trying to put a lid on it. We're not sure that we'll succeed. If not, I suppose the Agency will survive. But if something happens out here with Simms and all this comes out, well, it might be the last straw." He stopped his pacing to turn and face Durant and Wu. "Despite your sophomoric nihilism, can you bring yourselves to agree that this country does have need for a workable and effective intelligence-gathering organization?"

Wu sighed. "Don't make us a speech, Whittaker. Not us."

"No. Of course not. I should've known. We want him stopped."

Durant nodded slowly. "Fine. We'll stop him."

James stared at them for a moment. "You two don't need any frosting, do you?"

Wu stuck a fresh cigar into his mouth. "We never did."

"All right. Then I'll give you the tidbit that I've been saving. Simms and his new associate, Mr. Imperlino. I thought you might be interested in the fact that they were roommates at college."

Durant nodded, digesting the information. "That might explain a few things."

"Yes, it should, shouldn't it."

"At Bowdoin?" Wu said.

"Yes, Bowdoin." James brought a small notebook out of his pocket, tore off a sheet, and handed it to Wu. "When you have something to report, call me at this number."

Artie Wu glanced at the area code. "That's Santa Barbara, right?"

"Yes," James said. "It's a bit more civilized up there, don't you think?"

"Absolutely," Durant said.

Chapter Eighteen

If Pelican Bay was a long and grimy finger that poked itself up into what some often charged was the backside of Los Angeles, then that finger's dirty fingernail was Breadstone Avenue.

It wasn't an avenue really. It was just a street that served as a line of demarcation between the two cities, and for a long time it had been called simply Division Street. Then an unpopular Los Angeles city councilman, one Noah Breadstone, had died back in 1936 and the street had been changed to an avenue and named after him. The mayor of Los Angeles at the time had called it a fitting memorial. The Breadstone family had called it cheap, because Pelican Bay had had to pay half the cost of putting in the new street signs. Shortly thereafter the Breadstones had left Los Angeles—some said in a huff—and settled up north in San Luis Obispo.

Breadstone Avenue in its 2200 block had long been about half residential and half commercial. The residences were mostly fifty-year-old squatty bungalows jammed up against each other on forty-foot lots. Occasionally, there would be larger, two-story houses that usually wore a ROOM FOR RENT sign. Nearly all the houses boasted a porch or veranda of some kind, a sure indication that they had been built long before the almost twin advent of smog and air conditioning.

It was now a mixed block racially, integrated by economic necessity rather than choice. The Mexicans had come first, followed closely by some blacks, some Chinese, and now some Koreans. The sprinkling of whites who remained sighed often and kept their doors locked. As in nearly all poor neighborhoods, there were many children, most of them with enormous eyes.

Betty Mae Minklawn was one of the whites who still lived in the block, at 2220, a three-bedroom bungalow on the Pelican Bay side of Breadstone Avenue. The bungalow's mortgage had been paid off in full ten years before, just a month before her husband, J. B. Minklawn, a railroad engineer, had died of a stroke at the throttle of the Santa Fe Chief just outside La Junta, Colorado. J.B. had left his forty-year-old widow a small amount of insurance, the house, an almost new car, a modest pension, and $893 in a joint checking account.

At fifty, Betty Mae was still a large, handsome woman who worked hard at maintaining her big-breasted figure. She also kept her beehive hairdo an amazing shade of almost chrome yellow with the weekly help of Margarita, who worked at the Gonzalez Beauty Salon down at the corner next to the Honorable Thief Cocktail Lounge, whose Korean owner, Sang Ho Shin, was having trouble with his young wife.

As a cure for loneliness after J.B. died, Betty Mae had made friends with many of her neighbors. Those who didn't want to be her friends she had cheerfully turned into enemies, enjoying the resulting feuds quite as much as she did her friendships. One way or another, Betty Mae Minklawn knew everybody on her block and nearly everything about them. What she didn't know she quickly found out. She had recruited a network of superb spies, most of whom were nine and ten years old and got paid off in Sara Lee and Gatorade.

Of all the days in the week, Saturday was now Betty Mae's favorite. For on Saturdays she paid her weekly visit to Madame Szabo, a Hungarian seeress who had strayed into the neighborhood a couple of months before and whose intelligence gleanings were already nearly as good as Betty Mae's own. Then after Madame Szabo's it was down to the Tex-Mex Bar & Grill for a couple of beers, maybe three, and conversation with the Tex-Mex owner,

Madge Perkinson, and anybody else who happened to drop by. Most of Betty Mae's friends patronized the Tex-Mex. Most of her enemies hung out across the street in the Honorable Thief.

Betty Mae usually returned home on Saturdays about seven o'clock, which was in plenty of time to prepare a light supper which she ate on her lap before reruns of *Mary Tyler Moore*. Although she didn't watch the soaps on TV much because they weren't nearly as juicy as what went on in her own neighborhood, Betty Mae almost never missed an episode of *Mary Tyler Moore*. In fact, Betty Mae was now convinced that when younger she had very much resembled the actress—a conviction shared by absolutely nobody else.

After the program, Betty Mae always took a long bath and then retired to her bedroom to await the weekly visit from her roomer, Santiago Suárez, thirty-six, who drove a shuttle bus for Avis at Los Angeles International Airport and had a wife and three kids down in Mexico someplace. Suárez was trying to put by enough money to bring his family up North. Betty Mae at first had charged him $87.50 a month for his room, but after their first time in bed together, she had lowered his rent to $75 and then promised to lower it another ten if only he would do some rather peculiar things to her, which Santiago Suárez had cheerfully done.

Betty Mae was getting dressed in fits and starts that Saturday morning because she kept going to the window to inspect the car that was parked across the street. The car was a black four-door Plymouth Fury sedan. Betty Mae watched as little nine-year-old Sandy Choi sneaked up on its rear and wrote FUZZ in the dust on its trunk and then ran off giggling. Betty Mae was a little surprised that Sandy could spell that well.

She had known it was a cop car from the moment she had spotted it an hour before. But she couldn't quite decide at first whether it was the Pelican Bay or the L.A. police. Then she put on her glasses and took a better look at the pair who sat slumped in the car's front seat, wearing the patient, bored look of men who get paid to wait and watch.

The two men seemed to be in their forties, and because of the sour look that one of them wore Betty Mae classified them as belonging to the Pelican Bay force. Vice cops maybe, she thought. They look mean enough.

Betty Mae kept going back to the window, half dressed, to see whether she could figure out whose house the cops were watching. Maybe it's mine, she thought, and since the notion gave her a small thrill she decided to expand on it. Maybe Santiago has killed somebody at work and they're waiting for him to come back. She discarded the idea almost immediately, because she knew that except in bed, Santiago Suárez was one of God's gentlest creatures.

After one final peek out her window, Betty Mae got dressed. She was wearing what she thought of as her drinking uniform. It was a teal green polyester pantsuit with a tight white nylon blouse. On her feet she wore a pair of old and comfortable huaraches that she had picked up down in Mexicali one time.

Betty Mae made sure that her front door was securely locked and then moved slowly down to the sidewalk and turned right. It was out of her way, but she wanted a better look at the two cops. As she moved past them she saw that the one at the wheel was the younger of the pair—probably forty. The other one was maybe forty-nine or fifty.

Their eyes slid over her as she went past, and Betty Mae shivered a little, wondering what the older one would be like in bed. He was a heavy-shouldered man with a big head and not much neck. He had a lot of hair, a sort of dirty gray, that he wore long at the sides to compensate for his jug-handle ears. His face seemed to have been made out of mismatched parts and then given a coat of boredom. There was a lot of jaw and nose and very little mouth, but what there was looked sour and disappointed. He had tiny slitlike eyes that seemed to have been stuck so far back into his head that almost nothing could be seen of them except their glitter. It was a seamed, cruel face, and Betty Mae shivered a little again because on Saturday nights she liked a little cruelty.

The other man in the car, the younger one, wasn't worth a second glance in Betty Mae's estimation. He was big and blond and pug-nosed and blue-eyed with one of those upturned mouths that Betty Mae thought probably lied easily and often.

She jaywalked behind the car and crossed Breadstone Avenue into Los Angeles. She thought she could feel the policemen's eyes on her as she turned into the cracked cement walk that led up to Madame Szabo's two-story frame house. A covered wooden porch ran around its front and right side. The porch, like the house, had been painted gray many years back, and Betty Mae could remember when it had boasted some rather nice wicker furniture. Now the only porch furniture was a junked Kelvinator refrigerator, its door removed, that sat next to the window with the big sign that advertised Madame Szabo's powers. The sign was a red hand, palm outward. Down the side of the palm, in vertical red letters, ran the one word READINGS.

Betty Mae looked at her watch and then knocked at Madame Szabo's door. It was eleven o'clock—only a little after, really—which meant that Betty Mae was almost on time. Nearly seven weeks ago Betty Mae had been fifteen minutes late for her appointment and Madame Szabo had cancelled it without explanation, warning Betty Mae that in the future she must be exactly on time.

It was the book, of course, Betty Mae had decided. Madame Szabo accepted only a limited number of clients because she was writing a book that demanded nearly all of her time. The book, Madame Szabo had hinted darkly, would set the scoffing scientific world on its ear. Betty Mae believed it, because Madame Szabo certainly had told her a strange thing or two. Betty Mae figured that the Madame had a little money put by, because sometimes days would go by without a single client's visiting the gray frame house at 2221 Breadstone Avenue. Betty Mae knew because she sort of kept watch.

Of course, Madame Szabo probably made a little money off those four boarders of hers, Betty Mae had decided.

They were polite kids, two boys and two girls, all of them in their mid-twenties. They were gone most of the day, Betty Mae had noted, and when they came home at night they usually stayed there, although occasionally you would see them picking up some groceries down at Patty Pow's Markette on the corner.

Madame Szabo opened the door to Betty Mae's knock and then stepped back. "Welcome, madame," she said in her deep voice that seemed to come from far down in her throat, the heavy accent turning her W into a V.

"Not late, am I, honey?" Betty Mae said.

"Not at all," Madame Szabo said, although the accent made it come out something like "not tat tall."

Privately, Betty Mae felt that Madame Szabo used too much makeup. Especially too much green eyeshadow. She could have been sort of pretty if only she'd have got rid of that black wig she always wore, which came down low over her forehead, almost reaching her eyes. It was hard for Betty Mae to tell just what color those eyes really were because Madame Szabo always wore a pair of wire-framed glasses with heavily tinted rose lenses.

Madame Szabo was about five feet six. That was plain enough. But it was difficult for Betty Mae to decide whether she was fat or thin or maybe sort of in between, because she always wore that very loose caftanlike thing that covered everything up except her hands, and they had all those rings on them that Betty Mae thought looked cheap.

The caftanlike robe was of dark green velvet, and it had a high turned-up collar that covered Madame Szabo's throat and made Betty Mae suspect that the seeress might be sensitive about her neck's turning crepey. But if that was true, then Madame Szabo had to be at least forty. Of course, she had once hinted to Betty Mae that she had narrowly escaped from Hungary back in '56 when they were having all that trouble with the Russians, and that would make her about forty now maybe, but it sure was hard to tell with all that heavy makeup.

The two women moved down the hall until they almost reached the flight of stairs that led up to the second floor.

There wasn't much furniture in the hall, just a few pieces that looked hand-me-down. There was also a strip of carpet that had some worn traffic spots, especially around the stairs. Madame Szabo paused at a pair of sliding doors that opened into what had once been the dining room. She slid them apart, stepped back, and said, "Please," although it came out "Pleece"—or almost. For some reason, Betty Mae loved to hear Madame Szabo talk.

The room that they entered was dimly lighted by a lone fringed floor lamp that had a weak bulb. The windows were entirely covered with heavy dark red draperies. There were a few pictures on the walls, mostly steel engravings of vaguely European street scenes. There were a worn brown couch and a couple of upholstered chairs, one green, the other sort of a wet sand color. A flowered rug, not new, was on the floor, and near the lone lamp was a small, round polished table with two chairs drawn up to it. The chairs looked as though they might once have belonged to a dining-room set. Spotted here and there about the room were some useless knickknacks—a plaster bust of somebody unimportant; a stuffed bird, probably a falcon; a single goldfish swimming aimlessly around in a square fish tank with a china cat clinging to its edge; and in a far corner a tall blue jar with some pussywillows sticking out of it. It looked like a fortune-teller's room done by a cheap advertising agency with a low budget. Betty Mae thought it looked just great.

Madame Szabo waited until Betty Mae sat down in one of the chairs drawn up to the small round table. Then she slowly lowered herself into the chair opposite. She sat with her head bowed for a moment, then raised it slowly and stared intently at Betty Mae through the heavily tinted glasses. Betty Mae shivered a little in anticipation.

"The man Suárez," Madame Szabo said after a moment.

Betty Mae nodded. "Santiago."

"I have had signs."

"What kind?"

"There is another woman."

"His wife, huh? I've been expecting that."

"No. Not his wife. This woman has red hair."

"That son of a bitch."

"Please do not swear. It interferes."

"How'd you know about her?"

"Please," Madame Szabo said, and held out her hand for Betty Mae's own. Madame Szabo examined Betty Mae's palm for several seconds. Then she nodded and said, "Here, you see."

"Where?"

"There. Your fidelity line."

Betty Mae bent over to look. "Oh, yeah, that one."

"The slight interruption—just there."

"Yeah. Un-huh. What's it mean?"

"Her name is Red—no, not Red. Rusty. Yes, Rusty."

"Rusty Portugill," Betty Mae said. "Little bitch works weekends down at the Thief. Santiago swore he wasn't gonna see her anymore."

"I'm afraid that that is not true."

"When?"

"Two nights ago."

"Bastard."

"Please do not swear."

"Sorry, Madame Szabo, but it just makes me so damn mad. I don't care if he sees her, but she's gonna take him for every dime he's got and probably give him a dose while she's doing it. And Santiago's got this real nice wife down in Mexico, and three kids, I've seen pictures of 'em, and he's been trying to save enough to bring 'em all up here and I've been trying to help him out, you know, and now he's messing around with her. You know about her, don't you?"

"I have only the signs to go by."

"Well, let me tell you about Rusty Portugill. She was a hooker working Hollywood until about six months ago and then she got shacked up with Donnie Sumpter, that big mean spade who lives about three doors down—or did until they busted him a couple of weeks ago. He's still in jail and now Rusty's looking to shack up with somebody else, and lemme tell you, she's got her cap set for Santiago on account of he's got a steady job and he hasn't exactly got too much of the smarts, if you know what I mean. But he's sweet."

Madame Szabo threw her head back and gazed up at the ceiling. Her lips moved soundlessly for a few moments. Then she whispered, "Sumpter . . . Sumpter . . . I am getting something . . . Sumpter . . ."

"Donnie Sumpter," Betty Mae said helpfully.

"Yes . . . yes . . . he was in—inside this place—"

"In jail."

"Do not interrupt, please."

"Sorry."

"He was in . . . yes, inside . . . and now, there is something else, it is difficult . . . and now he's out. Yes, that is it. He is out." Madame Szabo's head dropped abruptly so that her chin almost rested on her breast.

She raised her head slowly. Once more she examined Betty Mae's palm. "Yes, it is here, see?" She pointed to a line. Betty Mae nodded.

"You will have no more trouble with the redheaded woman. This man—Sumpter?"

"Yeah, Sumpter."

"He has taken her away."

"No shit," Betty Mae said.

"Please do not swear."

"He busted out, I bet. That's why the cops are out there now. Of course, you knew about that, didn't you? The cops, I mean."

"Cops?"

"Police," Betty Mae said. "We call 'em cops in this country, but shoot, I bet you know that. Well, they're outside now. I thought maybe they had an eye on your place, but I guess what they're really looking for is old Donnie."

Madame Szabo rose quickly and went to the window, drawing back the heavy red draperies just enough to peer out. Betty Mae was now beside her.

"See 'em?" Betty Mae said. "That black Plymouth over there."

Madame Szabo almost spun around from the window. Her

usual composure, almost implacable, seemed shattered. She bit her lower lip hard. "I'm afraid we will have to cancel the rest of today, my dear," she said and almost, but not quite, lost her accent.

Betty Mae looked at her curiously. "You're not gonna charge me five bucks just for this, are you?"

"No, of course not. I have this headache—yes, this headache—it just suddenly came. The pressure from the signs, you know." Madame Szabo's accent was now firmly back in place.

"Well, okay, if you say so," Betty Mae said.

"You will excuse me?"

"Sure."

"I must go now. Goodbye."

Madame Szabo turned quickly and left through the swinging door that led from the former dining room into the kitchen. Betty Mae hesitated, then turned to leave. She was almost at the sliding doors when she stopped and turned back. She could hear a phone being dialed in the kitchen. Maybe she's really sick, Betty Mae thought, inventing a handy excuse. She tiptoed back to the swinging door and pushed it open slightly. There was nothing to see—just the old kitchen. She pushed the door open wider. And when she did, her eyes met those of the seeress.

Madame Szabo was standing at the wall phone, her black wig discarded, her rose-tinted glasses shoved up on top of her honey blond hair. A cigarette was in her right hand. Her eyes, now almost as wide as Betty Mae's own, were a curious, almost golden brown color. It was the first time Betty Mae had seen them plainly.

"I've got to go," Madame Szabo said hurriedly into the phone without any accent at all. She hung it up as Betty Mae moved back and let the swinging door close. Betty Mae started moving toward the doors that led to the hall. Madame Szabo came through the swinging door quickly and stepped between Betty Mae and the sliding doors.

"I have to talk to you," Madame Szabo said, the accent all gone.

Betty Mae's mouth was open and full of amazement. A funny, tingling sensation kept running through her body as she stared, almost transfixed, at the other woman.

"You're . . . you're . . . I mean, you're not—"

"No."

"Good Lord, honey, you're—I mean—you're—"

"That's right, Betty Mae," Madame Szabo said. "I'm Silk Armitage."

Chapter Nineteen

It was a wondrous yarn that Silk Armitage spun for Betty Mae Minklawn over a cup of tea. It involved a crooked agent and a conniving business manager and an embezzled $1.3 million. Silk confided that the rascally pair had been cheating her for years and that she was now in hiding while she got her records and proof into shape for the impending court battle. She dredged up old gossip, invented more, and dropped as many famous names as she could think of as she bounced her tale from Sunset Boulevard to Las Vegas to London and New York and back to Beverly Hills and Malibu. It was a heady potion that Silk Armitage served up along with the tea, and Betty Mae drank in every drop and thirsted for more.

"And those four young kids that live here?" Betty Mae said.

"One of them's my bodyguard," Silk said. "You know, the tall one."

"And the other ones?"

"Well, the two girls are researchers, and the other one— you know, the young guy with the glasses—well, he's a lawyer who's with this big law firm that's handling everything."

"You really need a bodyguard?" Betty Mae said, hoping that the answer would be yes.

Silk Armitage didn't disappoint her. "We figure that there's a million, three hundred thousand dollars involved. These two guys are desperate, and they've got some funny connections that, well——" Silk let her sentence trail off.

"Mafia?" Betty Mae almost breathed the word.

Silk nodded.

Betty Mae had read the gossip about Silk and the late Congressman Ranshaw, who had been her lover. She thought of asking Silk about the Congressman, but decided not to. Not yet, anyway. Instead, Betty Mae pressed her thighs together in excitement and delight. This was better than any old *Mary Tyler Moore Show*. This was the real stuff, and here she was sitting in this tacky old kitchen drinking tea with Silk Armitage, who was in all sorts of trouble, real danger, and there was just no telling what might happen next.

"Where'd you ever learn to tell fortunes like that, honey?" Betty Mae said, determined to scrape up every last crumb of information.

"Down home."

"You're from Arkansas, aren't you—you and your sisters? I read that some place."

"Uh-huh," Silk said. "Arkansas."

"And that's where you learned it?"

"There was this real old lady down there. Some folks said she was a witch, but we never believed it. She taught me and Ivory—that was my oldest sister. Lace, that's my other sister, you know; well, Lace never was much interested."

"Ivory's dead now, isn't she?"

"Yes."

"Was she in the same kind of trouble like you're in now, honey?"

Silk closed her eyes. Forgive me, Ivory, she thought.

Then she opened her eyes and said, "It wasn't quite like this. Not exactly, I mean."

"Sure, I understand. But how'd you get all your dope about what's going on around here?"

Silk smiled. "Kids. The same way you do."

"I never saw any come in here," Betty Mae said, and immediately wished that she hadn't because Silk might get the wrong impression and think she was a snoop.

"The back door," Silk said, and smiled again. "They came to the back door. You know that little Chinese boy, Sandy Choi?"

Betty Mae nodded. Sandy was one of her best sources.

"Well, he was sort of the ringleader. There was a whole bunch of them. They started out charging a quarter; then they went up to fifty cents. But they sure know what's going on."

Betty Mae felt somehow betrayed by the defection of her spy ring. But she decided to ignore her resentment, because there was something else that she wanted.

"Honey, I was just thinking," she said.

"Yes?"

"I was just wondering if maybe I could still come and see you sometimes. I mean, you don't have to be a palm reader or anything anymore. But you know how I keep a pretty close check on what's going on around here, and if I saw something suspicious—like those cops out there this morning. Well, you didn't know about that. But if I spotted somebody else nosing around, maybe you oughta know about it."

Silk smiled. "I'd like that, Betty Mae." She looked at the big blond woman searchingly. "But you can't tell anyone about me. You understand that, don't you?"

"Oh, sure, honey," Betty Mae said. "You don't have to worry about me. I know how to keep my trap shut."

Silk Armitage drew the heavy red draperies back just enough to watch Betty Mae Minklawn as she hurried down the walk toward the Tex-Mex bar. Forty-eight hours, Silk thought. She'll tell somebody as soon as she hits that bar and it'll take forty-eight hours for the word to spread. Maybe seventy-two, if I'm lucky. She watched Betty Mae move past the parked black Plymouth that contained the two watchers. Once again their eyes brushed over Betty Mae as they classified and filed her away. I'm not even going to have forty-eight hours if those two guys over there aren't really looking for Donnie Sumpter, Silk thought. She tried to think of where she might hide next, but her mind—usually so inventive and even fanciful—refused to function. And for the first time in weeks, Silk Armitage felt the quick, shuddering chill that was fear. It seemed to make everything inside her turn cold. So she did what she always did when she was afraid. She sat down at the small round waxed table, clasped her hands before her, and began to sing softly to herself. And as she sang, she thought and planned and schemed.

Betty Mae Minklawn had almost reached the Tex-Mex bar when her resolution evaporated. She had grimly resolved—sworn, really—that she wouldn't tell anyone about Silk Armitage's being Madame Szabo and all. But the excitement of her morning's adventure had been too much and now she had to tell someone or burst. Well, she would tell Madge Perkinson and that was all. And she'd make Madge swear not to tell anyone else. She'd make her swear it on a Bible. Betty Mae crossed the street and hurried into the Tex-Mex wondering if Madge still kept a Bible in the place.

The older man in the black Plymouth that was parked across the street stirred and fished an unfiltered Camel out of his shirt pocket. He lit it with a paper match and blew the smoke out the open window.

"Well?" he said.

The other man, who was behind the wheel of the car, yawned and stretched. "Somebody's going to have to get inside."

The older man thought about that for a moment. Then he said, "Maybe. Maybe not."

"What else?"

The older man rubbed his big nose. "Maybe if we squeeze a little, she'll scoot."

The other man nodded. "Yeah, that'd be good, wouldn't it?"

"Good?" the older man said. "I don't know if it'd be good. All I know is that it'd be better than the fuck-all we got now, which is nothing but an anonymous tip from somebody who doesn't seem to like the way she tells fortunes. I don't much like to count on people who go to fortune-tellers. Most of them are whackos." He brooded about it for a moment and then said, "Let's go find a phone."

The other man straightened up and turned the key to start the engine. "How you gonna work the squeeze?" he said, and pulled the car out into Breadstone Avenue.

"You don't seem to understand."

"Understand what?"

"The problem's not how we're gonna do it. The problem's *if* we're gonna do it. And since I'm just the chief of police and you're just a piss-ant homicide lieutenant, then it oughta be clear to you by now that we don't make important decisions like this. This is a very delicate situation, in case you haven't noticed. Very delicate. I mean, a situation like this calls for a lotta thought and study. You and me, Lake, we come across something like this and we're liable to just go ahead and, you know, do it. Just like we'd take a shit or get a haircut. I mean, you don't think about that too much either. But this. Well, this has probably gotta have what they call a feasibility study."

"You're letting 'em get to you, Oscar."

The big man, whose name was Oscar Ploughman and who was Pelican Bay's chief of police, smiled briefly, exposing his square yellow teeth that seemed too large for his small mouth. It was a bitter, sardonic smile that seemed to be Ploughman's response to some awful private joke.

"I'd sort of appreciate it if you'd call me Chief Ploughman, Lake. Just because we've known each other for fourteen, maybe fifteen years and even used to chew on the same pussy sometimes, that's no reason why we can't have a touch of formality. They're awful big on formality in this town, in case you haven't noticed. Awful big. So maybe you oughta try calling me Chief Ploughman. Start out with once or twice a day and then sort of work up to it. I don't want you to go into shock or anything."

"Go fuck yourself, Chief Ploughman," Lt. Marion Lake of Homicide said.

Ploughman flashed his bitter yellow smile again. "That's better, Lake," he said. "Much better."

They found an outside phone booth at the corner of Wyoming and Thirty-third. Ploughman got out and went into the booth. He was so big that he had trouble closing the door until he turned and pressed himself back against the opposite wall. He dropped the dime and dialed, and when his ring was answered, he said, "This is Chief Ploughman. Lemme talk to Mr. Simms."

He waited until Reginald Simms came on to the phone. "I think I might have something," Ploughman said.

He listened for a moment, and then he said, "That's why I wanted to check with you." He listened again, and before responding he let his bitter smile come and go. "Well, maybe if I used the siren, I could make it in five minutes." The grin came back and stayed in place while Ploughman listened to Simms' response. "No, sir, I'm not really going to use the siren. It was just a joke, sir. A very, very small joke. Tiny, almost." The smile went away as Ploughman listened to Simms. "Yes, I think I can make it by then. . . . No, sir. No siren."

After he got back into the car Ploughman said, "One thing you gotta say about Mr. Simms, Lake."

"What?"

"He's got this terrific sense of humor. I mean, he's nothing but giggles and chuckles and ho-ho-ho. A regular Jolly Green Giant."

"You're letting 'em get to you, Oscar."

"You think so, huh?"

"Yeah, you're getting like you got back in Jersey when the DA started dumping on you. All mean and sarcastic, and then you start switching that nasty smile on and off, which sorta makes you look like a caution light."

Ploughman rubbed his teeth with a forefinger and then twisted the rearview mirror around so he could examine the results.

"Irium," he said.

"Who's she?"

"It's not a she, it's an it."

"I don't know what the fuck you're talking about."

"You're not all that young," Ploughman said. "They used to put it in Pepsodent. Don't you remember? 'You'll wonder where the yellow went when you brush your teeth with Pepsodent.'" Ploughman sang the jingle in a harsh bass voice.

"I don't remember that."

"They put Irium in Pepsodent. It was a magic ingredient that some guys in this advertising agency dreamed up. Of course, it wasn't no magic ingredient. It was just the same shit they put in all toothpaste. Pumice or whatever. But they needed a three-syllable word that sounded kinda scientific, so these guys came up with Irium and everybody rushed out to buy it."

"I don't remember that," Lake said.

"It happened back in the '40s. Things were better back then. I was younger. And a hell of a lot smarter."

Lake shook his head and twisted the rearview mirror back into place. "You're letting 'em get to you, Oscar."

Ploughman flashed his yellow grin on and off once more, and then all the way down to the Plaza del Mar Towers he sang over and over again, "'You'll wonder where the yellow went when you brush your teeth with Pepsodent.'"

The Plaza del Mar Towers was a symbol of what some thought of as Pelican Bay's civic schizophrenia. It was located on the beach side of Seashore Drive just across the street from what at one time had been the heart of the city's downtown section. The section was still there and it was still downtown, but in a typical one-block stretch there were two vacant department stores, two empty jewelry stores, a vacant specialty shop or two, and a large motion-picture theater that advertised CLOSED on its marquee. The block was not much different from the rest of downtown Pelican Bay. A few businesses with a slippery look to them and EASY CREDIT signs had moved into some of the vacated stores. A couple of older, established businesses still hung on glumly, either too tired or too despondent to move on or give up. Only the banks still seemed solid and imperturbable.

To get to the Plaza del Mar Towers, Lt. Lake had to circle around Freddie, the twenty-one-foot-tall concrete pelican that had been built by the WPA back in 1937. Nobody could remember how he had come to be called Freddie, but that was his name now, and often people would say, "I'll meet you by Freddie at noon." At one time Freddie had had a clear view of the bay, but that was before the Plaza del Mar Towers had gone up a year ago.

The Towers were actually only one tower, which was perfectly round and twenty stories high and built mostly of tinted glass and as little steel as possible. It was an apartment building with suspect financing that had gone up as the downtown business section had declined. The apartments on the ocean side cost more, of course, than did the ones that had downtown Pelican Bay and Freddie to look at. And the higher the apartment the higher the rent until you reached the twentieth floor, where an apartment on the ocean side topped out at $2,000 a month. There was only one such apartment, however, and in it lived Reginald Simms.

Freddie was now the last pelican in Pelican Bay, and he sat, or rather stood, in a little round park in the middle of the intersection. The park had a few benches and some grass, and it was a good place to meet people or just to sit and watch the traffic. The real pelicans had disappeared from Pelican Bay some years ago, killed off by the DDT that ran down from the farms into the rivers and then into the sea. The DDT had done something to the shells of the pelicans' eggs—made them too soft, some said—and so there were

no more pelicans in Pelican Bay, even though DDT had
since been banned. There were no more pelicans, that is,
except Freddie.

"Hello, Freddie," Ploughman said as Lt. Lake drove
around the concrete bird and then turned right into the
curved drive that led up to the entrance of the Plaza del Mar
Towers.

Chapter Twenty

From a professional standpoint, Ploughman had to admire
the Plaza del Mar's security setup. Although the uniformed
doorman who admitted him didn't look like much, Ploughman knew that he was a retired street-smart Pelican Bay
policeman whose suspicious sixty-year-old eyes were almost
as good as an electric scanner.

But if trouble somehow got past the old ex-cop, its next
hurdle was the reception desk, which was manned by a retired thirty-nine-year-old former CID major who wore a
carefully concealed .38 Chief's Special on his left hip.
Ploughman knew that the gun was there because he had
signed the permit for it. And he knew that it was the ex-
major's left hip because he had once watched him fire it at
the indoor police range and the ex-major had fired left-
handed and hit what he aimed at.

Behind the reception area was another room which,
Ploughman remembered, contained a bank of closed-circuit
television receivers that poked and pried into almost every
exposed nook and cranny of the building twenty-four
hours a day. Of course, in a round building there weren't
too many nooks and crannies; in fact, hardly any at all

except down in the underground garage. Even so, the closed-circuit television setup was constantly monitored, which added considerably to the rents of the Plaza del Mar tenants, who seemed quite content to sacrifice privacy for security.

Although the ex-major knew perfectly well who Ploughman was, he still very politely asked the police chief to wait while he called upstairs to make sure that Mr. Simms was really expecting him. As Ploughman waited, he inspected the rather flashily decorated lobby, which had a lot of low, comfortable-looking chairs and couches that nobody ever seemed to sit in.

Once cleared, Ploughman took the high-speed elevator up to the twentieth floor and moved down the curving hall until he reached Penthouse B. He rang the bell, and the door was opened by a reserved black man in a white mess jacket, who ushered Ploughman down a tiled hall that was covered with Oriental throw rugs. The hall led into the living room.

Penthouse B was shaped like a wedge of pie with its first bite already gone, and the living room ran along about three-fourths of the pie's outer crust, where all the glass was. It was a large, strangely subdued room, almost sparsely furnished with good, but undemanding pieces. There were only two paintings, both mild abstracts, and Ploughman dimly perceived that the room had been carefully decorated so that nothing would detract from its magnificent view.

There was blue ocean to look at, miles and miles of it, and to the right was the curving coastline that was edged in lace when the waves came in. Ploughman was staring out the window when the voice behind him said, "Rather spectacular, isn't it?"

Ploughman turned to find Reginald Simms standing by a small wet bar across the room.

"Yeah," Ploughman said. "That's what I was thinking. Hell of a view."

"Would you care for a drink, Chief?"

"Sure. Thanks."

Simms turned to the bar. "Let's see—you're a gin drinker, I believe."

"That's right. Gin."

"Nothing with it, right?"

"Nothing."

Ploughman watched as Simms made the drinks. Simms wore a soft tweed jacket of grayish blue, dark gray slacks, black loafers that were carefully underpolished, and a shirt that was too pale to be cream and whose open collar was filled by a paisley scarf. Fred Astaire, Ploughman thought. The son of a bitch tries to dress just like Fred Astaire.

When Simms handed him his drink, Ploughman saw that it was a generous double. Simms' own drink was a pale amber, and Ploughman put him down as a Scotch drinker. Over the years Ploughman had found that he got along more comfortably with those who drank bourbon rather than Scotch. He felt most at home, of course, with gin-heads like himself, but there weren't too many of those around anymore. He was automatically suspicious of anyone who drank vodka; he believed that vodka drinkers had something to hide. Ploughman had many such prejudices which he enjoyed because of their certitude.

"I think over here, don't you?" Simms said, gesturing slightly with his drink toward a corner that was formed by a long pale couch and a matching chair with heavy arms. Ploughman nodded and sat down in the chair after Simms chose the couch. There was a thick glass table with chrome legs in front of the couch and chair. Ploughman put his drink down on it while he lit one of his Camels.

"Well," Simms said, "I believe you said you had something."

Ploughman blew some smoke out, waved it away, and nodded. "A fortune-teller, maybe a Gypsy, that lives just over the line in L.A. We got a tip that maybe she isn't a Gypsy at all."

"What's her name?"

"Szabo. Madame Magda Szabo."

"Hungarian?"

"If I thought she was Hungarian, I wouldn't be here, would I?"

"And what makes you believe that she isn't?"

Ploughman stared at Simms coldly. "You really want to know?"

Simms smiled slightly. "No, I don't suppose I really do." There was a brief silence and then Simms said, "You're not completely sure, though, are you?"

"No."

"You'll have to get inside."

"Will I?"

"I would think so. Perhaps you could use a policewoman. She could pose as a housewife who wanted her fortune told."

Ploughman picked up his gin and finished it. Then he wiped his mouth, sighed his appreciation, and said, "I don't think this is a police matter, Mr. Simms. I mean, here we got this Gypsy or Hungarian or whatever reading palms over in L.A. and as far as I can tell, minding her own business. Now, if she should turn out to be somebody else, maybe even somebody famous, well, that's sorta interesting, maybe even kinda cute, but I can't see why it should interest the Pelican Bay Police Department."

Ploughman leaned back in his chair with the air of a man who was through for the day. Simms examined him for a moment, smiled faintly, and said, "Go on."

"Go on?" Ploughman said, trying to put something like surprise into his voice and succeeding fairly well.

"That's right. Go on."

"Oh, well, it sort of occurred to me that if somebody who said he was a reporter, or maybe even a private investigator, started nosing around the neighborhood over there on Breadstone Avenue—kind of asking questions about Madame Szabo and dropping a hint here and there that maybe she's not Madame Szabo at all, but maybe somebody else, maybe even somebody sorta famous—well, I was just wondering what would happen if word about all this got back to Madame Szabo."

"She'd run."

"You know, that's sort of what I figured."

Simms kept the patient, interested look on his face with effort. "And then?"

"Well, then it'd sort of be up to you, Mr. Simms, wouldn't it—seeing as how the Pelican Bay Police Department hasn't got the slightest official interest in some Gypsy fortune-teller who's not hardly bothering anybody over in L.A."

"No official interest, anyway," Simms said.

A stubborn, unbudging look spread across Ploughman's lined face. As though to give it emphasis, he shook his head slowly from side to side. "The Pelican Bay Police Department has got no interest—maybe I'd better repeat that—no interest, either official or unofficial."

Ploughman had never seen a more implacably polite smile than the one Simms gave him. It was a smile that made Ploughman grow tense and wary as he braced himself for the onslaught that he knew would come.

"How old are you, Chief Ploughman, if you don't mind my asking?"

"Fifty-one."

Simms nodded approvingly, the polite smile still in place. "A good age," he said. "I believe it's what's called the prime of life—probably because a man is well seasoned by then and at the peak of his powers." The smile went away and Simms shook his head a little regretfully. "Still, in this country, which puts such a premium on youth, it's sometimes difficult for a man who's past fifty —or even forty, for that matter—to relocate satisfactorily. Of course, you'd never have such a problem. You came out here from New Jersey at our behest—and on my personal recommendation, I suppose I should add—and what you did once you could easily do again. And although we'd hate to lose you, we certainly would give you a very warm recommendation."

For several moments the two men stared at each other. Then Ploughman gave Simms his bitterest smile and said, "You know what I think?"

"What?"

"I think it's time we cut out the shit."

"Good," Simms said, and looked at his watch. "You've got two minutes."

Ploughman hunched forward in the chair, his arms on his knees, his bitter grin in place, his voice rumbling and confidential. "You and me, buddy boy, are stuck with each other. Of course, like you said, I could probably find another job—maybe as a doorman or a rent-a-cop someplace. But hell, I like this job. I like the town and I like the climate, and my wife likes it so much that she ain't hardly ever home anymore, which is another blessing. Fact is, I'll probably even retire here in another nine years or so. Of course, the pension's not gonna be too much, but if things go the way they're supposed to, then I don't figure I'll have much trouble picking up an extra dollar or two here and there. Why, shit, I might even get me one of those Swiss bank accounts that you're always hearing about. I'm not exactly sure how'd you go about opening one up, but I can always look it up someplace, or maybe just ask you, because I figure you'd probably know."

Simms looked at his watch. "That's one minute."

Ploughman stubbed his cigarette out in a ceramic tray. He took his time. "Well, I'm out here from back East just a couple of months or so and what happens? I get a big case dumped in my lap. Congressman Ranshaw's wife gets drunk and shoots him in some motel and then kills herself. A hell of a thing."

Ploughman shook his head sorrowfully and then lit another cigarette. "So guess who's not more than a couple of blocks away at two o'clock in the morning when the squeal comes in? Me and Lt. Lake, and how's that for coincidence? Now, I don't know how many homicides Lake and me've handled—hundreds, probably—but this is the goddamnedest thing you ever saw. I mean, the Congressman's wife shoots him okay. No problem there. But then she shoots herself in the stomach and then I guess she changes her mind and crosses over to the door somehow, maybe going for a doctor or something, and then changes her mind again and puts the gun up against her nose and pulls the trigger."

Ploughman shook his head in wonderment. "Right up the nose, can you imagine? Well, there were a couple of other things that looked sort of funny—at least to a homicide cop. But almost anybody else could see it was an open-and-shut case, especially after Lake and I sorta tidied things up a little. And of course, since he was a Congressman we figured that maybe he had some important documents with him. Maybe even top-secret government stuff. But we didn't find a thing. Not in the room, anyhow. So we decided to go out and look in his car.

"Well, there wasn't any car. So this kid on the desk, the one that called it in, he tells us that just after he heard the shots he waits a little while and then goes outside and sees this car driving off. It's about two o'clock in the morning and dark, but the kid's seen a lot of TV and stuff, so he writes the license plate down. In fact, the kid heard another car driving off just after the shots, but he didn't get the license plate of that one. He was sort of scared to go out, probably. Well, there's a lot more, about who the plate checked out to and stuff, but I guess my time's up. Besides, you know all the rest."

Ploughman leaned back in his chair—not smiling now, but a relaxed, almost confident look on his face.

After a moment, Simms said, "You're very convincing."

"Well, you gotta be logical about these things."

Simms nodded. "Suppose we do it your way. Whom would you use—Lt. Lake?"

"We might as well keep it in the family."

"When?" Simms said.

"Well, that all depends upon how long you're going to need."

"We'll probably have to bring someone in."

"That makes sense."

"Today's Saturday. I think you could start Lake on his— uh—inquiries Monday. No later than Monday."

"Okay. Anything else?"

"There is one small matter."

"What?"

"I have reason to believe that we may be having a couple of unwelcome visitors."

"Oh? Who?"

"Two men. An Artie Wu and a Quincy Durant."

"That first one sounds like a Chinaman."

"Yes. A rather large one. Both in their middle thirties— around there."

"What do they want?"

"I'm not quite sure."

"Trouble?"

Simms nodded. "Possibly. Probably, in fact."

"I'll look into it."

"You might have to be rather convincing."

Ploughman rose. "I'll think of something."

Simms was also up now, and the two men moved across the room together toward the tiled hall. "I appreciate your frankness, Chief," Simms said. "It helped clarify several points that have been bothering me."

"Well, you've gotta talk things over every once in a while." Ploughman paused almost in mid-stride, turned toward Simms, and snapped his fingers as if just remembering something. "There is just one more thing," he said.

"What?"

"Whenever this help that you're gonna bring in gets done, you might tell 'em that they oughta dump everything over in Burbank. That's what the L.A. cops do a lotta times. Over in Burbank, well, over there they won't even hardly notice it."

Chapter Twenty-one

The old man who wore his long white hair in a ponytail was still holding down the reception desk at the Catalina Towers when Wu and Durant entered the lobby at 1:30 that Saturday afternoon. He leaned his elbows on the counter and nodded knowingly several times as the two men approached across the small lobby.

"You two guys again, huh?" he said.

"That's right," Artie Wu said.

"Looking for Overby, huh?"

Wu nodded.

The old man grinned, delighted with the bad news that he was about to deliver. "He skipped."

Durant sighed and looked around the lobby. "When?"

"About three hours ago. He and that other guy, the young one. No notice or nothing. Just waltzed out bag and baggage, except the young guy didn't have no baggage except one of those shopping-bag kind of things. Down on his luck, I figured."

"Just turned in his key and left, huh?" Wu said.

"That's it," the old man said, trying to keep the greed out of his voice.

"I don't suppose Overby would have left a forwarding address," Wu said with far too much reasonableness.

The old man was quick enough to sense the warning in Wu's tone, but avarice won out over common sense. "Maybe," he said in a smart voice, "and maybe not." He wore his greed now like a mask.

Wu drummed his fingers on the counter. Durant leaned on it, staring and smiling into the old man's face. "My fat friend here has a few kinks," Durant said. "One of them is beating up on old folks." He closed his eyes as if trying to shut out the horror of it all. "Terrible," Durant said, and opened his eyes.

The old man took a step back. "You're shitting me."

Durant solemnly shook his head, his white, almost warm smile now almost fixed. Wu continued to drum on the counter.

A whine crept into the old man's voice. "Jesus, fellas, it oughta be worth something."

Durant looked at Wu. "Not a dime," Wu said, still drumming his fingers.

Durant made his shoulders go up and down in a helpless shrug. "Well, I guess you got him mad," he said, and glanced at Wu. "Five bucks, maybe?"

Wu shook his head. "Not . . . a . . . dime," he said, spacing the words.

Durant shrugged again. "It's up to you now, Dad."

"I don't need your fucking money," the old man said. "I wasn't always just a piss-ant room clerk. I was a top salesman for Bender Brothers before they went broke. Had me a nice place over in Silverlake. All paid for. I was somebody then, by God. I don't need your fucking money."

"The address," Wu said.

Everything drained from the old man's face—defiance, pride, even greed—leaving only defeat behind. "The Sandpiper Apartments," he said. "It's down at Third and Seashore right on the beach. You can't miss it."

Artie Wu smiled and brought his left hand out of his pants pocket. In it was a crumpled ten-dollar bill. He smoothed it out on the counter. The old man looked at it for several moments, then bit his lip, sighed, and pocketed the money. "You guys were shitting me, weren't you?"

"You press it a little hard, Pop," Wu said.

The old man nodded. "Yeah, you're probably right. Sometimes when you run out of money, you run out of brains too." He leaned on the counter, the confidential look back on his face. "That place I was telling you about, the Sandpiper Apartments."

"What about it?" Durant said.

"Well, it ain't new, but it's still nice. Expensive, too. I figure that shit Overby must've come into some dough. Made a score somewhere, probably. He sure as hell didn't go to work." He sniffed. "Not him."

"Maybe a rich uncle died," Wu said.

The old man thought about it, his face now glum, almost despondent. "It's the shits like Overby that's got 'em, isn't it?"

"Got what?" Wu said.

"Rich uncles," the old man said.

The Sandpiper Apartments looked like quiet, solid money—the kind that comes from Triple A municipal bonds and ironclad trust funds. Careful money. Old money. Money that could afford the upkeep on the twenty-seven-year-old right-hand-drive tan Bentley that was now parked beneath the striped canopy that sheltered the building's arched entrance.

There seemed to be something vaguely Moorish about the Sandpiper Apartments. It might have been the pale yellow stone from which it was built, stone that looked as if it had been hacked out of the desert and then dragged to the edge of the ocean. The building rose seventeen stories above Seashore Drive and was topped off by four round, somewhat exotic towers that might have passed for minarets. The towers provided a touch of the South Mediterranean, a sly hint of Africa, but it was the only hint, because the rest of the building was as exotic as the gasworks.

After parking the Chrysler in a lot, Wu and Durant crossed the street. They watched an elderly uniformed chauffeur help an even older woman inch her way from the apartment's entrance to the Bentley. The old woman, wearing a dark dress, a hat, white gloves, and a determined expression, was only halfway to the car by the time Wu and Durant had crossed the street and were entering the hotel. The old woman looked up from her shuffling feet as Wu and Durant went past.

"Hell of a thing," she said with a grin. "Being old."

Durant grinned back. "Hell of a thing."

The Sandpiper's lobby was a dimly lit place with stuccoed walls and high vaulted ceilings and lamps in the form of fake torches that leaned out from the walls. There were some rugs on the floor, which was made out of big square polished red tiles. The two men's leather heels clacked on the tiles as they moved over to the reception counter, where a middle-aged woman with blue hair presided.

"Mr. Maurice Overby, please," Durant said.

"You'd like to see him?"

"That's right."

"Your names?"

"Mr. Wu and Mr. Durant."

The woman inspected Wu and Durant for a moment, then turned to an old-fashioned switchboard, plugged in, and worked a switch a time or two. When she received a reply, she turned her back on the two men and talked in a low voice into the phone.

"The poor man left word that they didn't want to be disturbed," she said as she turned back. "He's just in from Singapore, you know."

"Yes," Durant said, "we know."

"His jet lag must be something terrible."

"Probably."

"We usually don't rent our furnished places to people who just walk in off the street, but Mr. Overby has such excellent references from the Governor."

Durant nodded. "They're old friends."

"That's what Mr. Overby said. Well, he's in 1229."

"Thank you," Durant said.

The elevator was almost new and very fast, and it seemed almost to leap up to the twelfth floor. A few moments later Otherguy Overby opened the door to Wu's knock.

Overby stepped back and said, "It's about time."

Wu and Durant entered the room, stopped, and looked around.

"We had a little trouble getting your new address," Wu said.

"I gave that old guy five bucks to tell you where I was."

Wu looked at Durant, who grinned and shrugged.

"Well, how do you like it?" Overby said, gesturing at the large room.

Wu and Durant turned slowly, inspecting the room with its three arched windows that looked out over the sea, its thick carpet, high ceilings, glittering chandelier, rich draperies, and solid, well-maintained furniture that seemed to be at least thirty or perhaps even forty years old.

As they made their inspection, Eddie McBride came through a door that led down a short hall. "Whaddya say?" McBride said.

"Not much," Durant said.

McBride held out his arms slightly and glanced down at himself. "Whaddya think?"

"About what?" Wu said.

"His new clothes," Overby said. "I don't know just what you guys've got in mind, but if he's gonna work with me, he can't go around looking like some beach bum." He eyed McBride's new outfit critically and added, "A perfect thirty-nine regular."

"Very nice," Durant said as he admired McBride's new dark brown hopsack jacket, the yellowish garbardine slacks, the semi-turtle neck, off-white sweater-shirt, and the burnished new cordovan loafers. "A bit flashy," Durant added, "but nice."

"What's flashy about it?" Overby demanded.

"What I meant was springlike," Durant said. "Very springlike."

"How much, Otherguy?"

"Well, we bought him a suit and another jacket and a couple of pairs of slacks and the shoes and some shirts. Shit, he didn't have hardly anything. This store we found was having a spring sale and we got a good deal, especially since he didn't need any alterations on account of he's a perfect thirty-nine regular. The whole thing came to seven hundred and twenty-six bucks."

"Not the clothes, Otherguy," Wu said. "The apartment."

"Oh, yeah, well, that's running a shade high, but Christ, I had to get a furnished place with two bedrooms, and I've sort of had my eye on this spot ever since I hit town. I mean, this place is *respectable*."

"How much?" Wu said again.

"Eight hundred bucks, but that includes utilities."

"It's a hell of a nice place," McBride said.

"Where's my car?" Durant said.

McBride fished in a pocket of his new jacket and brought out a cardboard square. "I left it in a lot over by the other place," he said, and handed Durant the parking ticket.

"Well, you guys want a beer or something?" Overby said.

"Is it free?" Wu said.

"Look, Artie, if you want me to front for you, I'm gonna have to spend a little money," Overby said. "Don't worry, I got receipts and I got it all written down. I'm not gonna stiff you guys." He looked from Wu to Durant. "Well, you want a beer or not?"

"We'll take a beer," Durant said.

"I'll get 'em," McBride said, and left through a swinging door that led to the kitchen.

Overby jerked his head at the swinging door. "He's not a bad kid, you know, once we got a couple of things straightened out, such as the fact that he's gonna be my assistant."

"Let's promote him and make him your associate," Wu said.

Overby frowned. "Does that mean I'm still in charge?"

"You're in charge, Otherguy," Durant said. "Just don't overdo it."

"Nah, I won't. He's not a bad kid when you get to know him."

They sat down in three upholstered chairs with broad arms and thick cushions. The chairs were drawn up around a highly polished black walnut coffee table with a glass top.

On the other side of the coffee table against a wall was a long, four-cushion couch.

"You're going to have to get a maid," Wu said.

Overby shook his head and smiled. "Nah, the kid said he'd keep things picked up and dusted. He can't stand it when it's not neat. Like I said, he's not a bad kid once you get him squared away."

McBride used his back to push open the swinging door. He was carrying four cans of beer, two in each hand. He served Durant first, then Wu, and finally Overby.

"I opened them in the kitchen," he said, "because if I didn't the slob here would toss his top on the floor."

Overby grinned and nodded. "See, he likes things neat."

Durant took a swallow of his beer, lit one of his Pall Mall cigarettes, and looked at Overby. "What about your meeting with Simms, Otherguy?"

"I called yesterday afternoon," Overby said. "It's set for nine Monday morning. The guy I talked to, this Chuck West, made sure that I knew it was gonna cost ten thousand bucks just to talk."

"Jesus," McBride said. "What kind of deal have you guys got going?"

"Interesting, Eddie," Wu said. "Very interesting."

"When do I get cut in?"

"As soon as we get Otherguy settled." Wu looked at Overby. "I don't think you can do a single."

Overby nodded. "Yeah, I've been thinking about that. I think I'd better be point man for a small syndicate."

"Scatter it all over the Pacific," Durant said.

Overby grinned. "Run Run, maybe?"

"Run Run would be good," Durant said.

"Jane Arden?"

Wu smiled. "Yeah, he'd probably be impressed by Jane. Everybody else is."

"Who else?" Overby said.

"What about Pancho Clarke?" Durant said. "Is he still working out of Bangkok or is he in jail again?"

Overby chuckled. "Nah, he's still out."

"That's three," Durant said. "You need one more."

Overby thought for a moment. "Gyp Lucas," he said.

Wu nodded. "Good. You'd better call them tonight."

"All of 'em?"

"Just in case somebody checks. Simms might."

Overby frowned. "I'll have a little problem with Run Run."

Durant sighed. "Tell him you're wiring him what you owe him."

"What about the rest of them?"

"Five hundred bucks each," Wu said.

"And when I see Simms how much have I got to play with?" Overby said.

"Mention a million and see what happens," Durant said.

"And just one more thing, Otherguy," Wu said.

"What?"

"This Simms is no dummy."

Overby smiled—a predator's smile. "Neither am I."

"Who's Simms?" McBride asked.

Durant glanced at Wu, who frowned and then shrugged in a kind of acquiescence.

Durant leaned forward toward McBride, who was sitting on the long couch. Durant smiled in a curiously gentle fashion. "He's an old friend of yours, Eddie, except that his name wasn't Simms when you knew him."

"What was it?" McBride said.

'The last time you saw him, you were both skimming off twenty thousand from two million and his name was Luke Childester."

Durant watched closely as McBride's face sagged with surprise. Wu was also staring at McBride, who now sat quite still for a moment and then absently began to stroke his taped-up left thumb. His face lost its sag and stretched itself into a tight, sullen expression that seemed to border on rage. Even Overby was staring at him now. Overby looked puzzled.

When McBride spoke, his voice was flat and almost toneless.

"It wasn't Solly, then, was it?" he said, directing the question more to himself than to anyone else. "I mean, out there in the canyon, that wasn't Solly's idea, it was his. That's the only way it makes sense. He wants it all, doesn't he?"

"He's got it all, Eddie," Wu said.

"What do you mean?"

"Just what I said. You were on the last chopper out of Saigon, right?"

McBride nodded, his face now pale and strained.

"An hour after you'd gone he had the money and was on his way out, probably by boat."

"How do you know?"

"We know," Wu said, and took out one of his long cigars.

"And you guys, you guys knew all the time, didn't you?" McBride said.

"We only suspected," Durant said.

"But you're going into some kind of deal with him, aren't you? You and Otherguy here."

Wu went through the ceremony of lighting his cigar. When he had it going he looked at Durant.

"Don't wink at each other and trade off those cute little nods," McBride said, his voice rising. "You guys have been fucking me over so you can do a deal with him."

Wu blew a smoke ring, a fat one. Then he looked at McBride and smiled, and there was warmth in it, even affection. "We're not going to do a deal with him, Eddie," Wu said, and stuck the cigar into one corner of his mouth. "We're going to take him. We're going to pick him clean."

There was no sound for a moment until Overby said, "Aaaah!" in a long contented sigh. A big, hard smile appeared on his face as his eyes narrowed and glistened with anticipation. It was beginning to have the sound and the feel of his kind of operation, because picking somebody clean was what Otherguy Overby knew he did best.

Chapter Twenty-two

It took a while to mollify Eddie McBride and convince him that his stolen plunder was indeed gone. It took almost half an hour, in fact, and the clincher came when Otherguy Overby served up his own testimonial.

"Kid, let me tell you something," Overby said. "I've known these guys for what is it now, ten years maybe?"

Wu nodded. "About that."

"Since I got out of the Air Force in the P.I.s eighteen years ago I've worked a lot of scams with all sorts of guys out there." Overby jerked his head west in a gesture that seemed to take in everything on the far side of Honolulu. "And Artie and Quincy and me've gone in a few times together on some sorta cute deals and I never had no regrets. But let me tell you this—and you can ask anybody out there." Again, Overby seemed to scoop up the entire Pacific in a single nod. "These guys never stiffed nobody," Overby said. "But nobody." There was a brief pause and then an afterthought that was almost a codicil: "Unless they deserved it."

"Jesus, Otherguy," Wu said. "I think I'll have that on my tombstone. 'He Never Stiffed Nobody Unless He Deserved It.'"

"Well, it's a fact," Overby said. "I oughta know."

The sullen anger was almost gone from McBride's face now. In its stead was a bleak look of reduced expectations and near resignation. He stared first at Wu and then at Durant as he absently stroked his taped-up left thumb.

"What do I get to do, Durant?" he said. "Polish the silver and take out the trash?"

"Can you speak English, Eddie?" Durant said.

"Yeah, when I have to." McBride smiled a little, but not much. "They like you to talk good in the embassies."

Durant looked at Overby. "You got a paper man here, Otherguy?"

"In Long Beach."

"He any good?"

Overby smiled. "He fixed me up with a hell of a nice letter from the Governor."

"We heard about that. How is he on ID?"

"Tops."

"I think," Durant said slowly, "that we're going to turn Eddie into a reporter." He looked at Wu.

The big man nodded. "An out-of-town reporter," he said. "Way out of town."

"You want the whole kit?" Overby said.

"Everything," Durant said. "Driver's license, Social Security, a couple of credit cards, the works. But the main thing will be a press card."

"Credit cards come awful high."

"We know," Wu said.

Overby shrugged. "Okay. What name and what paper?"

"What name would you like, Eddie?"

McBride thought about it. "Maybe one with an x in it. For some reason I've always liked names with x's in them."

"What about Max?" Wu said.

"Anthony Max," McBride said. "Anthony C. Max."

"What's the C for?" Overby said.

"How the fuck should I know?"

Overby grinned. "What paper?"

"You know Washington, Eddie?" Wu said.

McBride nodded. "They had me at Arlington for six months. It was good duty except for the chickenshit."

"Make it *The Washington Post*, Otherguy," Wu said.

Overby's eyebrows went up. "That's a little rich, isn't it?"

Wu shook his head. "I have the feeling that people out here probably think that talking to a *Post* reporter might well be their—uh—gateway to stardom." Wu wrapped the phrase in heavy irony.

Overby didn't notice. "Gateway to stardom. That's kinda nice. And shit, you know something? You're probably right. What else?"

"How hot are you now, Eddie?" Durant said.

"The cops aren't looking for me. We checked. Or Otherguy did."

"What about Solly Gesini?"

"He hasn't been around his place. At least, not today. We checked on that too."

Durant studied McBride for a moment. "You willing to take a chance?"

McBride looked down at his taped-up thumb and then back up at Durant. "What's the payoff?"

"Five hundred a week instead of three, free rent, and a guaranteed ten thousand when it's over. Plus a percentage of the net take, if there is any."

"How big a percentage?"

"Ten."

"Ten percent of how much?"

"We don't know yet," Wu said. "Maybe nothing."

McBride once more looked down at his left thumb and began to stroke it gently. After a moment, still stroking and staring at his thumb, he said, "I'm in."

"One more thing, Otherguy," Durant said.

"What?"

"That reporter who works on the paper here, the one you dug up."

"Herb Conroy. What about him?"

"How hard did you squeeze him?"

"Pretty hard."

"Has he got anything left?"

It took a few moments for Overby to make up his mind. "Maybe. In fact, he might have a whole lot of stuff that he's been saving up."

"We want to make him prove how much he knows," Durant said. "And we had an idea that we'd like to try out on you."

Overby nodded.

"Suppose Conroy were to be offered a new job on a magazine by the magazine's owner, and suppose that the offer were to be made in very impressive surroundings. A rich man's club, for example. Would he bite?"

"Hard," Overby said.

"And would he talk?" Wu said.

Overby grinned. "Forever. He'd probably think it was his last shot at the big time. He'd tell you everything he knew and then start making it up. But you wanta know what else he'd do?"

"What?" Durant said.

"He'd get drunk and blow it."

Durant leaned back in his chair and looked up at the ceiling. "That would be too bad, wouldn't it?"

"Nah, not really. You gotta understand guys like Conroy, and I've known a bunch of them. Guys like him way down deep wanta blow it. They're hooked on fucking up the same way they're hooked on booze. You see, as long as they keep on blowing things, then they've got their excuse to keep on drinking. And of course, after he blows it he can go around telling everybody how he's been offered this big job and turned it down."

"What does he think you are?"

"Some kind of businessman."

"Could you set it up?"

"No problem."

Durant looked at Wu, who nodded. "Your phone work?" Durant asked Overby.

"Sure. It's not in my name yet, but they haven't cut it off."

Durant rose and crossed the room to the phone. He dialed a number and then talked softly into the phone for nearly five minutes. When through he returned to his chair.

"Okay, Otherguy," Durant said, "here's your pitch. You may want to write some of it down."

Overby nodded and took a small black notebook from his hip pocket and a ball-point pen from his carefully tailored blue shirt with epaulettes and a small flap pocket on the left sleeve where the pen was kept. "Let's hear it," Overby said.

"Conroy thinks you're a businessman, right?" After Overby nodded, Durant went on. "Okay, let's say at a meeting—or rather, dinner—that you had the other day with the owner and publisher of *The Pacific Magazine*, he just happened to mention to you how difficult it was to find seasoned writers and editors. I think you might even use 'seasoned.' It's a pretty good euphemism for hack."

Overby wrote down *seasoned* and after it *Pacific Mag*.

"Well, you mentioned Conroy's name. In fact, you did more than mention it—you made him sound like a potential Pulitzer Prize candidate. The owner-publisher of *The Pacific* is so impressed with your judgment, of course, that he expressed interest in meeting Mr. Conroy and asked you to invite him to lunch at one o'clock on Monday at the Woodbury Club in Beverly Hills."

Overby wrote down *1—Mon.—Woodbury Club* and then looked up at Durant. Overby licked his lips, smiled a little, and said, "I've gotta have a name, don't I?"

"Randall Piers," Durant said, and out of curiosity he watched Overby's reaction. Overby wrote *Randall Piers* down slowly without asking how to spell it. When he looked up again his eyes were narrow and glittering with suspicion and his mouth was stretched into a small, tight, stiff smile.

"You got a ring in my nose, don't you, Quincy?" he said.

Durant smiled. "A small one."

"And you're just leading me along."

"You're forgetting something, Otherguy," Wu said.

"What?"

"'We Never Stiffed Nobody Unless He Deserved It.'"

Overby made a curious sound that was half snort, half bark. "Yeah, shit, but when I mentioned Randall Piers's name to you guys before, you didn't bat an eye. You just sat there, all big smiles, and let my mouth run."

"We were listening, Otherguy," Wu said.

"Sure you were. Okay, I'll go along. I'll go along in the

dark because it feels fat and smells rich. But sooner or later you're gonna have to let me in—all the way in."

"We know," Durant said.

"Okay. As long as you know. Now, are you two gonna be at the lunch?"

"We wouldn't miss it," Wu said.

"Who're you gonna be?"

"I think we're going to be two of Mr. Piers's closest business advisers from San Francisco."

"You wanta be Dr. Wu, Artie?"

"Why not?"

"Yeah, you can rattle off some of that economic mumbo jumbo, the way you used to. It always impresses the hell out of people."

"Well, I guess that's it," Durant said, and rose.

"Except for one thing," Eddie McBride said. "Me. After I get to be a reporter, what do I do?"

"You start looking for someone, Eddie," Durant said.

"Who?"

"We'll let you know."

McBride shook his head slowly. "You guys," he said. "You guys don't give away hardly anything, do you?"

"As little as possible," Artie Wu said.

Wu and Durant left and took the elevator down and then got into the Chrysler and started off to pick up Durant's car. Twenty-six minutes later they were in jail.

Chapter Twenty-three

When Oscar Ploughman, the police chief, and Lt. Lake came out of the Hungry Horse restaurant at Fifth and Seashore Drive after a late, long, and somewhat liquid free lunch, they walked slowly toward their unmarked black Plymouth, which they had left parked by the customary fireplug.

Lt. Lake went around the rear of the car and noticed for the first time the FUZZ that had been written in the dust on the trunk by little Sandy Choi. Because Lt. Lake didn't like to get his hands dirty unless he had to, he asked Ploughman to hand him the dustcloth that was kept in the glove compartment.

While Lake got rid of the FUZZ on the back of the car, Ploughman out of habit quartered the street scene with his eyes, then divided it up into eighths; sifting the faces through his mind; separating them, as he always did, into thieves, potential thieves, and victims. Ploughman placed a great deal of faith in his physiognomical powers and often lectured Lt. Lake on the significance of such key features as too much earlobe or too little chin. Lt. Lake often told the chief of police that he was full of shit.

Ploughman was about to climb into the car when he noticed the big green Chrysler station wagon that came around the corner far too fast, narrowly missing a double-parked Coors beer truck. But it wasn't the driving that attracted Ploughman's attention. It was the driver. One word clicked into his mind: Chinaman.

"Let's go," Ploughman snapped, and slid into the car, slamming the door.

Lt. Lake got behind the wheel, too slowly to please Ploughman.

"For Christ's sake, shake a leg."

"Why?"

"That green Chrysler up there. I wanta take a look."

It took them nearly two blocks to catch up with the Chrysler. At the siren's low, tentative growl Artie Wu looked in his rearview mirror and saw the red light that Ploughman was flicking on and off through the Plymouth's windshield. "Ah, shit," Wu said.

"Just what we needed," Durant said as Wu pulled the station wagon over to the curb.

"What the hell was I doing?"

"You were behind the wheel," Durant said, "which should be a crime in any state."

Ploughman and Lake got out of the Plymouth and walked toward the Chrysler with the slow, measured, somehow ominous tread that all policemen seem to use when going to do their duty. Ploughman went around the left side, where Wu was; Lake, around the right.

"Good afternoon, sir," Ploughman said.

Wu nodded. "Afternoon."

"Mind if I see your license?"

"Sure," Wu said, and dug it out of the wallet that he had already taken from his pocket. On the other side of the car, Lt. Lake bent down for a look at Durant. They nodded at each other, but found nothing to say.

Ploughman examined Wu's license and read the name off slowly. "Arthur Case Wu. That's how you pronounce it, isn't it? Wu—like in, well, Wu."

"Yeah," Artie Wu said. "Like in Wu."

"You're from Santa Monica, Mr. Wu."

"That's right."

"Nice little town, Santa Monica. Quiet, pretty, not much smog. I wonder if you drive over in Santa Monica like you do here, Mr. Wu?"

"I drive about the same way everywhere."

"Do you realize that you were doing forty-two miles per

hour in a thirty-mile zone and that you were also weaving in what I'd have to call a dangerous manner?"

Artie Wu said what nearly everybody says to the arresting officer: "Who, me?"

Ploughman leaned down, stuck his head halfway into the car, and sniffed a couple of times—big, loud, ostentatious sniffs. He could smell the beer on Wu's breath, which pleased him. Wu didn't have to sniff to smell all the gin that Ploughman had drunk that day.

Ploughman straightened up and said, "Mr. Wu, I'd appreciate it if you'd get out of the car, please."

Wu got out of the car. The two men were nearly the same height and the same weight. They eyed each other for a moment, exchanging silent appreciations of each other's size.

"Mr. Wu, have you been drinking, by any chance?" Ploughman said, keeping his voice friendly and polite.

Wu tried to remember. There had been the beer at Overby's. But that was all. "I had a beer," he said.

"Just one?" Ploughman said. "Not a couple?"

"Just one."

"You hear that, Lt. Lake? Mr. Wu blames his driving on a single beer."

"From the way he was driving, I'd say he'd had a couple," Lake said. "A couple of dozen."

"Mr. Wu," Ploughman said, "I wonder if you'd be kind enough to walk ten feet in that direction placing one foot directly in front of the other, then turn, and walk back to me in the same way. Would you do that for me, please?"

Wu made the walk up and back without difficulty.

"Did you see that, Lt. Lake?" Ploughman said.

"Having a little trouble, weren't you, Mr. Wu?" Lake said.

Wu stared at Ploughman for a moment and then smiled a small, bitter smile. "You got any ID?"

Ploughman grinned broadly, almost merrily. "Absolutely," he said, and produced for Wu's inspection a small black folding case that contained his identification and enameled badge. Wu studied them for a moment.

"Just in case you're a little too squiffed to read, Mr. Wu, permit me to introduce myself. I'm Oscar Ploughman, your friendly, conscientious chief of police."

Wu nodded slowly. "And this is a roust, huh?"

"You hear that, Lt. Lake?" Ploughman said. "Our Mr. Wu seems to think that this is a roust."

"Drunks will say anything," Lake said.

"I wonder if you'd ask Mr. Wu's colleague to step out of the car—if he's able—and show us a little identification?"

Lt. Lake opened Durant's door. "Okay, Slim. Out."

Durant got out slowly and even more slowly reached into his coat pocket and yet even more slowly and carefully brought out his wallet. He found his driver's license and handed it to Lake.

"And who have we got there?" Ploughman said.

"Quincy no-middle-initial Durant."

"And how does Mr. Durant appear to you, Lt. Lake?"

Lake ran his eyes up and down Durant's lean frame, sniffed a couple of times, and then shook his head sorrowfully. "Drunk as a goat, Chief," he said.

"And disorderly?"

"Yeah," Lake said. "Now that you mention it. Disorderly."

"Well, suppose you slip the cuffs on Mr. Durant while I do the same for Mr. Wu and we'll take them in for their own protection."

While Ploughman was putting the handcuffs on, Wu twisted his head over his shoulder and said, "Did you ever hear of such a thing as a Breathalyzer?"

"Hear of it?" Ploughman said as he snapped the cuffs into place. "I practically begged you to take it, Mr. Wu. But you refused, and your refusal in this state is tantamount to an admission of guilt. Yessir, tant-a-mount, which is a word they kind of like to use for 'like.'"

Ploughman walked Wu back to the Plymouth, opened the

rear door, and said, "Okay, mister, inside and watch your head."

It was a short drive to the Pelican Bay civic complex where taxes were levied, births and deaths recorded, justice meted out, and wrongdoers locked up in steel-and-concrete cages.

To get there, it was necessary to go around the twenty-one-foot-high concrete pelican, and Ploughman, as he always did, said, "Hello, Freddie."

When they reached the civic complex, Ploughman twisted around in his seat and said, "Now, that's a pretty nice little city hall, you gotta admit."

Durant and Wu didn't admit anything. Instead, they looked silently at the five-story pile of cream-colored concrete that baked in the warm California sun. It had been designed by someone who liked slabs as form. Some slabs went up and down and some went sideways and some overhung others. There seemed to be very few windows.

"Maybe you're wondering why there aren't too many windows?" Ploughman said, twisting around in his seat again.

"It wasn't bothering me much," Durant said, "but Mr. Wu here was beginning to fret a little."

"Well, it's kind of an interesting story. You see, the more concrete that was used, the bigger the kickback that this certain city councilman got. So when the plans came up for approval he kept taking out a window here and a window there until there wasn't hardly a goddamn window left in the place. Well, that didn't bother another councilman, who had the swing vote on account of he was getting a kickback on the air conditioning, and the fewer windows, the more air conditioning. It all worked out real nice. They both bought a couple of fifty-foot cruisers and keep 'em in Marina del Rey, where they don't have to pay any taxes on 'em on account of they're both registered and licensed up in Oregon. Sweet, ain't it?"

"Very," Artie Wu said.

Ploughman nodded comfortably. "I thought you'd think so."

After they reached the civic center, Wu and Durant were neither mugged nor fingerprinted. Instead they were whisked up to Ploughman's office on the fourth floor.

It was a large, almost square office with a single, rather narrow window that looked out over a seedy strip of the city that boasted some tattoo parlors, a couple of hot dog stands, several grim-looking bars, and a string of small shops that were in the unlikely business of selling souvenirs of Pelican Bay.

But just beyond all that was compensation. It was the Pacific, of course, looking just as elegant and expensive as it did at Malibu or Santa Barbara. To Durant, who stood now, still handcuffed, before Ploughman's gray metal desk, the Pacific always seemed like a beautiful, over-priced whore who promised far more than she could deliver.

Ploughman went behind his desk and sat down in a high-backed swivel chair. Lt. Lake stood next to Durant and Wu. Ploughman swung around in his chair, as though to make sure that his ocean view was still there, and then swung back. While studying Durant and Wu, he ran his hand over the lower portion of his face, squeezing it a little as if trying to mold its rather mismatched parts into some kind of symmetry.

"You notice I got a window," Ploughman said, and then twirled around in his chair to check up on the fact again.

"We noticed," Artie Wu said.

Still admiring his window and its view, Ploughman said, "You also notice I ain't read you your rights."

"We noticed that too," Wu said.

"You wanta know why?" Ploughman said, his back still to them.

Durant and Wu said nothing.

Ploughman spun around in his chair, his face split by a hard, yellow grin. "Because you ain't got any, that's why." He shook a Camel out of a pack and lit it. After he blew the smoke out, he said, "Time was, you know, when if cops wanted to make a point, well, they'd take a guy into a back room and work him over a little. Rubber hoses. That's what they always claimed. Well, shit, did you ever hit anybody with a rubber hose?"

Durant cleared his throat. "Not lately."

Ploughman, pleased, nodded at the answer as if Durant were an especially bright and promising student. "Exactly. If you wanta work a guy over, you don't use a rubber hose. That's bullshit, movie stuff. You wanta know what you really use?" He put the cigarette in his mouth and then held out his hands, palms up, clenching and unclenching them into big fists. "You use these, that's what."

Artie Wu sighed. "Get to it," he said.

Ploughman smiled again, as though Wu had reminded him of some pleasant but unfinished task. "Well, we don't do any of that kind of stuff around here anymore because we don't have to. You know what we do now when we wanta make a point? Well, we just put guys down in the Hole, and you know what we keep down there?"

"Animals," Durant said.

Durant remained Ploughman's star pupil. The yellow grin appeared again, this time not only pleased, but also appreciative. "Yeah, I'd imagine that you two would've spent a little time in the Hole. Not our Hole, of course, but somebody else's Hole. Every town's got its Hole that they use to drop guys like you into." Ploughman nodded encouragingly. "Now, you two have spent some time in a Hole—*¿es verdad?* as the Mexican folks say?"

"*Es verdad*," Artie Wu said.

"Then you kinda know what to expect." Ploughman looked at Lake. "Who we got down there, anybody interesting?"

"The Turk, he's still in," Lake said.

"What about Jimbo?"

Lake nodded. "Yeah, he's still there."

Ploughman looked at Durant. "Like you say, animals. Real animals." He shifted his gaze back to Lake. "Lieutenant, I think you can take Mr. Durant and Mr. Wu down now so they can get a little rest. And maybe when they've sobered up, well, maybe they can come back up here and we'll go on with our little talk. I don't know about you two," he said, looking at Durant and Wu again, "but I'm finding it real interesting. Are you?"

"Extremely," Artie Wu said.

Chapter Twenty-four

At approximately the same moment that Wu and Durant were being pulled over to the curb in Pelican Bay, Reginald Simms was turning his light brown, three-month-old leased Jaguar sedan right off Sunset into Bel Air's west gate entrance.

Simms didn't care much for Bel Air, finding it a bit gauche and showy, although certainly not so much so as Beverly Hills. At least in Bel Air the thick shrubbery afforded some vestige of privacy. In Beverly Hills, of course, it was simply naked wealth screaming to be envied.

Simms felt that power and wealth needn't be advertised—indeed, shouldn't be. His idea of city living was the quieter reaches of the East Sixties and Seventies in New York or Georgetown in Washington. And London, of course—almost anywhere in Mayfair.

But this, however, was California—Southern California, at that—and here, Simms felt, you were what you appeared to be. It was a section of the country that put a very high premium on face value.

Simms was on his way to a meeting with his former college roommate and present business associate, Vincent Imperlino, whom he always thought of as Imp. Simms was fairly sure that he was the only person in the country who still called Imperlino by that diminutive; doubtless the only one who dared to. Both men had traveled a far distance since their days at Bowdoin, but Simms was not at all surprised by their joint destination, which, when he thought about it, seemed somehow almost inevitable. During the years he had spent in Southeast Asia, Simms had acquired a hard streak of fatalism, which he now found comforting.

He and Imperlino had several matters to discuss, but the principal one would be how best to go about killing Silk Armitage. Simms made his mind form the word "murder" and derived a trace of sardonic amusement from the fact that the word made him experience no discernible revulsion. It had been a long time since the word or its concept had made him feel anything at all, and he promised himself that during the discussion with Imp he would use the word itself rather than some euphemism. He decided that Imp's reaction—if any, of course—might prove amusing.

The turn that Simms was looking for was about two miles up into the hills. It was a narrow, twisting road with a sharp grade, and at the top of it were the huge iron gates that had come from France, and in front of them was the guard, one of the three who kept a constant twenty-four-hour vigil.

The guard wore no uniform—unless, of course, you thought that a Shetland tweed jacket and gray flannel trousers were a uniform: a kind of preppy one that somehow smacked of the 1950s and lost innocence. However, there was nothing innocent about the guard or his too careful eyes that stared down at Simms from a thirty-year-old face as dubious as a question mark.

"Mr. Simms?" the guard said, nothing but doubt in his voice.

"Yes," Simms said.

"Would you mind?" the guard said, and held out his hand.

Simms produced his driver's license and handed it to the guard, who looked back and forth several times from the color photo on the license to Simms. He had seen Simms before and knew who he was. But in this job you didn't make mistakes. If you made a mistake, you got buried. Or worse.

The guard, Simms's license still in his hand, moved over to the gate and used a house telephone to call somebody. As he talked into the phone, he kept his eyes on Simms. Finally, he hung up the phone, went back to the Jaguar, and grudgingly handed Simms back his license.

"Okay, Mr. Simms," the guard said, and returned to the massive stone gatepost, pressing a button that swung the iron gates open. Simms drove through slowly, the carefully combed gravel of the drive crunching loudly under his tires. But that was what the gravel was there for—to make a noise. A loud one.

The nearly ten acres of grounds that formed Imperlino's estate were carefully landscaped, but all Simms saw was green trees and shrubs and bushes with flowers that were either yellow or red or orange or blue or purple. Simms had never been interested in vegetation and knew the names of hardly any flowers other than roses and tulips. But he didn't pride himself on his ignorance. It was simply that green, growing things had never interested him.

Simms preferred things that were built and made by man. That was why it was with some anticipation that he approached the crest of the hill, for on the other side of it, down in a kind of knell, was Imperlino's dream, the childhood fantasy that he had made come true: the house that was, Simms knew, an extremely private joke.

Reginald Simms was probably one of the four or five persons in the United States who knew that Imperlino had handed his architect a forty-year-old volume of fairy tales, smeared with old chocolate and Crayolas, turned to a page, pointed to a picture, and said, "Make it look like that."

"Exactly?" the architect had asked.

"Exactly like that," Imperlino is supposed to have said. "But bigger."

Simms didn't stop his car when he reached the crest of the

hill. That would have been unwise. But he slowed down enough so that he could enjoy the view.

The house was really too big to nestle, but that was what it seemed to do. Perhaps it was because of the trees that surrounded it down there in the knell, big tall pines and eucalyptus that were almost as high as the south tower where, in the fairy story, the good old witch had lived.

The roof, although made out of thick shake cedar shingles, somehow looked as though it were thatched, perhaps because of the way that the shingles curved back in under the eaves. The windows were all mullioned and irregularly, almost haphazardly, placed, and the brickwork seemed to be at least two hundred years old, which most of it was, having been salvaged from old houses in Boston and Richmond.

The house was two stories high in spots, one and three stories in others, and almost four stories where the tower was. It was the house where the good witch had lived a long time ago somewhere in England, and it was a triumph of practicality over whimsy and God knew how much it had cost. A lot, Simms thought. A whole hell of a lot.

After Simms parked his Jaguar behind a dark green Lincoln Continental, he got out and started toward the heavy oak door with its curious carvings and its heavy iron straps. The carvings were supposedly the cabalistic signs of magic, but no one was really sure of this because they too had been copied from the book of fairy tales.

The door opened before Simms reached it. The opener was a medium-sized man of about fifty-five with a hard, lined face, gray hair, and sure moves. He wore a black suit, a white shirt, and a dark tie. He was called Mark, although his name was Marcello Balboni, and he seldom spoke, if ever, because someone had forced most of a can of Drano down his throat in 1946 during a dispute on the Hoboken docks. He had been given to Imperlino as a college graduation present in 1952 and he did whatever Imperlino told him to.

Balboni nodded at Simms and then beckoned to him to

follow with another kind of nod. Balboni had an extensive repertoire of nods and shrugs and gestures, which he used instead of words because his voice sounded very much like a parrot's speech.

Simms followed Balboni down a hall of dark slate slabs. The hall, paneled in some kind of old, very dark, almost purplish wood, angled and twisted this way and that. Hung on the paneling at carefully spaced intervals was a series of old portraits of long-dead, thin-nosed people dressed in the clothing of the fifteenth and sixteenth centuries who all looked as if they might be kin to either Machiavelli or the Borgias.

After another confusing turn, the hall went up three steps. A few paces beyond the steps Balboni stopped, knocked once on a door, then opened it and with a jerk of his head indicated that Simms should go in.

Simms entered a large, book-lined room with leaded windows that looked out over a small, pretty English garden. It was a strongly masculine room with an ancient, trestlelike table that served as a desk. The rest of the furniture was mostly heavy stuff made out of dark leather and even darker wood. An Oriental rug, very old and very thin, covered most of the polished oaken floor.

Vincent Imperlino stood by the blazing fireplace beneath the oil portrait of a woman. He held a book in his hand, his place marked by a finger. It was difficult for Simms to remember when he had seen Imp at home without a book in his hand.

Imperlino smiled at Simms as they shook hands. He had an engaging smile, very white, very confident—an interesting contrast to Simms' own warm but strangely shy one.

"It's good to see you, Reg," Imperlino said, and Simms said something equally polite and then watched as his former roommate turned and stared up at the portrait of the woman whom Simms now recognized as Ivory Armitage.

Imperlino stared at the portrait for several moments. He was a tall man, almost as tall as Simms, and sturdily built, but not yet heavy, although he might get that way in a few more years. He had one of those thin, handsome noses that saved his face from being brutal, although his eyes helped too. The eyes had the color and sheen of melted milk chocolate, and they were too soft and too gentle for the rest of his face with its heavy, thrusting chin and wide, nearly lipless mouth that, unless it was smiling, looked cruel and unforgiving.

Imperlino's hair was nearly all of the same length, graying at the roots, and it hung down over his head like some medieval cap. It seemed to have been carelessly combed with his fingers, but it went well with the book in his hand and the dark green cashmere slipover sweater, the white open shirt, and the dark gray trousers. He could have been some professor of comparative literature at a large California college—a ruthlessly ambitious professor perhaps, with designs on the chairmanship of his department.

Still staring at the portrait of the late Ivory Armitage, Imperlino said, "What do you think?"

"It's quite good."

"Yes, it is, isn't it? I had it done by the same chap who painted one of her sister Lace—the one who's the actress now. He had to do it from photographs, of course, but he had met Ivory once or twice, so he was able to draw on that too. I'm really quite pleased with it."

Imperlino turned from the portrait. "Well, a drink? I have some sherry that you might like."

"Good."

Imperlino seemed to remember the book that he held in his hand. He looked at it and smiled fondly. "Rilke. I've been trying to read him in German with the help of a dictionary and the English pony that's printed on the facing page. But my German is almost lost, and I tend to cheat. Do you read Rilke much anymore?"

"No."

Imperlino put the book down and moved over to a nearby tray that held some cut-glass decanters and several glasses. "You should," he said, pouring two drinks. "He improves with age. My age, I mean. I tried reading Rupert Brooke the other day, for no very good reason, and found him unbearably young; but then, of course, he was."

He turned and handed Simms his drink. "How are you finding your middle years, Reg? I don't think I've ever asked."

Simms smiled. "Tolerable. And you?"

Imperlino shrugged. "I live in this rather splendid isolation which I more and more prefer, but I've been thinking about you and your new and rather romantic role as the disillusioned patriot turned renegade. Do you find it comfortable?"

"Both comfortable and profitable."

"And you don't miss the other—all that derring-do and arcanum and hugger-muggery?"

"Most of it was dull," Simms said. "Dull and often pointless. What I do now I find amusing, even intriguing. Plus there's a comforting absence of personal risk. I don't miss that at all, which must be a sign of some sort of maturity."

"And the fate of the republic?" Imperlino's tone was more amused than sarcastic.

If it was bait, Simms refused to rise to it. Instead he smiled and said, "That weight seems to have been shifted to other, surprisingly sturdy shoulders."

"You know," Imperlino said, gesturing Simms to one of the wing-backed chairs that were drawn up before the fireplace, "you should have come in with me right after college."

"Your hindsight is almost as good as mine."

Now seated in one of the chairs, Imperlino crossed his legs and examined Simms in a rather speculative manner. His chocolate eyes seemed to harden and cool. "So," he said, "no regrets?"

"None."

"And your former colleagues?"

"Fuck the fuckers, as a number of my new associates seem fond of saying."

Imperlino smiled slightly. "Yes, some of them are a bit awful, aren't they? Particularly that little man, the one who runs the gymnasium in Venice—uh—" Imperlino snapped his fingers as if trying to recall the name.

"Gesini," Simms said. "Solly Gesini."

"Yes. What happened there?"

"I have to assume," Simms said, "that he's incompetent. I offered him twenty thousand to murder young McBride, and his people apparently botched the job." Simms watched carefully to see whether Imperlino would react to the word and was amused when he didn't.

"No problem with the police, though?"

Simms shook his head. "None."

"But McBride could still be embarrassing, couldn't he? But nothing more than that."

"No, nothing more."

"Then I suggest that you have Gesini himself kill McBride."

"Is he capable?"

"Killing is his trade—or perhaps I should say murder." A small smile ran about Imperlino's thin lips—more of a twitch than a smile, really—and Simms realized with some small, odd pleasure that he had been caught out.

Imperlino sipped his sherry and went on. "Surprised? Well, back in the '50s and early '60s our little fat friend was the top assassin on the West Coast. I don't think he's demented enough to enjoy it, but he kills absolutely without compunction."

"Then I'll put him on it again," Simms said.

"You might invoke my dread name. He's frightened to death of me for some reason."

"I can imagine."

"Now, then," Imperlino said, "we seem to have a couple of other visitors from your past, the ones you mentioned over the phone."

"Durant and Wu."

"Yes. Should they concern us?"

"I'm not sure," Simms said. "They might want to repay me for something that arose a few years back out of a misunderstanding—carelessness on my part, really. But they're not exactly the 'don't get mad, get even' types—unless they could make a dollar or two out of it."

"They've learned to cut their losses, I take it?"

"A long time ago," Simms said. "But anyway, I've heard that they've been in touch with young McBride, although, knowing them, they must have found his scheme rather ridiculous."

"So what do they want?"

Simms shrugged and drank some of his sherry. "They may have heard about the pickings," he said. "I've asked Ploughman to look into it should they come nosing around Pelican Bay. Ploughman, incidentally, had some interesting news."

"Which you've been saving."

"Yes, that's like me, isn't it? The best at the end."

"You have a strong streak of the dramatic in you, Reg. You always have had. I rather enjoy it."

"Yes, well, the news is that Ploughman thinks he might have turned up the girl."

Almost involuntarily Imperlino's eyes went toward the portrait on the wall. "Might, you said."

"He's checking it out."

"Will he kill her for us?"

"No."

"Did you ask?"

"In a way."

"And he refused?"

"Yes. His argument was rather good."

"I trust he has no objection if we kill her—or have her killed."

"None. He even suggested how we might dispose of the body."

"Over in Burbank?" Imperlino said with a small smile.

"Yes, as a matter of fact. In Burbank."

"The Chief learns fast." Imperlino was silent for a moment. "Have Gesini kill her and for the same price—as penance."

"All right."

"Right away."

"All right."

"Tell me something, O friend of my youth," Imperlino said, almost tasting the posied phrase, "does it bother you—all this talk of murder on such a pleasant spring afternoon?"

"No. Does it bother you?"

Imperlino rose and stood before the fireplace, gazing up at the portrait of the dead sister of the woman whose murder he had just arranged. "Yes," he said finally, "it still bothers me."

Chapter Twenty-five

The huge Armenian would have to be dealt with first, of course: the one with the historically imprecise nickname of Turk. For the past twenty or twenty-five minutes he had been describing the delights of Chinese pederasty to the five other men who were on his side of the large, windowless cell in the Pelican Bay jail.

There were no benches or bunks in the cell, only a toilet without a seat and a drain in the middle of the floor where the drunks' vomit could be hosed away. The cell, with its concrete floor and metal walls, was about the size of a large living room, and Artie Wu and Quincy Durant sat leaning against the wall on one side, the five other prisoners across from them.

When Wu and Durant had first arrived, there had been only two other prisoners in the cell—a couple of middle-aged early-afternoon drunks who had been sleeping it off. Now one of the drunks was half awake and listening without much interest to the Armenian tell of the sexual delights that he had in store for Artie Wu.

In addition to the two drunks, the Armenian had as an audience a big, wise-looking black called Jimbo and a slim, young, almost pretty Mexican with a silky, deadly smile. The Mexican was called Dolores. All three men had been brought into the cell together shortly after Wu and Durant arrived.

Turk, the Armenian, had started in almost immediately on his sexual monologue, interrupted only occasionally by Jimbo, who kept staring at Durant and muttering something about the closer the bone, the sweeter the meat. The pretty Mexican had only smiled silkily and said nothing. Wu figured the Mexican for a knife.

After another five minutes the Armenian was beginning to repeat himself. Artie Wu closed his eyes, leaned his head back against the wall, and without moving his lips, said, "Well?"

"Let's," Durant said.

"Watch the Mexican."

"Right."

Wu opened his eyes and got up slowly. So did Durant. They moved over to where the other three men sat. The two middle-aged drunks were still sprawled on the floor. The one who had been awake had gone back to sleep. Wu stopped about a yard from the Armenian and stared down at him. Durant yawned and let his gaze wander, but kept bringing it back to the pretty Mexican called Dolores. The Mexican smiled at him sweetly. Durant smiled back.

"Gentlemen," Wu said, "permit me to introduce myself."

"You don't have to introduce yourself, Chinaboy," the Armenian said. "I know who you are. You're my sweet candy ass, that's who."

"Candy ass," the black said, and smiled hugely. "Sweet as sugar, I swear he is."

The Mexican only smiled some more.

Artie Wu rocked back on his heels a little and shook his head slowly as if saddened by some misunderstanding. Then he bent forward a bit, stared down at the Armenian, and grinned wickedly. Durant watched the Mexican.

"You got it just a little wrong, friend," Wu said softly. "You see, what I really am is the new chief motherfucker around here." He jerked his head at Durant. "And he's the new assistant chief motherfucker, and we're sort of sick of listening to your mouth run."

"Well, now," the Armenian said, and got up slowly, keeping his eyes on Wu. The black called Jimbo also got up and gave his pants a hitch. The Mexican, still smiling, rose and with his eyes on Durant, started to sidle around to Wu's rear. Durant turned with him. The Mexican was no longer smiling. Wu stepped back until he felt Durant's back touch his. Then Wu relaxed and the smile reappeared on his face. Durant raised his hands slowly until it looked as if he were showing the Mexican the size of some just-caught fish.

Turk, the Armenian, had a long, spiked mustache, and he stroked it once as though to make sure that it was still there. The Armenian was as big as Artie Wu, perhaps even a little bigger, although Wu was older by several years. The Armenian had thick, hairy arms and there didn't seem to be much fat on him anywhere.

"You ain't the new chief motherfucker around here, Chinaboy," the Armenian said; "you're just my very own sweet candy ass, that's what." Then he threw the left.

Although Artie Wu had been expecting it, it still came far too fast—a hard, much-practiced blow with all of the Armenian's weight behind it. Wu caught some of it on his forearm, but the rest slipped by, and it hit him hard just below his throat. Wu dropped into a crouch, and the Armenian's follow-up right slid past his ear. Wu drove two quick, hammering rights low into the Armenian's stomach. Very low. The Armenian's breath rushed out of his lungs with a harsh rattling gasp, and he bent over, clutching at his stomach. Wu clenched his hands together up high and hammered them down hard on the bent-over man's neck.

The Armenian sprawled on the floor and lay there twitching and gasping.

The knife had appeared in the Mexican's right hand suddenly with a magician's deceptive movement. It had been shaped from a spoon, and its handle was a kind of papier-mâché made out of wet bread and newspaper, molded to fit the Mexican's grip and then dried. It was a very personal knife, and Dolores, the Mexican, seemed fond of it.

He didn't wave it around unnecessarily. He came at Durant with a slick, fast lunge, the blade aimed for just under the rib cage. Durant caught the pretty Mexican's right hand, found the nerve in the wrist just below the pad of the thumb, and pressed hard. The Mexican screamed, but didn't drop the knife. Durant twisted the arm up behind the Mexican's back and broke it. The Mexican screamed again, and dropped the knife.

Jimbo, the big black, had been debating about whether to try a move on Wu. But when the Mexican screamed the second time, Jimbo frowned, hitched up his pants again, moved back to the wall, and settled down into a seated position on the floor.

He looked up at Wu, grinned without any mirth, and said, "Okay, Chinaboy, I reckon you is the new chief motherfucker around here."

The Mexican kept on screaming, holding his broken arm, until a jailer opened the door and took a quick look around. Five minutes later Wu and Durant were back up in Ploughman's office.

The chief of police was seated behind his desk when the two jailers brought Wu and Durant in. Ploughman stared at his prisoners for a moment and then dismissed their jailers with a go-away nod. After that he gestured for Durant and Wu to sit down in the two chairs that were pulled up to his desk.

Ploughman silently studied the two men for a moment or two longer, then smiled yellowishly, opened a desk drawer, and brought out a bottle of Gordon's gin and three Kraft cheese glasses.

"You drink gin?" he said.

"We drink gin," Durant said.

"Warm?"

"Any way at all."

Ploughman poured about two ounces into each glass and slid two of them across the desk one at a time. He then picked up two thick manila envelopes and tossed them toward Wu and Durant.

"Your stuff," he said, and took a swallow of gin.

Wu opened his envelope, found a cigar, and stuck it into his mouth. He then transferred his wallet and keys and change to his pockets. After that he had a drink of gin and then lit his cigar. Durant had a drink first, then transferred his possessions to his pockets, but not before counting the money in his wallet. After that he lit a Pall Mall. Ploughman watched them idly.

"I got curious," Ploughman said.

Wu nodded. "Oh?"

"So I did a little checking. You two are a couple of cuties. I had to call San Francisco and then some guy at home in Washington." He shook his head gloomily. "Nobody in L.A.'s ever heard of you."

"Why didn't you just talk to the guy who told you to roust us?" Durant said.

Ploughman eyed Durant thoughtfully, swiveling a little in his chair. "Now, that's a pretty good question," he said, and swung around to check on his view again. "You know what's wrong with this town?" he said after a moment. He was still staring out the window at the Pacific, which was beginning to turn purple in the late-afternoon sun. Or perhaps just dark blue.

"You want a list?" Wu said.

"Nah, just the main thing."

"What?"

"It's too skinny," Ploughman said, and spun back around. "I'm not kidding," he added in response to the doubting looks that he got from Wu and Durant. "It's shaped like a sharp stick that somebody stuck up L.A.'s rear end. Now, when they founded it, all the business section got built down by the beach. And behind the business section came the rich folks' section, then the middle class, and then the poor folks. The poor folks got stuck as far away from the ocean as possible, of course. Well, you know what happened then?"

"What?" Durant said.

"The niggers started moving in, that's what. Then the Mex, and then the Chinese and the Japanese and the Koreans and God knows what all. So the whites, at least the rich ones, took off for the suburbs or Balboa or Newport or some place, and then all those shopping centers started going up and the downtown section just went to hell, and what you got left here is a town without any industry to speak of, a business district that's almost a ghost town, a lot of folks who're poor or damn near that way, and a crime rate that's practically out of sight. Sound familiar?"

"Very," Wu said.

Ploughman nodded. "It's happening all over the country. But what you've really got here, if you look at it from just the right angle, is a very ripe, very juicy plum."

"So who's going to pick it?" Durant said.

"You get right to the point, don't you, Slim?"

"He's very direct," Wu said. "Honest, too."

"Halfway," Ploughman said.

"Halfway what?" Durant said.

"You guys are about halfway honest is the word I get, which means in this town they might put up a statue to you."

"Bent, huh?" Wu said.

"Outa shape."

"But ripe, you said."

"Juicy."

"So who's going to pick it?" Durant asked again.

It took a while for Ploughman to answer. He had to smile first—a big, wide, yellow, nasty smile.

"Me," he said, and went on smiling.

"Aaah, so," Wu said in his best Chinese voice. Or perhaps Japanese.

"Tell us, Chief," Durant said.

Ploughman spun around in his chair to check on the ocean again. "They brought me out from Jersey to be their tame police chief," he said. "I don't have to tell you who they are, do I?"

"Simms?" Wu said.

"He fronts for them."

"And sort of runs things," Durant said.

Ploughman nodded at the ocean and then turned around to face Wu and Durant again. "And sort of runs things. Well, I get out here and, by God, I like it. I like all this sunshine and the half-naked girlies in their bikinis and good stuff like that. So I figured I'd better lock myself in. But to do that you've got to have a base—a political base; and you know what?"

"You couldn't find it," Wu said.

Ploughman nodded slowly. "You nailed it, friend. There was one in the process of being built, but it went to pieces when the guy who was building it got himself killed."

"Congressman Ranshaw?" Durant said.

"Yeah. Congressman Ranshaw. He used to be a cop too. A good one, so I hear. Smart. His wife killed him."

Artie Wu blew a smoke ring. "Did she?"

Ploughman stared at him. "You hear any different?"

"Maybe."

"You got any hard evidence, friend, you're committing a felony by withholding it."

Wu blew another smoke ring. "No hard evidence."

"Just talk, huh?"

"Idle chatter. Very idle."

"Tell us some more about the plum, Chief," Durant said.

Ploughman nodded and smiled again. "Let me ask you this: you know what makes a city work?"

"Politics," Durant said.

"And you know what politics is? Favors. That's all. Favors. You do something for me and I'll do something for you. You vote for me and I'll get your idiot brother-in-law a job with the city. Or on a higher level, let's you and me do each other a favor and gang up on Russia. Favors. Cities used to work, you know. Look at Chicago."

"Daley," Wu said.

"And before Daley, Kelly-Nash. Kansas City, the Pendergast machine. Crump in Memphis. Boss Hague in Jersey. I could go on. But let's get back to Pelican Bay. Here you got a town of about a hundred and fifty thousand. Not a big town, but not little. And most of 'em are registered Democrats—I mean the ones who bother to register at all. And what do they want? Well, they want jobs, or to get on welfare, or to get their mother on welfare, or get the street light fixed, or their property-tax mess straightened out. Favors. That's what they want. Favors. So who can they go to—the precinct committeeman? Who the fuck's he? They don't know. The ward boss? Never heard of him. The city councilman? Forget it. But what about the cop, the one who walks the beat?—and you can walk a beat in this town; it's small enough. Suppose the cop on the beat was the guy who could get the pothole filled or Grandpa into the veterans' hospital. Well, the folks'd be grateful, right? So grateful that when election time came around, they wouldn't mind voting for who the cop on the beat recommended. So here you get a town with maybe a hundred thousand eligible voters and you get maybe eighty percent or eighty-five percent of them registered Democrat and then get damn near ninety percent of them to vote. And vote right. So up in Sacramento when election time comes around, the pols take a look at the map and say, What about Pelican Bay, what can we come out of there with? So somebody says, Maybe we'd better check with the man down there and see what he wants, because he's got a lock on eighty, maybe ninety thousand votes and in a close election they could just make the difference—except they don't talk like that, of course."

And what does the man want?" Durant said.

Ploughman decided it was time to check out the ocean again. He turned in his chair. "A little industry, maybe a new post office, maybe a state headquarters located here. Maybe a couple of Federal programs. A slice of the pie, really; that's all." He turned back again, a large, yellow smile on his face. "Like it?"

"The Ploughman Machine," Artie Wu said.

A look of pure delight spread across Ploughman's face. He tried the new name out, almost breathing it. "The Ploughman Machine. Now, by God, that's got a ring to it, I must say. You like it, huh?"

"What?" Durant said.

"What I just told you."

"Oh, sure," Durant said. "You run the cops and the cops run the city and you've got it wired. Maybe a little touch of fascism here and there, but what the hell, who's to notice?"

"I can think of some people," Artie Wu said.

"Them, you mean?" Ploughman said.

"Yeah, them," Wu said. "Are you going to deal them in or out?"

"Well, now, that sort of brings us up to where we are right now, doesn't it?"

"Where's that?" Durant said.

"Well, they've kind of got some plans for this town—plans that maybe I don't necessarily go along with on account of they would sort of have me running errands. Well, these plans they've got, they're sort of secret, and Congressman Ranshaw was kind of poking around in them before he got himself killed. In fact, I had a few lines out to the Congressman to see if he and I couldn't work something out together. But then he went and got himself killed before anything came of it."

"You keep saying 'sort of,' 'kind of,'" Wu said. "Does that mean you're on the outside looking in?"

Ploughman grinned. "Sort of. Kind of."

"But you've got some pretty good ideas of what they're up to?"

"Yeah, I do. And so when somebody like Mr. Simms suggests that maybe I oughta keep an eye out for you two, I get a little bit curious. I wonder just what Mr. Simms has in mind. I mean, maybe you two guys are gonna upset his honey wagon and get shit all over his face, which would be too bad."

"Yeah, wouldn't it?" Artie Wu said.

"But I went and did what he told me to, of course. I threw you in down there with the animals, although I hear they didn't give you too much trouble. But I can tell Mr. Simms I did my duty—just in case he asks. But you know something?"

"What?" Durant said.

"Mr. Simms, he's still sort of worried about Congressman Ranshaw."

"Oh?"

"Yeah, it seems that the Congressman had a girl friend who he was awful tight with. And this girl friend maybe knew everything that the Congressman knew before he got himself killed. Now, guess who this girl friend was?"

"Who?"

"You guys don't know?"

Durant shook his head. "We didn't say that."

Ploughman picked up the bottle of gin and poured another drink into each of the three glasses. He then held his up and looked into it as if perhaps its contents would explain life's mystery.

"You wanta know when this country started going bad?"

"When?" Wu said, and tried some of the warm gin.

"When the fucking Beatles came on the scene, that's when. First the Beatles and then Kennedy got shot, or maybe it was the other way around, and then the war got going pretty good and then the whole damn country went to hell and there the Beatles were like some smart-ass chorus in the background. I never bought any of their records. You know whose records I used to buy?"

"Whose?"

"The Armitage Sisters, that's who. Ivory, Lace, and Silk. Now, those girls knew how to sing. I mean, they might've been kind of loud, but by God, you gotta admit they could belt out a song. And the words made sense and rhymed and didn't make you wanta go jump off a bridge, although they could make you a little sad, too, sometimes."

Ploughman finished his gin in a gulp. "Silk Armitage was Congressman Ranshaw's girl friend."

"We know," Durant said.

"Mr. Simms would sort of like to find her. Before anybody else does."

Artie Wu blew a smoke ring. The three men watched it rise toward the ceiling, disintegrating along the way. "So would we," Wu said.

"So that's it, huh?" Ploughman said.

"That's it," Durant said.

"I'm sort of walking a tightrope, you know."

Durant nodded. "Yeah, we know."

"What would happen to Simms and all those nice fellas he's fronting for if you found Silk Armitage before they did?"

"Nothing good," Wu said.

"That a fact?"

"That's a fact."

Ploughman nodded and spun around for a quick look at the ocean. "Why don'tcha give me a ring Monday? Maybe Monday morning, and I might tell you where you oughta look."

"Will it be a race?" Durant asked. "Between us and them?"

Ploughman turned back around. "Maybe."

Durant and Wu rose and moved toward the door. Ploughman watched them. "Monday morning," Durant said. "We can count on it?"

Ploughman grinned, much the way that old wolves sometimes grin. "You've got the word of the Ploughman Machine." He shook his head with pleasure. "By God, I do like the way that sounds."

Chapter Twenty-six

In the kitchen of the fortune-teller's house on Breadstone Avenue the four young persons, two men and two women, watched silently as Silk Armitage wrote out the last check for $5,000. The tip of Silk's tongue peeked out from one corner of her mouth as she signed her name, tore the check out, and handed it to Cindy Morrane, a pretty woman of twenty-six with glasses, a deadly earnest expression, and thick blond hair that she kept cut short.

The five of them were seated around the big table in the kitchen. The table was covered with worn oilcloth. Cindy looked at the check for a moment and then placed it on the table before her. The three other young persons had done the same with their checks.

One of the men, John Butler, a lawyer who was twenty-five and very tall with a rather ugly, horse-sense face, cleared his throat and said, "You don't have to do this, Silk."

"You all've done all you can," Silk said. "I want you out of the way, somewhere safe. Saint Thomas is nice. Really it is."

"And you?" Cindy Morrane said.

"I don't want you to know where I'll be. If somehow something goes wrong—well, I just don't want you to know where I am. It's better for you."

The other young woman seated at the table picked up her check and placed it in her purse. She was Joan Abend, at twenty-seven the oldest of the four young persons and an economist who had earned her doctorate at Berkeley. She had a round, pleasant face, streaked brown hair, and calm, wise hazel eyes. Like everyone else at the table, she had built her faith on the slippery rock of socialism, and there was nothing she liked better than baiting Maoists, assorted Communists, and old-line Trotskyites with her biting logic. Conservatives weren't nearly so much fun, because they usually got mad before they got to the point. As for liberals, well, liberals were the kind who worked for Exxon during the day and then snuck off to stuff envelopes for Common Cause at night. Liberals, in Joan Abend's opinion, would file docilely into the corporate concentration camps wearing buttons that read, WE MEANT WELL.

After she placed the check in her purse, Joan Abend snapped it closed with an air of finality and said, "Silk's right. As usual. We've gone nearly as far as we can go."

"Two names," the other young man at the table said. "We came up with two names in two months. That's all."

"The same two names," Silk said. "That's what's important."

The big, blond young man frowned and shook his head. His name was Nick Tryc, which he pronounced "trice" instead of "trick," although the sportswriters had dubbed him "Nick the Trick" when he had played quarterback at the University of Southern California while maintaining a 4.0 grade average in political science. In August he would be going back to Oxford as a Rhodes scholar. He was twenty-two.

"We put a T. Northwood in Chicago on the right date and in Miami on the right date," Tryc said. "But it could be a coincidence."

"You want me to figure the probabilities of that for you?" Cindy Morrane said. Cindy Morrane was a mathematician; a genius, her professors at UCLA had thought, and they had been saddened when she abandoned her graduate studies. Cindy's implacable logic had led her to the peculiar brand of made-in-America, down-home socialism that was now embraced by 1,974 other visionaries in the United States. Cindy had counted them up after she had been elected the movement's treasurer in Chicago last fall at their convention in a Holiday Inn. The Holiday Inn had put up a sign on its marquee reading, WELCOME U.S. SOCIALISTS. The day before, the sign had read, WELCOME JOHN BIRCH SOCIETY. The Holiday Inn didn't care.

"You're both right," Silk said. "We know a T. Northwood was in both of those places on the right dates. If that old bat across the street hadn't been such a snoop, maybe we could've had another month here to work on it. Maybe even two. And maybe that would have been all we would've needed. But she's going to talk, if she hasn't already, and they'll come looking for me next week. Next week at the latest."

"You should get out of here today, Silk," John Butler, the young lawyer, said.

"I want to wait for the letter," Silk said. "It should've been here today. He said he mailed it Wednesday, so it should've been here today. That's four days. It's got to be here Monday."

The letter was to have been sent by Cindy Morrane's brother, computer expert (some thought a genius) and dedicated socialist who lived in Miami and had connections with most of the nation's major airlines.

"All it is is a Xerox copy of the airline records," Joan Abend said.

"I know what it is," Silk said.

"Where will you go, Silk?" Cindy Morrane asked.

Silk Armitage shook her head. "I'm not sure yet. But if I did know, I wouldn't tell you. I want you all out of the country. At least for a month."

"Can't your sister help you?" Tryc said.

"She'd be glad to help me. So would her husband. But I love my sister and I'm kinda fond of my brother-in-law and I'm not going to see them dead on my account."

"Jesus," Tryc said, "you're beginning to get me scared."

"I want you scared. I want you all good and scared."

"Don't wait for the letter, Silk," Joan Abend said. "For God's sake, don't."

"I want that letter," Silk said.

"All it will prove is that a T. Northwood was in Chicago and Miami on the right dates."

Silk looked at the young lawyer. "That's a big step, isn't it, John?"

"Well, it would help establish opportunity, I suppose."

"And God knows there was motive," Silk said. "The Congressman figured that out." In her polite, Southern way, Silk always referred to her late lover, U.S. Representative Floyd Ranshaw, as the Congressman. "They gave T. Northwood this whole damn city to kill the Congressman and his wife. That was the motive."

John Butler massaged his big chin, lawyerlike. "And that leaves what seems to me to be an insurmountable legal obstacle."

"You mean proving who T. Northwood really is?" Silk said.

The young lawyer nodded.

"I'll prove it," Silk said, her pretty face going curiously hard and stubborn. "I don't know how, but I'm going to prove that T. Northwood was in Chicago and Miami and that he killed them both and that they gave him this city to do it and that T. Northwood is Vincent Imperlino."

"He's going to kill you first, Silk," Cindy Morrane said. "Or have it done. You'll be dead. Just like the Congressman."

"Then that'll be all the evidence I need, won't it?"

Silk Armitage looked around the table at the two men and two women and smiled weakly to show them that she was joking. After a while they made themselves smile back.

Solly Gesini was so nervous that he arrived fifteen minutes early for his appointment with Reginald Simms. He was so nervous, in fact, that he had ordered a shot of Scotch to go with the Tab that he was now drinking in the back booth of the Sneaky Pete Bar & Grill—the same booth where Eddie McBride had had his thumb broken.

When Reginald Simms had called nearly an hour before and requested a meeting, Gesini had been so shaken that when Simms had asked Gesini to suggest a place, the only one that had come to mind was the Sneaky Pete—probably because Gesini owned thirty percent of it, although it hadn't made him a dime in two years. Despite the fact that he had the books audited twice each year, Gesini still suspected that his two partners were somehow cheating him. The fuckers've got ways, he had darkly warned the auditors, ways you guys ain't even thought of yet.

Reginald Simms arrived at the bar in Venice straight from Imperlino's. Simms didn't like cheap bars, never had, and decided to punish Gesini a little for having suggested it. He was still trying to decide what form the punishment should take when he reached the back booth. Gesini scrambled up out of it awkwardly, nodding and grinning foolishly at Simms as he tried to decide whether he should offer to shake hands. You never can tell with these ninety-nine-centers, Gesini thought. Some of them don't like to go around shaking hands all the time. But maybe Mr. Simms would expect it. Gesini stuck out his hand. Simms looked at it for a moment as though it were deformed, nodded coldly at Gesini, said his last name in an equally cold tone, and then slid into the booth.

Oh Jesus Christ, it's gonna be even worse than I thought it was, Gesini told himself as he sat back down in the booth.

"What *are* you drinking?" Simms said, eyeing the glass of Scotch and the Tab.

"Scotch and Tab."

"Scotch and Tab," Simms said, pronouncing the words as if they were the name of some dread and newly discovered disease.

"I don't drink very often," Gesini went on, the words tumbling out of his mouth, falling all over themselves in clumsy haste. "I don't drink very often, like I said, but when I do, I like something sorta classy like Scotch."

"And Tab," Simms said.

"Yeah, I drink a lot of Tab. You know, for the weight. What can I getcha, Mr. Simms? I get pretty good service here on account of I own a piece of the place."

"A piece of this?" Simms said, looking around with obvious distaste bordering on revulsion.

"Well, you know, it's just sort of a sideline."

"I suppose a bottle of beer would be safe. Can you arrange that along with a fairly clean glass?"

"Sure, no problem," Gesini said.

But there was a problem, because the waitress was mooning over some customer at the bar and didn't see Gesini's waves that eventually turned into wild gesticulation. Finally, the bartender, who was one of Gesini's two partners, saw the now frantic signals and sent the waitress back. She took her time returning with Simms' beer, and Gesini decided to have her fired that very night.

He watched as Simms inspected the glass, then took out his breast-pocket show handkerchief and wiped it carefully. Simms poured his beer slowly, examined it carefully, and then tasted it with extreme caution. After that he turned his eyes on Gesini and stared at him coldly for several long seconds. Gesini squirmed.

Still staring at Gesini, Simms took out his case, lit a cigarette, and smoked it for several seconds, his eyes still fixed on the luckless Gesini, who squirmed some more and sweated.

"Mr. Imperlino," Simms said, and then paused. It was a very long pause, one that made Gesini think Oh Jesus Christ Mary Mother of God now it's coming and it's gonna be bad, it's gonna be awful.

"Mr. Imperlino is deeply disappointed with you, Gesini. Deeply."

No "mister," Gesini thought. He didn't call me mister. That means he thinks I'm a fuck-up, nothing but a nickel-dime guy. To Gesini there was no worse fate.

He tried to think of something to say, something smoothly explanatory, but all he could come up with was "Well, I sort of tried to explain that to you, Mr. Simms. I mean I didn't handle it personal is what I mean, you know."

There was another silence as Simms let his cold stare bore its way into Gesini's marrow. Simms knew what a stare could do. Sometimes it was better than words, much better.

"Mr. Imperlino," Simms said, and then employed another cruel pause. "Mr. Imperlino was not only very disappointed with you, Gesini, he was also extremely angry. Yes, I would have to say extremely."

Gesini tried to think of something to say, but nothing came to mind except "I'm sorry," and what the fuck good would that do?

"Mr. Imperlino was not at all sure that you should be given another chance," Simms said, and watched with amusement the wave of hope that rolled across Gesini's face. "I, of course, interceded in your behalf." Even insects and toads can be useful at times, Simms thought.

"Jesus," Gesini said, "I appreciate that, Mr. Simms. I mean I'm much obliged to you, I really am."

"Even though you haven't heard what Mr. Imperlino and I have decided that you will do."

"I'll do anything you and him say, you gotta know that. Anything."

Simms glanced around for eavesdroppers and, finding none, leaned across the table toward Gesini. He lowered his voice until it was not quite a whisper. "We want you to kill two persons for us, Gesini. We want you to murder them."

The proposed deed didn't bother Gesini, but the words did. That wasn't class, using words like that. There were a lot of other words that could be used—nicer words, smoother words, words that had sort of a wink to them. For the first time Gesini was a little disappointed in Mr. Simms. But he was careful not to let it show. Instead, he simply said, "Sure. Who?"

"Sure. Who," Simms said. "An excellent response, Gesini. I'll have to tell Mr. Imperlino about it. He'll be very much . . . pleased. Sure. Who." Simms gave his head a small amused shake and for the first time smiled.

Now, what the fuck did I say? Gesini wondered.

"Now to whom—or who, as you say. First, of course,

McBride. Eddie McBride. Find him and murder him. Can you do that—personally, I mean?"

"Yeah. Sure." Eddie McBride would be no problem. Gesini just wished Mr. Simms wouldn't keep on using words like that. It wasn't just a matter of class; it was also a matter of, well, good taste. Yeah, that's what it is, Gesini decided. Good taste. For a moment Gesini was comforted by the notion that he had better taste in some things than Mr. Simms.

"The second person we would like you to murder is a young woman."

"Uh-huh," Gesini said to show that he was both alert and willing. The idea was, as a matter of fact, kind of interesting.

"Uh-huh," Simms said. "Another excellent response. Mr. Imperlino is going to be highly pleased, I can assure you. The young woman whom you will murder is Miss Silk Armitage."

Gesini knew who Silk Armitage was. His wife was always buying her records and before that the records that she'd made when she was singing with her sisters, the one called Lace and what was the other one? Ivory. There was something about Ivory that Gesini thought he should remember, and then it came to him. A rumor he had heard about her and Mr. Imperlino. She and him had been shacked up together, hadn't they? Well, now, by God, this was something. This was an opportunity to get back in good with Mr. Imperlino by taking care of something personal for him. And with Simms—him too, of course. But it was gonna have to be worth something. You just didn't go around doing it to somebody famous like Silk Armitage for nothing. It was gonna make a lot of noise. A lot more risk than some dumb fuck like Eddie McBride who nobody gave a damn about. It was, Gesini decided, time for him to be both smart and smooth.

So very smoothly he said, "Where does she live?"

Gesini liked the big smile that appeared on Simms' face. It was a smile of both delight and warmth with just a touch of amazement. I must've said something right, Gesini thought, but couldn't figure out either what or why.

"Where does she live?" Simms said, savoring the question. "That was the absolutely perfect reply, Mr. Gesini. Absolutely perfect. No hesitation, no senseless caviling, just the sturdy soldier's automatic response to duty. Mr. Imperlino is going to be most pleased."

He called me mister again, Gesini thought, so that's some progress. "What I mean is, you got her address?"

"We'll have it for you by Monday at the latest. In the meantime, perhaps you could kill McBride and get that out of the way."

"Yeah, sure, no problem there. I was just sort of wondering, though, Mr. Simms, about what the compensation will be for these two items."

"You mean how much are we prepared to pay you for murdering both McBride and Silk Armitage?"

"Yeah, that's kind of what I was getting at."

"Penance, Mr. Gesini. Penance."

"Peanuts?" Gesini said.

Simms sighed. "You made a mistake, Gesini. Now you'll have to pay for it. Mr. Imperlino insists. So you will commit the two murders for the same price that we agreed previously, twenty thousand dollars. Two for the price of one, to make myself clear. It is clear, isn't it?"

"Yeah," Gesini said unhappily. "Two for the price of one."

"And you will kill them both yourself."

"Yeah, I'll take care of it personally."

"Good." Simms rose. "We'll be in touch with you Monday with the address for the woman."

"Fine."

"And do try not to bungle it this time, Mr. Gesini. Please."

"Sure, Mr. Simms."

Simms nodded, turned, and left. Gesini sat in the booth thinking. He was going to have to make some phone calls, a lot of them, to get the word out on McBride. Well, he might as well get started. He rose and moved to the bar, choosing a spot that was safe. The bartender who was one of the partners saw him and moved down the bar toward him. He was a thin, sour-looking man of about forty who didn't drink and despised those who did.

"You want something else, Solly?"

"Yeah, Gobie, I want something else. I wantcha to keep your hand out of the fucking till."

"Don't get on my case about that again."

"Also I want you to start putting the word out."

Gobie Salimei's lean face acquired a wise, knowing look. "On who?"

"A nobody called Eddie McBride."

Salimei nodded. "How much?"

"Five hundred bucks for his address. No, make it a thou. I'm in a hurry."

"He owes you, huh?"

"Yeah, that's right, he owes me."

Salimei gave the bar a wipe. "Anything else?"

Gesini pointed his forefinger at the waitress who was in deep conversation with a customer. "You still fucking her?"

Salimei shrugged. "Now and then."

"Well, you ain't anymore, because I just fired her ass tonight."

Chapter Twenty-seven

The knock on Durant's door came just after midnight. It was more of a light, hesitant tap than a knock. Durant closed the book he had been half reading and turned off the small Sony television set with its old movie that he had been half watching. Then he rose, went to the door, and switched on the deck lights. Lace Armitage was smiling at him uncertainly through the door's glass.

Durant opened the door. "Well, come in."

"I saw your light," she said as she came in. "Isn't that what they always say, 'I saw your light'?"

"Who're they?" Durant said.

"I don't know. Just they, I reckon. Those who come calling at midnight. Actually, I've been standing out there for fifteen minutes trying to get up the necessary nerve."

"To do what?"

"To say 'I saw your light.'" Lace looked around hesitantly, as though not at all sure what she should do next. Durant asked her to sit down. She chose the suede armchair where she had sat before. She was wearing dark green pants and tan sandals and a thin white velour sweater-shirt. The nipples of her breasts seemed to thrust and poke at the thin fabric.

Durant, who was still standing, said, "Can I get you anything? A drink, maybe?"

"Will you have one?"

"Sure. Scotch?"

"And a little water."

Durant made the drinks in the kitchen and carried them back into the living room. He handed Lace hers and then sat down on the couch. Lace brought a box of Shermans out of her sweater-shirt pocket, extracted one, and lit it quickly, almost nervously, with the table lighter, not waiting for Durant to make an offer to light it, apparently not even aware that he might.

Then, remembering something, perhaps her manners, she offered him the box. He shook his head and thought, Well, she's got the drink and the cigarette, the props; now she can get on with the scene.

Lace sipped her drink, took some of the cigarette's smoke far down into her lungs, blew it out, and said, "Anything about my sister yet?"

"Monday maybe."

"Really?" Durant couldn't decide whether the interest and

excitement in her voice were real or merely acting. With her it was hard to tell—probably even for her.

"There's a slight chance that we might learn something Monday, but very slight. Don't count on it. That's why I didn't call you. Or your husband." You do remember him, don't you, Durant thought, the distinguished-looking guy with all the money?

"I'm very worried about my sister," Lace said.

Durant nodded.

Lace smiled—a wry, rather lopsided smile which didn't at all mar her beauty. "You don't believe me, do you?"

"I believe you're worried about your sister."

"But you don't believe that's why I came here tonight."

"You saw my light," Durant said.

"That's right. I saw your light and I started wondering."

"About what?"

"About whether you still have those clean sheets on your bed."

Durant nodded slowly, staring at her. "You want to fuck, is that it?"

"Yes," she said, looking away from him, "that's it."

"Why me?" he said. "Why not your husband—or the pool man?"

"He's not available," she said, still looking away, this time toward the glass wall and beyond that the ocean.

"Your husband?"

She looked at him then with a direct, level gaze. "The pool man. Or the gardener. Or the chauffeur. Or even the guy who delivers the booze."

"It's like that, huh?" Durant said after a moment.

"It's exactly like that."

"I'm sorry."

Lace's face softened. "You sound like you really are."

"I am."

Something passed over her face, something that seemed both bleak and stiff. "Well, you don't have to be sorry; all you have to do is take me to bed."

"That's partly what I'm sorry about."

"You mean you won't?"

Durant shook his head slowly, even sadly. "It's not that I won't." He paused. "I can't."

Lace's eyes went wide. "Are you saying—I mean, what you're saying is that you can't get it up?" There were sorrow and real compassion in her tone, and Durant decided that this time she wasn't acting.

"That's one way to put it," he said. "A little inelegant maybe, but graphic."

"Oh, Jesus, I'm sorry," she said, and there was no acting this time either. Only more genuine sorrow and more compassion.

Durant grinned. "It's sort of funny. I mean, you and I together are sort of funny, if you go in for heavy irony."

Lace didn't smile. "How long have you—well—had it?"

"You don't have it. It just happens. It's been about five years now, a little more."

"Did something, well, happen to you?" Lace's interest didn't sound prurient to Durant. She sounded more like a doctor who was anxious to prescribe a remedy once he diagnosed the disease.

"I think so. At least, I can date it from a certain time, a certain event."

"What?"

"There was a girl, or a woman rather, whom I was rather fond of. A French girl—woman. I got her into a place in Cambodia during the war where she shouldn't have been. She was a writer, a journalist. She got killed because of my stupidity and carelessness, and since then God has been punishing me."

"You don't really believe that," Lace said.

"About God?"

She nodded, very, very seriously.

"No, but I like to blame it on somebody."

"Have you seen anybody about it—a doctor, I mean?"

"Have you?"

Lace looked away again. "Yes. A lot of them. It doesn't do much good, does it? They don't have any answers or any cures either. And they try to be so fucking objective and above it all and God-like, but they still make you feel like what's really wrong with you is that you're just a nasty little girl with rotten morals."

"It sounds rough," Durant said.

"At least I can still do it. God, I don't know what I'd do if I couldn't. Did you—well—try much?"

"Incessantly."

"Was it bad?"

Durant nodded. "Pretty bad."

She looked out toward the ocean again. "Would you like to try with me?"

"It wouldn't do any good."

"I know a lot of—well—tricks." She looked at him almost beseechingly, and the only apparent desire in her eyes was a desire to help. Still looking at him, she unbuttoned her sweater and slipped it off. She ran her hands over her breasts. "You like that? Some men like to watch me do that."

Durant took it all in clinically. He commanded his brain to send some signal down to his groin. And when the command didn't work, he willed it. But there was no response, only an indifferent emptiness that still managed to ache. Durant shook his head slowly at Lace, who smiled at him encouragingly, ran her tongue over her sensual lips, and with her eyes promised all kinds of unimaginable delights. Durant wanted to believe. He wanted to very much, but he simply couldn't.

Lace unbuttoned the top of her pants and slipped them off quickly. Now she was completely naked. She rose and moved over to Durant and stood before him, moving her hands slowly over her body. Durant swallowed.

"You want me to talk to you?" she said. "You want me to tell you things?"

"No," Durant said, leaning back on the couch and closing his eyes. "It's not you, but it's no good. I'm sorry—it's just not going to work."

"Look," she whispered. "Please, just look."

Durant looked. It was one of the most totally erotic things he had ever seen. Her body writhed as her hands moved over it, caressing herself, offering to herself and to him.

But there was nothing. No, you're wrong there, Jack, Durant told himself, there's less than nothing. He watched dully now as Lace Armitage drove herself toward some sort of climax. Just as she was achieving it, the door from the deck opened and Randall Piers walked quietly into the room.

Piers stood watching his wife for a few seconds, a look of almost infinite sadness on his face. Sadness that mingled with affection and pity and love. After a moment he said very quietly, "Let's go home, Lace."

She turned toward him casually. "Oh, hello, sugar. You shouldn't have bothered to come out."

Piers stood waiting, a small, stiff half smile on his face. Finally, he nodded at Durant. Durant rose.

"My wife has a problem," Piers said, trying not to sound embarrassed.

"I'm sorry," Durant said.

Lace picked up her pants and started putting them on. She had one leg into them when she stopped and looked at Durant. "You don't have to worry about my husband, Mr. Durant," she said. "He—well, he understands."

Durant nodded.

The two men watched as Lace Armitage got dressed. Durant, staring at Lace, said to Piers, "Nothing happened."

"No, of course not. I understand."

"I'm not sure I do."

"It's a difficult thing to understand really well, I suppose," Piers said. "The first thing you have to do is accept it, and then you have to live with it."

Lace Armitage was now dressed. Piers moved over to her, put his arm around her waist, and kissed her very gently on the cheek. "You all right?"

"Fine," she said. "It just sort of got out of hand and I'm afraid I came bothering Mr. Durant."

"No bother," Durant said because he felt he had to say something.

"I'm sorry about—well, about everything," Lace said. She turned to her husband. "Mr. Durant thinks he might have some news about Silk on Monday."

"Is that right?" Piers said.

"Maybe," Durant said. "There's a chance."

"We have that lunch date Monday, don't we?" Piers said to Durant.

"That's right."

"Well, until Monday, then," Piers said. He took his wife's arm and gently guided her toward the door.

"Monday," Durant said as they went through the door and closed it softly behind them.

PART
III

Chapter Twenty-eight

A very wet, very unseasonable low-pressure system that had been lurking out in the Pacific for nearly a week finally decided to make its breakthrough late that Saturday night. By four o'clock the next morning, just as Quincy Durant's uneasy doze was turning into fitful sleep, a hard rain began falling over much of Southern California. It was a Sunday, the nineteenth of June.

By the time Aggie Wu arose that morning in her house on Ninth Street in Santa Monica, the hard rain had turned into fine mist and fog. Aggie Wu immediately decided that it was a perfect day for a picnic at the beach.

It took a while to convince her husband of the suitability of her notion, which he described as goddamned weird, but by ten he had made the call to Durant and got the Wu clan invited to the beach. By eleven the huge picnic hamper was packed, and by noon Artie Wu was parking his Chrysler station wagon at the far end of the Paradise Cove parking lot, which, because of the weather, was virtually deserted.

Durant watched from the deck as the Wu family proceeded across the parking lot to the driveway and up to the deck—Wu in the lead, of course, his big stomach relaxed and poking proudly at his tent of a white sailcloth shirt, his face beaming; very much the family man; very much, indeed, the patriarch.

Behind him came the two sets of twins, first the boys, then the girls, barely two, barely able to toddle. And last came Aggie Wu, tall and almost radiant in the Scotland-like weather, carrying the big picnic hamper. Since Artie Wu had created the delicacies that filled it, he had automatically assumed that his wife would do the carrying.

Durant greeted the twins by name, although it was sometimes hard for him to tell Angus and Arthur apart. The girls were easier. One was pretty; the other one, prettier.

"They've got a poem for you, Quincy," Aggie Wu said as she placed the hamper on the redwood table.

"Hell of a poem," Artie Wu said. "They picked it up from one of the neighbor kids." He nodded encouragingly at his two sons.

It was all the encouragement they needed. In unison they chanted in voices tinged with an odd Spanish-Scottish-American accent:

> Chinka, chinka Chinaman eats dead rats;
> Chews them up like gingersnaps.

"Like it?" Aggie Wu said.

"The rhyme's a little off, but the meter's pretty good," Durant said.

"And they've learned some new Spanish," Aggie Wu said. "Say your new Spanish for Quincy, Angus."

Angus Wu, the elder son, the one who, if things turned out just right, might someday be both Emperor of China and King of Scotland, smiled sweetly at Durant and said, "*Chinga tu madre, loco cabrón.*"

"And the same to you, pal," Durant said.

"Come on, kids," Aggie Wu said. "Let's go take a walk along the beach so we can be cold and wet and chilled like God intended people to be."

Wu and Durant watched the mother and her bundled-up children head down toward the beach. Wu then picked up the hamper and followed Durant inside. Wu put the hamper down and poured two mugs of coffee from the big gallon pot and handed Durant one.

"You look like you could use a little something in yours," he said, studying Durant.

"That bad, huh?"

"It shows. Hard night?"

Durant nodded.

"I've got big ears."

"I don't know," Durant said. "It's sort of kiss-and-tell stuff."

"What'd you do," Wu said as he moved into the living room, "pick up some broad?"

"Not exactly."

"One picked you up?" Wu said, sitting down on the couch.

"Something like that."

Artie Wu shook his head in a gesture of kindly commiseration. "And it turned out as usual."

"As usual."

"Bad?"

"Yeah. Bad."

"Who was she?"

Durant debated whether to tell Wu. It might help a little to talk about it. Sometimes it did, and of course, he knew it would go no further. It wasn't something that he wanted to go any further.

"Lace Armitage," he said.

Artie Wu lifted his face heavenward and flung his arms out beseechingly. "Oh, Lordy, let it happen to me!"

Durant told Wu what had happened, adding nothing, editing much. "And then came her big moment—"

"And you sitting there not even able to get your tongue hard."

"Yeah. Well, who should walk in on us but the husband."

"Piers?"

"That's the only one she's got."

"Christ. What happened?"

"Nothing. He seemed used to it—or as used to that kind of thing as you can ever get, I suppose. He seemed more sorry for her than anything else."

Artie Wu produced a cigar and lit it with his usual ceremony. "I guess for a woman like that you could put up with just one hell of a lot."

"I guess."

Wu examined Durant several moments. "You still want to go through with it?"

Durant nodded.

"We can cut and run."

"No."

"You're still counting on what that doctor told you in London?"

"He was a pretty expensive doctor. Thirty-five guineas an hour."

"The retribution theory."

"Yeah," Durant said. "Retribution, not revenge. There's a difference."

"She's dead, Quincy," Wu said, his voice gently reasonable.

"I know. I've finally got around to accepting that. But I should've done something about it. According to our Harley Street friend, it really wouldn't have mattered much what I did as long as it was something. But I didn't do anything. So it all started festering inside some place, the feelings that I wouldn't let myself have, the guilt I wouldn't admit; then the conflict and the payoff in the form of a permanently limp dick, which for us grown-ups isn't much fun."

"It's some theory," Wu said.

"You don't buy it?"

"I don't know. Retribution." Wu shook his head. "If you fix Simms, who was responsible for Christine's dying, then you fix up the family jewels. It's a little pat."

"The shrink's theory was that it doesn't matter what I do to Simms. I can slap him on the wrist or drop him off a cliff. What he meant—and this part I do buy—is that it doesn't matter a damn what I do now as long as I believe that it's what I should have done then. You follow that—or is it too murky?"

"Yeah, I follow it."

"It's all a matter of confidence."

"Impotency?"

Durant nodded.

"Well, shit," Wu said, "we can't have you going around like this for the rest of your life."

"No, that's a bit long."

"So let's get on with it, then." Wu looked past Durant to the ocean, still gray from the overcast, although the horizon, for some reason, was clearly defined—so clearly, in fact, that Catalina was plainly visible, which it seldom was, even on clear days. "I've had a couple of ideas," Wu continued, "which, when you hear them, might help you to understand why they used to call us Oriental folks wily."

"Shifty, too."

"Well, this is one of the shiftiest ideas I've ever had, but it might make us a little money."

"How much is a little?"

Wu blew one of his smoke rings. Durant watched it rise toward the ceiling and said, "That much, huh?"

"How can you tell?"

"Whenever you come up with something really rotten, you blow a smoke ring first. It's sort of like italics."

Wu blew another smoke ring and said, "A half a million. Each. Cash."

Durant leaned back in the suede chair and looked at the ceiling. "Well, now. A slight risk involved, of course."

"We might wind up in jail. Or dead."

"As I said, a slight risk."

Wu blew his third smoke ring. "Your ears always get pointy."

Durant touched his right ear. "When?"

"Whenever I mention a bit of money, they start growing points." He sighed. "Greed, I suppose."

"I didn't think it showed. Tell me about how we're going to get rich, Artie."

Wu looked at his watch. "Let's call Otherguy first and get him and McBride out here for a small conference." Wu rose and went over to the telephone. He reached Overby on the third ring. Overby said that they could make it by two that afternoon. Wu hung up the phone and went back to the couch, sat down, and blew a final smoke ring.

Then he looked at Durant and smiled. "Let's go after the two million."

"Eddie McBride's two million?"

Wu nodded.

"That means we'll have to go after Simms."

Again Wu nodded.

"I like it already," Durant said. "But half of two million is a million each. You said half a million."

"We might have to divvy it up with a couple of people."

"Well, fair's fair. Let's hear your rotten plan."

Wu grinned. "It's really rotten."

"Good," Durant said, and lit a Pall Mall, his second for the morning. "Let's hear it."

It took Artie Wu nearly an hour and forty-five minutes to outline his ideas. It took that long because Durant immediately began poking some rather large holes in them, which together they plugged up. Then Aggie Wu and the children came back and they decided to have the picnic early out on the deck. After the picnic, the children were put to bed for a nap on the twin beds in the spare bedroom. Aggie Wu decided to take a nap in Durant's room.

When the children and their mother were finally asleep, Durant and Wu went over the scheme again, probing for weak spots, for holes, and for gaping inconsistencies. They found quite a few and patched them over, mostly with improvisation.

Finally, Durant locked his hands behind his neck and gazed up at the ceiling again. "By God, it's rotten, isn't it?"

Wu smiled. "I thought you'd like it."

"You know what the odds against it are?"

Wu shrugged. "We've got a Chinaman's chance."

"That bad, huh?"

Wu stuck a fresh cigar into his mouth and around it grinned a big, wide, white, merry grin. "Nah," he said. "That good."

Chapter Twenty-nine

Otherguy Overby fell in love with Durant's house. In fact, nothing could begin until Overby was given a tour of the place. Aggie Wu had taken the children for a last, damp walk along the beach, this time toward Santa Monica, and Overby went through the house like a prospective buyer, opening closets, flushing the toilet, and making sure that the garbage-disposal unit in the kitchen worked properly.

After that, Overby stood in the middle of the living room, looking around with a proprietary air. "How much you paying, Quincy, if you don't mind my asking?"

"Six-fifty."

Overby stuck his lower lip out a little, turned the corners of his mouth down, and nodded his approval. "Not bad, not half bad. Your furniture?"

"Yes."

"What about the utilities?"

"Another fifty or so."

"Not bad at all. And you got the ocean."

"Plus the beach."

"Who cares about the beach?" Overby said. "All a beach is good for is tracking sand in all over the place." Overby nodded to himself, still looking around, and said in a voice that was clearly a self-addressed promise, "One of these days."

"One of these days what?" Artie Wu said.

"One of these days I'm gonna make a bundle and buy me a place like this and then tell the world to go fuck itself."

"You want a beer in the meantime?" Durant said.

"Yeah, I would, thanks."

"What about you, Eddie?"

"Sure," McBride said.

After each had a beer, he selected a place to sit in the living room, Overby claiming a spot on the couch so that he could keep an eye on the ocean. McBride sat in the leather Eames chair which he had bled on a little a few nights before. Durant chose the suede chair, and Wu sat on the couch with Overby.

"All right," Durant said, "let's see what we've got scheduled." He looked at Overby. "You've got an appointment with Simms tomorrow at nine, right?"

"Right."

"How long do you think it'll take?"

"An hour probably. Maybe a little more."

"And you've got the reporter—what's his name?"

"Conroy," Overby said. "Herb Conroy."

"Yeah, Conroy. You've got him set for the lunch tomorrow."

"I'm going to pick him up at twelve, maybe a little before."

"He still thinks it's about a job?" Wu said.

"Sure."

"I think," Durant said slowly, "that we'd better get a rundown from you, Otherguy, on your meeting with Simms before we get into the lunch."

"Where're you gonna be about ten or ten-thirty?"

"Anywhere you say," Wu said.

"My place?"

"Yeah, that's good," Wu said.

Overby nodded. "If I'm not there, the kid here'll let you in or I'll leave word for somebody to."

"What about Eddie's ID?" Wu said. "Any problem there?"

Overby shook his head. "We picked it up this morning. It's a nice job."

"How much?" Durant said.

"One thousand even."

"Jesus," Artie Wu said. "I can remember when you could get a whole set for three hundred."

"Not with credit cards and a *Washington Post* press card," Overby said.

"What's that name you're going to use, Eddie?" Durant said.

"Max," McBride said. "Anthony C. Max, and maybe, in a couple of hours or even maybe a couple of days, you guys are gonna get around to telling me what the fuck this is all about."

"Five minutes, Eddie," Durant said. "That's all you've got to wait."

"Show him your stuff, kid," Overby said.

McBride took a wallet out of the breast pocket of his jacket. From the wallet he extracted a folding, accordionlike plastic case and holding it up, let it unfold itself as the nine or ten connected compartments tumbled down toward the floor.

Overby rose, took the case, and showed it almost proudly to Durant and Wu. "Maryland driver's license, Social Security card, American Express, Carte Blanche, Gulf Oil, D.C. public library card—I thought that up—and the press card."

Wu examined the press card carefully. "Is this really the way it looks?"

"Who the hell knows?" Overby said. "What this guy did was go down and buy a copy of the *Post* somewhere and then take its name, the way it is in Old English type here, and shoot it and then ink it in good and reduce it. He had a press card that he'd got somehow from the *Sacramento Bee* and he used that as a kind of model and then got a color Polaroid shot of the kid here and put that in and then laminated the whole thing with plastic. I think it looks damn good."

Wu looked at Durant, who nodded. Wu handed the folding case back to McBride and then looked at Overby. "One more thing, Otherguy."

"What?"

"We need a couple of pieces."

Overby's face went very still. Only his eyes moved as they flicked from Wu to Durant and then back to Wu. "Well, now," he said. "If you two guys need pieces, how about me and the kid here?"

"You've already got one, Otherguy," Durant said. "It's a belly gun, a thirty-eight, and when you carry it, you carry it cute—around in the small of your back."

Overby's hand went around to the small of his back and touched something through his jacket. "You remember," he said.

"Yeah, we remember."

"What've you got in mind?" Overby said.

"Pistols," Durant said. "Revolvers. No smaller than a thirty-two, no larger than a thirty-eight."

"There's a guy over in Hollywood that—"

"Otherguy," Wu interrupted.

"What?"

"We don't want to know."

Overby nodded thoughtfully. "Yeah. Okay. But I'm running a little short."

Wu sighed. "How much?"

"Five hundred."

Wu sighed again, took out his roll with the oversized silver paper clip, peeled off ten fifties, and handed them to Overby. "Make sure they've got firing pins in them and everything."

"Firing pins," Overby said as if making a note, and stuck the money into his pocket.

"Just make sure they shoot. And get some bullets for them, too."

"How many rounds you want?"

"Just enough to load them," Wu said. "We're not starting any war."

"What the hell are we starting?" McBride said. "You guys all need pieces, but I don't. I'm going to be the boy reporter, which I know fuck all about being. I think your five minutes are up, and if I don't hear something that makes sense in one minute flat, I walk."

"Okay, Eddie," Durant said. "We're going to get to you right now."

"You know, the kid's got a point," Overby said. "He and I've sort of been talking things over."

"About what?" Durant said.

"Well, you know, you guys've got your deal going, and I mean, you don't have to tell us every last detail, but we would kind of like to get a look inside."

"How'd you like a peek at two million dollars?" Durant said.

Again, Overby's face went still. "Cut how many ways?"

"Four," Wu said. "Possibly five."

"Even?"

Durant nodded. "Even."

Overby looked at McBride. "What do you think, kid? With that kind of money we could maybe do what we were talking about."

"What's that?" Wu said.

"Well, I'm not getting any younger and I could probably use an associate—a partner, really—and the kid here has got all the right moves, so he and I were sort of thinking about going in together out there when this is all over." Overby nodded toward the Pacific Ocean, again indicating that out there could be anything from Seattle to Singapore.

"Two million," McBride said. "That's a pretty familiar figure."

"It's the same one, Eddie," Durant said.

"So what do I have to do?"

"You have to look for somebody."

"Where?"

"We'll know tomorrow morning, probably around nine," Wu said. "It may be an address, it may be just a neighborhood."

"And what do I do when I find whoever I'm looking for?"

"You call us," Durant said.

McBride nodded thoughtfully. "And that's all you're going to tell me, isn't it?"

"For now," Wu said.

"Except who I'm going to be looking for. You're going to tell me that."

"Silk Armitage," Durant said.

The name made McBride look down at the floor. For several long moments he seemed to be studying the intricate pattern in the Oriental rug. When he looked up his face was set, thoughtful. "If I'm looking for her," he said, "that means she doesn't want to be found."

"That's right, Eddie," Wu said. "She doesn't want to be found."

Chapter Thirty

At 3:30 P.M. on that damp, cool Sunday afternoon, a failed pimp turned part-time car thief was killing an otherwise dull day by bar hopping down the Pacific Coast Highway. The car thief's name was Joe Crites, and he had already been in three bars by the time he hit the Sneaky Pete in Venice and ordered a Virgin Mary.

There wasn't much of a crowd in the place, and Crites had grown bored and was almost ready to leave when Gobie Salimei, one of the Sneaky Pete's three owners, came down to Crites's end of the bar, leaned on it, and offered his opinion of the weather.

"You'd think, Joey, on a day like this people'd be flocking in here, wouldn't you?"

Crites looked around and shrugged. "You got a crummy joint here, Gobie. They ain't gonna flock in here rain or shine."

"Maybe I oughta get a string of ladies and let 'em work outa here."

"It's an idea, except the oney kind you're gonna get are gonna be dogs and they'd drive more bidness away than they'd bring in."

"You think so, huh?"

"I know so."

Gobie Salimei nodded gloomily. Then he thought of something that might elevate him a little in the bankrupt pimp's estimation. It was information, inside stuff, and you never could tell. Crites knew a lot of people.

Salimei leaned across the bar and lowered his voice. "The word's out on a guy."

Crites nodded and made his tanned, thirty-three-year-old face look interested.

"A guy name of McBride. Eddie McBride. Ever hear of him?"

Crites shook his head. "How much?"

Salimei looked around and made his voice grow even more conspiratorial. "A grand. Just for his address."

"Who's putting it up?"

"Solly Gesini. You know Solly?"

Crites nodded. "I know who he is. What'd you say this guy's name is?"

"McBride," Salimei said. "Eddie McBride."

Five bars, two ginger ales, and three draft beers later, Joe Crites found himself on the outskirts of Pelican Bay. Because he had grown bored with bars, Crites decided to go calling on a former business associate. He decided that he would drop in on Brenda Birdsong, whose pimp he had once been back in the old days in North Hollywood. The old days to Crites were eighteen months ago. Brenda was one of the reasons that Crites had failed as a pimp. She was pretty enough, but she was lazy and had a smart mouth and didn't like to take baths. Dirty ankles, he remembered. Brenda always went around barefoot and had dirty ankles, and that sort of turned guys off unless they were some kind of freaks.

Crites had no trouble getting past the old man with the white ponytail who held down the reception desk at the Catalina Towers. A few minutes later he was knocking on the door of 521, which was just across the hall from 522, where, until recently, Otherguy Overby had lived.

"Who is it?" Brenda asked through the door.

"Joey."

"Joey who?"

"Come on, Brenda."

She opened the door, and Crites saw that she hadn't changed any since the old days. She had on an unbuttoned man's white shirt and blue nylon panties and that was all, except for too much mascara around her wise-ass eyes and a pretty good coat of grime around her ankles.

Inside the apartment, Brenda turned to Crites and said, "No freebies, Joey."

"Aw, hell, Brenda. I just dropped by for a drink and a few laughs."

"What've we got to laugh about?"

"We'll think of something. Here." He took a pint of White Horse Scotch out of his jacket pocket and handed it to her. "Make us a drink."

Brenda shrugged, took the bottle, and went into the kitchen. She came out a minute or two later with two glasses. "No soda," she said. "So I used water."

Crites accepted his glass. "Water's okay." He took a taste of his drink and looked around the shabby apartment. "So how's hustling?"

"How's car stealing?"

He shrugged. "I get by." Crites sat down in an upholstered chair and poked at a cigarette burn in the fabric of its left arm. "I was just talking to a guy over in Venice."

"Don't poke at it," Brenda said. "It'll just make it worse."

Crites stopped poking at the burn. "This guy over in Venice I was just talking to is thinking of letting a few ladies hustle out of his bar."

Brenda made a face. "In Venice?"

"What's wrong with Venice?"

"Fifteen- and sixteen-year-old dopers, that's what's wrong with Venice. They give it away over there for the price of a joint. You talk about turning a trick in Venice for fifty bucks and you get laughed out of town. You wanta know what Venice is? It's the pits."

"Well, maybe you're right," Crites said, "except I think probably you oughta move back to Hollywood."

"I'm doing all right here."

"Yeah, I can see," Crites said, looking around the room.

"I got some regulars," Brenda said. "I turn five or six, maybe seven tricks a week and I can get by. The cops don't bother me, not in this town, and I don't have to keep some fucking pimp in nine-hundred-dollar suits."

Crites made a small deprecatory gesture with his drink. "Hell, it was just an idea. I mean, about Venice. I was over there and this guy happened to mention it so right away I thought about you. He also told me something else kinda interesting."

"What?"

"The word's out on some guy."

"Anybody we know?"

"I never heard of him. Some nobody called Eddie McBride."

Brenda's face changed. Her eyes lost their wise-ass look and turned cunning instead. A small, tight smile appeared on her face. "Who's Eddie McBride?" she said.

"I don't know. Some guy that Solly Gesini's looking for."

"Is that the Gesini who runs the muscle factory over on Lincoln Boulevard?"

"You know him?"

"I just heard of him."

"Well, Solly'll pay a little money to find out where this here Eddie McBride is keeping himself."

"What's he offering?"

Crites looked at her carefully. "You sure you don't know him?"

"Who?"

"McBride."

"Nah, I don't know him. How should I know him?"

"Well, I just thought in case you did we might split the two hundred bucks that Gesini's offering—just for his address."

"Well, if I hear anything, I'll let you know. I could sure as shit use the money." She finished her drink, put it down, then turned to Crites. "You wanta ball—just for old times' sake?"

"I don't mind," Crites said.

After Crites had gone it took a while for Brenda to get someone to give her Solly Gesini's unlisted home phone number. But finally she got it from Gobie Salimei at the Sneaky Pete. Gesini answered his phone with a hello on the third ring.

"Mr. Gesini?" Brenda said.

"Yeah."

"You don't know me, but I hear you're looking for a certain party whose last name begins with an M."

"Yeah, I might be looking for somebody like that."

"How much is it worth to you?"

"You got the address, it's worth one grand."

"A thousand?"

"That's what I said."

"How do I know I'm gonna get the thousand if you get the address?"

"You got a name?"

"Brenda."

"Well, let me tell you something, Brenda. I'm a businessman and I got a reputation to keep up. I say I'll do something, I'll do it. You can ask anybody."

"How soon can I get it—the money, I mean?"

"You give me the address, you can get it tonight. You know a place called the Sneaky Pete in Venice?"

"Yeah."

"Well, you give me the address and then give me an hour to do a little checking, and if everything works out, then there'll be an envelope for you at the Sneaky Pete. An hour from now."

"Well, he's living in another guy's apartment."

"Where?"

"In Pelican Bay."

"What's the name of the apartment?"

"The Sandpiper Apartments. It's on Third and Seashore Drive."

"Yeah, I know where it is. What's the name of the party he's living with?"

"Overby. Maurice Overby—although nearly everybody calls him Otherguy."

"Otherguy?"

"That's what they call him."

"Okay, Brenda, if this checks out, you just made yourself a thousand bucks."

"And I can pick it up in an hour?"

"That's right. In an hour at the Sneaky Pete."

After she hung up the phone, the excitement of what she had just done hit her. She looked around the apartment trying to think how she might kill half an hour before she started for the bar in Venice. She didn't want another drink —not just then. But she wanted to do something, though, something that would help keep the excitement and anticipation under control, but still not spoil it. So Brenda Birdsong decided to do something that she hadn't done in quite some time. She decided to take a bath.

Chapter Thirty-one

On that following morning, the first day of summer, a Monday, Randall Piers was at his desk at seven o'clock after having walked and run the six greyhounds for their usual mile along the beach.

Piers tried the large cup of coffee that Whitlock, the butler, had left for him on the desk. It was good—very good, in fact—but still not quite as good as the coffee made by the tall, lean man with the scars. Thinking of Durant, Piers remembered how the day before, Sunday, Lace Armitage had described Durant's impotency. She had made it a sad, even poignant story, and her obvious compassion and sympathy had irritated Piers a little, and still did, although he was careful not to let it show.

When Piers had married Lace he had known what he was getting into, because she had told him very carefully and with much graphic detail, explaining that she wanted him to know exactly what to expect.

"I just can't seem to help it," she had said. "I try, but somehow it happens anyway."

"But you want to do something about it?"

"Of course I do."

"Then we'll work on it," he had said.

And they had, and things had seemed to be getting better until this business with Silk started. After Silk disappeared, things had gone to hell again. Randall Piers very much wanted to find his sister-in-law because he had decided that it just might somehow save his marriage, and he was very much in love with his wife.

After another sip of coffee, Piers rang for his executive assistant. Hart Ebsworth came in a moment later and took his usual seat.

"Well?" Piers said.

"It cost."

"How much?"

"The Senator said to tell you that as far as he's concerned he doesn't owe you a thing now."

"He thinks it's worth that much, huh?"

"That much."

"So what did he come up with?"

"Just the bare bones," Ebsworth said. "But it cost him plenty, or so he said. But you know how he lies."

Piers nodded.

"Durant and Wu had a contract to furnish supplies to a hush-hush hit-and-run outfit in Cambodia. There was a girl involved, Durant's girl. She was a reporter, French. She got killed along with some CBS guy, and Durant got captured. That's how he got the scars. Wu went in and got him out. Then they went to Scotland. And that's it, except for one thing."

"What?"

"The hit-and-run outfit. It was a bunch of CIA-paid mercenaries, illegal as hell. The guy who ran it was one Luke Childester. The Dirty Duke, they called him. Well, when the war ended, Childester went sour, turned renegade or something, and now he's running things for Imperlino in Pelican Bay using his real name, which is Reginald Simms. It seems Imperlino and Simms went to school together. Bowdoin."

Piers turned his swivel chair slightly and stared out at the ocean, which had gone pewter gray under the overcast. "And suddenly Wu and Durant just happen to turn up in Malibu and we just happen to meet on the beach, Wu and I."

"They worked it pretty slick, didn't they?"

"Yes, very slick. Are they connected with the CIA now— or anybody else?"

"The Senator says they're not. Swears they're not, in fact."

"Well."

"What're you going to do?"

Still staring at the ocean, Piers said, "Do? I'm going to let them find Silk, that's what I'm going to do."

At seven-thirty that morning Solly Gesini arrived at the asphalt-covered parking lot across the street from the Sandpiper Apartments and bought four spaces for his Oldsmobile 98 from the surly attendant, parking it himself. The spaces that he bought gave him a clear view of the apartment building's entrance and almost instant access to the lot's exit.

Next to him on the Oldsmobile's front seat was a stack of country-Western tapes. He chose one and shoved it into the tape deck. Gesini liked country-Western music, mostly because he could understand the words, which usually told a story, and that too he liked.

Next to the tapes on the seat was an almost frozen six-pack of Tab. The Tab was for his weight, and the five packets of M & M chocolates next to the Tab were for his hunger. Gesini felt that they sort of balanced things out. He popped open a can of Tab and held it between his knees while he tore open one of the M & M packets and tossed a handful into his mouth, letting them melt a bit before he washed them down with a swallow of the cola.

Gesini then settled back in the seat, his eyes fixed on the apartment entrance, his soul soothed by the country-Western music, his inner needs satisfied by the diet cola drink and the candy-coated chocolates, and his mind pleasantly engaged by the interesting task that lay ahead, which was the murder of Eddie McBride.

Across the street and up on the twelfth floor in apartment 1229, Eddie McBride was sprawled half dressed in an easy chair in the living room. He had a cup of instant coffee in one hand and a Camel in the other as he listened with no little interest to Otherguy Overby's lecture on the proper dress, appearance, and grooming of the successful mountebank.

Overby stood in the center of the living room dressed in jockey shorts, shoes, a white shirt, dark tie, and no pants. He held a suit up by a hanger, as though offering it for McBride's inspection and possible purchase.

"Now, look what I got on, kid. A white shirt, custom made, with no breast pocket and never, never any fucking initials where the pocket's supposed to be. You wear initials, it means you're not sure who you are and that you gotta have something to remind you—and probably everybody else. Now the tie. Whaddya think about the tie?"

McBride shrugged. "It's dark, not much color."

Overby shook his head. "It's ugly. That's the important thing. Ugly, but expensive. What you gotta do is find the ugliest, most expensive tie you can, like this one, which cost me sixty-five bucks. But somebody else sees me wearing it and they think, 'Hey, there goes a guy who can afford expensive bad taste.' Not flash, kid, but expensive, conservative bad taste. There's a hell of a difference."

"Yeah, I think I know what you're saying," McBride said, and sipped his coffee, not taking his eyes off Overby.

"Now the shoes and socks—what about them?"

McBride shrugged again. "Black shoes, black socks, the high ones that come up almost to your knees."

"Okay, first the socks. You sit down and cross your knees and you're wearing short socks and you show a little patch of white, hairy leg and lemme tell you something, there's nothing nastier looking. I mean nasty. The way it affects some people it'd be better if you took your cock out and waved it around. I don't know why, but that little white, pasty patch of hairy leg—unless you got just one hell of a tan—looks *diseased* to most people. So whatever you're talking about, they're not gonna be listening. Instead, they're gonna be thinking about that horrible disease on your leg. Okay?"

"Sure," McBride said. "Okay."

"All right, now the shoes. Guess how much they cost?"

McBride looked at them. They were ordinary-looking black low-cut shoes with capped toes—the kind once referred to as Oxfords. McBride decided to go high on his estimate. "Eighty-five bucks," he said.

Overby shook his head, pleased by his pupil's low guess. "Two hundred and forty-eight dollars," Overby said.

"For them?" McBride didn't believe it.

"Handmade by a little old English guy in Hong Kong. He must be close to a hundred now and he makes 'em just like they did thirty, forty, even fifty years ago. Now what else about 'em, except that they're kinda ugly?"

"They don't shine much."

"They're not supposed to. They sort of glow, but they don't shine. The only place shoes are supposed to shine, kid, is in the Marine Corps, although sometimes I like a good spit shine on my loafers. And that's the other thing—these aren't loafers. They lace up. Loafers, and boots that zip up, and shoes that buckle, and pimp flash shoes with five-inch heels—well, they indicate a weak moral fiber."

"A what?"

"A weak moral fiber," Overby said very seriously. "I

mean, if you're too lazy to lace up your shoes, there's gotta be something wrong with you."

"Jesus, Otherguy, I feel I oughta be writing all of this down."

If it was sarcasm, Overby chose to ignore it. Instead, he put on the dark blue suit that he had held up throughout his lecture. The suit had some very faint gray stripes, and when Overby had it on and its vest buttoned—except for the final button, of course—he looked very much like a smart, hard, tough, prosperous banker from a medium-sized city—which was exactly what he wanted to look like.

"Well, whaddya think, kid?" he said.

McBride examined him carefully. "The suit," he said finally. "It don't fit."

"One size too large," Overby said. "Like maybe I had the guts and determination to take a little weight off and keep it off, right?"

"Yeah, maybe."

"So what does that tell you about me?"

McBride nodded slowly. "Yeah, I see, like maybe you're the kind of guy who does what he sets out to do."

"Exactly. One size too large. Remember that."

"What about out there?" McBride said, unconsciously imitating Overby's westward nod that embraced the entire Pacific. "Is this the way you do it out there too?"

"Not exactly, kid. I'll have to show you when we get there. But out there," he said, his voice almost dreamy, "well, out there it's kind of different."

As Artie Wu was getting dressed that morning in his bedroom in the house on Ninth Street in Santa Monica, his wife had summoned his children to observe and learn.

"Watch Daddy, darlin's. He's puttin' on his gittin'-outa-here-and-gittin'-us-some-money suit." Agnes Wu had expertly copied both the voice and the admonition from the wife of an Anadarko, Oklahoma, tool pusher whom she had known in Aberdeen.

It was a resplendent outfit that was intended to be noticed, and Solly Gesini noticed it immediately and the man it clothed as soon as Artie Wu climbed out of Durant's Mercedes coupé.

Jesus, Gesini thought, it's gotta be the Chinaman. And the other guy, the skinny one, must be Durant.

The cream-colored raw-silk suit and its double-breasted vest with black silk piping fitted Wu to perfection. Stretched across the enormous mound of stomach, made even more pronounced by the vest, was a heavy gold watch chain. Wu's glistening white shirt had been hand tailored in Singapore out of handkerchief linen with a high, rounded, almost Hoover-like collar. His tie was severely narrow and no-nonsense black. Dash, if that, indeed, were needed, was supplied by the black-banded Panama hat with the enormous brim turned down all the way around.

"Hell, Artie," Durant had said when he picked Wu up that morning, "you forgot your ivory-handled fly whisk."

It was a little after nine when Wu and Durant got out of the Mercedes, which they had parked in a two-hour meter zone on Seashore Drive across from the Sandpiper Apartments.

As they jaywalked across the street, Wu glanced at the fat gold watch that he kept tucked away in a vest pocket. "We're going to miss Otherguy," he said.

"He doesn't need any last-minute advice."

"No," Wu agreed. "Not him."

"But McBride?"

Wu shrugged. "We'll see."

McBride, after his early-morning lecture by Overby, was visibly impressed by Wu's attire when he let the two men into apartment 1229. He studied it all for several moments, trying to decide who Wu was supposed to be. He had no trouble with Durant in his conservative lightweight glen plaid with the blue shirt and black knit tie. Durant was exactly what he seemed to be: smart, competent, and a little hard. Even, perhaps, a trifle ruthless. But Wu—well, Wu, McBride decided, was something else. So he gave up and asked.

"What the fuck are you supposed to be, Artie?"

Wu smiled and made his eyes become two curved sparkling slits. "Mysterious, knowledgeable, highly intelligent, and a bit eccentric. Mild eccentricity, by the way, inspires confidence."

"No shit?"

"No shit." He turned to Durant. "You want to call him?"

Durant glanced at his watch. "Okay." He went over to the phone, dialed a number, and asked for Chief Oscar Ploughman.

Lt. Marion Lake of Homicide watched as Ploughman let his private outside line ring twice. Then the police chief said, "This has gotta be them," picked up the phone at the end of the third ring, and said hello. When Durant asked for Chief Ploughman, the chief said, "You've got him."

"This is Durant. You said for us to call."

"I'm going to give you all I can," Ploughman said.

"All right."

"Breadstone Avenue. Somewhere in between the 2100 and 2300 blocks."

"That's all?" Durant said.

"That's all," Ploughman said, and hung up. Then he smiled a large, yellow smile and turned to Lt. Lake. "Let's give 'em until three o'clock."

"Then?"

"Then you get over there and find out for sure."

Lt. Lake nodded. "Who do you think I oughta be this time?"

Ploughman thought about it as he studied Lake for several moments. "A reporter," he said finally. "You do that pretty good."

When Durant hung up the phone he turned to Eddie McBride. "Okay, here's what we've got. She's somewhere in the 2100 to 2300 blocks on Breadstone Avenue. And that's all we've got. You know what to do?"

McBride nodded slowly. "I've been talking to Otherguy about it. He gave me a lot of ideas. I'll hit the bars and the stores and dry-cleaning shops and things like that and ask questions."

"And if you find her?" Wu said.

"I call you guys."

"Right. Now, we're going to be at a meeting between one and two-thirty probably. But we'll be back here after that."

McBride cleared his throat a little nervously. "How do I look?" he asked, his voice full of self-consciousness.

The two men inspected the well-cut jacket, the dark slacks, the tasseled loafers, and the gray oxford-cloth shirt with the slightly loosened foulard tie. Durant thought McBride looked about as believable as Steve McQueen would look playing a reporter, but he didn't say what he thought. Instead, he said what Eddie McBride wanted to hear: "You look like a reporter, Eddie. A smart one."

McBride looked at Wu for further confirmation. Wu nodded slowly, even judiciously. "Get me rewrite, sweetheart," Wu said.

"What the fuck's he talking about?" McBride asked Durant.

Durant smiled. "A very old play."

"You look great, Eddie," Wu said. "Just right."

As if in need of additional evidence, McBride opened the door of the living-room closet and examined himself in its full-length mirror, pulling the loosened tie down another careful half inch.

While McBride was inspecting himself in the mirror, Durant said, "When you and Simms—or Childester—were lifting the money in Saigon, did you help him make the actual switch?"

McBride shook his head, still examining himself in the mirror. "Nah, he had that part all done. What he needed me for was to take down the screens over the air-conditioning ducts. We had exactly two minutes the way he had it figured."

"But he had the money all switched and ready, right?"

"Yeah, why?"

"I was just curious how you worked it," Durant said.

McBride turned and looked at Durant for a moment, the younger man's skepticism obvious. But then a thought struck McBride. "Jesus," he said, "I almost forgot."

He turned and went into the kitchen. When he came back

he was carrying two packages of frozen vegetables. He handed Wu a package of Green Giant frozen peas, and Durant got the same brand of frozen broccoli.

"What's this?" Wu said.

McBride grinned. "Overby said you might have to warm 'em up a little—you know, like in a pan."

Wu ripped open the box of peas and took out a short-barreled .38 Colt revolver. Durant's box of broccoli contained the same thing.

"That's where the guy kept 'em," McBride said. "He had this little store over in North Hollywood and he kept them in the back in a refrigerator. He—"

"Eddie," Wu said.

"Yeah?"

"You'd better get going."

"Yeah, okay."

McBride examined himself for the last time in the full-length mirror and then went to the door, where he paused and looked back at Wu and Durant. "What do I do if I don't find her?"

"You'll find her," Durant said.

"Yeah," McBride said. "Sure." And left.

When the door closed, Durant looked at Wu. "What do you think?"

"About the purloined two million?"

Durant nodded.

"I think," Wu said slowly, "that it's all beginning to make just a little more sense."

"Just a little," Durant said.

When McBride came out of the Sandpiper Apartments that morning at 9:32, Solly Gesini was on his second can of Tab, having already polished off most of the M & Ms. When he saw McBride he turned down the country-Western music, as though the absence of sound would help him see better.

Gesini watched as McBride crossed the street and took an overparking ticket from under the windshield wiper of his 1965 Mustang convertible, the someday-soon classic that he had rescued from its abandonment in Venice. As he watched

McBride stuff the ticket away in a pocket, Gesini started the engine of his Oldsmobile.

McBride got into his car, started it, and pulled away from the curb. Gesini waited until another car came by and then shot the Oldsmobile out of the lot after the car of the man he was going to kill, with any luck at all, that very morning.

Chapter Thirty-two

Otherguy Overby sat patiently in the chrome-and-leather chair and watched the man who looked like a male model count the ten thousand dollars. Every time his count reached another thousand, Chuck West would look up at Overby and smile a little helplessly, as though to say that while he knew it was all there, he still had to make sure, and he was confident that Overby would understand and bear with him.

West was counting the money onto the top of his grimly contemporary desk in the sizable office that he held down for Reginald Simms, Inc., Consultants, on the fifteenth floor of the Ransom Tower. Overby thought that West was as grimly contemporary as his office, and he had already dismissed both as being second-rate Sunset Boulevard.

When he finished counting, West looked up at Overby and gave him his beautiful-person smile. "Right on the nose, Maurice."

"Maurice?" Overby said with a puzzled smile. "Did you call me Maurice? Not many people call me Maurice anymore."

"What do they call you, Maury?"

"They call me Mr. Overby," he said in a flat tone. "Sometimes for years."

Chuck West stared at Overby for a moment, and behind the beautiful hair and the beautiful tan and the beautiful teeth Overby caught a glimpse of something else that was not so beautiful, but instead quite ugly and just a little sinister.

"I'll call you anything you like, mister," West said. He picked up his phone and dialed two numbers. When the phone was answered he said, "Mr. Overby is here and we've just finalized his consultation fee." There was a pause and then West, "No . . . cash." After another pause, West said, "Yes, how very true."

After he hung up the phone, West didn't tell Overby what was very true. Instead, he rose and said, "I'll take you in to Mr. Simms now."

Overby liked the view that Reginald Simms had of the ocean, but that was about all he liked. He immediately marked Simms down as a smooth, smart bad-hat, which didn't bother him at all because Overby found smooth, smart bad-hats an interesting challenge. But anyone who would have a fire in his office in June must have a few soft spots that Overby decided might well be worth probing. Overby thought the fire a silly affectation.

After Chuck West made the introductions and left, Simms gestured Overby toward one of the high-backed leather chairs that flanked the fireplace.

"Do you like a fire even in June, Mr. Overby?" Simms said after waiting for Overby to sit down.

"They're comforting anytime," Overby lied, choosing his words carefully.

"You approached us first—let's see, when was it—two months ago?" Simms said, pouring coffee into two bone-china cups from a silver pot that rested on a table near his chair.

"About then," Overby said, accepting a cup.

"And you represent a small syndicate of investors?"

"It's not so small."

"I mean the number of investors, of course, not the amount of their proposed investment. A million dollars is still a very respectable sum."

"You're not exactly dragging your investors in off the

street by the arm," Overby said. "Not if you charge ten thousand dollars just to talk."

"Try to think of it as earnest money," Simms said. "It separates the idly curious from the totally serious. You are totally serious, aren't you, Mr. Overby?"

"I'll let the ten thousand dollars speak for itself. I didn't drop by just for the small talk."

Simms drank some of his coffee, produced his cigarette case, offered Overby one, and when Overby accepted it, lit it for him. After he had lit his own, Simms blew the smoke out, fanned it away before the air conditioning had a chance to get at it, and said, "You've been looking around our little town these last two months, I understand."

"That's right."

"And what have you discovered that's interesting?"

Overby decided to see how Simms would handle a hard, fast one, low and inside. "What I've discovered that's kind of interesting is that Vince Imperlino has a lock on this town and you've got the key to the lock."

Simms put his oval cigarette out carefully after having smoked no more than a quarter of an inch of it. He leaned back in his chair and made a steeple of his fingers and gazed thoughtfully over them at Overby. A small, nearly whimsical smile came and went from his almost chiseled lips.

"Otherguy Overby," Simms said, and shook his head in a small gesture of appreciation that was almost mocking, but not quite. "To use a phrase that I intensely dislike, almost a legend in your own time—at least"—and Simms gave his head a small nod toward the window—"' out there.'" From the tone, Overby realized that Simms was quoting him, even mocking him a little now. Overby smiled, but said nothing. It was getting interesting.

"We did some checking on you, of course," Simms said, examining the steeple that his fingers still formed.

Overby produced another small smile, but again said nothing. He too had long ago learned the many uses of silence.

"And your syndicate of 'investors,'" Simms went on with another small shake of the head. "Run Run Keng, Jane

Arden, Pancho Clarke, Gyp Lucas, et al." Simms sighed happily. "As merry a band of freebooters as one could hope to find anywhere." He paused and smiled again. "And, I should add, our kind of people."

"Yours and Imperlino's," Overby said.

"That's right. Mine and Mr. Imperlino's."

"So what're you and Imperlino selling that up until now has cost me ten thousand dollars for nothing more than a cup of coffee and a seat by the fire?"

Simms seemed to consider Overby's question quite seriously for several moments. "I suppose," he said thoughtfully, "what we're really offering is licenses to steal. Interested?"

"Very."

"What about hotels, Mr. Overby? Are you also interested in them?"

"I've lived in a lot of them."

"We're going to build in this town on ten acres of the finest beach property left in the world what may very well be the world's largest hotel. We're not quite sure about that because there may be one in Moscow that has a few more rooms. Do you know the Bayside Amusement Park?"

Overby nodded.

"That will be the site. We already have clearance from the Coastal Commission, we have the necessary environmental-impact studies completed and approved, and we, of course, have the necessary financing."

"So what's left, the hatcheck stand?" Overby said. "There's no money in that anymore. The linen service? The ladies? The booze?"

"All very small change, Mr. Overby. Very small indeed. Of course, you haven't quite thought it through. When one builds a hotel of five thousand rooms, one has to fill it with paying guests. So what do we have to offer? An excellent hotel with a fine beach, immaculate service, wonderful food, and Disneyland not much more than an hour away. But one can get all that in Miami Beach or a number of other places. No, what fills a hotel is conventions, Mr. Overby, people getting together once a year or so to trade information, elect new officers, find new jobs, get away from their wives or husbands, and also, perhaps most important of all, have a little excitement. And that, Mr. Overby, is what we intend to provide: excitement."

"What kind?"

Simms rose. "Let's go over to my desk and I'll show you something."

When they reached his spindly-legged desk, Simms opened a large leatherbound folder—about the size of those that commercial artists keep their samples in. The first page was a detailed map of the downtown section of Pelican Bay.

"Here we have the amusement park where the hotel will go up," Simms said, using his finger as a pointer. "And here, just across the street from it, we have this four-block area that's now largely made up of second-rate apartments, small, marginal businesses, and one-family homes, most of them deteriorating. With the city's official blessing and the enthusiastic backing of the local newspaper and the various civic groups, including the labor unions, we're going to raze that entire four-block area."

"And put up what?"

"Whatever people dream about in their wildest fantasies."

"You mean a whorehouse that's four blocks square?"

"Not all fantasies are sexual, Mr. Overby, although we will, of course, provide sex in all of its many delightful forms. But what we're really going to provide is sin without sorrow and thrills without danger. Good, wholesome licentiousness, one might say, with no regrets."

Overby thought about it for a moment. Finally he said, "Either you are or you aren't. You can't have it both ways. Either it's going to be real or it's going to be a gyp."

"A good point. An excellent point, in fact. But take a look, Mr. Overby, and then decide."

Simms turned another page in the folder. It was a street scene done in skillful watercolors, and Overby somehow knew that if he went down that street with its small sidewalk cafés, its intriguing-looking doorways, its cobbled pavements, he would find all sorts of stimulating, possibly erotic things to do and see. He lifted his eyes from the rendering and stared at Simms for a moment, thinking, The fucker's not all flash after all.

Simms turned another page. This time the scene was again vaguely European, but more tawdry, more decadent. "Berlin in the '30s," Simms said. "The first one was Paris in the '20s, the Pigalle section—idealized, of course. You can go from Paris to Berlin"—Simms started turning more pages—"to Singapore to Hong Kong to Marseille to London's Limehouse to San Francisco to New Orleans to New York to wherever you have ever dreamed of going. It will all be within this four-block-square area, and whatever you have dreamed of finding in those places you will find here —carefully sterilized for safe consumption."

"Gambling?" Overby said.

"Our one problem. Gambling is against state law except for draw poker, which California, with its usual omniscience, has recognized as a game of skill, not chance. But real gambling will come to California, sooner probably than any of us think. The voters will decide that they'd rather have legalized gambling than confiscatory property taxes. It's wonderful, don't you think, how flexible one's lifelong convictions usually are?"

"Sure," Overby said. "Wonderful. But what's still bothering me, is there going to be any action or not?"

"Action?" Simms said, as if he liked both the sound and the taste of the word. "You will see things that you have only heard whispered rumors of before—not you, of course, Mr. Overby, but the average person. Let your imagination run rampant; it will all be there."

Overby bored in again. "Can I get laid, for example?"

"Laid? Laid. If during your wanderings down these delightful streets you spy a young woman who strikes your fancy, you need only whisper to her the number of your hotel room. And she will whisper back the time. And then, at that exact time, she will appear as if by magic in the comfortable surroundings of your room—perhaps accompanied by a friend, if you should so desire. Yes, Mr. Overby, you can indeed get laid."

"What about the law?"

"The law, Mr. Overby, will be present to protect the customer. Nobody will get rolled, nobody will get mugged, nobody will have his pockets picked or his body harmed—except, of course, through his own self-indulgence. The policemen on duty will, in fact, cheerfully steer the adventurous into even more intriguing pursuits."

"Dope?"

"Perhaps an opium den or two—the height of wickedness, don't you think?"

"Real opium?"

"Who's to say—as long as the beautiful young Chinese girls prepare the pipes?"

"Has it got a name?"

"A working one, because not all of us are delighted with it. We're tentatively calling it The Barbary Coast."

"Okay, you're offering four square blocks of broads, booze, gambling—sort of, anyway—food, a little action probably, maybe a three-way exhibition with a donkey or something like that; but it still doesn't sound much better to me than Havana in the '40s and '50s. In fact, it sounds like a shuck."

"It *is* a shuck, Mr. Overby. A safe, antiseptic, quite expensive, carefully immoral shuck that the average person will remember for the rest of his days because he will have convinced himself that he alone of all his fellow conventioneers actually experienced the real thing. The Japanese will go absolutely crackers over it."

Overby nodded thoughtfully. "What it really is is sort of a dirty Disneyland, right?"

"Excellent, Mr. Overby, excellent. A dirty Disneyland for people with normally dirty, normally twisted minds. You see, in many cities they have set aside certain sections for legalized vice. Amsterdam comes to mind. The Reeperbahn in Hamburg. The Combat Zone in Boston, which was a recent, rather unsuccessful experiment that made the mistake of trying to offer the real thing. People don't want the real thing, Mr. Overby, because the real thing has bad breath, and smelly armpits, and sometimes steals your wallet and makes you hurt when you pee. What people want is vice and sin that look the way that they look in the movies—and that's exactly what we intend to give them. I would not be at all surprised if many a budding movie star will receive his or her first big break at The Barbary Coast."

"How many people?"

"On the payroll?"

Overby nodded.

"Approximately five thousand, we believe, including the hotel staff, all organized by the same union whose pension fund, incidentally, is providing much of the capital."

"The Teamsters?"

Simms only smiled.

"What will my million dollars buy me?"

"In."

"How far in?"

"A cabaret perhaps. Half of a poker parlor even."

"What would the return be?"

"Fifteen percent the first year. Between nineteen and twenty-one after that."

"Guaranteed?"

"Not quite."

"But you've worked these figures out pretty carefully?"

Simms made a gesture that indicated that they should resume their chairs before the fire. As they sat down, Simms said, "This is not someone's sudden bright idea. It's been on the boards for almost ten years. Teams of psychologists, cost accountants, designers—some of them from Disneyland, by the way—gaming experts, crowd-flow specialists, and even one rather well-known writer with a particularly salacious imagination have all been working on it for nearly a decade. We had to find the right town in just exactly the right stage of development—or perhaps I should say decline. Pelican Bay is ideal."

"What about the Feds?"

"What about them?"

"Aren't they interested?"

"No reason why they should be as long as the proper taxes are paid. We are not involved in interstate commerce; our business will cross no state lines."

"When do you start operations?"

"The groundbreaking on the hotel will begin in approximately six months. Construction of The Barbary Coast—do you like the name?"

"Not much."

"Well, it will begin at about the same time."

"When would I have to say yes or no?"

"I'll give you some figures to look over—some projections. Then you will have one month."

"That's not much time."

Simms rose, signaling an end to the interview. "No, it isn't. But there are many applicants who want to get in on what will be a very profitable ground floor. We have to decide which ones to select."

Overby was also up now and noticed that he was being very politely steered toward the door. "I should add, I suppose, Mr. Overby, that this is only a pilot project. A billion-dollar pilot project."

"You mean there're going to be more of them?"

Simms smiled agreeably. "All over," he said. "All over these United States—wherever we can find a suitable city. And I must say, there are additional candidates every day."

"But you're starting here?"

"In Southern California, you mean?"

Overby nodded.

"Doesn't everything start here?" Simms said.

Chapter Thirty-three

Otherguy Overby had drawn a rough map of Pelican Bay's downtown section, which he had used to show Wu and Durant where the enormous hotel and what he called "the dirty Disneyland" would be erected.

"And all this goes, too," Overby said, indicating another large chunk of Pelican Bay's blighted commercial district. "They're gonna turn practically the whole fucking downtown into one big parking lot. But that's not all."

"What else?" Durant said.

"Jobs. How many working stiffs would you say there are in Pelican Bay?"

Wu thought about it. "Maybe fifty or sixty thousand."

"And suppose you created maybe five thousand new jobs with the absolute power to hire and fire. Translate them into votes and political clout and it means somebody's gonna have Pelican Bay in their hip pocket."

"The Ploughman Machine," Durant said softly, and smiled to himself.

"The what?"

"Just somebody's dream," Durant said.

Overby tossed aside the pencil he had been using as a pointer for the rough map he had drawn and leaned back on the couch. Since his return to his apartment it had taken nearly an hour for him to describe the meeting with Simms. It had taken that long because he had left nothing out and he had quoted Simms verbatim most of the time, even down to Simms' shrugs and steepled fingers and half-whimsical smiles.

"So," Durant said, still looking at the map on the coffee table, "what it adds up to is a billion-dollar pilot project for sanitized licentiousness." He looked at Wu and frowned slightly. "What the hell's wrong with that?"

"Not enough," Artie Wu said.

Durant nodded slowly. "Not nearly enough."

While Otherguy Overby was describing the curious fate that awaited Pelican Bay, fifty-one-year-old Herb Conroy, the reporter who would be lunching at the Woodbury Club that afternoon, was throwing up his breakfast into the kitchen sink under the watchful, sympathetic gaze of his sixty-three-year-old mother-in-law, Netta Gambling, who over the years had by default become Conroy's favorite drinking buddy.

Conroy's breakfast that morning had consisted of a large, warm glass of Manischewitz Concord-grape wine, which was about the only thing that would stay down long enough to soothe the uncontrollable shakes that Conroy woke up to nearly every morning.

"You don't look so good, Herb," Netta Gambling said, and took another swallow of her breakfast beer, her second can of the morning.

Conroy turned from the sink. Tears caused by the vomiting streamed down his puffy cheeks. He wiped them away with a hand that shook. "How bad?"

Netta studied him judiciously. "Well, not as bad as last Saturday. Last Saturday was kinda bad, if you remember."

Conroy took a deep breath. He was a thin man, medium tall, who would have been wiry except that he long ago had lost all muscle tone. His face was pasty and splotched with gray, except for the tip of his nose and two round spots high up on his cheekbones where years before the capillaries had burst into rosy bloom. The shape of his nose was ordinary, and his mouth was gray and almost thin, and his chin was virtually without character of any kind.

"Well," Netta said, "this is gonna be your big day, huh? You took the day off from work and everything."

"Yeah. You know who Randall Piers is?"

"You told me last night. Maybe fifty-eleven times."

"Well, this is the one, the real fat chance, Netta. It's almost as good as that time I could've gone with the *Daily News* in Chicago, except you wouldn't leave this horseshit town."

"You could've gone without me; I didn't hold you back."

"Yeah, but Doris wouldn't go without you."

"You should've left her. Of course, I don't know what you'd've left her for, because after that lunch you had with that guy from Chicago suddenly there wasn't no job offer anymore. You got pissed. You're not gonna do that this time, are you?"

Conroy took a swallow of his first vodka of the day. "Not this time. No way. This time I'm just going to coast. You know, just enough to keep the edge off."

"Yeah, sure," Netta said. "What're you gonna wear?"

"My blue suit?"

Netta nodded. "Yeah, you always look nice in that."

Eddie McBride started his search for Silk Armitage on the wrong end of the three blocks on Breadstone Avenue. If he had started at the other end, near the Tex-Mex Bar & Grill, things might have turned out differently. But perhaps not, because Eddie McBride never did have much luck.

Once he established his pattern of operation, McBride soon learned to his surprise that people were more than willing to talk to him about almost everything, but particularly about themselves. Even though he told them that he was from *The Washington Post* and looking only for Silk Armitage, nobody had seemed much interested in that, and none had seen her around anyway. What they really wanted to talk about, however, was the world they lived in, a world that, McBride soon found, was made up largely of sickness, divorce, apprehension, unpaid bills, shattered ambition, suspicion, resentment, quite a lot of hate, and not much hope.

So far that morning McBride had been in nine bars, two liquor stores, four gas stations, a Seven-Eleven, three beauty parlors, two dry cleaners, a laundromat, three cafés, a pet shop, a five-and-dime, and two drugstores, and he was about to enter a small Italian bakery called Angeletti's.

From his car, parked about one hundred feet up the block and across the street, Solly Gesini watched McBride enter the bakery. Gesini had quickly figured out that McBride was looking for something or somebody, but he hadn't been able to fathom what or whom.

Gesini noted the Italian name of the bakery, and it decided his course of action. After McBride left, he would go in and try to find out what the hell McBride was up to. If he couldn't, well, he could use some cookies, maybe some of those kind with the walnuts and the chocolate frosting. The M & Ms were long gone, and Gesini was hungry again as well as curious.

Angeletti himself was behind the counter in the bakery when McBride entered. The proprietor was a short, tubby man with sad eyes who looked as if his feet might hurt and as if he might be fond of opera. He had one playing not too softly in the background: Verdi's *Rigoletto*, the first act.

Angeletti was waiting on a customer, so McBride inspected the glass cases of pastry and bread, which didn't interest him much because he wasn't fond of sweets. Angeletti went to the cash register to make change, but paused and cocked an ear as the tenor tried for a high one. When he made it, as he always did, Angeletti nevertheless smiled with relief and punched the cash-register key.

When the customer had gone, McBride moved over to the cash register.

"You like opera?" Angeletti said.

"I don't know. I never listened much."

"Listen to that."

The tenor was at it again, reaching for yet another high one, and when he caught it neatly, Angeletti smiled and said, "Something, isn't it?"

"It's pretty," McBride said.

"So what can I sell you nice?"

"Actually, I'm not buying, I'm looking for somebody."

"Oh? You a cop?"

"No, my name's Tony Max and I'm a reporter with *The*

Washington Post." McBride brought out his fake press card and showed it to Angeletti, who glanced at it and handed it back.

"No kidding—Washington, huh? Who the hell you looking for in this crummy neighborhood?"

"Silk Armitage."

"The singer?"

"The singer. Have you seen her around here?"

"You mean the singer who made all those records with her sisters, what was their names—Ivory and Lace? Yeah, Ivory and Lace. And *she's* living around here? Huh."

"We got a tip that she might be."

"What'd she be living around here for?"

"That's what I'd like to find out."

"With her money, she can live someplace nice. Beverly Hills. She in trouble?"

"I don't know, but she's dropped out of sight. We'd like to find out why."

Angeletti settled himself down on the counter on his elbows. He again cocked his head as if listening to the recorded opera. "You know something, I remember the first time I heard them sing, those girls. It was back in what, the early '60s? Yeah, about then. On the Sullivan show, Sunday night. I turned to my wife and said, 'That little one'—Silk was the little one, you know—well, I said, 'that little one can *sing*.' And by that, I meant she could sing this." He straightened up and jerked his thumb at the speaker. "Of course, she would've had to've had a whole lotta training, you understand. I mean, you don't start singing opera without a whole lotta training. But she had the—the quality, you understand?"

"But you haven't seen her?" McBride said.

"No, but you wanta know something? My wife died of cancer six months to the day after we heard her sing. I started to get married again about four years ago, but then I thought, 'What the hell you wanta go and get married for? At your age, who needs it?' I'm sixty-four."

"You don't look it."

"Well, I feel it. Standing up all the time is what gets you.

I been standing up since I was fourteen years old. I tried to get my two kids interested in coming in with me, but hell, you think they wanta work? One of 'em turned out to be a drummer. What kind of musician is that, now, I ask you? A drummer." Angeletti shook his head in sorrow for the lost son.

"Well, thanks for your help anyway," McBride said.

"Sure," the baker said.

Less than two minutes after McBride left, Gesini entered the store and bought a dozen cookies, the kind with the chocolate icing and walnuts. As he paid for his purchase he said, "You know, that young guy that was just in here, he looks familiar."

"You from Washington?" Angeletti said.

"Nah, I'm from around here."

"Well, he's from Washington. He's a reporter for *The Washington Post* and he's looking for somebody."

"Who?"

"Silk Armitage. You know who she is, don't you?"

"Sure, the singer."

"Yeah, well, he says she's supposed to be living around here someplace."

"Around *here?*"

"That's what *I* said. You know, you don't sound like you're from around here."

"What do you mean, I don't sound like I am?" Gesini said.

"You know, you sound like the way I do, like you're from New York. You from New York—I mean, originally?"

"Yeah, New York, originally."

"Me too, originally," Angeletti said. Then a thought struck him. "I wonder if they got many Italians in Washington?"

Solly Gesini said that he didn't know.

Chapter Thirty-four

The Woodbury Club was just off Camden Drive on Little Santa Monica in Beverly Hills, and it looked like a bank, which was exactly what it once had been. When Franklin D. Roosevelt declared the bank holiday in 1933, the Liberty Bank and Trust Company had been one of those that never reopened, the victim of some poor loans it had made on a lot of land that nobody then wanted out in a place called Westwood.

The bank building had been bought cheaply by a group of wealthy men who founded the club because they wanted somewhere convenient and pleasant to go where they wouldn't be bothered by picture people, which could be decoded into Jews. So the Woodbury Club became an Aryan haven and didn't admit its first Jew until 1951. It still had no picture people as members, because it was felt that some standards simply had to be maintained. No one was now quite sure how the club had got its name, but most were content with the story that the founding members couldn't agree on a name until one crusty old party went to the bathroom, washed his hands with a cake of Woodbury soap, came back to the meeting, and rammed the name through.

Durant and Wu arrived at the club at a little before one o'clock. There was no sign on the two-story granite building, only the street number and a small plaque that read PRIVATE. But if you looked very closely, you could still just barely make out the faint LIBERTY BANK & TRUST CO. above the entrance although it had been sandblasted away in 1933.

Inside the club there were a lot of old walnut paneling, thick carpet, leather furniture, and the hushed atmosphere of wise investments soundly made. Randall Piers, wearing a neat gray suit and tie, met Wu and Durant in the reception area, where they signed the guest book.

Artie Wu then asked for directions to the men's room, partly because he had to go and partly because he wanted to see what it looked like, since Aggie Wu always demanded all the details whenever he went someplace interesting.

Piers drew Durant to one side, out of earshot of an old gentleman who kept glancing at his watch impatiently and then ducking his head back into a copy of *The Wall Street Journal*.

"I've got a question," Piers said.

"About the other night?"

Piers shook his head. "That's past and forgotten—all right?"

"Fine. What's your question?"

"Who are you, Durant, you and Wu?"

Durant took a moment before answering. "We're pretty much what you see."

"The pretty much is what bothers me."

"Let me put it this way," Durant said. "We're going to get your sister-in-law back and then get whoever's on her neck off of it. Permanently. She won't have to hide anymore."

"Silk was the key all along, wasn't she?"

Durant nodded.

"Imperlino's also involved somehow, right?"

"Up to his neck."

"And this guy Simms—the one they used to call the Dirty Duke?"

Durant smiled a little. "You've been busy."

"When you get roped as slickly as I got roped, you like to know who did it and why."

Durant nodded in mild approval. "Artie said you'd make us in five days. I said four. It's four and a half, so we were both right."

"How big is it?"

"We're not quite sure, because some of it doesn't make any sense yet. But it could be pretty big."

"You mean a national mess?"

"Maybe." Durant took out a Pall Mall and lit it. "Your sister-in-law probably has a big piece of it. This reporter who's coming to lunch may have another, smaller piece, and Artie and I, we may have the key piece. If you're still willing to play along, then when you get your sister-in-law back she can tell you all about it. If she wants to."

Because he had a brilliant mind and liked to use it, it took less than a second for Randall Piers to make it up. "Okay," he said. "I'll play."

"Good."

"This reporter—you want me to dazzle him, right?"

"Right," Durant said. "Would you like me to hum a few bars?"

Piers smiled for the first time. "No," he said, "I think I've played it before."

Shortly after Wu returned from the men's room, Otherguy Overby arrived with the guest of honor, Herb Conroy, who was wearing his good blue suit and a mild vodka glow.

Piers bored in on Overby. "Maurice," he said warmly to the man whom he'd never seen before in his life. Otherguy Overby was up for it.

"Randy, it's good to see you."

They shook hands the way men do who genuinely like each other but who meet all too infrequently. Piers swung around to Conroy. "And this must be Mr. Conroy, whom you've been telling me about." Piers gripped Conroy's hand and studied him for a moment. "I've been hearing a lot of excellent things about you, Mr. Conroy. Really remarkable things."

"Well, thank you," Conroy said, and allowed himself to be turned by Piers toward Wu and Durant.

"These are two of my closest advisers, Dr. Wu and Mr. Durant. Gentlemen, Mr. Conroy—do you mind if I call you Herb?"

"Not at all."

"And I'm Randy, of course," Piers said as Conroy shook hands with Wu and Durant.

After the introductions were completed they filed into a small private dining room that Piers had engaged for the occasion, along with a small bar and a carefully instructed bartender. Still playing the expansive host, Piers suggested double vodka martinis all around. When those were drunk to the accompaniment of some highly flattering small talk aimed dead on at Herb Conroy, Piers insisted on another round of doubles, and by the time Conroy sat down at the table for lunch he was quite pleasantly in the bag, which was exactly where Wu and Durant wanted him.

When Conroy ordered a shrimp cocktail, a filet steak with Béarnaise sauce, a baked potato, and a salad for lunch, everybody flattered him further by ordering the same thing. Durant, however, said he would like some wine with the meal and ordered that and also another martini, but this time a single. Herb Conroy, his voice beginning to slur just a little, said he thought another single might be just the ticket.

"You know my magazine, *The Pacific*, don't you, Herb?" Piers said.

"Yeah, I've read it."

"What do you think of it? Be honest, now."

"I think it's pretty fucking dull," Conroy said, and polished off the last of his second double martini.

"We're thinking of making some changes, some rather drastic ones. We want to turn it into a hard-hitting, no-holds-barred kind of thing. Would you be interested in taking charge?"

"I could do a job on it," Conroy said. "A real job. The only thing you've got in it now is who's ruining the redwoods and where to eat and who's screwing who in Hollywood."

"You'd need a pretty big story for the first new issue," Overby said.

"There're plenty of big stories lying around that nobody's got guts enough to print," Conroy said. "Plenty of them."

"Pelican Bay, for example?" Durant said.

"Yeah, for example."

"We understand that there're going to be certain, interesting changes made down there—economic changes," Dr. Wu said in a rather academic tone.

"You don't understand half of it, Professor. Not half."

"Why haven't some other newspapers or magazines sent in some reporters yet?" Durant said. "The L.A. *Times,* for example."

"Why? You wanta know why?"

"Yes. Why."

"Because they don't know how far back it goes."

"And how far back does it go?" Wu said.

"Back to '53, that's how far back. They haven't connected now with back then, the way I have." Conroy tried some of his fresh martini, the single. Then he tapped a forefinger significantly against his temple. "I've got it all up here—names, dates, the lot. And I've got files, too—confidential files that could blow it all out of the water."

"I've been thinking in the neighborhood of fifty thousand dollars a year for the new managing editor," Piers said. "Does that seem adequate to you, Herb?—with an expense account, of course, and a few other perks. It's not a firm offer yet, of course, but I'd like to know if that's in your ball park."

Conroy thought about it. Finally, he nodded judiciously. "Yeah, fifty'd be about right." He was making $16,345 that year.

"Suppose for the first issue you were going to do a story on, say, Pelican Bay," Durant said. "Where would you start?"

Conroy finished his martini first. Then he held up the glass and looked at Piers. "You think I might have another one of these, Randy?"

"Certainly," Piers said, and signaled the bartender, who quickly brought a fresh drink over.

"So you wanta know where I'd start, huh?" Conroy said. "Well, I'll tell you where I'd start. I'd start back at Bowdoin in '53, that's where, because that's when a couple of roommates were voted 'most brilliant' and 'most likely to succeed.' And you wanta know who those two guys were?"

"Who?" said Durant to keep it going.

"Vince Imperlino and a guy called Reginald Simms, who you probably never heard of. But you know who Imperlino is, right? At least *you* oughta know," he said to Piers.

"I know."

"Well, they got out of college, right? And Imperlino goes into the family business, which I don't have to spell out for you, and this guy Simms goes into the CIA. And by '61 they've both gone up in the ranks. So some CIA biggie about that time gets the bright idea that maybe somebody oughta slip something into Castro's toothpaste—curare, maybe—who the fuck knows? Well, it's just one hell of an idea, but who's gonna do it? So the really heavy thinkers at the CIA decide to turn it over to some people who lost a lot when Castro took over, and that's the mob, naturally. Well, now, who in the CIA is buddy-buddy with somebody in the mob? Simms, of course. Hell, he roomed with one of them. So Simms is told to get in touch with his old roomie, and Imperlino gets in touch with two other, older guys, real mob heavies by the name of Sam Consentino and Johnny Francini—you heard of 'em?"

"They're dead," Durant said. "Both of them."

"Yeah, that's sort of interesting too," Conroy said, "but I'll get to that in a minute."

Artie Wu wasn't at all sure that Conroy was going to last that long. The reporter's voice was thick now and his eyes were wearing a bright glaze. But still he went on talking. And drinking.

"Well, the word is that Consentino and Francini tried three or four times, maybe even more, to snuff out Fidel, except it didn't work out. But the Feds were so grateful anyway that they let both of them off the hook on a couple of tax matters that could've put 'em away in Atlanta for ten, maybe even fifteen years."

"Mr. Conroy?" Wu said.

"Yeah?"

"I think I read most of this in the *National Enquirer* last week. Or maybe last year."

"What you're saying is that it's not anything new, is that right, Professor?"

"Close, Mr. Conroy. Very close."

"Well, lemme try this one on you. What would you say if I were to tell you that I've got incontruov—incontriv—that

I've got solid evidence that would place Consentino and Francini in Dallas the same week that Kennedy got killed? What would you say to that, Professor?"

"I would, I think, ask how you happened to come by it."

Conroy nodded wisely and then leaned over and wiggled a finger under Wu's nose. "I've got certain sources, Professor. But they gotta be protected. You always protect your sources."

Otherguy Overby, who always liked to get to the heart of any matter, said, "Are you saying these two guys killed Kennedy?"

This time Conroy looked arch, then crafty. "I'm not saying anything. I haven't heard any firm offers around here yet, so I'm not saying whether they did or not."

It was time for Piers to go into his buck-and-wing again, and he came on smoothly. "You know, Herb, in a town this size the man who holds down the job we've been talking about would be spending a lot of time in his car. Unproductive time. I've been thinking that perhaps a limousine with a driver and a phone and tape recorder would be a wise investment—from an efficiency viewpoint, of course. Even perhaps a small bar so the poor guy could relax once in a while. What do you think?"

"Yeah, that doesn't sound too bad."

"But I'm interrupting you," Piers said. "Why don't you continue?"

"I'm gonna jump ahead a little bit," Conroy said. "After Dallas, well, Consentino and Francini couldn't do anything wrong—not as far as the Feds were concerned. Consentino operated out of Chicago and Francini out of Miami, and they got rich and they got older. In the meantime, Imperlino's moving up out here on the Coast. Then Watergate happened and all bets were off."

"What do you mean?" Durant said.

Before Conroy could answer, the waiter started serving the shrimp cocktails. Conroy stared fixedly at his, convinced that one of the shrimp was still alive and wiggling. He picked it up with his fingers and bit it in two. He thought he could still feel it wiggling in his mouth, so he chewed it up and swallowed it. Any appetite he might have had deserted him.

"What do you mean about Watergate?" Durant said.

"I mean that the kid gloves came off. That Consentino and Francini were suddenly the focal point of a whole lot of interesting speculation. You see, almost ten years had gone by since Dallas. The people they'd been tight with in government, well, those people, some of them anyway, had died. Or retired. Or got fired. Instead of being sacred cows, Consentino and Francini had become just so much raw meat. So there they were, almost sixty then and looking forward to retirement, and all of a sudden they've got new tax problems, bad ones, and a Senate committee is breathing down their necks. So they decided to take immunity and talk."

"But they didn't," Wu said.

"No, Professor, they didn't. Before they could, Consentino gets shot in his basement in Chicago and Francini winds up in a fifty-gallon oil drum off Miami Beach."

"And Imperlino?" Durant said.

"Well, Imperlino was having his own internal problems out here. But after Consentino and Francini aren't around anymore, Imperlino all of a sudden gets anything he wants —including Pelican Bay. They handed it to him on a platter."

"Who?" Wu said.

Before Conroy could reply, the waiter took away the shrimp cocktails, which nobody had seemed to want except Otherguy Overby, and started serving the steaks and the rest of the meal. Conroy eyes his steak with near revulsion. Overby watched him carefully. Five minutes, Overby told himself. He's gonna last about five minutes more. Conroy looked around and focused finally on Piers. "Hey, Randy, you think maybe I might have another small one?"

"Sure," Piers said, and signaled for another martini, which was brought almost instantaneously.

"Who gave Imperlino Pelican Bay?" Durant said.

"On a silver platter," Conroy said, and swallowed some of his drink. "That's how they gave it to him."

"Who?" Durant said again.

Conroy was having trouble staying upright. He weaved a little in his chair. He peered through his alcoholic fog at Durant. "So guess who he brought in to help him divvy up the pie in Pelican Bay? His old college roomie, that's who, Reginald Simms, and nobody knows that except me and now maybe you guys." He turned to Piers. "You ever think of getting a Learjet for your magazine? Might be a good idea."

"Who gave him Pelican Bay?" Piers said.

"I'll tell you who knew the answer to that and a lot of other questions. I'll tell you who knew the whole fucking story, even more'n I do. Congressman Ranshaw, that's who, but the fuckers killed him." Conroy stared down at his steak and the glistening Béarnaise sauce. It looked warm and comfortable.

"Who gave Imperlino Pelican Bay, Herb?" Artie Wu said in a gentle, almost coaxing voice.

Conroy looked at Wu and smiled and then closed his eyes and lowered his head onto the steak and the warm Béarnaise sauce and went to sleep.

Piers looked at Wu and Durant. "Well?"

Durant shook his head thoughtfully. "I think he told us everything he knew."

"Did he have the piece that you were looking for?"

"Dallas," Durant said. "We didn't know about Dallas."

"That doesn't make any sense," Piers said.

"Maybe it will when we talk to your sister-in-law," Artie Wu said.

The cab driver shook Herb Conroy awake.

Conroy sat up and looked around. He knew he was going to be sick. So did the cab driver. "Where am I?" Conroy said.

"This where you live, Jack?" the driver said.

Conroy looked. Yes, this was where he lived. He tried to remember what had happened, but then decided that he didn't want to remember. Not just yet.

"How much do I owe you?" he asked the driver.

"It's all paid for, fella; just get out of the cab before you

barf all over it. Here." He handed Conroy an envelope.
"They said for me to give you this."

Conroy took the envelope and got out of the cab. He
started toward the front door, wondering if he would make it
before he got sick all over everything. He tore open the
envelope. In it were five one-hundred-dollar bills and a card
that read, *Too bad, but thanks anyway. Overby.*

Chapter Thirty-five

It was two o'clock that Monday afternoon when Eddie
McBride, his search for Silk Armitage so far a failure, realized that he was hungry. Because McBride cared little about
where or what he ate, he saw no reason why the Honorable
Thief Cocktail Lounge wouldn't do just fine.

Nobody in the Honorable Thief had seen Silk Armitage
around either, and so after a bacon, lettuce, and tomato
sandwich and a glass of beer, McBride went outside and
paused on the sidewalk, wishing that he had a toothpick and
trying to figure out where he should go next. After a few
moments of hesitancy, McBride decided that the place across
the street, the Tex-Mex Bar & Grill, would probably do as
well as any.

When the knock came at her back door, Silk Armitage
thought about putting on her wig and the rest of her Madame
Szabo disguise. But then she realized that that didn't make
any sense, not any longer, so she went to the door just as she
was, dressed in the tailored jeans, the high, expensive boots,
and the cream silk blouse that came from Paris. Silk Armitage was ready to travel.

Little Sandy Choi's eyes went almost round when Silk opened the door.

"Hey, man, you're not—"

"Hello, Sandy," Silk said, using her Madame Szabo accent.

Sandy Choi, all of nine, ran his discovery through the abacus that was his mind, estimating its cash value. It might be worth four bits across the street at old Betty Mae Minklawn's. Yeah, she'd pay four bits. At least that.

"What've you got, Sandy?" Silk said in her normal voice.

"A dollar," Sandy said, holding out a sticky hand.

Silk took a dollar from a pocket of her jeans. "You go first," she said. "Then we'll see."

"There's a guy going in every place and asking everybody questions. He says he's a reporter from the Washington something."

"*Post?*" Silk said.

"Uh-huh, *Post.*"

"What kind of questions?"

"He wants to know if anybody's seen Silk Armitage around." Sandy Choi smiled winningly; said, "That's you, ain't it?"; snatched the dollar bill from Silk's hand; and raced down the back-porch steps and into the alley.

After he ordered his draft beer, which he wasn't going to drink, Eddie McBride decided to hit on the old blond broad who was talking to the female bartender. The old blond broad was Betty Mae Minklawn, who was in deep conversation with her friend and confidante Madge Perkinson.

McBride picked up his beer and moved down to the end of the bar, keeping a respectable two stools between him and Betty Mae. The two women looked at him, and McBride nodded and said, "Afternoon, ladies."

Betty Mae liked good-looking young men, especially those who looked a bit the way Alan Ladd had looked back in the '40s and '50s, except that this one wasn't quite that pretty and soft. So she said, "Afternoon" and touched a hand to her chrome yellow beehive hairdo, just to make sure it wasn't messed up.

"My name's Tony Max," McBride said, "and I'm with

The Washington Post." He took out his identification with an easy, practiced movement and showed it to Betty Mae, who looked at it carefully, because it was kind of interesting, and passed it over to Madge.

When Madge handed the identification case back to McBride, Betty Mae said, "What in God's name you doing way out here?"

"We're looking for somebody."

"You on a story?"

"That's right."

"Who you looking for?"

"We received a tip that Silk Armitage might be living around here someplace. She's dropped out of sight and we'd like to find out why."

Something happened to Betty Mae's face, something that told McBride that he had scored. Her eyes narrowed and her mouth grew prim, almost disapproving. Cagey, McBride thought. She's trying to look like she doesn't know anything, but instead she looks just the opposite. Cagey.

"Silk Armitage, the singer?" Betty Mae said, trying to sound indifferent.

"That's right."

"What in the world would somebody like that be living around here for?"

"That's what we're trying to find out."

"She in trouble?"

"If she is, we'd like to help her."

"You mean do a big story on her."

"Yes, ma—" McBride had started to say "ma'am," but he thought better of it. Instead, he gave her a smile, the one that he thought of as his whorehouse smile. Betty Mae seemed to like it.

"You think it's a big enough story for them to make a picture out of it?"

"Well, you never can tell about that," McBride said. "We'd have to find her first, of course. But if it turns out to be a big story, well, sure, they might make a picture out of it."

"You know something?"

"What?"

"She could play herself, couldn't she?" Betty Mae turned to Madge Perkinson. "What do you think?"

Madge did some judicious mental casting before committing herself. "Well, I guess she could do it, but you know who could really do it?"

"Who?"

"Lace Armitage. Her sister."

"God, yes!" Betty Mae said. "And think of the publicity." She turned back to McBride. "Who do you think might play you?"

"Well, I haven't even thought about it," McBride said.

"You know who could play him?" Betty Mae said to Madge.

"Who?"

"Steve McQueen."

Madge shook her head. "McQueen's too old."

"Yeah, well, maybe." Betty Mae again faced McBride. "But I suppose when they make it, they'd have to have somebody play the part of whoever it was who gave the reporter the big tip, right?"

"You mean who told him where Silk Armitage was?"

"Uh-huh," Betty Mae said. "They'd have to have somebody pretty good play that part. I mean, it wouldn't be a big role or anything, but it'd be a hell of a cameo part for somebody." Betty Mae gave her beehive another unconscious feel.

"Yeah, they'd have to do that, all right," McBride said, and watched as Betty Mae and Madge exchanged glances full of secrets and significance.

"Maybe Mary Tyler Moore even?" Betty Mae said.

"She'd be great," McBride said, and took out a ball-point pen and a small notebook that he had purchased on the advice of Otherguy Overby. "Where's Silk Armitage?" he said.

"We didn't say we know," Betty Mae replied, her voice now coy.

"You know," McBride said, and smiled. "By the way, I'd like to get your names to use in the story. You're—uh?"

"Betty Mae Minklawn, that's spelled with a y in Betty, an

e in Mae, and M-i-n-k-l-a-w-n, and this is Madge Perkinson and Silk Armitage is living right across the street from me, just a block from here at 2221 Breadstone."

McBride tried to keep it from showing, the elation that roared through him as he wrote it all down. He made himself ask the two women a few more questions, mostly about themselves, and they responded eagerly now, vying with each other to be the first with the most details. Finally, McBride thanked them both, slid off the bar stool, turned, and started for the door.

Just as he was going out of the Tex-Mex another man came in, a fairly big blond man, dressed in a bright plaid polyester jacket, dark slacks, and a blue shirt with a loosened tie. The big man and McBride eyed each other, and through experience and possibly instinct one word automatically popped into McBride's mind. Cop.

As the big man's eyes took in McBride and memorized him for future reference, a single word came quickly to his mind: Trouble, although he wasn't quite sure what kind. The big man was Lt. Marion Lake of Homicide.

Lt. Lake sized up the bar and automatically designated Betty Mae and Madge as his two most likely prospects. He moved down to them, ordered a beer, and then in a conversational tone said, "My name's Bill Warren and I'm with the L.A. *Times*."

Betty Mae and Madge looked at each other and then held a hurried whispered conversation.

After the quick consultation, Betty Mae turned back to Lt. Lake and said, "We're not talking to any more reporters until we see him first."

"See who first?" Lt. Lake said.

"Our agent."

This time Solly Gesini had to get out of his car to follow McBride. But before he did he unlocked the glove compartment; took out the .38 Smith & Wesson Centennial; inspected it quickly, although he had done so only an hour before; and dropped it into his coat pocket.

McBride walked up Breadstone Avenue toward 2221 until

he found what he wanted, a drugstore. He went inside and used the pay phone to call Otherguy Overby's number. He let it ring five times and was about to hang up when Overby answered the phone, sounding a little breathless.

"It's me," McBride said.

"It's the kid," Overby said to Durant and Wu, who had just followed him into his apartment. Durant took the phone.

"Durant, Eddie."

"I think I've found her," he said. "But I think a cop may be right behind me."

"What's the address?" Durant said.

McBride told him the address and said, "What do you want me to do?"

"Get inside and keep her there for ten minutes."

"You'll be there then?"

"We'll be there," Durant said.

"What'll I tell her?"

"Tell her you like the way she sings," Durant said, and hung up.

When McBride reached 2221 Breadstone Avenue, he puzzled for a moment over the sign that said READINGS. But then he shrugged and went up onto the porch and knocked at the door. Through the door came Silk Armitage's voice. "Who is it?"

"Tony Max, Miss Armitage," McBride said. "I'm with *The Washington Post*. I'd like to talk to you."

Inside, behind the door, Silk Armitage stood with her head bowed. Maybe this would be the best way after all, she thought. Maybe I'll just tell them and then let them track it all down—all those loose ends. She'd give them what she had and then let them do it. I'm tired, she thought. I'm just too damn tired. She leaned her forehead against the door.

"Have you got any identification?" she said.

"Sure," McBride said.

"Put it through the mail slot."

McBride did as he was told. After a moment, the door opened. She was prettier than McBride remembered her as being from the photographs he had seen. Prettier and older and tireder.

"Come on back in the kitchen," Silk said. "I was making myself a sandwich."

"Sure," McBride said.

In the kitchen McBride watched as Silk used a sharp chef's knife to slice a tomato. "So you're from the *Post*, huh?" she said.

"That's right."

"You want a sandwich?"

"No, thanks."

"What about some coffee?"

"Yeah, sure."

"Instant?"

"Instant's fine."

Silk made McBride a cup of coffee and then went back to her sandwich. "Well," she said, "what do you want to know? I haven't got much time. Not here, anyhow. I'm just waiting for a letter."

McBride tried to think of what a reporter would say, but nothing came to mind, so he said, "Why don't you just start at the beginning and tell it from there?"

Silk used the knife to cut her cheese-and-tomato sandwich diagonally. "All right," she said after a moment, "that's probably as good a place as any to start."

Solly Gesini studied the house at 2221 Breadstone Avenue and had a difficult time believing his good fortune. They've both gotta be in there, he told himself. I can do 'em both and be outa here and down the alley and into my car in less'n five minutes. Gesini knew the alley was there because he had checked it earlier.

Getting into the house presented no problem. From where he stood he could see that it was just an ordinary lock on the door. The lock would be a snap unless she had a bolt on the other side. Well, he would just have to see.

Gesini looked around to determine whether anyone was watching, and when nobody was he moved quickly up the steps of the porch to the door. He listened for a moment, then took out a case of picks and easily snapped back the lock. He took one more fast look around and then cautiously opened the door and slipped inside.

He heard the voices then. Or rather, the woman's voice. It was coming from the rear of the house. Gesini went through a pair of half-open sliding doors and into what he thought was a funny-looking room. It was the room where Madame Szabo had given her infrequent readings.

Gesini took the pistol out of his pocket. The voices were coming from the room on the other side of a swinging door. Gesini knew from experience the advantage that surprise gave him in situations like this. They freeze first and can't do anything. Not for a couple of seconds. And that's plenty of time.

He went through the swinging door fast, banging it open, and shot Eddie McBride twice in the back.

McBride knew it was coming. He had been given just a split second of warning by the startled expression on Silk's face. And just as the bullets struck he grasped the chef's knife.

He turned somehow, despite the pain, and saw Gesini, and the rage hit him along with the third round that Gesini fired, this time into McBride's left arm just beneath the shoulder. McBride made himself move. He staggered toward Gesini for three feet and then lunged the final foot. The fucker won't go down, Gesini thought, backing away. I hit him three times good and he won't go down.

At the end of his lunge, McBride drove the chef's knife deep into Gesini's stomach, and as he did he cried a wordless cry, the one that the Corps taught in bayonet practice, the one that was half screech, half scream, and when that was done, McBride ripped the knife up until it ran into bone. And then McBride, in a curiously conversational, almost solicitous tone said, "Tell me where it hurts, Solly."

McBride staggered back then and sat down on the kitchen floor with a thump. Solly Gesini looked down at the knife that was protruding from just below his breastbone. He dropped the pistol and touched the knife handle gingerly. Oh Jesus, does it hurt! Oh, why does it have to hurt so much? After asking the silent question that nobody ever answered,

Solly Gesini sank to his fat knees and then toppled over on-to the floor and went into shock and bled to death.

McBride, sitting on the floor, watched Gesini die. He heard the girl say something, but he couldn't quite make out what. Something about if I'm hurt. I wonder why she's asking that? McBride thought, and then lay down on the kitchen linoleum because he was tired and he hurt. He wondered again why the girl kept asking if he was hurt and then Eddie McBride died, as he had lived, just a bit puzzled.

Silk Armitage stood with the cheese-and-tomato sandwich still in her hand. She put it down on the kitchen table and then sank slowly into a chair. She licked her lips nervously, folded her hands almost primly before her on the table, closed her eyes, and began to sing softly. She would sing until she decided what to do.

She was still singing when Durant, Wu, and Overby came into the kitchen. She opened her eyes and stopped singing and said, "Who are you?"

Artie Wu looked up from his study of Eddie McBride's body. "We're your friendly local samurai," he said, and went back to his study of McBride. "But a bit late, as usual."

Durant took his eyes away from McBride and said, "Your sister sent us, Miss Armitage." Durant handed Silk the letter that Lace Armitage had written. Silk looked at the letter for a long moment before she tore it open and began reading.

While she was reading it, Otherguy Overby knelt down by the dead body of Eddie McBride. His hard face softened, and he looked up at Artie Wu and said, "The kid and me, we'd been talking about going in together, partners, sort of; you know, like you guys."

Wu nodded. Overby, still kneeling, stared at McBride for a long time. Then the tenderness in his face went away and the hardness came back. He stood up.

"Well, hell," Otherguy Overby said. "It was only talk."

Silk Armitage finished reading the letter and looked up at Durant. She's going to cry in a moment, Durant thought. She's either going to cry or go mad.

"I can't do any more," Silk Armitage said in a too reasonable tone that to Durant seemed to lie just this side of madness.

"You'd better let us take over," he said.

Silk Armitage looked around the kitchen. For a moment her eyes rested on the two dead men. Then she smiled and said, almost brightly, "Yes, I think I've done just about everything I can, don't you?"

And after that, she began to cry.

Chapter Thirty-six

Chief Oscar Ploughman and Lt. Marion Lake beat the Los Angeles police to the house on Breadstone Avenue by nearly ten minutes, which was plenty of time for Ploughman to have a brief but extremely interesting and even profitable chat with Otherguy Overby.

Ploughman had been on his way to meet Lake when the shooting report came over the radio. When the two men entered the fortune-teller's house, pistols drawn, they discovered Overby sitting calmly in the room where fortunes had been told, smoking a cigarette and drinking a can of beer that he had found in Silk Armitage's refrigerator.

"Who're you, fella?" Lt. Lake said.

"Overby," he said, and jerked a thumb at the kitchen, which lay beyond the swinging door. "I'm with Durant and Wu, and there're a couple of dead ones in there."

Ploughman turned to Lt. Lake. "Take a look," he said, "and take your time." When Lake went through the swinging door, Ploughman turned on Overby. "And you, make it fast."

"They've got the girl," Overby said.

"She hurt?"

"No."

"So?"

"They're gonna move on Simms and Imperlino and they wanta know if you wanta be in or out. If in, then they told me to tell you that they might be able to make a little contribution to your political hope chest."

Ploughman studied Overby for a while, perhaps ten seconds. "How little's a little?"

"Not so little," Overby said. "Half a million."

"And where do you come in?"

"I run errands," Overby said. "And stick with you—if you decide to sit in."

"Cash contribution?"

"Is there any other kind?"

Ploughman nodded. "I'm in," he said, and then went back to his study of Overby. After a moment he nodded and smiled his big, yellow smile as if pleased with himself. "San Francisco," he said, "1965, the Intercontinental Assurances swindle. Maurice Overby. You were the bag man."

Overby smiled. "They never proved it," he said. "They never proved it because it was some other guy."

Silk Armitage had finally stopped crying by the time they reached Durant's yellow house on the beach. Inside, Silk looked around and said in a small, almost indistinct voice, "Why here? Why not over at Lace's?"

"Because we'd like to talk to you first," Durant said.

"Would you like something?" Wu said. "A drink—or maybe some coffee or tea?"

"Have you got anything to eat?" Silk said. "I know I shouldn't be hungry now, but I just can't help it."

"What about a nice grilled cheese sandwich with maybe a few sliced stuffed olives sort of worked into the cheese?"

Silk smiled weakly at Wu. "Sounds good."

"And tea?"

"Tea would be wonderful."

Artie Wu went into the kitchen and Silk sat down on the

couch. Durant chose the suede chair. Silk looked at Durant for a moment and then bit her lip, as if trying to decide how to phrase her question.

"I know who you are—I mean, from Lace's letter. But I don't understand what you want to do now."

"We'd like to finish what Congressman Ranshaw started."

"Did you know Floy—I mean, the Congressman?"

"No."

"Are you with the government?"

"No."

Silk shook her head. "I don't understand."

"It's a rather personal matter for me," Durant said. "As for Artie, he's in it for—"

"Personal gain," Wu called from the kitchen. "Don't saddle me with anything more high-flown than that."

"A grudge?" Silk asked.

"You can put it that way."

"Against who?"

"Reginald Simms."

When Silk continued to look puzzled, Durant told her as much as he thought she should know about his and Wu's prior association with Simms. By the time he was finished, Wu came in from the kitchen with the sandwich and the cup of tea. Silk started to eat the sandwich with small, neat, hungry bites.

When she was finished she wiped her mouth delicately with the paper napkin and looked first at Wu and then at Durant. "And you want me to tell you what the Congressman knew?"

Durant nodded.

"You know about how far back Imperlino and Simms go?"

Again, Durant nodded.

"And about Castro and the attempts to poison him and all that?"

"Yes," Durant said.

"And Dallas—do you know about Dallas?"

"We heard something about it," Wu said.

"They were sent in, you know, by Simms, those two men."

"Sam Consentino and Johnny Francini?" Durant said.

Silk nodded. "Simms got Imperlino to send them in."

"But not to kill Kennedy?" Wu said.

Silk's eyes went wide with surprise. "Oh, Lordy, no! Is that what you thought?"

"That's what some people think," Durant said. "At least, we think that's what they think."

She shook her head. "Consentino and Francini didn't even get there until after Kennedy was dead."

"Then why were they sent in?" Durant said.

"The Congressman said that nobody really understands how they work."

"Who's they?" Wu said.

Silk shrugged. "He just called it 'them' or 'they'—I reckon he always meant the people who really run things."

"The CIA?" Wu said.

"They were just part of it. You see, right after Kennedy got shot, nobody really knew just what had happened. You remember all the confusion. But some of them thought they knew—so they acted. Or reacted. They got in touch with Simms and he got in touch with Imperlino. And Imperlino sent in Francini and Consentino because they'd known him in Havana back in '58."

"Known who?" Durant said.

"Why, Jack Ruby," Silk said as though addressing some small and not very bright children.

"They needed a cleanup man," Durant said in a soft, thoughtful voice, staring at Wu.

Artie Wu ran it through his mind. "Yeah, they would do it like that, wouldn't they? That's how they work. They operated from one assumption: that Kennedy was supposed to get shot. After that it was just routine. They had to keep Oswald from talking. You say Francini and Consentino knew Ruby in Havana?"

"In '58," Silk said. "He was in jail there for a while."

"The perfect sap," Durant said.

"So Imperlino sends in Francini and Consentino," Wu

said, "and they remember this dope they'd known back in Havana and they work him over good and get him all fired up and he takes Oswald out in a burst of glorious patriotism on live TV."

"They paid him," Silk said.

Wu looked at her. "Is that what the Congressman thought?"

She nodded. "They paid Jack Ruby fifty thousand dollars."

"Could he prove it—the Congressman?"

Silk shook her head.

"How much could he prove?" Durant said.

"He could place Consentino and Francini in Dallas. That was all he could prove—about that, I mean. But then when they got old and were thinking about taking immunity and getting themselves off the hook, then the Congressman could almost prove that Imperlino went to Chicago and then to Miami and killed them both."

"How could he almost prove it?"

"He knew that Imperlino sometimes used an alias. Always when he traveled. He used it that time when he went down to Miami after Ivory died. The alias was T. Northwood. Terence Northwood. The Congressman was checking the airline records when he got killed. Afterwards, that's what I was doing. We almost had it. I mean, it was supposed to be in the mail this morning, but the mail never came, did it?"

"And the airline records would prove what?"

"That Imperlino was in Chicago and Miami right when Francini and Consentino got killed," Silk said.

Wu shook his head. "That's pretty sketchy."

"He was a cop," Silk said. "Or had been. You have to remember that. What he was really after was who gave Imperlino his town. Pelican Bay."

"Did he ever find out?"

Silk shrugged. "It was just 'they' again. When Imperlino bought the newspaper in Pelican Bay, nobody objected. When he needed the environmental-impact approval for that hotel he's going to build, it went through in record time. When he needed the Coastal Commission's approval here in

California, that sailed through. The fix was in. That's what the Congressman always said. The fix was in."

"So now only Imperlino knows the real story?" Wu said.

"Imperlino and Simms," Silk said. "They were at college together—did you know that?"

"We knew," Durant said.

"The Congressman was trying to find out about Simms when he got killed. Simms'd been with the CIA, you know, but he turned bad or something. It wasn't quite clear. All the Congressman knew was that suddenly Simms showed up in Pelican Bay with a lot of money and went in with Imperlino. Simms ran things while Imperlino played hermit in that house of his in Bel Air."

"Who killed the Congressman?" Wu said.

Silk looked at him. "His wife."

"You don't believe that," Durant said.

"No, I don't believe that. I was outside in the car. I heard the shots. Then I waited and a car drove off. I couldn't see who was in it. Then I went in and there they were. Dead. He'd left his briefcase in the car—with all the stuff he had, his evidence. Most of it, anyway. So I panicked, I reckon. I thought they might have seen me. So then I tried to finish what he started. But I didn't get very far. Can I call my sister now?"

"Not yet," Durant said.

"How much longer?"

"A day," Durant said. "Maybe two at the most."

"Then it'll be over?" she said.

Durant nodded. "Then it'll be over." He looked at Wu. "You'd better call our friend up in Santa Barbara. Tell him to get down here with his mop."

"Who?" Silk said. "Am I supposed to know who?"

"A guy with three names," Wu said. "Whittaker Lowell James."

"What does he do?" she said.

"Well," Durant said, "I suppose what he does best is to go around with his mop and tidy things up."

* * *

At two o'clock the following morning, a Tuesday, the twenty-first of June, Durant lay in his bed, his hands behind his head, staring up into the dark and listening to the sobs that came from the spare bedroom. He had been listening to them now for almost an hour.

Finally, Durant got up and went down the short hall and into the bedroom, where he switched on a dim night-light. Silk Armitage was curled up in one of the twin beds crying into her pillow.

Durant stared at her for a moment and then went over to the bed and sat down on its edge. He put his hand out and tentatively, even hesitantly, began to smooth the blond hair back from her eyes.

"I'm so—so damned scared," she said.

"It's almost over."

"I—I don't know how it feels anymore, not to be scared."

"Just a little while more—two days at the most."

As he continued to stroke her hair, the sobbing subsided. She twisted around in the bed, snuggling up close to him. And then came the feelings that Durant thought he had forgotten how to feel. It was desire—and something else. A feeling of protectiveness that was very close to pity. Too close, probably. Durant stopped analyzing and let it happen, if, in fact, it was going to happen. It came on stronger then, almost purely sexual now, moving down to his groin, where it took over completely.

Durant's hand moved from Silk's head down over her body. She was wearing one of his shirts, and his hand went under the shirt and moved over her breasts and then down between her thighs. She sighed and curled up closer around him. He sat there for a moment and then he bent over and kissed her, wondering if he had forgotten how to do it. But he hadn't, and the kiss went on, open mouthed and pleasantly moist, and full of mutual sexual promise that had Durant wondering whether he could live up to what he was advertising.

When the kiss was over he picked her up.

"I think we're going to need more room," he said.

She nodded and smiled, but said nothing. He carried her

down the short hall into his bedroom and gently put her down in the bed. He stood there for a moment, looking down at her. She smiled up at him.

"Did you change your mind?" she said.

"No," he said. And then he got into the bed and they made love, and if it wasn't perfect, it was still much better than Durant had expected.

When Durant awoke the next morning, Silk Armitage was lying on her stomach, propped up on her elbows, her chin in her hands, studying him.

"Hi," she said.

"Morning."

"Can I ask you something?"

"Sure."

"Are you a virgin? I mean, were you?"

Durant smiled. "Yeah, I suppose I was. In a way."

"I'm not complaining," she said, "but I think you could do with a little practice."

"So do I."

"Now?"

Durant smiled again. "Sure," he said. "Now."

Chapter Thirty-seven

They brought in Otherguy Overby to baby-sit Silk Armitage, who was still in the shower when he arrived.

"Ploughman's all set?" Durant said.

"Yeah, he's set. You know, he's a pretty interesting guy."

Durant nodded. "I thought you two would get along."

"What about the girl?"

"No phone calls in or out," Durant said. "And nobody leaves and nobody comes in. Absolutely nobody except either Artie or me."

"What am I supposed to do with her?"

"Tell her some stories," Durant said.

"Does she know why I'm here?"

Durant nodded. "She knows. You just make sure she doesn't change her mind."

Durant picked up Wu shortly before noon at the house on Ninth Street in Santa Monica. Wu started to get into Durant's Mercedes, but paused, bent down, and stared in at Durant, who was already behind the wheel.

"What happened to you?" Wu said.

"What do you mean?"

Wu examined him some more. "I don't know. Maybe it's the chipper air, the confident smile, the flashing eyes. If I didn't know better, I'd say you got laid."

"Unngh," Durant said.

"What does 'unngh' mean?"

"It means I don't want to talk about it."

"We'll celebrate," Wu said, settling his big body into the seat next to Durant. "I'll buy us lunch at El Charro's."

"Jesus," Durant said, "not again."

"Sure," Wu said. "Why not?"

"You know what you are, Artie?"

"What?"

"A closet Mexican."

"Yeah," Wu said, nodding comfortably at the suggestion. "I probably am."

Durant, who had finished his guacamole salad, watched as Artie Wu polished off the last morsel of the enormous $4.25 platter of tamales, enchiladas, burritos, frijoles refritos, rice, and salad.

Wu leaned back with a sigh, patted his big belly, and said, "Jesus, that was good."

Durant lit a cigarette. "She doesn't know all of it," he said, and dropped his match into the ashtray.

Wu nodded. "I wonder if the Congressman did?"

"I'm not all that sure that he did either. But what he did know might have made a hell of a tabloid headline."

"You mean, CIA ORDERED MOB TO SNUFF OSWALD, something like that?"

"I'd read it," Durant said.

"Yeah, so would I, but it would be just a one-day story unless you could prove who gave Simms his orders."

"Everybody seems convinced that the Congressman knew that."

"By everybody you mean Imperlino and Simms."

Durant nodded. "And now they're apparently convinced that she knew everything the Congressman did—and maybe even more."

Wu smiled and stuck one of his long, slim cigars into his mouth. "Let's not disillusion them."

"No, let's do something else," Durant said, also smiling. "Let's go be rotten to Reggie."

Chuck West didn't like the way they looked or the way they talked or the way they smiled.

Wu and Durant were standing in West's office on the fifteenth floor of the Ransom Tower. West had invited them into his office, but he hadn't asked them to sit down. Instead, he was explaining why it would be impossible for them to see Mr. Simms. Mr. Simms, it seemed, was tied up in conference.

Artie Wu puffed on his cigar. "Tied up in conference," he said, savoring the phrase. "Well, we're old friends so we'll just wait."

"I'm afraid that's impossible," West said. "The conference could go on all afternoon."

Durant smiled. "We'll wait all afternoon."

West dropped his polite pretense, which was seldom, if ever, very firmly in place. He pointed to the door. "Out," he said. "Now."

"Us?" Artie Wu said, apparently surprised, if not shocked.

"You."

Wu smiled. "No."

West nodded thoughtfully. "I think I'll arrange for some-one to show you to the elevator—or maybe down the stairs, just to see how high you bounce."

West started toward his desk, but Wu stepped in front of him. They were both about the same height, but Durant gave Wu the advantage of at least thirty pounds. On the other hand, West was younger by at least seven or eight years. Durant watched carefully because it promised to be rather interesting.

Artie Wu put his cigar back into his face. Then he exam-ined West carefully, admiring the beautiful hair and the tan and the marvelously cut suede jacket, the beige shirt and dark brown knit tie. Wu nodded, as if well satisfied with his inspection, and hit West very hard in the stomach. Twice.

The whoof came as West bent over and his hands went to his stomach. But his right hand started inside his jacket. Wu caught it, held it, reached inside the jacket with his other hand, and brought out a small automatic pistol.

He looked at it and turned to Durant. "Jesus," he said, "a real Beretta."

"Nice," Durant said.

West straightened up, glaring at Wu.

"Now, then," Wu said, waving the Beretta a little. "Let's go surprise Reggie."

West used the plastic card to open the steel sliding door into Simms' office. With a nod of his head Wu indicated that West should go first. West went in, followed by Wu and then Durant.

Simms looked up from his spindly-legged desk. A smile, very warm and very white, appeared on his face. "Well, Artie," he said. "And Quincy, too. What a pleasant sur-prise."

"We didn't want to disturb you when we heard you were busy, Reg," Wu said, "but your Mr. West insisted."

"I didn't—"

Simms interrupted. "That's all, Charles."

"Are you sure, sir? I mean—"

"No. That's all."

"Here, kid," Wu said, and handed him the Beretta. West

glared again at Wu and left. Simms was up now, the white, almost shy smile still there. Durant studied him, trying to analyze how the older man made him feel. Durant discovered a mild, almost detached dislike, but no hatred, and that surprised him. He wasn't at all sure whether it was a pleasant surprise or not.

"Well," Simms said, "this calls for a bit of a celebration. Do sit down." He indicated two chairs in front of his desk. As Wu and Durant sat down, Simms asked, "Now, what can I get you?"

"You still drinking Armagnac?" Durant said.

"Of course."

"Then we'll begin with some of that."

Simms went to his bar and poured three glasses from what seemed to be a very old bottle. He brought the glasses back on a small silver tray and served Durant first, then Wu.

Simms lifted his own glass and said, "Well, to prosperity."

He sipped his drink, watched as Durant and Wu tasted theirs, and then went back behind his desk and resumed his seat.

"I heard you were in town, of course."

Durant smiled, but said nothing. Wu puffed on his cigar and tried some more of the Armagnac.

"Here on business—or just passing through?" Simms said.

Durant smiled again and said, "Two million dollars."

Simms nodded, almost encouragingly. "An interesting sum."

"We want it," Durant said.

"Of course you do. And doubtless deserve it."

Durant sipped his drink. "We've got the girl."

"Well, now."

"You can have her for two million."

"Indeed."

"She's got some interesting information, Reg," Wu said, "about you and Imperlino and Dallas and Jack Ruby and all that good shit. The Congressman seems to have been an awfully fine snoop. But then, he used to be a cop, didn't he? And a pretty fair one, I hear."

"Clever," Simms said, nodding his appreciation. "Not only clever, but also cunning, and totally out of character."

Durant nodded agreeably. "It does make us feel a little rotten, but we'll probably get over it."

"The money should help," Wu said.

"Of course, I believe you have the girl."

"Well, if you don't," Wu said, "we can always bring you an ear."

"That's not quite what I meant. You have the girl, of course, but what does she have that's so dreadfully expensive?"

Durant finished his drink and put the glass on Simms' desk. Simms picked it up and put it on the silver tray. Durant lit a cigarette and blew the smoke up in the air.

"Well, let's see, what does she have?" Durant said. "She has some airline records concerning a couple of trips that a Mr. T. Northwood took to Miami and Chicago. The T is for Terence. Terence Northwood. To start with, she has that."

"Well, now, that is interesting," Simms said.

"We thought you'd think so," Wu said. "By the way, how is your old roomie?"

"How nice of you to ask, Artie," Simms said. "He's fine."

"Good. You know, it might be nice if you brought him along tomorrow when we pick up the money."

"Tomorrow?" Simms said. "That soon?"

Durant nodded. "That soon. Ten o'clock tomorrow morning."

"You know something," Simms said, "I'm beginning to believe you're serious."

"That's very perceptive of you," Durant said.

Simms examined Durant more closely. "You've changed, Quincy, haven't you? You're more—well—determined, I suppose."

"Very determined."

"Interesting. Well, of course, I can't make this decision myself."

Wu rose, picked up Durant's glass and his own, and moved

over to the bar. "We'll drink some more of your booze, Reg, while you go call good old Vince. You might tell him he has twenty minutes to make up his mind. It's the usual setup. Nothing original. If we're not heard from by then, the girl, files and all, go public. She should make quite a splash."

Simms rose. "Yes, well, do enjoy your drinks and I'll be back shortly."

He was back in less than ten minutes. "Would you like to haggle a bit over the price?"

"No," Durant said. "The price is firm."

Simms sighed. "That's what we were both afraid of. It's something romantic to do with poor Eddie McBride and all that, I suppose."

"You're close," Durant said.

"Well, we do insist on picking the place."

"Okay," Wu said.

"It's a beach house here in Pelican Bay, quite remote. It was used as an office while all the houses on either side of it were being razed."

"Whom does it belong to now?" Durant said.

"The city, but I have access. I've also drawn you a rather rough map." He handed it to Durant, who looked at it, nodded, and put it away.

"Well, then," Simms said. "Until ten o'clock tomorrow."

"Will Imperlino be there?" Wu said.

"Indeed, yes."

Wu rose, and so did Durant. "Just one more thing, Reg," Durant said.

"What?"

"I bring the girl in and Artie waits outside. If anything tricky happens, Artie runs. But he'll come after you—sometime. You know how Artie is. Mean. Think of it, waking up nights and realizing that somewhere out there the last of the Manchus is waiting." Durant made himself shudder. "Jesus."

Simms smiled. "I'll keep it in mind."

"Do that," Durant said.

Chapter Thirty-eight

At four minutes until ten the next morning, which was a Wednesday, the twenty-second of June, the big Chrysler station wagon, Artie Wu at the wheel, stopped along the deserted, closed road approximately fifty yards from the gray, two-story frame house that looked as if it properly belonged on Cape Cod rather than on a strip of Southern California beach.

Spaced at regular intervals on either side of the house were the remains of the foundations where other beach homes had once stood. Parked in the gray house's driveway was a late-model Ford LTD sedan.

"It looks as though they're already here," Durant said, glancing carefully around. "How does it look to you?"

Artie Wu studied the house for a moment. "Like a setup," he said, and then looked at his watch. "You ready?"

"What time is it?"

"You've got a minute or two."

"Let's be early," Durant said.

Inside what had once been used as the living room of the gray house, Vincent Imperlino watched as Reginald Simms tied the strong, waxed black thread around the trigger guard of the .38 Colt automatic. He then took an ordinary thumbtack and used it to suspend the pistol in the well of the old battered desk that faced the door through which Durant would come.

"It's one of those dirty little tricks that they taught us," Simms said, now down behind and almost underneath the desk. He stuck the pin into the wood, wrapped the thread

318

securely around it, and then let the pistol dangle. He rose, brushing his hands.

"It hangs upside down, of course, but still quite handy."

"Do you think we'll actually need it?" Imperlino said.

"One can take comfort in a hidden advantage whether one uses it or not."

"Is that what they taught you too?"

"No," Simms said. "I do think I just made that up."

Artie Wu got out of the station wagon, opened the rear door, and stripped back the blanket. The rear seats had been lowered to form a deck space. Stretched out on the hard surface was Silk Armitage, her hands tied behind her back, her mouth taped, her eyes wide and very frightened.

Wu pulled her up into a sitting position and then lifted her out of the car and set her on her feet next to Durant, who glanced at her once and then looked around again.

"They sure as hell chose one deserted spot," he said.

Wu, also looking around, nodded his agreement. "The next few minutes are going to be pretty interesting."

"Uh-huh," Durant said. He took Silk by the elbow. "All right," he said, "let's go."

Wu watched as Durant walked Silk Armitage down the cracked cement of the abandoned road, up the driveway, and into the condemned house. When they were out of sight, Artie Wu lit a cigar.

Just before he went into the house, Durant took the .38 revolver out of his pocket. He held it in his right hand down by his side. His left hand was on Silk Armitage's elbow.

The door to the house was already open, so Durant went in, Silk Armitage slightly in front of him. Reginald Simms came out of the living room and stood in the small reception hall. Like Durant, he casually held a pistol in his hand down by his side, an automatic, which to Durant looked like the Beretta that Chuck West had had the day before.

"Well, Quincy," Simms said. "I see that neither of us trusts the other very much."

"Hardly at all."

"We're in here," Simms said, indicating the open door that led into the living room.

"You first," Durant said.

Simms smiled and nodded. "Of course."

Simms went into the room and Durant guided Silk in, following closely behind her. He glanced around the room quickly. The tall, not quite heavy man who sat in the straight wooden chair in the corner would be Imperlino. There were a couple of other chairs, cast-off wooden ones, but except for them, and the one behind the old, scarred desk, that was all the furniture the room contained, except for the two suit-cases on the floor, apparently brand new and about the size of large overnight bags.

"Well, I think everyone knows who everyone else is," Simms said. "So any introductions would probably be un-necessary as well as tactless."

"Let her sit down," Imperlino said.

Durant guided Silk to one of the wooden chairs. She sat down in it, her eyes even wider and more frightened than before. She looked at Imperlino and then at Simms and finally at Durant. She stared at him for a long time and then closed her eyes wearily and slumped back in the chair. After a moment she opened them and stared out the window at the ocean, which seemed crisply blue and sparkling under the warm June sun.

"Let's get to the money," Durant said.

"The two cases there," Simms said.

Durant went over to the cases, knelt down, and opened one of them. He kept his pistol in his right hand. The case was filled with fifty- and one-hundred-dollar bills, bound in neat bundles by heavy red rubber bands. Durant pawed through the stacks with his left hand, taking some of the packets out from the bottom and riffling through the bills.

"You *are* suspicious, Quincy," Simms said.

"Very."

Durant closed the case and then opened the other one and made the same kind of inspection. When satisfied, he closed the second case and rose.

"Well," he said, "I think that takes care of everything."

"No," Imperlino said, and stood up. He had a pistol out now, one that looked to Durant like a Luger. Durant didn't examine it too carefully because it wasn't aimed at him. It was aimed at Silk Armitage instead, but rather casually.

"What do you mean, no?" Durant said.

"For our own protection, Mr. Durant, you are going to have to be a party to the murder of the young lady," Imperlino said in a quiet, reasonable tone.

"I'm not going to kill her," Durant said.

"No, of course not," Imperlino said. "I shall do that—with much regret, although such a comment from me at this time must seem rather tasteless. But since you've sold her to us—and will witness her death—then in the eyes of the law you will be held just as guilty of her death as either Reg or I." Imperlino paused. "Morally, I should think, even more so."

Durant nodded. "They told me you were smart."

Imperlino ignored the remark. "Let's get it over with."

"Most brilliant, too, I understand," Durant said. "At Bowdoin, I mean."

"Do you have a point to make, Mr. Durant?"

"Well, if I'd been voted most brilliant at Bowdoin, I think I'd be smart enough to be a little suspicious when my old college roommate suddenly shows up on my doorstep with a hot two million dollars that he's stolen from the Saigon embassy. Two million dollars that nobody was even looking for because it supposedly had been burned. And my old roomie, the eternal company man, has suddenly, unexpectedly turned apostate, even renegade. Now, that would have given me pause. Yes, sir, it would have."

Imperlino stared at Durant. Finally, very carefully, he said, "Why?"

"You mean, why be suspicious? Well, let's look at it this way. The war was ending in Vietnam just as you were making your first moves into Pelican Bay. We'll call that a coincidence, but it's the last one you'll have to put up with. So your old roommate comes back to Saigon from the wars—embittered, cynical, maybe even burnt out. He sees the opportunity to steal two million dollars with virtually no chance of being discovered. Well, he stole it. Who wouldn't? And to help him do it, he enlisted the help of somebody called Eddie McBride, not too bright, not too dumb. Just average.

"So after they've stolen the two million and hidden it away for future recovery—and here comes the part that really bothers me—well, Simms makes a date to meet McBride in, of all places, L.A. Or rather, Beverly Hills. But he never shows up, and poor Eddie wanders all over town trying to sell his map of where he thinks the two million still is to whoever'll pay him a few thousand for it.

"So why did your old roommate do that, Imperlino? Why didn't he just meet Eddie and buy him off with a sweet stall and a few thousand? It wouldn't have taken more than that to make Eddie happy. But instead Eddie flits around L.A., a walking, talking advertisement to the fact that the money was indeed stolen.

"So whom was your old roommate trying to convince?" Durant shook his head sadly. "You, I'm afraid."

"You're saying that they didn't steal it?" Imperlino said softly.

"What I'm saying is that somebody let them steal it."

Imperlino looked at Simms. "Well?"

Simms shrugged easily. "He's trying to talk himself out of a hole, Imp."

Imperlino nodded and turned back to Durant. "Go on."

"It's obvious. The same somebody that let them steal the money decided to send Simms in after you. But they knew he'd have to get all the way inside. So they figured that he'd have to come to you with unclean hands. The dirty money out of Saigon would be perfect. Somebody back in Washington heard about the six million that had to be burned, so they set it up. It was perfect. Unaccountable bait money. And Eddie McBride wandering around as a living testimonial to the fact that, yes, it sure enough had been stolen. You bought it, of course, along with your new partner—although from now on, if I were you, I'd sort of watch my back."

Imperlino smiled politely, as though thanking Durant for some useful but not terribly important information. Then, still smiling a bit politely, Imperlino turned quickly toward his old roommate and was raising his pistol when Simms shot him twice through the chest.

The polite smile went away and then came back and then went away again, this time forever, as Imperlino stumbled back, slid down the wall, and died sitting on the bare wooden floor, in the dust, staring at Simms and wearing a look of deep disappointment, one that not even death could quite erase.

"Okay, Reg," Durant said, his pistol now aimed at Simms. "Nothing quick or cute. Just turn around and put it down on the desk. Take all the time you want."

When Simms turned, Durant was surprised by the look of almost total grief that had distorted his face. Well, how are you supposed to look, Durant thought, when you kill your best friend? He has a right to it.

Simms did exactly as he was told. He put the Beretta down on the desk and slid it slowly toward Durant.

"Now sit down and put your hands on the desk," Durant said, moving cautiously over to the Beretta. He picked it up and put it into his pocket.

"I was going to have to do it sooner or later, of course," Simms said in a thoughtful, reasonable tone that bore no resemblance to the tortured lines that he still wore on his face.

"Were you?" Durant said, and looked quickly at Silk Armitage, who was staring down at the dead Imperlino. She started shaking her head slowly and was still shaking it when Durant looked back at Simms.

"You don't believe me?" Simms said.

"It doesn't matter much what I believe."

"You were right about poor Eddie McBride, of course. He was my bona fides, so to speak."

"Who sent you in, Reg?"

Simms shrugged, some of the grief now gone from his face. In its place was a questioning look. "That doesn't matter," he said. "What I'm intensely curious about right now is what you intend to do with me."

Durant stared at Simms for several seconds and then said, "What I'm trying to decide is whether I should pull the trigger."

"Should or can?" Simms said.

"The should's the hard part," Durant said. "Can presents no problem."

Simms smiled, apparently quite cheerful now. "You'll never do it, Quincy. Never."

"I might enjoy it."

"Nonsense. You'd never kill your own brother. Half brother actually, of course."

The gun wavered in Durant's hand as pure shock hit him like a cruel, totally unexpected blow. He automatically rejected the idea in self-defense, then accepted it, rejected it again, and then accepted it forever as a lifetime of speculation about his identity ended. And suddenly, Durant realized that he hadn't wanted it to end. And he was thinking about this, puzzling about it, when Artie Wu walked quietly into the room.

"I was just telling Quincy, Artie," Simms said, "about us being brothers. You do look shocked, Quincy. But think about it. Why do you think I nursemaided you all these years after you first popped up on our green sheet down in Mexico that time? I got you out of jail and then into the Peace Corps and later kept you in tow and mostly out of trouble. Mother made me promise, of course. Incidentally, her maiden name was Quincy. It was one of those dreadful deathbed scenes—you know what I mean."

As if to make his point, Simms' right hand performed a graceful flourish, an actor's practiced gesture actually, which ended with the hand resting casually on his right knee, almost beneath the desk. Simms moved the hand cautiously until he had it wrapped around the butt of the automatic that was suspended out of sight beneath the desk top.

Simms tightened his finger and began, "You see, Quincy," in a conversational tone that ended when Artie Wu took his gun out of his pocket and shot Reginald Simms at close range once in the throat and twice in the chest, just about where the heart is. The bullets slammed Simms back in his chair, but then he slumped forward onto the desk and after a moment slipped awkwardly to the floor.

Wu moved over to the desk, reached under it, jerked the

hidden automatic free, and slid it across the desk toward Durant, who still stood in the center of the room, silent and stunned.

"You don't need a brother," Artie Wu said. "You got me."

Chapter Thirty-nine

Finally, Durant moved. He walked around the desk and stared down at the body of Reginald Simms. Well, brother, he thought, and wondered why he kept staring down at him.

Artie Wu had put his revolver back into a pocket of his resplendent silk suit. From its hip pocket he now brought out a small silver flask. He uncapped it and handed it to Durant.

Still staring down at Simms, Durant swallowed some of the brandy. He then moved over to Silk Armitage, put the flask down, carefully removed the tape that covered her mouth, and untied her hands. After that he silently handed her the flask. She took a small swallow.

"Oh, my God, I was scared!" she said. "Were you?"

Durant nodded. "You okay now?"

"I think so." She looked quickly at Simms and then even more quickly looked away. "He really your brother?"

Durant shrugged.

Silk put out her hand as though to comfort him with a touch. But she stopped and instead said, "I'm sorry, I really can't help it, but I'm just obliged to go to the bathroom."

"Try down the hall," Artie Wu said.

After she had gone, Durant continued to sip at the brandy while he stared down at Simms. But finally he turned to Wu and said, "You knew, didn't you, Artie?"

Wu nodded.

"How long?"

"About eight years. It was when we were in Bangkok that first time. Reg came through on some fruitcake mission. If anything happened to him, I was to tell you. Well, nothing happened."

"Who was he?"

"Who?"

"Daddy," Durant said, grating up the word.

"What do you care?" Artie Wu said. "Make him up. Pick anybody you like. Somebody swell, the way I did."

"Who was he, Artie?"

Wu sighed. "He doesn't know."

"You mean about me?"

Wu nodded. "She was a widow—your mother, Simms'. She got involved with a married man. When she found she was pregnant she went to San Francisco. Simms told me that she had you and a breakdown at about the same time, so you got left on the doorstep with the tag around your neck."

"So who was he?"

Wu sighed again. "James."

"Whittaker Lowell?"

"Whittaker Lowell."

"Well, now."

"Well, now, what?" Wu said.

"Well, now, isn't that too fucking bad," Durant said.

When Silk Armitage came back she hesitated at the entrance of the living room. "Do we have to wait in here?" she said.

"Yes," Durant said.

She came in slowly, not looking at the two bodies. She went up to Durant and said, "Look, I'm sorry about your brother, but I'm not sure if there's anything I can say."

"No," Durant said. "There's really nothing to say."

Silk went over to the window and stared out at the ocean. "How much longer?" she said.

Wu glanced at his watch. "Not much now."

It wasn't much longer, no more than a quarter of an hour, before they arrived right on time, the three of them. Oscar Ploughman came in first, followed by Otherguy Overby.

Last in was Whittaker Lowell James, sprucely dressed, almost dapper, wearing his usual brusque, no-nonsense air.

Ploughman took it in quickly. He glanced first at Wu and Durant and Silk Armitage and then went over to the bodies. He gave Simms only a cursory look, but when he reached Imperlino he smiled happily with his big yellow teeth. "Well, Vince," he said. "Hello, Vince." Then he turned to Wu and Durant. "Who got him?"

"Simms," Durant said.

Ploughman nodded. "Why?"

"Because Simms had been sent in to take him out."

"No shit?" Ploughman said. "Who sent him?"

"Ask him," Wu said, nodding at Whittaker Lowell James.

"What about it, Pop?" Ploughman said.

The man with three names ignored the Pop. Instead, he said, "As far as I know, Simms was acting on his own."

"Who shot Simms, then?" Ploughman said.

"Let's talk about money first," Artie Wu said. "Then we can talk about who shot Simms."

Ploughman nodded thoughtfully. "Yeah, that makes sense. There is some money to talk about, huh? I mean, you guys weren't just selling snowflakes?"

Durant nodded toward the two suitcases. "It's in there."

"Mind if I take a look?" Ploughman said.

"Why not?"

"Give me a hand, Otherguy," Ploughman said. The two men knelt down by the suitcases and opened them. As Durant had done, they took some of the packets from the bottom and riffled through them.

While Ploughman and Overby inspected the cash, Durant inspected the man who was his father. Artie is right, Durant finally decided, children should be allowed to pick their own parents.

Ploughman looked up from the money at Durant, his big yellow smile gleaming. "Two million?"

Still staring at James, Durant nodded. "Two million," he said.

"Four-way split?"

"Four-way split."

As Ploughman and Overby closed up the suitcases, James said, "It was a very clever scheme, Quincy. Ingenious."

"It was Artie's idea."

James nodded approvingly. "All very neatly done—and rather profitable, too, I should say."

"Of course, it still leaves Silk around," Durant said.

James smiled politely and bowed slightly to Silk. "I don't think anyone bothered to introduce us, Miss Armitage. I'm Whittaker James."

"The man with the mop," Silk said.

"Yes," James said with a small chuckle. "I suppose you might say that. And I'm sure that you and I can reach some mutually satisfactory accommodation."

Ploughman, back up on his feet, frowned. "What the fuck's he talking about—pardon me, lady?"

"He's trying to put the lid on," Artie Wu said.

Ploughman frowned some more and shook his head slowly, looking around the room. "We're gonna have to give 'em somebody," he said.

"The law, you mean?" James said.

"The law? No, I'm not talking about the law, Pop. I'm the law. Me. I'm talking about people who don't pay much attention to the law. I'm talking about Vince Imperlino's buddies, pals, friends, and associates. Them. You don't kill somebody like Imperlino in my town without hanging it on somebody. And it can't just be somebody you found down in the alley with a bottle of muscadoodle in his pocket. To make Imperlino's crowd happy, you gotta come up with somebody they'll buy. If you don't, then you're in bad, bad trouble with them, and that kind of trouble I don't need."

There was a lengthy silence, which lasted long enough for Artie Wu to light a fresh cigar with his usual ceremony.

He blew one of his fat smoke rings toward the ceiling and said, "Let's give them Otherguy."

"No fucking way, Artie," Overby said, and his right hand darted around toward the small of his back where he kept his snub-nosed revolver. But then his hand stopped. No, that wasn't the play, Overby realized. That was just the check before the raise, the bump. They're gonna sandbag somebody, Overby told himself with pleasure. So he smiled slightly; said, "No fucking way" again, but without much vehemence; folded his arms; and leaned against the wall, watchful and very much interested.

Ploughman frowned again, although this time it was more of a scowl than a frown. "Well, I'd sort of hate to lose Brother Overby here, on account of him and me've been talking about maybe going in together on a couple of small items after we get this mess here squared away. Which sort of reminds me, Durant. You know how to set up a Swiss bank account?"

"Sure," Durant said. "You want us to set one up for you?"

"Would that mean you'd have to take my cut?"

"Well, it's a little hard to open an account without any money."

Ploughman rubbed his big chin. "Well, I don't know," he said. "Lemme think about it. Right now we've gotta figure out who we're gonna give 'em."

There was another lengthy silence that lasted almost thirty seconds until it was finally broken by Durant.

"Let's give them Whittaker Lowell James," he said, a small crooked smile on his face, his eyes fixed steadily on the older man.

Artie Wu stared at Durant. Then he smiled a big, broad, happy smile. "By God, I like it. I do."

Ploughman chuckled. "These two guys are pretty funny, right, Pop?"

"Yes," James said. "Very amusing."

"He's perfect, Chief," Durant went on. "Think of the headlines. EX-DIPLOMAT SLAYS CIA TURNCOAT, MOB CHIEF. What do you think he'd get—a year, eighteen months?"

Ploughman again rubbed his big chin, staring at James. "If that," he said. There was a pause and then he said, "You know what, Pop, I think they're serious. I mean, they really want to set you up."

"Yes," James said, his voice calm, his gaze level. "So it would seem."

"The best thing about it," Durant said, "is that he can't talk. If he denies it, then he has to explain, and if he explains, then he has to explain everything, and he can't afford to do that, right, Whit?"

"There are reasons for not talking, which, I think, Quincy, you'd have a most difficult time understanding."

"You know," Ploughman said, "the more I think about this, the better I like it. Hell, Pop here comes off sort of a half-ass hero, I get the credit for making the collar, and Imperlino's buddies have all that honor shit of theirs taken care of." He turned to Overby. "What do you think, Otherguy?"

Overby smiled—a small, careful, crafty smile—as he stared at Whittaker Lowell James. "I say give 'em the old man."

Ploughman looked at Artie Wu. "Well?"

Artie Wu blew another fat smoke ring up at the ceiling. "Sure," he said. "Let's give them Whit."

"Well, I know how you feel, Durant," Ploughman said. "But what about the little lady here?"

"It's up to her," Durant said. "The whole thing."

Ploughman frowned again. "What do you mean?"

"Just what I said," Durant replied. "She has the yes or no vote. Whittaker Lowell James is probably as much responsible for the death of Congressman Ranshaw as anyone alive. You could probably never prove it, Chief, but it's almost a cinch bet that he and some of his R Street cronies sent Simms into Pelican Bay to silence the Congressman and then, at the right time, take out Imperlino. But I think Simms' loyalties got a little mixed up there toward the end. And when he showed signs of waffling, Artie and I were brought in—to find Silk and somehow stop Simms. If we found Silk, then Whittaker knew he could put a clamp on her one way or another. So you see, to him the whole thing was just one more rather big job for his mop."

"Why?" Ploughman said. "He's not with the government anymore."

Durant smiled. "He'll always be with the government," he said, staring at James. "The real government, right, Whit?"

"Are you almost through, Quincy?" James said in a bored voice.

"Almost," Durant said, and turned to Silk. "You can either let him loose and then try to get your story told, or you can put him away and then keep silent. You can't have it both ways. Because if you decide to put him away, then you become part of it—this conspiracy. But if you let him go free and then try to get your story told, he'll shut you up—and don't ever, ever kid yourself that he can't."

"You're babbling now, Quincy," James said.

"Probably," Durant said. "But there he is, lady, the Them and the They that the Congressman was always telling you about. You call it."

Silk Armitage, the product of the Black Mountain Folk School in the Arkansas Ozarks and millionaire socialist singer of songs, stared for a long time at Whittaker Lowell James, the product of St. Paul's, Yale, and years of quietly accumulated power. James returned her stare, on his lips a small, amused, almost aloof smile, the kind that a man wears when he has total confidence in himself and a kindly fate.

The long silence lengthened as Silk Armitage bit her lower lip and stared at Whittaker Lowell James. When she finally spoke, her voice was soft, but firm.

"Give them the old man," she said.

Chapter Forty

Chief Oscar Ploughman whistled and hummed "Harbor Lights" as he drove his black unmarked Plymouth sedan down Seashore Drive on his way to Police Headquarters with his distinguished-looking, gray-haired prisoner safely handcuffed in the seat beside him. When Ploughman reached the small circle that boasted the twenty-one-foot-high statue that was the last pelican in Pelican Bay, he gave it a small salute and said, "How the hell are ya, Freddie?"

Whittaker Lowell James stared straight ahead and didn't bother to ask who Freddie was.

Chapter Forty-one

The evening of that same Wednesday, late, when the sun was going down, Quincy Durant and Silk Armitage walked barefoot in the sand along the beach at Paradise Cove. They had walked from Durant's house up to Little Point Dume and now they were walking back. Silk wore white shorts and a soft blue sweater. Durant had on his sawed-off jeans and the faded sweat shirt that read DENVER ATHLETIC CLUB.

They had been walking in silence for nearly five minutes when Silk said, "That old man."

"What about him?"

"Was he evil?"

"Evil. That's not a word I use very much."

"You know what I mean."

"No, I don't suppose he was evil. Or is."

"What he did, he did because he thought he was right."

Durant shook his head. "He didn't just think it; he knew it."

"But he wasn't, was he?"

"Well, he's in jail," Durant said.

"But that doesn't mean we were right."

"No," Durant said, "it means that we got away with it."

"And that's what counts."

"Usually."

"You know something?" she said.

"What?"

"I should feel awful, but I don't."

"You just won one."

"Did I?"

"You'd better think of it that way."

They walked on in silence until they passed the pier and were approaching Durant's house. She wondered if he would ask her in again. They had spent most of the afternoon and early evening there in bed. Then she knew that he wouldn't. She wasn't quite sure how she knew.

"What happens now?" she said.

"I'm not sure."

"Will you go to Switzerland?"

"For a few days anyway."

"And then?"

"That's what I'm not sure about."

"Well, you have that number I gave you."

"Yes."

"Call it sometime."

"All right."

She looked up at him. "But you won't, will you?"

"I don't know," he said.

They walked on until they reached the marble steps that went up to Randall Piers's house. He kissed her then and held her quite close for a long time. Then she moved back and smiled up at him. "Goodbye, Quincy."

"Goodbye," he said, and turned and started walking along the beach back toward the yellow house.

She went up the steps and then paused and waited for him to turn and perhaps wave. But when he didn't, she went on up the remaining 175 steps made out of Carrara marble that led to the house of the man with six greyhounds.

The next morning, which was a Thursday, the twenty-third of June, Randall Piers and his six greyhounds came down the marble steps just after dawn.

They headed along the beach toward the Paradise Cove pier, the greyhounds clustered at his heels, watching for the signal, and when he gave it, the hard, almost chopping gesture, they grinned and raced one another to the pier, their ears hard back and joy in their eyes.

By the time the dogs had trotted back, Piers was abreast of the small yellow house with the green composition roof. He skirted by the dead pelican, which had lain on the beach for exactly one week and which nobody had bothered to get rid of yet, and climbed up the four-foot slope of sand, the greyhounds now bunched at his heels again.

When he reached the steps that went up to the deck, he hesitated, and then started up, the dogs just behind him. He moved around to the door that led into the kitchen and peered through its glass. The house was empty. Everything was gone, including the wall of books and the Oriental rug. Not even the usual trash and junk had been left behind.

Piers tried the door. It was unlocked, so he went in. He looked around the kitchen and noticed that something after all had been left behind. On the stove was the big gallon coffeepot. He thought he could smell coffee, so he went over and touched the pot. It was very warm, almost hot. Next to it on the tile sink were several unused Styrofoam cups.

Piers poured himself a cup of coffee and tasted it. It was as good as ever. He wandered into the empty living room and looked around, wondering where they had gone, the lean man with the scars on his back and the other one, the fat pretender to the Emperor's throne. Piers almost wished that he had known them better, because they were rather interesting men—certainly different, if not wholly admirable. But then, who the hell was?

Randall Piers discovered that he was very curious about what they would do next. As he stood there in the empty house, sipping the coffee, he decided to find out. But for many reasons, he never did.

MORE MYSTERIOUS PLEASURES

HAROLD ADAMS
MURDER
Carl Wilcox debuts in a story of triple murder which exposes the underbelly of corruption in the town of Corden, shattering the respectability of its most dignified citizens.   #501 $3.50

THE NAKED LIAR
When a sexy young widow is framed for the murder of her husband, Carl Wilcox comes through to help her fight off cops and big-city goons.
                                                        #420 $3.95

THE FOURTH WIDOW
Ex-con/private eye Carl Wilcox is back, investigating the death of a "popular" widow in the Depression-era town of Corden, S.D.
                                                        #502 $3.50

EARL DERR BIGGERS
THE HOUSE WITHOUT A KEY
Charlie Chan debuts in the Honolulu investigation of an expatriate Bostonian's murder.   #421 $3.95

THE CHINESE PARROT
Charlie Chan works to find the key to murders seemingly without victims—but which have left a multitude of clues.   #503 $3.95

BEHIND THAT CURTAIN
Two murders sixteen years apart, one in London, one in San Francisco, each share a major clue in a pair of velvet Chinese slippers. Chan seeks the connection.   #504 $3.95

THE BLACK CAMEL
When movie goddess Sheila Fane is murdered in her Hawaiian pavilion, Chan discovers an interrelated crime in a murky Hollywood mystery from the past.   #505 $3.95

CHARLIE CHAN CARRIES ON
An elusive transcontinental killer dogs the heels of the Lofton Round the World Cruise. When the touring party reaches Honolulu, the murderer finally meets his match.   #506 $3.95

JAMES M. CAIN
THE ENCHANTED ISLE
A beautiful runaway is involved in a deadly bank robbery in this posthumously published novel. #415 $3.95

CLOUD NINE
Two brothers—one good, one evil—battle over a million-dollar land deal and a luscious 16-year-old in this posthumously published novel. #507 $3.95

ROBERT CAMPBELL
IN LA-LA LAND WE TRUST
Child porn, snuff films, and drunken TV stars in fast cars—that's what makes the L.A. world go 'round. Whistler, a luckless P.I., finds that it's not good to know too much about the porn trade in the City of Angels. #508 $3.95

GEORGE C. CHESBRO
VEIL
Clairvoyant artist Veil Kendry volunteers to be tested at the Institute for Human Studies and finds that his life is in deadly peril; is he threatened by the Institute, the Army, or the CIA? #509 $3.95

WILLIAM L. DeANDREA
THE LUNATIC FRINGE
Police Commissioner Teddy Roosevelt and Officer Dennis Muldoon comb 1896 New York for a missing exotic dancer who holds the key to the murder of a prominent political cartoonist. #306 $3.95

SNARK
Espionage agent Bellman must locate the missing director of British Intelligence—and elude a master terrorist who has sworn to kill him. #510 $3.50

KILLED IN THE ACT
Brash, witty Matt Cobb, TV network troubleshooter, must contend with bizarre crimes connected with a TV spectacular—one of which is a murder committed before 40 million witnesses. #511 $3.50

KILLED WITH A PASSION
In seeking to clear an old college friend of murder, Matt Cobb must deal with the Mad Karate Killer and the Organic Hit Man, among other eccentric criminals. #512 $3.50

KILLED ON THE ICE
When a famous psychiatrist is stabbed in a Manhattan skating rink, Matt Cobb finds it necessary to protect a beautiful Olympic skater who appears to be the next victim. #513 $3.50

JAMES ELLROY
SUICIDE HILL
Brilliant L.A. Police sergeant Lloyd Hopkins teams up with the FBI to solve a series of inside bank robberies—but is he working with or against them?   #514 $3.95

PAUL ENGLEMAN
CATCH A FALLEN ANGEL
Private eye Mark Renzler becomes involved in publishing mayhem and murder when two slick mens' magazines battle for control of the lucrative market.   #515 $3.50

LOREN D. ESTLEMAN
ROSES ARE DEAD
Someone's put a contract out on freelance hit man Peter Macklin. Is he as good as the killers on his trail?   #516 $3.95

ANY MAN'S DEATH
Hit man Peter Macklin is engaged to keep a famous television evangelist *alive*—quite a switch from his normal line.   #517 $3.95

DICK FRANCIS
THE SPORT OF QUEENS
The autobiography of the celebrated race jockey/crime novelist.
                                                         #410 $3.95

JOHN GARDNER
THE GARDEN OF WEAPONS
Big Herbie Kruger returns to East Berlin to uncover a double agent. He confronts his own past and life's only certainty—death.
                                                         #103 $4.50

BRIAN GARFIELD
DEATH WISH
Paul Benjamin is a modern-day New York vigilante, stalking the rapist-killers who victimized his wife and daughter. The basis for the Charles Bronson movie.   #301 $3.95

DEATH SENTENCE
A riveting sequel to *Death Wish*. The action moves to Chicago as Paul Benjamin continues his heroic (or is it psychotic?) mission to make city streets safe.   #302 $3.95

TRIPWIRE
A crime novel set in the American West of the late 1800s. Boag, a black outlaw, seeks revenge on the white cohorts who left him for dead. "One of the most compelling characters in recent fiction."—Robert Ludlum.   #303 $3.95

FEAR IN A HANDFUL OF DUST
Four psychiatrists, three men and a woman, struggle across the blazing Arizona desert—pursued by a fanatic killer they themselves have judged insane. "Unique and disturbing."—Alfred Coppel.   #304 $3.95

JOE GORES
A TIME OF PREDATORS
When Paula Halstead kills herself after witnessing a horrid crime, her husband vows to avenge her death. Winner of the Edgar Allan Poe Award.   #215 $3.95

COME MORNING
Two million in diamonds are at stake, and the ex-con who knows their whereabouts may have trouble staying alive if he turns them up at the wrong moment.   #518 $3.95

NAT HENTOFF
BLUES FOR CHARLIE DARWIN
Gritty, colorful Greenwich Village sets the scene for Noah Green and Sam McKibbon, two street-wise New York cops who are as at home in jazz clubs as they are at a homicide scene.

#208 $3.95

THE MAN FROM INTERNAL AFFAIRS
Detective Noah Green wants to know who's stuffing corpses into East Village garbage cans . . . and who's lying about him to the Internal Affairs Division.   #409 $3.95

PATRICIA HIGHSMITH
THE BLUNDERER
An unhappy husband attempts to kill his wife by applying the murderous methods of another man. When things go wrong, he pays a visit to the more successful killer—a dreadful error.   #305 $3.95

DOUG HORNIG
THE DARK SIDE
Insurance detective Loren Swift is called to a rural commune to investigate a carbon-monoxide murder. Are the commune inhabitants as gentle as they seem?   #519 $3.95

P.D. JAMES/T.A. CRITCHLEY
THE MAUL AND THE PEAR TREE
The noted mystery novelist teams up with a police historian to create a fascinating factual account of the 1811 Ratcliffe Highway murders.

#520 $3.95

STUART KAMINSKY'S "TOBY PETERS" SERIES
NEVER CROSS A VAMPIRE
When Bela Lugosi receives a dead bat in the mail, Toby tries to catch the prankster. But Toby's time is at a premium because he's also trying to clear William Faulkner of a murder charge!   #107 $3.95

HIGH MIDNIGHT
When Gary Cooper and Ernest Hemingway come to Toby for protection, he tries to save them from vicious blackmailers.   #106 $3.95

HE DONE HER WRONG
Someone has stolen Mae West's autobiography, and when she asks Toby to come up and see her sometime, he doesn't know how deadly a visit it could be.   #105 $3.95

BULLET FOR A STAR
Warner Brothers hires Toby Peters to clear the name of Errol Flynn, a blackmail victim with a penchant for young girls. The first novel in the acclaimed Hollywood-based private eye series.   #308 $3.95

THE FALA FACTOR
Toby comes to the rescue of lady-in-distress Eleanor Roosevelt, and must match wits with a right-wing fanatic who is scheming to overthrow the U.S. Government.   #309 $3.95

JOSEPH KOENIG
FLOATER
Florida Everglades sheriff Buck White matches wits with a Miami murder-and-larceny team who just may have hidden his ex-wife's corpse in a remote bayou.   #521 $3.50

ELMORE LEONARD
THE HUNTED
Long out of print, this 1974 novel by the author of *Glitz* details the attempts of a man to escape killers from his past.   #401 $3.95

MR. MAJESTYK
Sometimes bad guys can push a good man too far, and when that good guy is a Special Forces veteran, everyone had better duck.   #402 $3.95

THE BIG BOUNCE
Suspense and black comedy are cleverly combined in this tale of a dangerous drifter's affair with a beautiful woman out for kicks.   #403 $3.95

ELSA LEWIN
I, ANNA
A recently divorced woman commits murder to avenge her degradation at the hands of a sleazy lothario.   #522 $3.50

THOMAS MAXWELL
KISS ME ONCE
An epic *roman noir* which explores the romantic but seamy underworld of New York during the WWII years. When the good guys are off fighting in Europe, the bad guys run amok in America.
          #523 $3.95

ED McBAIN
ANOTHER PART OF THE CITY
The master of the police procedural moves from the fictional 87th precinct to the gritty reality of Manhattan. "McBain's best in several years."—*San Francisco Chronicle*.   #524 $3.95

SNOW WHITE AND ROSE RED
A beautiful heiress confined to a sanitarium engages Matthew Hope to free her—and her $650,000.   #414 $3.95

CINDERELLA
A dead detective and a hot young hooker lead Matthew Hope into a multi-layered plot among Miami cocaine dealers. "A gem of sting and countersting."—*Time*.   #525 $3.95

PETER O'DONNELL
MODESTY BLAISE
Modesty and Willie Garvin must protect a shipment of diamonds from a gentleman about to murder his lover and an *un*civilized sheik.   #216 $3.95

SABRE TOOTH
Modesty faces Willie's apparent betrayal and a modern-day Genghis Khan who wants her for his mercenary army.   #217 $3.95

A TASTE FOR DEATH
Modesty and Willie are pitted against a giant enemy in the Sahara, where their only hope of escape is a blind girl whose time is running out.   #218 $3.95

I, LUCIFER
Some people carry a nickname too far . . . like the maniac calling himself Lucifer. He's targeted 120 souls, and Modesty and Willie find they have a personal stake in stopping him.   #219 $3.95

THE IMPOSSIBLE VIRGIN
Modesty fights for her soul when she and Willie attempt to rescue an albino girl from the evil Brunel, who lusts after the secret power of an idol called the Impossible Virgin.   #220 $3.95

DEAD MAN'S HANDLE
Modesty Blaise must deal with a brainwashed—and deadly—Willie Garvin as well as with a host of outré religion-crazed villains.
          #526 $3.95

ELIZABETH PETERS
CROCODILE ON THE SANDBANK
Amelia Peabody's trip to Egypt brings her face to face with an ancient mystery. With the help of Radcliffe Emerson, she uncovers a tomb and the solution to a deadly threat.   #209 $3.95

PATRICK RUELL
RED CHRISTMAS
Murderers and political terrorists come down the chimney during an old-fashioned Dickensian Christmas at a British country inn.
#531 $3.50

DEATH TAKES THE LOW ROAD
William Hazlitt, a universtiy administrator who moonlights as a Soviet mole, is on the run from both Russian and British agents who want him to assassinate an African general.
#532 $3.50

DELL SHANNON
CASE PENDING
In the first novel in the best-selling series, Lt. Luis Mendoza must solve a series of horrifying Los Angeles mutilation murders.
#211 $3.95

THE ACE OF SPADES
When the police find an overdosed junkie, they're ready to write off the case—until the autopsy reveals that this junkie *wasn't* a junkie.
#212 $3.95

EXTRA KILL
In "The Temple of Mystic Truth," Mendoza discovers idol worship, pornography, murder, and the clue to the death of a Los Angeles patrolman.
#213 $3.95

KNAVE OF HEARTS
Mendoza must clear the name of the L.A.P.D. when it's discovered that an innocent man has been executed and the real killer is still on the loose.
#214 $3.95

DEATH OF A BUSYBODY
When the West Coast's most industrious gossip and meddler turns up dead in a freight yard, Mendoza must work without clues to find the killer of a woman who had offended nearly everyone in Los Angeles.
#315 $3.95

DOUBLE BLUFF
Mendoza goes against the evidence to dissect what looks like an air-tight case against suspected wife-killer Francis Ingram—a man the lieutenant insists is too nice to be a murderer.
#316 $3.95

MARK OF MURDER
Mendoza investigates the near-fatal attack on an old friend as well as trying to track down an insane serial killer.
#417 $3.95

ROOT OF ALL EVIL
The murder of a "nice" girl leads Mendoza to team up with the FBI in the search for her not-so-nice boyfriend—a Soviet agent.
#418 $3.95

JULIE SMITH
TRUE-LIFE ADVENTURE
Paul McDonald earned a meager living ghosting reports for a San Francisco private eye until the gumshoe turned up dead . . . now the killers are after him.   #407 $3.95

TOURIST TRAP
A lunatic is out to destroy San Francisco's tourism industry; can feisty lawyer/sleuth Rebecca Schwartz stop him while clearing an innocent man of a murder charge?   #533 $3.95

ROSS H. SPENCER
THE MISSING BISHOP
Chicago P.I. Buzz Deckard has a missing person to find. Unfortunately his client has disappeared as well, and no one else seems to be who or what they claim.   #416 $3.50

MONASTERY NIGHTMARE
Chicago P.I. Luke Lassiter tries his hand at writing novels, and encounters murder in an abandoned monastery.   #534 $3.50

REX STOUT
UNDER THE ANDES
A long-lost 1914 fantasy novel from the creator of the immortal Nero Wolfe series. "The most exciting yarn we have read since *Tarzan of the Apes.*"—*All-Story Magazine.*   #419 $3.50

ROSS THOMAS
CAST A YELLOW SHADOW
McCorkle's wife is kidnapped by agents of the South African government. The ransom—his cohort Padillo must assassinate their prime minister.   #535 $3.95

THE SINGAPORE WINK
Ex-Hollywood stunt man Ed Cauthorne is offered $25,000 to search for colleague Angelo Sacchetti—a man he thought he'd killed in Singapore two years earlier.   #536 $3.95

THE FOOLS IN TOWN ARE ON OUR SIDE
Lucifer Dye, just resigned from a top secret U.S. Intelligence post, accepts a princely fee to undertake the corruption of an entire American city.   #537 $3.95

JIM THOMPSON
THE KILL-OFF
Luanne Devore was loathed by everyone in her small New England town. Her plots and designs threatened to destroy them—unless they destroyed her first.   #538 $3.95

DONALD E. WESTLAKE
THE HOT ROCK
The unlucky master thief John Dortmunder debuts in this spectacular caper novel. How many times do you have to steal an emerald to make sure it *stays* stolen?   #539 $3.95

BANK SHOT
Dortmunder and company return. A bank is temporarily housed in a trailer, so why not just hook it up and make off with the whole shebang? Too bad nothing is ever that simple.   #540 $3.95

THE BUSY BODY
Aloysius Engel is a gangster, the Big Man's right hand. So when he's ordered to dig a suit loaded with drugs out of a fresh grave, how come the corpse it's wrapped around won't lie still?   #541 $3.95

THE SPY IN THE OINTMENT
Pacifist agitator J. Eugene Raxford is mistakenly listed as a terrorist by the FBI, which leads to his enforced recruitment to a group bent on world domination. Will very good Good triumph over absolutely villainous Evil?   #542 $3.95

GOD SAVE THE MARK
Fred Fitch is the sucker's sucker—con men line up to bilk him. But when he inherits $300,000 from a murdered uncle, he finds it necessary to dodge killers as well as hustlers.   #543 $3.95

TERI WHITE
TIGHTROPE
This second novel featuring L.A. cops Blue Maguire and Spaceman Kowalski takes them into the nooks and crannies of the city's Little Saigon.   #544 $3.95

COLLIN WILCOX
VICTIMS
Lt. Frank Hastings investigates the murder of a police colleague in the home of a powerful—and nasty—San Francisco attorney.
                    #413 $3.95

NIGHT GAMES
Lt. Frank Hastings of the San Francisco Police returns to investigate the at-home death of an unfaithful husband—whose affairs have led to his murder.   #545 $3.95

DAVID WILLIAMS' "MARK TREASURE" SERIES
UNHOLY WRIT
London financier Mark Treasure helps a friend reacquire some property. He stays to unravel the mystery when a Shakespeare manuscript is discovered and foul murder done. #112 $3.95

TREASURE BY DEGREES
Mark Treasure discovers there's nothing funny about a board game called "Funny Farms." When he becomes involved in the takeover struggle for a small university, he also finds there's nothing funny about murder. #113 $3.95

■ ■